Fate Accompli
Murder in Quebec City

Miriam Clavir

BAYEUX ARTS
DIGITAL-TRADITIONAL PUBLISHING

FATE ACCOMPLI: Murder in Quebec City

Publication: April 2018

Published in Canada by
Bayeux Arts Digital - Traditional Publishing
2403, 510 6th Avenue, S.E.
Calgary, Canada T2G 1L7

www.bayeux.com

Cover design by JF Granzow
Cover photo credit: Jules-Ernest Livernois /
Library and Archives Canada / PA-023967

Book design by Lumina Datamatics, Inc.

Library and Archives Canada Cataloguing in Publication

Clavir, Miriam, 1948-, author
        Fate accompli / Miriam Clavir.

Issued in print and electronic formats.
ISBN 978-1-988440-19-4 (softcover).—ISBN 978-1-988440-20-0
(ebook)

        I. Title.

PS8605.L379F38 2018   **C813'.6**   **C2018-900299-9**
                                                      C2018-900300-6

The ongoing publishing activities of Bayeux Arts Digital - Traditional
Publishing under its varied imprints are supported by the Government of
Alberta, Alberta Multimedia Development Fund, and the Government of
Canada through the Book Publishing Industry Development Program.

Printed in Canada

Dedication

For Bruno Pouliot
And good friends and colleagues in Québec
And for John, always

Avertissement de l'auteure

Ceci est un ouvrage de fiction que se déroule dans la ville historique de Québec, la plus ancienne et vraisemblablement la plus captivante et la plus belle ville du Québec et du Canada tout entier. J'ai succombé à son charme quand j'y ai vécu et travaillé, comme j'imagine que le sont tous ses visiteurs. L'histoire, les rues, les quartiers, l'allure des édifices, l'atmosphère des cafés, le caractère québécois de la ville – tout cela est à la portée de tout le monde. J'ai changé seulement les noms des établissements commerciaux.

Je recommande aux lecteurs d'apprécier la vraie ville de Québec, et pendant que vous arpentez les mêmes rues ou voyez de vos propres yeux les endroits qui jouent un rôle dans ce récit, veuillez bien vous rappeler que le complot meurtrier ne s'est jamais produit et que les personnages impliqués sont fictifs, qu'ils sont le fruit de mon imagination et qu'ils ne représentent aucune personne appartenant au passé ou au présent, morte ou vivante.

Author's Note

This is a work of fiction set in historic Quebec City, the oldest and arguably most absorbing and beautiful city in Quebec and the whole of Canada. I fell under its spell when I lived and worked there, as I think all residents and visitors do. The history, the streets, the neighbourhoods, the look of the buildings, the atmosphere in the cafés, the Québécois character of the city—these anyone can experience. I have changed only the names of commercial establishments.

Readers are encouraged to enjoy the real Quebec City, and as you walk the same streets or see with your own eyes the places which play a role in this story, please remember that the murderous plot never occurred and that the characters involved are fictional; they are products of my imagination and do not represent any person past or present, living or dead.

CHAPTER ONE

Everyone knew there was important archeology to finish, and here it was, not yet mid-August in Quebec City, the year now 2000, the future in a new millennium, and the claws of winter already ripping into summer's fabric. Last night's ugly storm had slapped sheets of rain mixed with hail down the cliff that backed our historic site. The violence had torn up bushes, rocks, and soil, pouring the debris into the carefully measured trenches dug into this last undisturbed corner of Lower Town. The raised walkways used for photography had crumbled. To add to the disaster, another storm was wrecking the dig this morning. The furious swearing of my young conservation assistant, Meg Keane, had brought the whole site to a standstill, even those of us inside the workrooms.

"Son-of-a bitch, stealing my table and book. All fucking gone!" Meg was stomping around in the waterlogged yard in front of the office trailer, spraying the walls and windows with gobbets of wet dirt. The invective drenched us: table, notebook, man, guts, dog, all effing together in the same sentence. As her pitch rose I began swearing myself and, snatching up my red slicker, deserted the half-cleaned coins on my worktable. The rain was light now but still falling.

"What's happened?" I called out to Meg, my own voice hardly carrying through the dank morning. It was the abnormal intensity of the outburst that worried me.

Her arms opened wide to indicate 'isn't it obvious?' But in case it wasn't, I heard an anguished, "Berry, they're bloody fucking gone!"

"Meg . . ." I softened my voice. "There's got to be an explanation. Come have coffee and we'll figure it out."

"Don't 'come to Mammy' me," muttered my eighteen-year-old protégée, and louder, "Fuck!" This came out "*Phoque*" with her Irish accent. My lips twitched, hiding a smile. Meg still didn't know that the Francophone males on this dig traded dreams of *"leur phoque Irlandaise"*. Hearing them, she would have asked for the translation, been told 'the Irish seal', and it would have made no sense. The guys would have continued to smirk about the gorgeous creature with the mouth on her, their fantasy Irish "fuck".

I took a deep breath and coughed as the chill air penetrated my lungs. The cold bristled through my thinning hair and I found myself actually wanting one of my time-of-life hot flashes. Shit *de merde*. This was not the best morning for one of Meg's moods. My dwindling reserve of patience was just enough to keep my voice calm. "Someone stole your stuff?"

Meg stomped. "Gaetan," she snorted. "Seems he needed a drafting table to complete his drawings."

"Gaetan is sick."

"Hung over, right?"

Being staff, I held back my considered judgment that twenty-five-year-old Gaetan was already an alcoholic. "He's not on-site today."

Meg scowled. "Probably got to take the table home. Finish his illustrations in comfort instead of under this piss-poor awning."

"*Arrête*, kiddo. Enough. We'll solve it. Let's talk inside. It'll be more private. Isn't there a tour for some students this morning? Or did Professor Nadon cancel because of the storm?"

Jean-Paul Nadon had been visiting the dig every two, three weeks. The enthusiasm of this Quebec City historian for all things which illuminated the past, whether a single potsherd or a previously unknown building, energized us here as well as his own students. I welcomed this vibrant, charming man for another reason. Ever since his first visit to the site I'd recognized him. Over twenty years ago he spoke at my ex's university graduation, and into that dry ceremony Professor Nadon had injected an exuberant sense of life. For years I'd created fantasies about the kind of life I'd glimpsed through this remarkable man, and right when the dig began, he and that life crossed my path again.

"Meg," I said, trying a more supportive line and putting the brakes on my irritation. "You already do the best drawings of the finds from this excavation."

Meg smeared her black curls out of her face and a loud wail followed. "My notebook! That's the worst part. The photos being so dreadfully dark make my drawings the best record."

More than one drawing missing?

Meg's hand flew over her heart. "Oh, Berry, I sketched everything, not just the artifacts. There was one of Luc with his pipe identifying the finds at the end of the day. He was going to frame it. He'd even fussed about how to record why a page would end up cut out of an official notebook."

Yes, the bearded bull of a director fussed over details. He was an excellent archaeologist, a good site director and terrific with the young students. But Luc wanted his workers to obey. They admired him, and did.

"We'll hunt down your notebook," I said to Meg. "Where'd you last see it?"

"At the 'finds' table. I was drawing Sector 7 pottery. Right after lunch. The good light outside. Then *you* called me to the lab and I forgot it."

"So maybe the storm took your notebook and it's in a dirt pile somewhere. We'll find it."

"Oh, to be sure." Meg glared, and growled something.

"What?" I said. "Okay, you're right, I'm north of fifty and too old to hear anymore. What'd you say?"

"It's Irish for 'piss off'." She stomped away.

"The notebook isn't the end of the world." I yelled after her. "You're still a really good artist."

Meg swivelled and the wet on her face wasn't just rain. "Without a portfolio? Screwing up with Luc and my first chance in Canada? All I ever want is to go to the *École des beaux-arts*. And my French isn't even good enough to tell you to piss off." Her shoulders hunched as she turned her back.

"Go take a quick look then meet me in the lab." To convince her I added detail. "There's a 'just excavated' drawing I need a.s.a.p. on a wooden artifact that's drying out, and you're the only person who can do it."

I returned inside to my worktable and immediately the warmth and brightness of the artifacts lab lifted my irritation. The day was going to get better; I would talk to Meg when she arrived and we would plan the most effective way to handle the notebook situation together.

A half hour later Meg still not shown up. "Damn downside to independence." I dragged myself out of the warm room to search.

Excavating a historic site right in a city gave us the benefit of the lab being housed in luxurious accommodation by any archeological standard: high-ceilinged rooms rented for the summer at the back of nineteenth-century stone and brick buildings. Back stairways crisscrossed above a narrow street, Sous-le-Cap, to reach our doors on the second floor. The small dirt lots off rue Sous-le-Cap that we looked down on had been used for spare parking until we began the excavation.

On the dig's first day Luc had described how over three hundred years ago the one-lane Sous-le-Cap had been a high-tide-only path between the Intendant's palace and the village that had grown up around Champlain's original *Habitation*. Through the centuries infill had pushed the St Lawrence river back, wharves and warehouses had been built, and rue Sous-le-Cap had grown into a neighbourhood of coopers and other tradesmen who served the tall sailing ships. Garbage had accumulated. Luc had said to the crew that we would find all the evidence, whether we wanted it or not. Meg's trash talk this morning fit right in. Lame joke, Berry, I muttered.

Pausing on the landing outside the lab, I fought off my disappointment in my young assistant. Instead of showing up for pressing work, Meg had likely gone to Luc's office to receive the concern he always, in the end, showed for his students. I surveyed the dig site across the lane-like street below, the site's remaining grass chewed into ruts by too many boots and wheelbarrows. After the storm, it was swampland. Leaving the stairs' oasis, I zigzagged across to the on-site trailer Luc used, a "building" large enough for his desk and papers, boxes of supplies, and tables where, at day's end, the diggers at this field school excavation could complete their notes without dragging mud all over a good floor. In the short time it took me to hop on the tufts of green poking up out of the mud my slicker and jeans resembled the carapace of a pond turtle dripping with muck.

Sure enough, Meg was sitting in Luc's office. For him had she whimpered like a pup about the missing notebook and table? Would he deflect a boss's concern for lost records into anger towards her supervisor, me?

"Meg, I'd said you were urgently needed in the lab."

"I had to talk to Luc."

"Then let me know. Your help in the lab is essential." But Meg's common sense knew I could easily have wrapped up any wooden artifact so it wouldn't dry out.

"When has that happened?"

"That's for me to judge. You're my assistant."

"Just because I draw the artifacts doesn't mean I work for Ms. Berry Cates all the time."

Luc was smoking his pipe, eyes skimming from me to Meg and back. The pipe conveniently hid any expression as well as being a good excuse for silence. And Luc's sheltering presence had made Meg bolder. If I pressed further he might enter the conversation and it could get worse.

"Meg, I really do need to see you in the lab. Right after you're finished."

Luc interrupted with a wave of his pipe, my summary to a workmate later being, "Number one, Gaetan needed the drafting table and I authorized it. Two, find the notebook." Maybe because Meg was there he hadn't shouted at me about a lack of good supervision allowing my assistant's notebook to go missing.

I headed back to the Collections and Conservation Lab, Luc's door closing with a slam. In some ways I understood Meg's earlier tantrum too well. Outside in the mud I craved just one stomp, one magnificent flying spray of dirt porridge. Or a sodden lump flung at Luc's aluminum door. Like the cliff backing our dig, though, the slippery slope. It would be hard to stop.

Luc's expectations of unquestioning agreement got my back up, and our conversations often ended at cross-purposes. But I had come to accept that Luc's two front teeth didn't help, either. The space between them was exactly like my gap-toothed ex-husband's, buddy-the-jerk who'd walked out on me. Same teeth, same lips, the beard emphasizing their wet and pucker and the hairy halo guarding every smell it came near.

Ten minutes before lunchtime Meg did arrive, jean cuffs soaked, plaid corduroy jacket dirty and dishevelled, and a look on her face that said this better be quick.

"Shit *de merde*, Meg," I said before she could talk. "What's bugging you?" and pushed an empty chair towards her. "You're all wound up."

"Too much coffee."

"There's more. This morning you sat outside measuring pottery when you could've been drawing artifacts inside, and only later you started yelling about your table and book being gone."

Meg's hands crawled to her face. I froze. I'd set her off. Tears streaming, she bawled, "He stood me up!"

"Gaetan? Do you like him?"

Meg looked horrified. "You thought . . .? Fuck!" She launched herself towards the door.

For a second time this morning I'd hoped to connect with my young protégée and we'd gone nowhere. "So who then?" I shouted into the growing silence. "Who stood you up?"

The rain had let up slightly and I needed fresh air. I took my break under the shelter of the excavation's outside 'finds area', an old green-striped canvas roof sloping over two thick pieces of plywood held up by sawhorses. Rough sketches were worked up here and dirty artifacts laid out for Luc's preliminary inspection. Squatting on an overturned bucket, I wished I'd made a hot cup of Earl Grey before heading out. The chill was reaching my insides and I had better eat that green stripe on my sandwich or move. But something niggled in my brain as I gazed out over the bleak, sodden piles of dirt and debris removed from the archeology trenches after the storm, all shadowed by the dark grey face of *La Falaise* scoured down to its ancient metamorphosed sediments.

The cliff—*La Falaise*, as it was called in Quebec City, as if it were a person—dominated Lower Town and our dig. Rue Sous-le-Cap ran along its base, with the tiny dirt parking lots we were excavating squeezed out of any spare ground between the pavement and the rock. "Sous-le-Cap" meant "under the promontory", the headland of Cap Diamant. Upper Town spread out on top of the Cap, and Lower Town and our backstreet lay many steep steps below. The cliff remained a living presence, an unavoidable reminder of the city's four hundred years as a defendable fortress and a symbol of battles between French and English.

As I stared at the end of one dirt pile spilling out beside a stone wall, what was niggling away at me surfaced. The rocks on top of the heap of soil struck me as being too-exactly spaced. Could a notebook be hidden in that mound?

—◦◦◦◦—

CHAPTER TWO

I crept to the equipment shed and skulked back with brushes, trowel, and short knife, grateful for the continuing cold rain that had moved the archeology crew indoors. Six carefully placed rocks were my clue that something had been deliberately cached. In fact, to my eye, the whole mound looked like an artful arrangement in a *décor* magazine instead of soil dumped off of workers' wheelbarrows.

Nobody paid these dirt piles much attention during the dig; the barrow loads had already been meticulously examined for artifacts, so the soil was kept only to refill the trenches at summer's end. The perfect hiding place for pranks.

As I scrabbled around at the foot of the peculiar mound, my tools found no evidence of the blue plastic tarpaulins the diggers always layered between the heaps of excavated soil to make the dirt easier to move back. Neat rocks, no tarps: this mound was doubly bizarre. I gently moved two rocks aside so my trowel could create a smooth furrow across the pile, improvising on an art conservation technique I was familiar with, one that, with scalpels and brushes and tiny strokes, was used to reveal historic paint layers on frescos. I took the same care passing my broad trowel across the damp soil, a deeper cut this time but now going only nine-tenths of the way, so as I continued, a part of each layer would always be preserved intact. Never destroy evidence, particularly what the boss might want. On the eighth cut my trowel passed a yielding lump. Finally, a bag with Meg's missing notes?

Meg's notebook was indeed irreplaceable. It contained the only clear drawing of the weave pattern inside a rare Victorian rubber bathing slipper. The woven cloth lining had rotted away to leave nothing but an imprint in the burial mud. And the whole actual location of the find, the muddy soil itself, no longer existed. The "shoe" had been found in one of the dig's open trenches ruined by yesterday's storm.

Gently my fingers pressed against the lump. The mass was too soft. Spongy soft. This was no notebook.

But if Meg's records weren't found by the close of the excavation season, Luc would kill me and maybe even young Meg, too. Skewer me, for sure, or if I was lucky just bellow the roof off as he did often enough, but this time it would include the roof off any future recommendation for me as an artifacts conservator in charge of preservation on an archeological site. I absolutely needed a reference from him as well as the current paycheck I was desperate to keep coming.

My hands shook and the trowel dropped. I willed my mind to forget the only other time working as an artifacts conservator I'd found softness on an excavation. At a burial site from the 1800s, two large British pennies had closed the eyes of a corpse. My conservation job included removing the pennies for security until the skeleton would be reburied. Preserved by the copper salts, the eye flesh underneath had remained gelatinous, white-green.

A paintbrush now helped me go millimetre by millimetre further into the dirt mound. Underneath, slowly, two bloated human hands began revealing themselves, knit together under a chin and mouth, age-spotted, bloody skin contrasting with the granular earth.

Buried under slime and soil lay a man I recognized. Professor Jean-Paul Nadon.

Screaming, I collapsed on the ground, the earth that welcomes all remains.

A panicked voice was at my ear. "Berry! Berry!" and somebody was holding my arms, lifting me up off the damp soil. My English-language mind needed to fix on the French words to tell them that at our feet a man lay dead. Now Luc was at my side, shouting, and for once I was grateful. Workers scurried under his terse orders; more tools were brought as warm, soothing companions gently walked me away. Head down, I concentrated on moving my feet forward. And my coincidental role—or what was it, why me at this precise location to discover him?—in the death of a man for whom I'd had enormous respect. As well as other emotions I'd kept private.

My knees buckled. Unbidden, a much older but intensely remembered image of Jean-Paul Nadon surged into my mind and now glued itself onto what I'd just seen—a dynamic man giving a speech which had powerfully affected my sense of how life should be lived. Jean-Paul Nadon's glittering words flooded back. "Québec is a place whose citizens routinely say, not 'I like', but, '*Je me passionne pour*'".

Now, here, so many years later, on this prize job in a marvellous city, it was I who for a few short months had been saying and living, "I am passionate for". Until today.

I hugged myself inside the sweet comfort of dry clothes from the emergency stash. The warm flannel jacket held no memory of black mud, slaked rock, wet cloth, or blood. The tuque covering my wet hair reached my eyes and I buried my face in the clean, waterless scent of anonymous work clothes. Inside my safe cave my mind stayed put, another source of comfort. I wanted to go nowhere, especially nowhere near my heart.

But there was noise too close by—a man singing '*Frère Jacques*': no, my name. "Berry Cate-s, Berry Cate-s." The earnest English sounded so funny with its deliberate S's at the end, silent in French. Should I join in? But if I lifted my head from the flannel folds I would have to look at the real world. A hand smoothed my hat and hair, and another was finding its warm way along my cheek and chin. I knew these ancient loving gestures. Feelings pushed like rootlets through my body, bursting sobs deep inside.

The protective fog around me dissolved, reshaping itself into the lean, inviting form of my *beau*, Daniel. My heart's reason for seeking a job in Quebec had been in part to see if a close friendship begun last year in Vancouver with a Radio-Canada reporter, Daniel Tremblay, might develop into a deep *amour*. Now Daniel bent over my chair, one knee holding the seat steady.

Looking up in his eyes I managed, "*Merci*". Through my eyes' wet blur I saw a worried face, and brushed my fingertips against its cheek. Daniel smiled and rocked slightly on his heels, salt-and-pepper hair falling over his forehead. My body swivelled: my boss Luc's desk chair. I must be in the chief's archeology trailer. On my other side Luc's small electric heater was blasting out its own comfort.

Daniel whispered, "It's okay, *ma petite*." It was old banter, and usually I rose in fun to the bait—I was no "petite", in fact, a half-inch taller than him—but when I hardly smiled back, he repeated softly that it was going to be all right. He hugged me and said, "*Ma chère*, now I'll go sit with Meg. She's not in good shape. Actually, I'm not allowed to stay here."

Daniel kissed me once on each cheek *à la française*, and then a third time, as among intimates.

"The police want to speak to you," he made a half bow towards two figures. The blue background came into focus wearing uniforms. "I've already been interviewed and they want me out of the room for yours. I only knew Jean-Paul Nadon as a public figure, but you know him from visiting the dig."

I nodded my agreement and kept the rest quiet. Daniel would not be in the room to hear how else I knew Jean-Paul.

Meg—I understood Daniel's concern for her. My choice of Meg as conservation assistant had gotten Daniel's Irish second cousin a student placement on the dig. The seemingly perfect placement for us both until today.

"No interview," and I shook my head, bending back inside the big flannel collar. "Not yet."

"Madame Cates," intoned a male figure. "Sorry to bother you at this time. I'm sure you want to go home. Like the site crew has been able to."

He knew exactly what he was doing, this cop. He knew what a temptation the promise of release would be. How I'd agree to his, "We just need to ask a few questions first."

"Daniel, don't leave. It's not fair. I mean," I said, appalled at what sounded like begging, "I'm not myself." This was obvious. To me at least.

Daniel squeezed my shoulder. "I'll get Florence." He turned towards the cops. "A victim is allowed a woman with her." The young policeman said nothing in return.

Florence, the only woman close to my age on the dig site, had been seconded from the university lab that would permanently house the dig's collections to store and catalogue the artifacts as they were found. My first-day impression of her had come from her tight, tinted perm, her shirt with large embroidered flowers, and the tedious grey slacks. How would our different tastes play out on the job? Within a week it had become evident my happiness on-site would be due in large part to this companionable workmate.

"Tell Florence . . . please, tea." I managed a smile and sank back into the chair. "Strong. Hot." Watching Daniel as he opened the door, my heart made contact with my body again.

I took the risk of looking around the room, returning me to the world. Luc was sitting perched on the edge of a worktable. It was his office and obviously the police officers had not told *him* to leave. I didn't want to share my private life with my boss during an inescapable interrogation. For me and Luc, I'd also learned how easily "I don't like" fit its Quebec phrase, "*Je déteste*".

My hoarse sigh went unnoticed. Right now I had no strength for conflict, for anything that might turn bad. Upset and exhaustion submerged me when I needed instead to be strong.

Could I talk to Florence in private before the police ordeal began? The "ladies room" gambit worked.

"I'm feeling a bit nauseous," I lied in a low voice to the policeman. "Could Florence help me to the washroom?"

Three minutes later, Florence and had a scheme, including that if either of us pitched forward as if we were sick, the other would act anxious or whatever it took to pause the interview. My boss sat listening to what I would say. If I wanted time out, our plan meant I could get it.

Florence scored our first success by convincing Luc he was needed elsewhere, to secure the artifacts in the collections room in the midst of today's chaos. She stayed by my side.

The policeman began with small talk, routine questions about name, address, occupation. I clasped my cup, the tea sweetened for strength, and recited back. The questions were all easy. Until a woman taller than myself walked in. Like a model on the catwalk, thin body placing one foot in front of the other, perfect face blank and haughty, she advanced towards us. But her clothes were wrong. Creased, with police insignia? My interviewer leapt out of his chair and the woman sat. She began, in silence, to flip through the reports on the table.

"Which of you is Bérénice Cates?"

"Me." It sounded like the chirp of a newly fledged chick.

After a two-second stare at me over her papers she recited her name as if it were a chemical formula. "Detective Sergeant Laflamme." Her face bent back over the reports. Eventually I heard, "Describe to me how you found Monsieur Nadon's body." She lifted her head for good now, and any flame that had once burnt in those cold blue eyes had long ago been extinguished.

At the mention of the historian's death my mouth opened and my jaw must have moved, but no sound passed through my dry, constricted throat. Florence steadied my mug, settled her girth like an old owl watchful in the woods, and nodded encouragement. Detective Laflamme leaned over and said, "Madame, start from the beginning. When did you first meet Professor Nadon?"

CHAPTER THREE

No way would Detective Sergeant Laflamme hear that "the beginning" meant the secret I'd kept for decades, that Jean-Paul Nadon and his words had inhabited my world. That this summer the memory had reappeared face-to-face. Over two months ago on his first visit to our newly-begun excavation, Jean-Paul Nadon had spoken to me. Even more marvellous, several times he and I had met, just the two of us, for drinks and chats after work during the field season. For discussions about artifacts, I reminded myself primly. If the detective wanted more than Jean-Paul Nadon's interest in archeology for her "beginning", she would have to dig through the rubble for it.

Since our archeological site was in one of the oldest quarters of Quebec City, I described to Laflamme how I'd watched Luc's evident pleasure as he greeted the famous historian, Prof. Jean-Paul Nadon, on his first visit. My boss always looked the image of a chief archaeologist: large-brimmed canvas hat, plaid work jacket, jeans—that day more laundered than usual—scuffed boots, and pockets stuffed with all the archy paraphernalia: pens, notebook, jackknife, magnifying glass, and, proudly old-fashioned, a pipe and tobacco pouch. Jean-Paul Nadon's brown leather jacket, in contrast, looked trim and handsomely urban Québécois.

Luc embraced the older man with both arms wrapped around the dignitary's shoulders, and received a quick hug in return. A typical *à la française* greeting here, although this time also a photo-op designed by Luc to intentionally feed an assembled group of local media. I didn't reveal to Laflamme that my own shoulders tingled as I stood at the window of the lab, observing Luc welcome the popular Quebec City writer, speaker and scholar. A man I suddenly had recognized personally, because that same man's words at a long-ago graduation had surfaced.

"Luc greeted Nadon. Of course. Then what? Describe exactly what you saw next."

With his right hand collegially resting on Nadon's back, Luc had directed his gaze towards the dig's newly opened trenches. All at once I could see from my upstairs window that the story being told here seemed vastly different from that warm welcome. Luc's hand had curled into a ball from its initial open palm of friendship. His fist was creeping nearer Nadon's neck. Almost as if Luc might be ready to push the eminent professor into the open hole.

"Probably I'm misinterpreting," I said to Laflamme. "Otherwise, all I can think of is there's some hidden jealousy. That Luc's visitor enjoyed more recognition than him." Even though Professor Nadon would have been nearing seventy, and Luc, a quarter-century younger, still had ample time to achieve his own celebrity status. "I have to admit, I think Luc's just not got the public personality Monsieur Nadon has...had...his energy, his charisma." I didn't add, "Energy I'd love to have, battling a mid-life divorce slap that's left me determined to get the most out of my second fifty years."

But at least now a person with a potentially tantalizing relationship to the murdered man was planted in her mind, and that person wasn't me.

Laflamme said only, "And you? Did you yourself talk to Monsieur Nadon?"

I veered around her question. My assigned role the morning of that visit had been to make sure no one in the media scrum pocketed any of the artifacts in the conservation lab, especially the small gold cross discovered the year before in the exploratory trenches, a signature piece that had secured the site as archeologically significant.

"Yes. Luc brought Nadon up to the lab to see the gold cross."

I recounted the details to a pen-tapping Laflamme, how in the lab Luc had loudly explained to Nadon, although no doubt in reality it was to the media traipsing after, that every single artifact they were now seeing laid out on the tables had been found in the original place it had been lost or hidden centuries ago: the glazed and patterned ceramic sherds that I'd restored to show the vessels' shapes, green glass fragments from eighteenth-century wine bottles, wrought iron nails, and a thin copper coin. All found in the first week.

The cameras had jostled for close-ups.

"My concern is Professor Nadon. And you. Not artifacts, not the media."

Slowly I began a summary of the rest of the morning of that visit, being careful to distance my real feelings as the scene played out in my mind.

Laflamme heard my calm voice say: "Luc invited Monsieur Nadon to look at the gold cross under conservation's binocular microscope."

I remembered that the chief archaeologist's voice had boomed: excited, proud, uncontained. "A gold cross hundreds of years old in perfect condition! Here, look at it magnified. Stand back, cameras, let Professor Nadon in."

To Laflamme I said, "I'd set up the dig's surgery-quality microscope." Smiling like the excellent employee I knew I was, or at least could mime, I'd stepped aside while Luc moved the cross under the 'scope and the media pressed closer.

"But now my job was to watch the media people. For straying fingers." And my gaze fixed on Jean-Paul Nadon still bending over the ceramic sherds laid out on the table's far end.

"*Très beau*, Luc," he had said, "this nineteenth century Willow pattern."

I knew how common Willow pattern blue-and-white pottery was. Why was he intrigued? He had sounded amiable and genuine, though, not sarcastic. The impression I'd formed of him at that early graduation was reconfirmed. The historian still lived his "*Je me passionne pour*".

I know I grinned. His voice hadn't changed from that day my then-husband and I had fully celebrated at an expensive supper, hubby toasting his new degree and me raising a second and then a third glass to the hope of no longer being principal support for our household.

"Next, I think," I said to Laflamme, "Nadon caught sight of my white labcoat. He asked if I was the artifacts conservator."

Stepping forward, I'd made sure my boss Luc remained out of my sightline as his eager employee met her '*Je me passionne pour*'. And met as well, at full boil, the secret I'd been desperate to hide all morning: my stupid, decades-old, teenage-like crush on Jean–Paul Nadon. Ridiculous for a fifty-four-year-old woman. Doubly inane for someone here in Quebec professing love in two languages to *mon beau* Daniel Tremblay.

Staring back at Laflamme I checked that my smile was well-epoxied in place. What was she really after? Cops have tricky methods and why were they choosing to make this interview so long? Suspicions about me finding his body? About my swooning over the charismatic Jean-Paul Nadon? How could she already know that? I leaned back, the desk chair wheeling slightly, but enough physical distance increased between me and Laflamme to boost my emotional distance. I found my voice, and made it professional to hide any insinuations about passion I might inadvertently contribute.

"I introduced myself to Monsieur Nadon: 'Bérénice Cates.'" To the stone-faced detective I omitted my actual follow-up, "Please call me Berry" and said instead, "And Jean-Paul Nadon introduced himself to me." With a warm smile. "We shook hands." An ordinary greeting, no hug or cheek kissing *à la française*, but my heart gave a little swish.

"He said, if I'm remembering right but these aren't his exact words, 'in my experience, conservators are either more like scientists or more like artisans. Both take special training and experience. Which are you?'"

As with most people, had Nadon assumed my greying hair meant I'd had a long career in my field? My hair colour might be tattling on my age, but this summer on Luc's dig I was still only a few years past my 'mid-life-and-hubby-leaves, change-it-all' radical lifectomy. Nadon the expert academic didn't know he was talking to a recent student barely past graduation from art conservation school. Would it matter?

"Monsieur Nadon continued with something like, 'please understand, I'm not trying to be nosy. I'm just asking because, as a city historian, I've had to research material culture, but I'm no chemist. A restorer like yourself, you work with the same artifacts but you have a science background, yes?'"

"Luc," I continued my account to the Detective Sergeant, "interrupted my answer."

With a loud grunt. He was in his own world, though, not mine, fiddling with the microscope's focusing knobs and moving the gold cross to its best advantage for Nadon's appreciation.

I addressed Laflamme's sharp eyes. "Monsieur Nadon then asked me a few more questions about conservation."

And paused, suddenly voiceless, pain mounting at these memories. Florence handed me my tea and I took my time sipping.

Nadon had asked whether the best word was conservator, then, or restorer, and had glanced towards the high-tech microscope. His next speech was easy to remember. "I'll visit again, eh Luc? We'll talk further with Berry?" Turning back to a delighted me, he said he needed to know more about the science. And then, eyes alive with interest and phrasing his words politely, he asked, "Science or art? What made you go into conservation?"

I met his eyes. "Go into conservation? The honest answer? A divorce a decade ago. After that, I just wanted to make things last."

The minute my words were out I flushed. They were embarrassingly personal. Masking them with cool, I re-arranged those fragments of my life and continued, business-like, "Really, it's because I like puzzling out the stories the artifacts tell. In archeology, you know how the stories have missing bits? Like those ceramics? We rely on Luc's knowledge and he's very supportive of all his staff and their work." Wasn't I, by any standard, Luc's wonderful employee, crediting my boss in front of the media?

Jean-Paul Nadon seemed to think so, or at least nodded at my answer. And he didn't appear in a hurry for the conversation to end.

The way I saw it, this chat was happening between a highly celebrated, warmly smiling man and a wavy-haired, keen-eyed, next-year-officially-mid-fifties woman wearing a non-descript labcoat whose thickness over her jeans and work shirt only augmented another hot flash coursing up her cheeks. But the historian was genuinely interested in talking with me about art and artifact conservation. I'm sure my face gave away my pleasure as well as my time of life.

I found my actual voice for Detective Laflamme and managed a grave look. "Luc needed me to re-adjust the microscope's focus."

This one sentence was my discrete summary to Laflamme of what had immediately followed, Luc shouting, "*Merde!*" instead of paying attention to his guest and exemplary employee. Having pressed his head too hard against the microscope, Luc now looked like a mad sleepless raccoon with big red circles around his eyes, spittle on his dark beard, and his soft belly brushing against tables as he navigated the crowded room.

Pointing out the microscope's fine focus so the last adjustments could be made by each viewer to suit his eyesight, I stepped aside once more, but careful to listen while Nadon and Luc took turns peering at the gold cross. Personal adornment or worn by someone in a religious order? Had similar ones been discovered on any other site? Erudite colleagues enjoying their intellectual arm-wrestling.

"They discussed the cross. Nadon knew his history and Luc his archeology."

Moments later, still talking, Luc had glanced briefly in my direction and, fingers pointing to the door, steered Professor Nadon towards the exit. That day I'd had no chance to share my grad ceremony reminiscences, to pay the historian his deserved tribute, to wipe out the craziness now gluing my emotions and him to the romantic vision of *Québec* he'd drawn at that ceremony long ago. But Jean-Paul Nadon had said he wanted to speak to me again. Could I hold him to it?

"See you, *au revoir*," I'd said to their departing backs, almost forgetting to keep the gold cross in view, and was rewarded when Professor Nadon ducked his head around the gaggle of reporters and said with a friendly wave, "*À la prochaine*, Berry Cates. Until next time. Summer ends too quickly. You'll see me again."

I could not have guessed how unspeakably, hideously right he would be.

CHAPTER FOUR

My speech to Laflamme finished, my mind and memory inspected and investigated, my body's exhaustion became self-evident. Laflamme and the two cops silently sitting at the back of the room now knew enough, in my opinion, to satisfy a 'Berry-Nadon beginning'. I rose to leave, Florence pressing her support under my right arm.

Laflamme smiled and looked much less bored. "Sit down, Mesdames," she said. "Just a few more questions."

I kept the snarl off my face but noticed rather gleefully that when Laflamme lifted the case file, her hands shook as if shivering.

"Somebody needs a cigarette," I muttered. But not 'muttered' enough. Laflamme heard and fixed me with her cold stare. In an instant, I knew I was facing more interrogation. At least Laflamme couldn't go outside to have her ciggy until I was released. After staring like a cat fixed on a bird, the detective said, "You work in a lab. Why did you decide to dig in a dirt pile?"

"I was looking for a missing notebook."

"Whose notebook?" As I answered, Laflamme rechecked the constable's details.

"My assistant's. She couldn't find it after the storm."

"Your assistant is related to your friend Daniel Tremblay, *n'est-ce pas*? Tell me."

I knew Daniel would have gone over this in his own interview. So again I did a summary, but this time left out nothing. "Has Daniel mentioned his grandmother and her mother before her keeping in touch with the Irish side of the family who never emigrated? Meg contacted Daniel about spending a summer in Quebec, sent photos of her artwork. We both pushed her to apply for the dig. Why not use her art talent in archeology? Luc let her register as an overseas student for the summer."

Thinking of family made me wonder if Daniel had been like Meg at that age, all exposed heart and young passion, no big-urban cool or existential attitude. Most of the time I loved this in Meg, her being so blatantly alive, but I had to concede I'm no saint either, much as I try to put on that act, and some days her youthful mercurial moods tested my patience. Then again, admittedly, there were days when Florence reminded me I hadn't entirely grown up myself. But doesn't everyone secretly want to pick their pie slice after someone else has cut? Just because I'm brash enough to voice it.

I must have passed Laflamme's exam. Or the Detective Sergeant herself was now craving a smoke. After quick questions verifying the size, shape, and colour of the notebook, Laflamme slapped the papers on the desk.

"You will make a statement to the constable and sign it. I forbid you to leave town or change addresses." Laflamme's perfunctory monotone was at odds with the chilly glint in her eyes, almost daring me to answer back. "And whatever you think you know, you tell *us*. The police give out all public information. You *may* express your condolences that Monsieur Nadon died from a fall during the storm." She began gathering up her papers.

I stared at the police like a crab in a restaurant's tank. Just leave and don't touch me.

Minutes later, an unfamiliar man banged open the trailer door. He and a woman sheltered in the entranceway, half-supporting each other, and the woman called out, "Luc?"

In unison Laflamme and the two policemen turned. Florence rose immediately, stepping over to the strangers, murmuring, and gently placed her hands on the woman's shoulders. When Detective Laflamme addressed the man as "*Monsieur Nadon*", my whole body shuddered.

I scrunched down in the chair. Evidently distraught, the man still held himself tall, his ashen features strikingly handsome. He was wearing a long businessman's raincoat but I noticed muddy jeans poking out and work boots rather than city shoes. Was he an archaeologist? The woman appeared fragile, upset, her face thin and lined, framed by wisps of too-blonde hair. She was shivering in a stylish black coat. Her shoes looked Italian, shapely heels and almost immaculate. One officer ushered the couple out to find Luc, and the other lagged behind, speaking into a phone about being ready to officially identify the body. He took a brief statement from me, and left.

I was alone with Florence, and the name Nadon penetrating the room's sickly hot air.

"Nadon's family?" I whispered. "Identifying . . . ?" Florence nodded, hugged me, then bent me over as my guts retched out.

Florence cleaned up my puke, drove me home, searched my closet for comfortable clothes, practically dressed me and drove me to Daniel's. I gazed mutely at the streets. When we entered the Old City through the St. Jean gate in Upper Town, I said, "These Quebec City walls are hundreds of years old and I can't even weather the death of . . ." Words stuck in my throat. "An acquaintance."

"These ones only a hundred years old. Rebuilt. And yes, you are a mess."

"Hey, you're supposed to be supportive right now."

"I am."

"Supportive, not honest," I clarified.

"Now *is* the time for honesty, *ma chérie*. You can't avoid it. When your own walls are down, you aren't pretending everything's fine when it's not."

"You're okay and it looked like you knew that couple."

"How do you know I'm okay? I react differently. Get all efficient and bustle around, anything to make me think I'm doing something."

"Florence, sorry, I wasn't thinking."

"That's shock, *ma chérie*. You found the body."

I changed the subject to one I could face right now. The Nadon couple. "So who were they?"

"Haven't you met Antoine yet? He's Jean-Paul's younger brother, the biologist. He makes exquisite cheese from his herd of goats on Île d'Orléans. Odette teaches history at Laval. Every winter she brings her class to my workroom for a lecture on archeological artifacts."

"They're a handsome couple."

"They aren't together. That's a whole other story."

"Out with it, Florence."

"We're almost at Daniel's."

"Gossip! Please! I need distraction."

"Well, the story is that years ago Antoine lusted after Odette, but Odette admired the brother more, our Professor Jean-Paul. In the end, nobody got anybody. Odette eventually married a dull physicist who was supposed to be in line for a Nobel Prize and he ignored her all those research years. Antoine was out of the picture except as a friend."

"How do you know this?"

"It's a small town, this city."

"Who did Antoine marry?"

"He didn't." Florence pulled into a parking spot and idled the motor. "I've heard he likes the chase, but when it comes to making room in his life for another human, he finds excuses. 'You'd leave me if you had to live on a smelly goat farm' or 'I don't make nearly as much money as my famous brother.'"

"Excuses all right. Who wouldn't want to live in a rural paradise like Île d'Orléans?" The pastoral landscape of the large island lay an accessible thirty-five kilometers from Quebec City, the capital of the province. "But Odette and Antoine seem tight now."

Florence turned and unclasped my passenger seatbelt. "Common ground. They both wanted things out of life they never got."

"Not like the rest of us, eh?"

"Bravo, Berry. You're making jokes."

I noticed for the first time how exhausted Florence looked.

She said, "Your *ami* Daniel is a good one for making people laugh. You've landed a keeper there. Berry, three pieces of advice. Stop thinking about being a mess, laugh with Daniel, and get out of the car."

⚬⚬⚬

CHAPTER FIVE

The inner staircase up to Daniel's was narrow, the cream-painted plaster on both walls thick and smooth. The brass lamp hanging above gave the steps a sort of comfortable warmth, and the elaborate handrail, the wood cleaned of more than a century of grime, beckoned all comers to his apartment upstairs. But the day's details, the flashing images and voices, kept me leaning and thoughtful against the bottom wall. Gradually, though, the cozy space infiltrated my mind with the message that the world was not all bad, and I made myself think of the good I'd also seen today on the dig—the sympathy of the hard-working diggers, the gorgeous energy of youth revealed even in Meg's tantrum. I sat down on a step, absorbed in these moments. Until a door slammed like a gunshot.

An apparition hovered at the top of the stairs. "Stop!" I shouted and my fists flew up, half guarding, half ready to fight. But the large creature silhouetted by the light began thudding slowly down each step. Slowly the shape became human, a man, and then nearer, directly under the light, Daniel. My love Daniel, eyes dark, mouth set, not a glimmer of *amour* anywhere on his face.

"My God, Berry, where have you been?"

Sitting on your steps for a few minutes, maybe half an hour? When I didn't answer he continued, "Florence phoned to ask how you were. I said I hadn't seen you, weren't you with her at the police station?" Daniel stood inches from my face now. "How do you think we both felt then?"

"Like me," I finally answered. "Lousy, after today."

"Why didn't you . . ." but his voice had dropped. He lifted his shoulders in a kind of helpless shrug. "One knock. All I needed. Just to let me know you were here. If you need to be alone, fine." He opened his mouth to say more, but all I saw was the intensity in his eyes. "I was so worried," he whispered.

Worried that he didn't like I'd made him feel that way, or worried because I meant a lot to him? I'd find out.

"Daniel," I said, "I've had some bad stuff in my work life but nothing like today. My hands right there, in the earth. Touching. . . ."

Daniel hesitated. "I have to go and phone Florence. She needs to know you're okay."

That was all? He was heading back up? I folded my arms and deliberately made my voice solemn. "There *is* one more thing you can do, Daniel."

He stopped, hesitant, looking almost frightened.

I stepped forward and formally bestowed a brief hug to see how he reacted.

A huge smile gave him away. Daniel leaned closer and I could see the wet shine in his eyes.

"What had happened to you?" His shoulders lifted and his hands opened wide. "I began to panic. I needed a plan, what to do. Action, not just feelings."

He continued, "Now I do have a plan."

Daniel embraced me so close I could feel the tension in his chest as it released. "After Florence phoned, I knew you were alone facing today and I didn't know where."

Our embrace held while we kissed for, I don't know, a few minutes, maybe half an hour?

Upstairs, as he opened the door to his roomy apartment, Daniel put a finger to his lips. It was evident that

Meg was asleep in his bedroom and he had been making up the sofa for himself. A moment later he said, "I'm so glad you're here," and hugged me once more. I hugged him back, hard. But my mind strayed to the couch. It was not the kind that pulled out to be a double bed.

"How are you feeling right now? Better? Do you want to talk about today?" Daniel clasped my hand. He had learned to prepare himself for my sometimes unpredictable, and today unprotected, emotional responses.

Me, in this instant I lusted after avoidance. Anything to momentarily escape, to obliterate, to erase the images that were tearing at me.

"Do I look better? Could I look worse?" I joked, and immediately regretted asking. But bantering meant that for a few minutes death had again slipped from my thoughts.

Daniel grinned but knew enough not to respond. "Have you eaten?" Already prepared were slices of Brie and baguette, arranged enticingly on an artisan plate, and a large glass of Merlot.

"How's Meg?" I asked.

"Asleep."

"Good."

I was glad for Meg, and for myself. Meg and I still had to talk about her outburst this morning on the dig, but right now my body felt it might break like old fragile glass if words touched me wrong.

And they did. Daniel had his own news, and once I was seated he couldn't contain it. In my right mind, I would have been furious. Daniel, one of the top journalists at Radio-Canada, had been offered a job in the States.

"Just one season but a whole season, that's what Louisiana's proposing." Daniel was beaming. "I'd do the morning show. We'd exchange places, me and their regular host, and even carry some joint programs on both networks. *Radio Louisiane*. Bilingual programs, zydeco music, Cajun food. A warm winter! But it'll take months for the idea to get approved. You'll come? You could do whatever you want to down there."

"Except work, Daniel. They wouldn't give a non-American like me a green card so I could work."

"Well, what about just having fun? Mardi Gras in New Orleans?"

"Daniel, I'm not exactly in the mood right now to talk about this."

"Mille pardons, chérie. I'm so—how do you say it in English?—over the moon?— that they chose me."

After a tired pause I replied, "Understand one thing. You're making your life and I'm going to make mine."

He nodded an 'of course' but the shine in his eyes was not just for me.

Daniel and I chitchatted on easier topics while I drank, propped up in his modern, designer armchair. His furniture was all light wood and clean lines but placed on a floor where each old polished board was a foot wide. I glanced up at the high Victorian tinned ceiling, and across at the exposed brick wall stripped of its plaster and lath. "Sometimes I feel like such a foreigner in this city," I said.

"You grew up in Toronto. It's hardly the same as here."

I snorted, but it was true. The heart of Quebec City was ancient, a walled European town. Quebec Francophone culture, from the traditional to the ultra-contemporary, spilled out like music rich with colour and vibrancy. Besides, Daniel was a true insider; his family, the Tremblays, had been in Quebec for hundreds of years.

"It's hard not being part of the gang here," I said. "Everyone knows everyone, you all have the same touchstones."

"But your French is fluent. Maybe you can't rap in French, but you do okay."

"My Grandma Céline thanks you. And those Toronto years tutoring *le français* kept my grammar honed."

"Can I tell you a secret that your Grandma Céline and your tutoring didn't know? But you could hone more?"

My curiosity overcame good sense. In any case Daniel continued talking. He couldn't pass up this chance now he had an opening.

"My bilingual Westmount friends always said, 'Shit *la merde*, not shit *de merde*."

"*Merci*," I sighed. "Is that standard usage or a regional variation?"

"You're making real progress, you know. You're becoming as much a smart aleck in French as you are in English." He waited for my reaction, biting a smile.

"My grandma wouldn't be pleased about that, either." How to change the subject without sarcasm? Daniel beat me to it, and more gently.

"Is it the people here who make you feel . . . more like a tourist?"

"No. Not here. In Montréal maybe, they've subtly made the point I'm not *Québécoise*. Even with my French. How do they know?"

Daniel's lips moved without speaking while he considered what to say. "Your style's, well, different. Of course, your dig clothes aren't *à la mode*. But the running shoes? You have no other shoes for walking?"

The downside of being chic in Québec. Daniel had no idea what most women's shoes felt like. Why were only women the ones having to wobble on high heels and pinched toes? Avoiding any argument, I said, "This cheese's delicious."

"I found it on Île d'Orléans." Daniel matched my side-step. "When Meg . . ."

My gut clenched with images. The Brie on the dark ceramic, like slices of pale bits of fingers curling out of the dirt. The gaunt face of the brother, come into town from Île d'Orléans to identify the body.

"When Meg what?" came a strained voice from the door of the bedroom.

"When you went out to Antoine Nadon's farm on Île d'Orléans. When I drove you out to draw the plants for his botany book." Daniel spoke softly and Meg shuffled off to the bathroom, returning to bed with a vague good-night wave in our direction. But she had given me a wary look that left me uneasy.

"Mm, ice cream," I said just before the bedroom door shut.

Sure enough, Meg opened it again. "Is there any?"

Daniel shook his head.

"Daniel," I said. "I'm craving ice cream, too. Would you be a total sweetie . . ." He was already shaking his head and shrugging into his coat. The corner *dépanneur* stayed open late to serve the young crowds roaming the walled city's main street.

"Meg," I said as soon as he had left, "I need a hug."

We both did, and I knew it, and it felt good.

"You were so upset this morning," I said while I held her. "Your notebook, but there was also a guy who didn't show up. Was it," my voice choked on the next words, "Professor Nadon?"

"He never misses our rendezvous."

"You rendezvous with him? Regularly?"

Meg pulled back and looked at me. "That's what *he* calls it." Her eyes closed and she shook her head as the tears started. "Called it. He was bringing me more plants I'm illustrating. For his brother. The private contract, you know, I'm not supposed to talk about because of Immigration's rules? Overseas people can't work without the right permit except as registered students? The dig's good since I'm taking 'Summer Field School', but the paid contract . . . they'll throw me out of Canada. Or in jail."

I nodded in sympathy. What exactly would be the consequences?

"But I think it was just Jean-Paul's excuse to hear what's happening on the dig. '*J'aimerais t'offrir un café*,' he would say—in French it's so romantic—like we didn't have coffee most weeks."

What do I say next? That I'm Clueless Cates, not knowing this eighteen-year-old woman is regularly meeting a seventy-year-old man? Better not go there. Does her big cousin Daniel know? Better not ask right now. The same dig visitor I looked forward to having a drink with when there was the chance? Was. Never again. My swallow was audible even to me. Meg was saying something else about her rendezvous, but Daniel and Jean-Paul were whirling around in my mind until she shouted, "You aren't even bloody listening!"

"Sorry. I was thinking about your upset this morning."

"Like hell you were," she said, scrutinizing the fingers of my right hand as they picked away at my left.

"You're right. I'll stop the bullshit," I said. "I was figuring my chances of whether you knew I'd had a drink with Jean-Paul a couple of times, and if you'd tell Daniel."

Meg's clenched face dissolved into a sheepish smile. "I've already told him."

My face sparked crimson. No hot flash this time.

"In the interests of fucking the bullshite," continued Meg, "I told Danny before he heard it as a nasty rumour. Quebec City's a hundred times bigger than Ballyhaunis and twice as small. You see a parked car here, you know whose it is and what bar they're in. I was passing Café Le Temps and saw Jean-Paul with you. I told Danny how . . ." Meg's voice cracked, ". . . how kind Jean-Paul was to all of us who were new . . ."

Handing her a box of tissues, I tried to sound calm. "What did Daniel say?"

"Oh, he knew you were just having a drink. Jean-Paul's famous. He's old but he's still handsome, even without much hair. He could have any woman in Quebec he wanted. He's a grand friend to the dig is all."

I hung my head and chuckled. "Thanks, Meg."

When Daniel returned with chocolate ice cream I wolfed too much down.

After Meg had gone to bed I went to brush my teeth, leaving Daniel to figure out our sleeping arrangements. My mind moved back to Louisiana—an adventure? Alligators? Or maybe it should be crocodiles. I began musing about whether, if the tables were turned, I'd have proposed leaving for a year if a good job came my way, and would I expect Daniel to follow? No quick answer for 'expect'. Exactly what job, where, and anyway, when this blessed event happened, were Daniel and I still enveloped in *amour*? The phone rang. I stuck my head out the bathroom door.

I heard Daniel's jocular "*Bonsoir*" drop to a whisper, and silence followed. He was hunched over his phone, making his way to the kitchen. A cold tremor slithered up my legs, impossible to ignore, like Daniel's hushed tone.

He looked everywhere but at the armchair I'd returned to. Hesitating a moment, he walked back into the kitchen. The sound of a tap. When he emerged, a few strands of hair dripped water onto a cold-reddened face. He sat on the sofa, pouring more wine.

I remembered my conversation with Florence. The tragedy might affect us differently, but we had all been scarred. I found my sea legs and went to embrace him.

"*Ça va?*"

"*Non. Ça ne va pas.*" Daniel turned to look at me. "There's a new development."

"What?" I made my voice strong. "What happened, *mon cher*?"

"That was the police reporter for one of the papers." As a journalist, Daniel had an extensive network of contacts. "There's some buzz at the station that the death of Jean-Paul Nadon was definitely not . . . natural. Too early to say, but so and so talked to so and so."

I shrugged. "How could it be natural when he ended up in a dirt pile at the base of a cliff?"

Daniel's smooth radio voice held an edge. "The storm didn't make a wandering old man slip and fall so he ended up buried by debris? No landslide?"

"Maybe. But somebody else touched that dirt pile after."

Daniel looked horrified. "Berry, you know this? If it's not an accident, what in God's name do you know about this . . . murder?"

That one word sank home the unspeakable truth my brain had shut out. The possibility I hadn't let myself name. My head slumped on his shoulder and eventually I explained about the rocks on the dirt pile. And that I was sure the mound was from the day before.

"Did you tell all this to the police?" he said.

"I kind of fudged about moving the rocks," I admitted. "If they're evidence, I'm in trouble. And the rocks could have been one of the diggers tidying up after the storm. I did tell the police the dirt pile looked strange to me, way too neat."

"It's not some code, for God's sake, how the stones were placed." Daniel sounded almost desperate for me to understand. "It's not evidence like that. But maybe there are fingerprints or something. The police have to know the real story." Daniel's face was inches from mine. "Worse for Jean-Paul if they don't find his murderer."

I acquiesced. He phoned the station.

CHAPTER SIX

Laflamme was not appreciative that concerned citizen Daniel had called so late. I figured she had been summoned from home. The detective barked at an officer for coffee and hauled a fake cigarette out of her pocket. She chewed on it throughout the session. Here was a woman high up in a difficult profession who seemed to be doing everything possible to make people hate her. When the officer who delivered the coffee rolled his eyes at his mate as he set the cup down, my guess was confirmed. She didn't win any points from me, either. Laflamme shut Daniel out of the room before she asked me why the hell I thought these stones could be important. Or at least that's how her monotone sounded. Right now, the armour I'd developed over my fifty years had been thoroughly pierced by the shock of finding Jean-Paul dead. Laflamme seemed bent on making me feel worse.

Laflamme ordered the cops to take me down to the dig and show them the rocks and the dirt pile. "Write it up in detail. Photos." To me she said, "We bother you, not the other way around. Got that?"

Exiting with Daniel and two cops into the police car that had been commandeered, I saw Laflamme outside the station smoking a real cigarette. I liked that she was adding more harsh lines to her stunning face.

It was well past midnight by the time the police took us and strong lights down to the dig to photograph and collect the stones, which thankfully hadn't been moved further in the chaos of the afternoon's events. Sometime after one in the morning they drove us back to Daniel's. I staggered from the car but my head buzzed as if I'd run a marathon on caffeine. The ornate doorframe of his old building helped hold me steady while Daniel searched for his key. "At least now," he said, "it's not as if you're withholding a secret from the police."

There was still a hidden agenda, but it was between Daniel and me. Where would I sleep?

Daniel grinned. "I know what you're thinking," he teased. "I believe you're on the road to recovery."

He had the key in his hand now but had not yet opened the door. "Let's go for a walk!" he exclaimed. "You probably need to stretch and calm down."

"A walk? What about just going to bed? Have you been living too long with your cat?"

"But Faux Paws is with Aunt Adèle." Daniel sounded hurt. "Summer camp in the country."

Daniel's beloved aunt lived in her old family farmhouse just outside a small village on the south shore of the St. Lawrence River, less than an hour's drive from Quebec City. He had taken his cat out there, and Meg too, but had yet to introduce me. Over the summer Meg had gone out herself by bus for several weekends with her newfound relative, but no one had brought me into this picture. Exactly what this meant I wasn't sure. Daniel had promised to introduce me, and then he had been overloaded at work. It was true he not been out to St.-Édouard himself since depositing the cat, but he phoned his aunt every Sunday. Aunt Adèle was Daniel's last remaining relative of his parents' generation and his affection and caring concern for her touched me. He was no mama's boy, he was too independent, but it showed he had huge depths for love.

"Forget I mentioned Faux Paws. A short walk." It would help work off my frazz. And, I thought, you'll still have to decide where I sleep tonight. You can't sidestep this one like a cat that licks its fur when the bird is out of reach.

"Good. I'll just check that Meg's still asleep." Daniel opened the thick street door and ran up the staircase to his apartment. I sat on my now-familiar bottom step, wondering about hidden agendas. Was the walk a ploy to get me to talk about Jean-Paul? His death? Couldn't Daniel the journalist wait until morning? It was morning. Well, if he started, I would turn the conversation to the seesaw between friendship and relationship that Daniel and I had been bouncing up and down on ever since he'd been my upstairs neighbour in Vancouver a year and a half ago.

Although we rented separate apartments here it felt like we were living sweet and close. But there were times Daniel seemed to crawl back into a convoluted shell, or sidestep an intimate moment with a joke. Outwardly he was all affection, but there was also armour. Inwardly my heart spiked up and down in response. In Vancouver Daniel had been a warm neighbour for a short three months. In Quebec our friendship had swept into intimacy. Deep and desired, but with sidesteps and a few failures of lust. Was I in love with a man with a problem? A perfectly wonderful man nearing sixty who couldn't make a commitment or talk about it? There were some things I still wanted out of life. I told myself I would enjoy this city to the max without him if he didn't want a relationship. And, yes, I could always move on and work elsewhere. In Canada. But not in the States.

We walked through the darkness up rue Ferland, the sidewalk snug against two-and three-storey historic houses joined one to the next to buttress against the freezing winters. The tops of the trees that grew in walled back courtyards were visible behind the bricks. With the slope of the street, lamplight silhouetted leaves, dormer windows and mansard roofs against the night sky. Large, diamond-shaped metal shingles gleamed. Upper Town's unique beauty was peaceful here. Winter would bring a different, more wary peace: the cushioning silence of snow, and swords of icicles thrusting over sidewalks. Their reminders hung permanently on the houses: '*Danger—Chute de Glace*'.

Danger. Death. We were all connected to it and to each other. Rocks on a dirt mound laid in an abnormal way over the victim; a victim whom I'd uncovered with no witnesses present, and in doing so had carefully changed the position of two suspicious stones; Luc's apparent jealousy of and sparring for recognition with the man who became the victim; Meg's missing notebook, and the revelation of another missing event, the victim's rendezvous with her; my secret crush on the victim, but not as secret as I might have wished—Meg had seen us together over drinks and had told my lover Daniel; Daniel, going on suspicions from his radio colleagues, calling the death "murder; the police under the command of the cold Detective Sergeant Laflamme with their own suspicions about the crime and its perpetrator.

What was the one common denominator in all these connections? Me, Berry Cates.

The dig would end in a little over three weeks, and before today I'd tried to be Ms. Perfectly Pleasant Productive Employee while waiting to hear Luc's response about awarding me the contract to continue my conservation work. With it, I could settle here at least through the winter. Unless Daniel, in whatever way, indicated unequivocally that he was giving me the pink slip.

"I wonder if my contract will be extended." I slowed my step, waiting to see how he would respond.

Instead Daniel lobbed the question back at me. "What do you think?"

"What do you think of Luc?" I parried.

"I hardly know him," Daniel replied honestly. "Meg says he takes care to mentor the students as well as the archeology. She likes him a lot. And you? Do you want to stay on working?"

I loved my work of preserving heritage despite any dis-agreements with my current boss, but I needed to hear this answer from Daniel. Did he want me to stay on? I responded with an observation about Luc, not Daniel's question to me. "You know how some people look like animals?" I began. "Well, Luc reminds me of the bears circuses used to have. He can look tame and charming on the outside, but jerk his chain too often and you know who really holds the power."

A chuckling Daniel took my hand and gazed up at the stars.

"I really do want to keep working," I said, knowing full well that this didn't in fact answer his phrase "stay on". The unknown remained hidden; whether Daniel would quit Quebec for Louisiana.

My mind returned to Luc. The episode I'd witnessed between Luc and Meg earlier in the day, when her missing notebook had been our biggest worry, had not helped this assessment. Like a tune you can't get out of your head, the scene replayed in my mind. But now it focused on Luc, and the almost unnoticed details of his small acts of power.

I'd found Meg by instinct after juddering open the aluminum door to Luc's office. Inside the trailer Meg hunched in a chair, grasping a steaming mug, Luc's personal one. He sat surrounded by artifacts, boxes and battered furniture, the image, as always, of a field archaeologist. A sweet haze of tobacco radiated throughout the room. In Luc's trailer, Luc smoked.

Conversation had stopped immediately. Meg and I argued irritably about her not coming back to the lab. Luc intervened, breaking the awkwardness with a wave of his pipe. "It's all true, Berry, I'm at fault. Gaetan needed a drafting table and I needed Gaetan to finish the stratigraphy drawings. *C'est ça.*" The end. He not invited me to sit down.

The motion in the room had then become Luc's boots crossing and uncrossing, steel showing through the toes, while his soiled fingers rummaged in his workshirt's pockets. A tobacco pouch surfaced. Silence continued through the pinching and tamping of more brown nicotine into the pipe's bowl, until Luc murmured, "Problems?"

"What about the notebook?" I said, and directly scrutinized Meg's face for any reaction, but she had bent over her mug.

"I'll call Gaetan," Luc said. "That is Meg's property on this dig, and it's important. If he took the notebook, I'll deal with it. But if not, I want you to find it." Meg's eyes lifted and their hunger betrayed her gratitude.

My own surprise at Luc's mild response to me and to the missing notebook was overtaken by another realization. I gritted my teeth rather than blurt out my assessment of this cozy 'young woman admires Great Man' scene. I respected Luc as an archaeologist, but his strong, controlling charm had already pushed me to the brink several times.

"Thanks, Luc," I'd grimaced, my mouth not quite managing the manoeuver of smiling.

The cold and wet of the excavation had seemed a minor irritant as I slogged back to the artifacts lab.

In the early morning that was still night, Daniel and I walked on, keeping to the small residential streets, crossing Côte du Palais to stroll in silence down quiet McMahon past the Celtic cross erected to honour Irish settlers in Quebec. We were holding hands, walking in rhythm in the soft closeness of the night. We avoided Rue St-Jean with its bistros and laughter. Even so, we were far from being the only people out late enjoying the night. Circling back on Rue des Remparts, we took in its amazing view of the St. Lawrence River, the lights of the port, a docked cruise ship, the south shore, and far off in the distance, the bridge to Île d'Orléans. At the top of the street Montmorency Park was a green space that would give us an even more spectacular view. We found late-nighters lingering there, gazing out from the battlements and historic cannons over the wide St. Lawrence. Warmth had crept in with the night and people had stayed out gathering its last blooms. Monday's storm had warned us all to harvest as much as possible.

Daniel breathed in the night air. "Let's just go past the Ursuline Convent, then home. Follow the scent of history." He beamed, and squeezed my hand.

I'd heard architects talk about a sense of place, and I smiled back. This walk was working for us both. I felt much calmer, maybe not in the same way as Daniel with his sense of belonging in this solid history, but with my awareness now of simply being in a good place with him. Literally and lovingly. We ambled across the street hand-in-hand.

A man and his dog slipped around us towards Montmorency Park, the man whispering and smiling down at the fur gleaming pure gold under the street lamps. A late-night group of happy teenage tourists noisily clambered up Côte de la Montagne from Lower Town, surging around the statue of Monsignor Laval, founder of the seminary opposite. We backed into the portico of the old stone post office to let the crowd pass.

"You know the Golden Dog?" said Daniel.

"Over in the park?"

"No, *ma belle*, overhead. Haven't you noticed the dog? He's our landmark. Everyone in Quebec City knows him. '*Le Chien d'Or*'."

Daniel dragged me out of the shadow of the doorway and pointed. Inset above the portico was a large stone relief of a gilded hound chewing a bone, surrounded by four lines of inscription. The spelling and the uneven letters using "v" instead of "u" looked hundreds of years old. I'd heard about the nineteenth-century novel "The Golden Dog", but I'd no idea the dog was real, as real as being carved in stone, or famous. Daniel read aloud,

Je suis un chien qui ronge l'os
En le rongeant je prends mon repos
Un temps viendra qui n'est pas venu
Que je mordrai qui m'aura mordu

I could read the older French, too, and knew what it meant.

I am a dog who gnaws a bone,
As I chew, I take my rest,
A time will come that is not yet here,
When I will bite him who has bitten me.

My shoulders slumped. In Quebec, was lingering resentment over the English winning New France written in stone? If everyone in Quebec City knew the Golden Dog, is that what this corner in the centre of town kept fresh in their minds?

"1759, the Plains of Abraham, right?" I said. *La conquête* as it was still called in French but rarely now in English. The Conquest.

"What are you talking about?"

"This," I pointed up to the inscription. The calm intimacy I'd felt with Daniel not five minutes ago had disappeared. Gone, and the gnawing question I harboured about the nature of our relationship had resurfaced.

"This . . . golden doggerel." I hoped Daniel took it as a joke, "Just a joke," I added, in case he hadn't. "It's not bad verse, but isn't it saying the same as '*Je me souviens*', the motto of Quebec? You know, *I remember* . . .what you bastards did, *la conquête*, but Quebeckers will get back at the English one day."

"By now, we have," said Daniel. I would have told him he looked like the Cheshire Cat if it hadn't meant sidetracking into another unshared cultural reference.

"Supposedly—anyway, what we were taught—," he continued, "'*Je me souviens*' means the opposite. We remember both the English rose and the French *fleur de lys*."

"Is that what you think of when you see the motto?"

"I remember my home, Québec."

I put my arm in his to change the subject, and stepped smartly off the granite curb. "*Aux Ursulines*! Let's go. As Shakespeare said, 'Get thee to a nunnery'."

"To be precise, Hamlet said that to Ophelia." Daniel stifled a grin.

Back at the apartment, her face stained with tears, Meg made quick work of the walk's pleasure. "Where the hell were you?"

Daniel attempted hugging her, explaining in his soothing radio voice that he'd checked just before leaving and she was asleep.

"You could've left me a note," she yowled. Florence had been the first to pinpoint Meg's drama queen personality, while this summer I'd tried to excuse her emotions with the words Irish, exuberance, and teenager. We were both right.

Daniel stage-whispered an apology, followed by "the neighbours!".

I moved into the kitchen and poured a glass of water as my excuse, propping myself against the sink. The warmth of the room brought waves of exhaustion. If the theatrics in the next room continued any longer I would sneak around the players and collapse on the sofa. Let Daniel figure out where he was going to sleep. It must be close to three a.m. I stumbled back into the living room.

"You look like *le Chien d'Or* whose bone has been snatched away," said Daniel.

Meg frowned, as if wondering whether I'd be on her side or Daniel's.

"I am one golden bitch right now, Daniel," I said. "I'm so tired. *Je me souviens de ton sofa,* and like the dog said, *je prends mon repos.*" I added, "Pronto." I threw myself on the couch, pulled the duvet over my head, and curled up with my back to the room. He had a foamie for camping he could pitch somewhere for himself.

"Hey," Daniel chuckled, "you can't sleep now. The next line is, '*Un temps viendra qui n'est pas venu.* A time will come that is not yet here," he translated for Meg's benefit.

He didn't need to, but it was a way of ensuring she was part of our banter.

He should have left her out. A high moan fled Meg's lips.

"*Quoi, ma petite*? Daniel embraced his cousin. "What's wrong?"

Meg's voice cracked. "That's exactly what Odette said."

"Odette?"

"This afternoon I was working with Luc when Antoine and Odette came into the artifacts room looking for him. Just before they had to go identify the body. While Antoine talked to Luc, Odette sat down right beside me. She wasn't really, like, saying anything to me, more to herself. Really slowly, I guess she was in shock."

"What?" I raised my head and made my voice carry from the couch. "What did she say?"

"'I guess I'm the Golden Dog now,'" she said. 'My time has finally come.'"

"That's it? Out of nowhere?"

"Then she recited some verse in French like what you just said. Odette repeated and repeated the last line, only at some point a few words changed. She shook her head with each line, like she was keeping time to music. But it was dreadful. Slow, like the drumbeat in a dirge."

"And the words?"

Meg closed her eyes and then recited, "*Il est mordu qui m'a mordu.*

"He is bitten who bit me," Daniel muttered.

CHAPTER SEVEN

꧁ ꧂

Meg stayed on at Daniel's. Me, I forced myself to go to appointments as well as the dig. One doctor suggested sleeping pills, another grief therapy. Both might dive me into long, swampy ponds. I avoided the wine bottle, not out of any inner strength but because it made me feel worse. Movies helped, their images replacing the other one, the still photo in my mind of dirt, fingers, hands, face.

Movies ended in resolution. I, too, needed a *dénouement* to the story I'd uncovered. Knowing exactly what had happened to those fingers, that hand, that life.

If the night could be bad, my emotions during the day were not much better, try as I might to control them. Quick mood changes skittered this turtle between slow and snapping. I heard from too many people that shock affects you in so many ways. Shit *la merde,* what about death under suspicious circumstances? What if the only probe into that death is being done by a supercilious, uncommunicative cop? PTSD or not, I vowed that Laflamme's would not be the only investigation. First, though, to be effective, I needed to look after myself, my own wellbeing. Everyday life, not everyday death, had to be faced.

But one good night's sleep remained impossible. On the third day of my first full work week Florence began to resuscitate my tired spirit. She lovingly described a handsome shepherd who would help me count sheep. My cure started with laughter, Florence the physician. She would ask what movies I'd watched the evening before and at break go on the web for film gossip. She borrowed a book from the library with rotten jokes and bad puns. Each morning of that week, however sleepless I felt, I went to work to talk with my closest woman friend there.

Friday morning Florence, sunk into one of the ragged armchairs that made our coffee corner comfortable, eyed me approvingly over the rim of her instant. I was attempting distracting conversation, to be drawn into the problems of ordinary daily life.

"Half the time I don't know how to deal with that assistant of mine, Florence. One day she's sweet rosy Meg from County Mayo, and the next she acts like a pouting two-year-old."

"She's spunky, talented, rebellious," said Florence. "What do you expect?"

"From a legal adult? Less drama queen. A bit more self-control. In most places she can drink, drive, and vote."

"And have hormones. And have independence. And have sex. She's entitled."

"What's sex got to do with this?"

"What planet do you live on, Berry Cates?" Florence grinned. "Gaetan's been hanging around her like a tomcat. Did you think it was just convenience, him bringing her morning coffee and croissants? Haven't you seen them together after work at La Taverne? What about the St-Jean-Baptiste-Day concert on the Plains?"

"Shit *la merde*." I'd been practicing the right words. "I thought she didn't like him. I really am Clueless Cates."

"Don't trash yourself. I think Meg's mainly annoyed by his attentions."

"She was horrified when I asked if they were together." At the time, unknowing, I'd been tickled it wasn't the twenty-five-year-old beer-guzzling Gaetan who had upset Meg with a missed rendezvous. I coped with this memory by backtracking.

"Maybe Gaetan did take the notebook," I said. "He knew that would really get Meg's attention."

"He's not as dumb as you think."

"Great. A smart alcoholic. Wise choice, Meg. Way to go."

"She doesn't like him."

"Okay, but she's not entirely mature. She has tantrums. She acts like a kid."

"Unlike yourself?"

I would have stuck my tongue out at her except it would prove her right. My voice softened, the epitome of dignified reason. "Maybe we just don't know the 'Emerald Isle' folk."

"Of course I do." Florence proffered a tin of biscuits. "Half of us in Quebec have Irish Catholic blood in our families."

"Meg's direct from Ireland. Daniel isn't."

"There you go. The Irish aren't just fighters and good musicians."

"Florence," my finger wagged in her direction, "*Faut pas stéréotyper*."

"I never stereotype," replied Florence, laughing, "Not like you just did, waving your schoolmistressy finger at me. And of course, the Emerald Isle's no stereotype either."

I stuck my tongue out.

"As you were observing," Florence continued, "Some people regress to two-year-old behavior when they get frustrated."

"Shaddup. So, okay, you win."

"Those are golden words." Florence beamed. "I come from a large family."

"Seriously, how do I deal with Meg's dramas?"

"No idea, *ma chère* Berry." Florence poured a little water from the kettle into her empty cup, swirled it, and moved towards the door to empty it onto the mud below, our otherwise perfect workroom lacking all plumbing. She looked back at me. "One thing I do know is you're not her mother, and you've never been a mother, so a word of warning—don't try it with Meg. Your assistant needs to treat you like a hockey player looking up to his coach."

"Her coach."

Florence smiled. "Okay, agreed, no stereotyping, eh?"

Florence became my coach in many ways. She answered with good humour my repeated, innocent-sounding questions about Quebec City and everything about the Nadon family from the time they were born. Then she started guiding me through details I wanted to forget. "What about the funeral— do you have clothes?" We looked through my closet together and Florence found nothing that wasn't too dig-like, too summery, or set aside for good memories. I would have made do with my one plain dress, but Florence was adamant that while the dress might be fine for a desk job in Toronto, square and navy was not cool in Quebec.

"*Bien, ma chérie*, tomorrow you buy me a nice lunch, and we buy you clothes. Right after work, so wear something you can try stuff on with. Are you working outside, in the dirt? You'll need dress shoes tomorrow. Got any?"

"No. Yes. They hurt. Anyway Florence, your sense of style, it's . . ." Pausing, I came up with the words, "not really mine."

Florence turned her back and began rooting around in the closet. I counted the minutes in silence. She emerged holding, at arms-length as if they were contaminated, one dusty loafer and a pair of worn black heels.

The dress shoes had been expensive so I'd kept them but dumped in a forgotten dungeon recess, black reminders of nights dancing all over town with my now ex. "Too small and I hate them."

"*Ma chère* Berry," Florence dropped the shoes and folded her arms. "I wear what's me. You choose what's you. I don't care what it is, as long as it honours Jean-Paul at his funeral."

"So what *is* me?" I said, aware my voice was rising towards a Meg-like pitch. "English Canada dresses name brands, French Canada dresses chic. Except on a dig where being overdressed is just so not with it."

"Look, Daniel's seen you dressed up or casual, primped and gorgeous or coated with dirt. He's still in love with you. Besides, I've seen you dressed up a little fancy. You look good."

My cheeks flooded red. On those few special occasions when I met Jean-Paul Nadon after work, my outfits had been chosen with care. For dig clothes, that meant clean and colourful. The perceptive Florence had invariably commented, and I'd been torn apart, pleased my clothes looked nice and embarrassed by a rendezvous I wanted the outside world not to notice.

I turned my head and pointed to the closet, wiping my wet eyes with the sleeve of the other arm. My voice lowered. "What if fancy isn't the real me? My steel-toed workboots are in there, too."

Florence replied, "Berry, your taste in shoes is . . . unusual, so if you want to try on dresses in your boots, it won't surprise me. But I won't allow you to get out of buying clothes for Jean-Paul's funeral."

I dread black clothes. The glass half full says they're hip, they're artsy, and they can be worn anywhere, anytime. The glass half empty says: especially at funerals. Sad, wrenching, voyeuristic events that somehow never do justice to the life that is gone. Happily, I won't be aware of my own.

"New shoes too, then," I said, giving up. "You'd think at this start of a new millennium there'd be black pumps comfortable enough for walking," I said, "but I don't hold out much hope."

Florence picked up my black shoes and dangled them in front of my eyes. "What you'd better hope for is you don't have to wear these."

At six in the morning the thought of shopping for horrid clothes woke me. I dressed in bright work gear to fight a sinkhole of depression forming in my mind. The black clothes for funerals; when would I be wearing them again? Who would die next? I decided to pack away all dark, grim reminders so they wouldn't hang in a closet I opened daily. Right now, though, I needed to implement the "look after myself" plan. Dressing rapidly, I headed out to start the day with a treat: croissants and an extra-chocolaty mocha in a sunny café.

It was early, so I ambled along St.-Jean, peering down side streets to find a good café that was open. The Café Croissant—perfect. Until a man came out of the church opposite loudly calling my name. I was caught, and this was not my morning for chitchat. But curiosity triumphed. Gaetan running towards me? He was not the sort I imagined going to church, and on weekday mornings? Unless he was confessing something. Like hiding a notebook. I smiled. He could be the ideal source for other dig information as well.

Gaetan asked if he might walk to work with me. I suggested we had time for coffee and croissants instead. We sat at a small round table by the café's window and I waited for the right time to ask him about the notebook.

We didn't know each other well and the conversation began awkwardly. The young man fidgeted as he made small talk, asking if we used technical drawings in our conservation records. My answers were brief, safe, and, I hoped, supportive enough to create a positive ambience. "Gaetan, conservation might be a wonderful career option for an artist like you."

Eventually my own questions became less round-about. "Do you often go to church before work, Gaetan?"

He shrugged, mumbled something noncommittal and drank more coffee. "Is Meg Catholic?" he blurted.

"Yes, she's Irish Catholic. Why do you ask?" I smiled a little too wolfishly at the small pleasure of already having Meg's name introduced into the conversation.

Gaetan smiled back and whispered, "I'm giving her a present."

"She's not actually religious."

"It's nothing like that. But a priest gave me some advice, and it's not cool, but I'm going to try, and if Meg's Catholic she won't mind it came from him."

My brain kicked in and my stomach cramped with the thought that the priest had advised Gaetan to ask for some traditional something, like Meg's hand in marriage. "Is that the present? The advice you're going to try?"

Gaetan laughed and shook his head. "Luc says I can share my drawing supplies with her if she'd like. I've got pigments ground with walnut oil where the colour's really intense. So maybe she'll like them even if me, if I'm kinda not cool anymore."

I kept my mouth shut about the 'anymore' and kept wraps on my curiosity about what would make him so uncool, because Gaetan had handed me the perfect segue.

"But Meg's missing her notebook. You know anything about where it could be?"

"Nothing!" Shock at my suggestion and then misery contorted his face. He suddenly looked so young, so exposed. "Honest, Ms. Cates, I would've told her. Why would I hide anything? Meg'd thank me if I found her notebook."

His words were true, his reaction genuine. I was glad to have this one small insight into the puzzle and a positive insight into Gaetan, and we chatted about the dig and the finds as we walked down the steep street to work.

We arrived at the site but I didn't get to work. A cop, arms crossed, was waiting to take me for another interrogation by Laflamme. The morning is not my best time and D.S. Cunning Cop had found out. I observed, though, that the morning was not her best time, either. Maybe it was her cold soul which had whitened her face and weakened her eyes. Motioned to the hard chair opposite her desk, I was astounded when her first words were "Would you like a coffee?" and before I could answer she had instructed the constable sitting at the side of the room with, "*Deux cafés au lait, s'il vous plait.*"

Laflamme consulted her notes and, to my continued astonishment, smiled. Although, whether at me or the arrival of the coffee, I couldn't tell. I clued in: the good cop bad cop routine. My lips rose in a return smile that today Laflamme was playing good cop. Even the room was furnished more like an office than an interrogation cell, with a nondescript landscape scene on one wall, Laflamme's table a desk made of wood, and the requisite filing cabinet. Would the constable at the room's side, sitting but without a coffee, act the bad cop?

"Berry Cates, thank you for all the information you've provided."

Laflamme sat back, waiting for a response.

"*Merci*," I said, staying away from, "*Merci beaucoup*." I waited for her next move.

"We'd like your further help," Laflamme continued. She rose, cup in hand, and as if on cue the cop who'd gotten the coffee moved two chairs over to my side of the desk until she, I and Laflamme formed a small circle. The constable sat back in a relaxed posture, watchful but saying nothing, while Laflamme, crossing her long legs, leaned forward.

"Berry, you've been very helpful," she repeated again, "and you play a key role in this investigation. But I have the feeling you're hiding something."

I parlayed this "thanks for your help" as an opening for me to ask my own question. "Did you call me in because you suspect me of being involved in Jean-Paul Nadon's death?"

"Not really, no. But before I continue, would you confirm for me please where you were the night before you found Monsieur Nadon."

I said, "The previous night? With Daniel and Meg at Daniel's," while I thought, "not really", is it?

"Of course. Monsieur Tremblay said the same. You were together the whole time?" Her voice kept a mild, smooth tone.

I paused, my face as blank as I could make it, but I knew I was snookered in this match.

"Daniel did get a call from Radio-Canada at about nine that night. Some big mess with the next day's early morning show, so he went into work for a few hours."

"Thank you. Monsieur Daniel said that as well, and also as a journalist, he knew Jean-Paul Nadon as a public figure and had no reason to cause him harm. But we have information about you and Monsieur Nadon. A *tête-à-tête* over few drinks is nothing to worry about, *n'est-ce pas*? I can't divulge the source, but it was not Monsieur Daniel. Have you talked with him about your meetings with Jean-Paul Nadon? Does he know the details?"

Shit *la merde*. Meg said she had mentioned a sentence or two to Daniel, but I hadn't. I shook my head and was about to retort that nothing had happened at those meetings except professional discussion when a memory of Jean-Paul rose, the image of a dead hand under wet dirt. I shuddered, and knew Detective Sergeant Cunning had gained another advantage.

"What are you hiding, Berry?"

I had to cut a deal if I was to gain anything out of this interview. "I'll tell you what you may or may not already know, but on condition that information is reciprocal. What do the police know about the cause of death?"

Laflamme's mask of a friendly face closed down. "You tell me the truth about what you've been hiding. The truth about you and Jean-Paul Nadon. I'll judge what comes next."

There would be no deal. Why did I ever think there would be? Stalling any longer was impossible, so in a deliberately emotionless voice I began to reveal the whole history of my crush on Jean-Paul Nadon and my enjoyment of the personal *rencontres*. I finished with, "That's it," and tried again. "Your turn, Detective Sergeant Laflamme. What was the cause of death?"

She was scowling. "Is that all, unrequited love indulged over wine and old bits of pottery? We'll see. Now, tell me who you think might have killed your matinee idol."

"Can't. I'd need more information from the police." No deal from me, either.

Her eyes closed for an instant. "We'll be releasing a public statement. Monsieur Nadon had extensive injuries and died from them."

I said, "From a fall? His foot slipping? Or was someone else . . .?"

Laflamme cut me off. "Undetermined."

"Signs of a struggle?" I probed. "In the mud, maybe?"

"What, after a storm that violent?"

"Maybe the coroner could tell."

"The autopsy is not finished. Monsieur Nadon's body will be released to the family when we have completed our investigation."

Her speech did sound like a press release. She still hid details, and so did I in not speaking about Meg's relationship with Jean-Paul.

Back at work I focused intensely on cleaning fragments of glass through the microscope so I didn't have to talk to anyone. Florence caught the signal and left me alone for the rest of the day. By the end of the afternoon I felt human again, my soul more restored and my body telling me it still existed by the crick in my neck and backstrain from hunching. Distraction would help even more, and Florence, picking up on my mood, renewed her offer to take me clothes shopping.

There is no shoe department at SiBelle-SiBon in this city, so Florence and I stopped first at one of the small stores along St. Jean. They tried to sell me two different pairs, dress and walking being totally incompatible in their opinion.

Indignant, I refused, thinking, "Of course you want me to spend more money."

The pumps I ended up with had elegance and a shaped heel low enough for city trekking. Half an hour after I'd put them on, though, my wide toes began to speak. Much later, Meg would ask me where the awesome shoes had come from, and my pride temporarily corrected my newly-acquired limp.

The real find at SiBelle-SiBon came in Women's Clothing. Florence had been pulling dark outfit after outfit off the racks, holding them up under designer lights while she extolled their qualities, the smiling salesclerks wondering who would get this commission. Florence being no fashionista did not matter to us right now. She was looking for anything in my size that would do for a funeral, and I was looking for anything to keep my mind occupied. But the dark clothes were making me increasingly depressed.

"Let's call it quits and get something to drink," I said, but Florence would not let me escape.

"Just try on two you like, so at least you'll have something."

"For God's sakes, Florence, that one's for students. An empire waist for the overweight teenager, that's the big market these days."

"So it's Indian cotton. The pattern is gorgeous. I'd wear it myself."

"Showing your bra straps? How *au courant*. And that one's awful—look at the embroidery."

Florence huffed and pulled out another choice.

"Look, Florence, today's not a good day for me, and I don't really want funeral clothes."

"*Ma chérie*, you need funeral clothes."

"I want a drink."

"Just buy something. Anything you can live with."

"Living for the dead. What a life."

Our bickering continued through the racks. Florence let me be irritable because it was an escape valve for my sadness. I let her lead me through countless gloomy clothes to soothe her own grief. Like an alcoholic and an enabler, our co-dependency meshed.

I was snarling barefoot in front of a mirror at my dispirited, caterpillar-like figure in a charcoal Italian dress. One of the salesclerks commented on how this light wool outfit was perfect in any season and looked terrific on me.

I glanced at the store tag. "It costs as much as I take home in a paycheck."

"Then Luc isn't paying you what you're worth."

I whirled around to see who not had trouble recognizing the *Anglaise* from the dig. Maybe they knew me as the one whispered about: "There she goes, she found the body."

My eyes met Odette's. The woman who had accompanied a grieving man to identify his brother's corpse. The death I had unearthed.

CHAPTER EIGHT

"Shit *la merde!*" I gasped. "I didn't know it was you!"

Odette smiled. "Some days I worry about that myself."

Florence laughed for the first time in hours. "I'm discovering who the real Berry is right now. Including what clothes she won't wear." She stepped over to Odette and the two embraced. "Are you here for . . .?"

"Same thing you are, I imagine."

They stood for a moment in silence, Odette elegant in perfectly fitted, smooth beige linen. Florence, in wrinkle-free shirt and slacks that had pilled across her thighs where artifact boxes had rubbed, said, "Well, let me show you what I've found so far. This is the fall stock and there's a good size range in most." Then she introduced me formally.

Odette held my hand longer than necessary, hearing in Florence's words that Jean-Paul had meant something to me as well. Whether or not Odette recognized me as the huddled figure in Luc's lab, I guessed that even before this introduction in the store she had known the name of the person who had found Jean-Paul. As for me, I'd heard Meg repeat what Odette had sung that day, "I'm the Golden Dog now. And my time has come." And then her satisfied refrain, "He is bitten who bit me".

"My deep condolences," I managed. "I believe you were a friend of Jean-Paul's for many years."

The wetness in Odette's eyes answered me, but all she said was that between us it wasn't necessary to use the formal "*vous*".

I needed more. Here was an elegant woman who had some reason, it appeared, to want Jean-Paul gone. Was she crying because her old friend had died, or from regret at a death she had a hand in? Florence ran her arm through Odette's, and walked her over to the outfits I'd earlier disparaged.

Ridiculously, I felt abandoned. The afternoon had made me disgruntled and now here was Odette. Key questions hid just below the surface but I had no way to ask them. Florence wouldn't let me, anyway, without first buying the clothes we had come here for. I took out my indignation on the Italian dress, ditched it, and each time the two of them sorted through my discards and went to look for the same in Odette's size, I retried the outfit they had gone to find. In the end, Odette, at least two sizes smaller than me, looked stunning in the Italian wool. I found myself urging her to buy it.

"You think *I* can afford it?" she said, laughing.

"If I looked like you in that dress, I'd take out a loan."

"Berry has invited us out for a drink," Florence announced to my astonishment. "After you've both bought something." She was now the irritated one, letting me know to get a move on. None too soon, I said to myself.

"I *will* get the dress." Odette posed in front of the mirror. "*Merci*, Berry. Just what I need right now, a drink and some girl talk. A pact, okay? No mention of anything serious."

Hah. Chitchatting over a glass of wine about hairdos? "Yes, for a funeral I prefer a layered bob." My mood darkened. My chance for information had just been neatly deflected. Shit *la merde*. I corralled Odette and Florence into admiring an outfit my emotions could barely stand but did look good on me. The bolero jacket and skirt that flared at the bottom already had a silk scarf and blouse picked out for the display mannequin. Loudly I complimented the saleswoman who had made those choices and bought the whole reckless ensemble.

We headed towards the bar.

Small talk is not my forte, especially with suspicions about Odette occupying my mind. Florence carried the conversation. I drank. One of the delights of Quebec is the excellent wine served at even an ordinary bistro. A second delight is that 'girl talk' turned out to be code for gossip. Although most of the people Florence and Odette chatted about were not familiar to me, when Luc came up for consideration, I was an avid listener. Not knowing Odette's connections in this small town, though, my own opinions remained guarded.

Good thing, too. Odette extolled the work Luc had done with her on the prehistory of Quebec City.

"Prehistory?" I couldn't help commenting, "like there was no history before the white guys came and wrote it down?"

Florence gave me a look, but Odette replied, "I know what you're saying, and I agree. It's one of those convenient words that replaces a long explanation. We historians need to get our act together. Find *le mot juste* that says the same thing."

"Try 'contact'. 'Before contact'."

"With whom? Indigenous people contacted each other." Odette was answering with enthusiasm as if a good student had been challenging her. "People also intermarried, of course. And many had European-style goods through trade before they'd ever seen a European. Not to mention all those who had seen Vikings or Basque fishermen on their shores." She reached over with an apologetic expression, her hand resting near mine. "Excuse this historian, please, for telling you things you probably know already."

Odette had handled my smart-ass pedantry perfectly, and my cheeks flushed. She had kept our girl talk comfortable after I'd prodded with a sharp point. But how could I get her to tell me the things I really wanted to know?

Odette asked if I was aware that Luc's real expertise was in the history of Indigenous peoples before the arrival of Europeans. His archeological background had been broader, though, and apparently he had been top choice for our dig in historic Lower Town to replace the prof on sabbatical.

The point of interest for me in all this wasn't how good Luc's reputation was or his field; it was how long the other prof was away. "So Luc might not be here overseeing the artifacts this winter, if the other prof comes back? Who's teaching the winter session?"

"Don't get your hopes up, Berry." Florence laughed. "Luc's here for the whole school year." To Odette, Florence said, "Berry finds him a demanding boss," and left it at that.

"He does like to control the details," agreed Odette, and we were all satisfied with our versions of Luc.

With Luc out of the way and me knowing better what could and could not be said in this conversation, my spirits revived. When Odette had showed up at SiBelle-SiBon, my sourness had masked the small thrill that we might all be chatting together. And now, right here across the table, loosening up with drink, was the self-proclaimed Golden Dog. Trapped. With me burning to find out what she meant when she'd spoken that verse aloud, Meg hearing every word. I decided to tackle my mission in pseudo-girly talk.

"I loved that gold top you tried on," I began.

"The shimmery knit? Too scratchy with all those metallic threads."

"But your blonde hair looks great with the deeper gold."

"Really?" She was taking me seriously and I'd better watch it.

"Gold should be a favourite colour." Fashionista advice straight from the running shoe.

Florence had no idea what was going on, but she knew something was up from my sudden interest in clothes, and sat back, watchful, ready to spread her wings over any fire in the nest I might ignite.

"Sure. I kind of picture you golden. Do you?"

Odette laughed, but with a sort of raw throat cough. "About forty years ago, maybe." She reached for her glass of Sauvignon Blanc, turning it in the light. "Pale, isn't it? Not even yellow. I must be going." She finished the wine quickly, picked up her parcels, and with brief kisses on cheeks, left.

Florence leaned across the table. "Well, whatever you were trying to do, it sure backfired."

"I was just making small talk," I said. "And you know how lousy I am at it."

That appeased Florence and she shoved the bill towards me. Even though she'd put me up to it by inviting Odette, I'd planned on paying the minute I attempted to bribe my dig companion out of the clothing store. In the end, all the good this outing had done was to buy me dismal clothes for the horrible funeral of a friend.

We walked slowly down Rue St.-Jean towards the old city walls. Florence was uncharacteristically silent and it worried me. Should I ask in girly talk or could I resume our normal relationship? "What's wrong?" squeaked out in a voice neither girly nor normal.

Florence gave a weak laugh. "Ah, *ma chère* Berry, you know me too well. I was going to ask Odette about something, but she didn't want anything serious. There's new information on Jean-Paul."

"What?" I stopped and made a conscious effort to stand tall, but found myself leaning impatiently towards Florence.

When she didn't answer, I said, "How did you find out?"

"My brother's son is in the *Sûreté*. He's not one of the cops on the case, but he has friends who are."

"Well? Come on, Florence, you'll feel better if you don't hold it in."

"Lucky for you that's true. But this isn't public knowledge, so keep it quiet. You know the police are trying to find anyone who saw a man out in the storm Monday night? So they went to the Beau-Port restaurant to see who were the diners that evening, to call them with the numbers they phoned in with making their reservations. But the storm was so bad, people cancelled or didn't show. Except for one man who dropped in about seven to see if they were staying open. He made a reservation for two for a late drink and meal. After the theatre, the waiter at the Beau-Port assumed. Around eleven. But the man never showed up, either. The reservation was in Jean-Paul's name."

"Was it Jean-Paul?"

"The waiter identified a photo, and he was positive because . . . he knew his name as a celebrity. Apparently Jean-Paul gave no indication who the other person would have been, man or woman."

"You said, 'Positive because . . .?'" She had been going to say something else.

Florence put one arm in mine. "Because he described exactly the coat Jean-Paul was wearing when you found him."

Vivid images of that day erupted inside me. Florence and I said our goodbyes. Dazed, I wandered along Rue St.-Jean. Wine and bad memories did not mix, and all I wanted now was to put one foot in front of the other long enough to arrive *chez moi*. Get to my own tiny apartment in the St.-Jean-Baptiste neighbourhood just outside the walls where I didn't have to answer to anybody. I would pull myself together tomorrow. Right now, ten more minutes and I could collapse at home.

The imposing city walls screened my view of St.-Jean-Baptiste. So I'd gone nowhere in the last how long? Steep, crowded streets still lay ahead. I turned abruptly towards the nearest café, some tea, coffee, a croissant, any stopgap for my buckling legs. Daunted by my normal walk home? Maybe something to do with not eating since lunch and the full glasses of wine? But I knew it was the flickering of images pulling me under, Jean-Paul's hand in the sleeve of a dark blue coat and the cold clinging dirt. A man for whom I'd had a teenage crush, looked forward too much to chatting with over a glass of wine, whose fresh corpse had suddenly lain inches from my face.

I glanced through the windows of a bar as I shuffled past, and for an instant did buckle over, only the building's wall catching me upright. Meg sat inside. At a corner table spread with papers. With an older man whose back was to me. They were holding hands. Adrenalin stiffened my legs and propelled them into the entranceway where I had a better view.

Meg's eyes were glistening under the lights and I could read her lips. "I'm so sad," she was saying, pausing between each word. "You?" He must have replied, because Meg smiled and placed her other hand on top of his. Then her mouth opened, in fear or surprise at me finding them together like that, but she freed one hand to wave. The man turned. His eyes narrowed. The furrows of grief I'd once seen on his face molded themselves into anxiety.

The man immediately stood up, his shoulders stiffly high against his collar while he gathered up the papers. His height made him bend halfway over to kiss Meg good-bye. An air kiss on each cheek. As the man strode towards the door I backed out and hid in the adjacent tourist shop, a complete act of cowardice, but I had no reserves to meet his mood. Especially when Meg's earlier words about sadness could have come from me. The tall gaunt man, Jean-Paul's brother Antoine, left the bar, and when he had gone down the street I snuck back in, to the corner table, to confront Meg.

CHAPTER NINE

Confusion brought a halt to my normally direct 'shit *la merde*' approach; "Meg, what, WHAT, is going on?" remained unvoiced. She was sobbing. I sat down quietly, pulled out a few tissues, and very gently covered her hand with mine, then almost withdrew it when I remembered Antoine and her doing the same. At my touch, Meg's head snapped up and she flung herself across the small table to hug. I slid my chair closer and we held tight, her weeping finding a home in my exhaustion. I was glad she had chosen a table off to one side for her clandestine rendezvous, and that the café's music covered our conversation.

Why was she hugging me so close and why had Antoine looked anxious? I'd better find out. This was not the only time Berry Cates had jumped feet first into business that was none of her own. Hoof-and-mouth disease was a comfortable, chronic condition.

"Is everything okay?" It patently wasn't. I tried again, circling around my concerns. "Was that the biologist you do the illustrations for?" Meg nodded. "Were those drawings on the table?" Another nod. "I wish I'd seen your work."

"It was his." Meg sniffled and reached for a tissue. "He wanted to show me angles I could try out. Antoine's a brilliant artist. But he has to write the text so I'm doing the rest of the pictures."

"He's thinking about his book? He just lost his brother."

"He's devastated!" Meg grabbed more tissues, half-crying, blowing her nose the only interruption to a cascade of words. "He came into town to show me the drawings, but it was his excuse. He felt so dreadful, so lost without his brother, and hoped when he'd phoned I would understand and spend a little time with him. I think he just needs a friend. He lives out there all alone, Berry, and I don't know who he's close to except Odette, he's never mentioned any names or anything except business when I've seen him about the pictures, and he's so upset about his brother." Tears flowed. "Could he have my permission to rendez-vous with him instead of Jean-Paul, he asked, ever the gentleman, he wanted to keep this family tradition going, so of course I said yes. He's such a lovely man, so much like his brother, Berry, no man's ever been old-fashioned like that to me, he even asked if it would be all right if he took my hand, he just wanted some human contact."

"So do I." I squeezed her fingers. "I'm sorry I inter-rupted." This was a lie, white or otherwise, but I was curious to keep the subject going and find out what had caused Antoine's anxiety. When Meg didn't answer except to ask for more tissues, I said, "Was Antoine upset when you waved at me? Did it come at a bad point?"

Meg shook her head. "I could tell he was feeling bet-ter than when he'd arrived, but when I waved, all he said was, 'I shouldn't have done this. I'm keeping you from your afternoon.' He sounded so depressed again, I assured him it was just you, but he got up. You'd gone by then, though, so I figured you'd understood, and he'd come back, but it was like the clouds had settled on him and if I hadn't known he was feeling so dreadful I would have said it was rude to leave like that. Not a glance back or a wave?"

"He's on a rollercoaster of emotions. I wonder if he's even sleeping at night. Grief, it magnifies feelings, like exhaustion." I spoke from experience.

"Poor fella." Meg's Irish origins came through with feeling. "He's always seemed so happy out on his farm the few times I've gone. Now this horrid . . ." She couldn't finish. "I wish there was something I could do."

"No," I said, too quickly. "Antoine must be three times your age. He has Odette and there's no reason anyway he should have told you about his friends or the rest of his family." My voice steadied. "What exactly is his relationship to Odette?" Meg shrugged. I added, "He shouldn't have to lean on an eighteen-year-old through this."

"Oh, so eighteen's no good?" Meg glared and an instant later she smacked back her chair, muttered her "piss off" Irish phrase, with "Mammy" pointedly added on the end, and stood. "You smart people can be stupid too, you know."

"Hear me out!" I hadn't let go of her hand. "You're grieving as well. You had a special relationship with Jean-Paul." Not that I was going to venture into it at this point. "Antoine didn't come here to help your sadness, he was trying to deal with his own."

"So? So?" But Meg was no longer pulling away. Her free hand occupied itself instead with twisting stray strands of hair.

"So, he needs, well, a comfort, like patting a furry lapdog would be. And you need to look after yourself."

"Lapdog? Jaysus!" Meg snapped. "You're the dog!" she muttered, but not low enough so I couldn't hear. "A dog who digs in everyone's business. Fuck!" This was loud. "No wonder doggie found Jean-Paul in the dirtpile." She jerked her arm, grabbed her bag and headed for the door, turning only to shout, "Your time's going to come, too, when somebody bites *you*."

The eyes at several tables were on us.

I said calmly, "And you have just shown exactly what I'm talking about."

Meg slowed in the entranceway.

"Rollercoaster of emotions? Grieving? Magnified feelings?"

Meg's cheeks reddened but the rest of her face was too pale. She stood for a moment, ghost-like in the doorway. I'd been prepared for her to run. But, one hand clutching her bag while the other pulled at her hair, she dragged herself back to our table, eyes wet, and murmured, "That was rubbish what I just said."

"Me too."

"I do know things at eighteen, you know."

"I know."

"I don't think you trust me sometimes."

"Meg, you're right. I don't know many people your age. I haven't had much practice in this particular *pas de deux*. My steps, well, either I'm lurching forward like a toddler or I feel so old it's like my age is in dog years." I grinned. "Woof woof!"

"*Wouf wouf*," replied Meg in French. "Don't worry. I won't ever fetch his slippers."

Saturday morning I willed myself to get to Daniel's on time. Before the funeral—memorial service was the official word—we were driving out to St.-Édouard, and my impression of Aunt Adèle could seal my fate. Daniel's parents were both dead, like mine, and the matriarch who would be inspecting me was the adored eighty-year-old aunt. Despite my dark "good clothes" I swung my arms and quickened my stride, adding more purpose and ignoring the glances at my running shoes from the native pedestrians. I was determined to have walking comfort. But one of the runners must have reached the point of public embarrassment and stumbled on the uneven pavement, lurching me against a lamppost and upending the bag hiding my new pumps and a box of tissues. I swore under my breath.

I'd been ruminating again on why Daniel hadn't introduced me to his aunt long before this. Because he was leaving anyway, to go to Louisiana? Now I was forced into a loaded meeting the day of Jean-Paul's memorial. Aunt Adèle had heard Jean-Paul lecture, admired his understanding of traditional Québec, and wanted to attend the service. "Damn!" I picked my personals up from the sidewalk and remembered Grandma Céline making me put a penny in a jar each time I used a bad word. So much time had passed since then that the government of Canada had stopped making pennies. "Shit *la merde*," I said again with satisfaction.

Daniel headed the car out of the city in the opposite direction from Île d'Orléans, crossing the St. Lawrence on the suburban bridge whose road eventually led to Montreal. Aunt Adèle had lived much of her life in the old farmhouse outside St.-Édouard, her son Réjean and his family now in the bungalow next door. Soon enough we passed its driveway. A bike with training wheels, a pink ten-speed and a pickup large enough for an ATV took up half the length of the gravel. Between the bungalow and the farmhouse a vegetable garden flourished.

Aunt Adèle's house gleamed white trimmed in blue. Its steep Quebec snow roof curved out over a wide shady veranda. A woman who could have belonged to any of the last few centuries, and maybe did except for her hemline, stood pinching unwanted suckers from tomato plants. Daniel jumped out of the car to kiss her, as did Meg, and Aunt Adèle removed a large sun hat to receive her due. Turning to me changing my shoes by the vehicle, Daniel made a theatrical bow towards his aunt.

"*Tante Adèle, je te présente l'autre 'incorrigible' dans ma vie*, Berry Cates. Berry, *je te présente l'Incorrigible, la soeur de mon père.*"

"*Une Incorrigible, elle aussi*?" Aunt Adèle's eyes shone. "Daniel has spoken very highly of you." As I approached, the old woman gave me an obvious head to toe, nodded, and broke into laughter, saying, "She makes it past the sentry." I didn't know how, because I was staring at her bun of jet-black hair that couldn't help but accentuate her wrinkles and pallor.

"Yes, of course I dye it." The woman's eyes held amusement. "Welcome, Bérénice, *dite* Berry." She extended a bony hand.

My face flushed crimson. Uncontrollable blushing—what an asset to a secret investigator. Aunt Adèle gave my hand a firm shake. I almost winced.

"*Pardon!*" she exclaimed. "It's a daily fight at my age to remain a part of the world. Sometimes I exaggerate." Aunt Adèle gently brushed one finger against my cheek, then kissed me on both of them.

I said, "I'm very glad to finally meet you, Mme ..." and blushed, again. Daniel had never called her anything but Aunt Adèle.

"Please, from you, too, I'd like 'Aunt Adèle'. Come in. I'll just wash and find my good hat. I would not feel right going to a funeral without a hat." We walked towards the house, hatless me wondering if I needed to borrow one. Aunt Adèle set a good pace with the explanation, "Berry, when you get to the age when you're called shrunken instead of '*ma petite*', don't give in." She added, "And whenever you want more unsolicited advice, come to Aunt Adèle. I've got more than my family can handle."

"I'd love to," I grinned. "Especially if you'll tell me what Daniel was like as a boy."

"God help me," Daniel groaned. "You know those sorts of leashes you once saw toddlers harnessed in so they couldn't run more than six feet? I need one for Aunt Adèle, but I've been told they're politically incorrect these days."

A young voice whimpered as we entered the house, letting in a reality the pleasant banter had camouflaged. Meg had already flung herself on a low brocaded couch.

"I can't go. I don't want this day to happen."

Aunt Adèle swept through the door to embrace her.

CHAPTER TEN

While Aunt Adèle and Daniel soothed Meg, I looked around this quintessential Quebec farmhouse. The old kitchen had kept its original cast-iron cookstove, magnificent with chrome curves and rose-beige enamel insets, a wood box still close by for fuel. Why discard a source for winter heat? The room's windowsills were deep, and the back door screened a porch, clothesline, and, in the distance, fields of hay. Over the years the kitchen cupboards and counters had been modified to install new appliances; an old wooden icebox housed a microwave. All the rooms on the main floor—the two front ones, the narrow hallway between them, and the kitchen at the back—had doorways that opened onto a square floral-wallpapered room at the very center of the house. You could go anywhere from this central room: the entire main floor, the basement with its steps closed off by a utility door, or up an elegant set of stairs with a turned handrail to the bedrooms.

Of the two front rooms on either side of the narrow entrance hall, it was obvious Aunt Adèle lived most of the time in the smaller sitting room rather than the more formal living room. There, beside a worn padded chair, were knitting and newspapers. Family photographs hung on the walls and brass and china bric-a-brac filled a corner cupboard. A box of chocolates and a porcelain figurine sat on the side table: birthday gifts to an old lady? Like Aunt Adèle, though, this small original parlour, easier to heat in winter than the living room, was not the archetypical picture of age. The walls were a bright buttery yellow, the knitting basket a funky artisan box, and the floor brightly covered. Aunt Adèle had made a graceful change from the world of carpet slippers and vestibules to that of wall-to-wall broadloom.

"You can snoop upstairs, too," I heard from the other room. Aunt Adèle added, "I want a little more time here." Daniel had warned me his aunt didn't mince words.

"Thanks," I yelled back, "I figured the floorboards might creak anyway and give me away," and bounded upstairs as fast as my dress shoes would allow.

"So this is why they call them dormers," I said out loud as I opened a door to a cozy bedroom lit by its one window jutting out through the steep roof. "*Dormez-vous? Dormez-vous?*" I hummed, then stopped, remembering when I'd last thought I'd heard '*Frère Jacques*'. The second dormered bedroom was like the first, a neatly made up, dusty guest room with a painting on one wall. At the front right was Aunt Adèle's bedroom: larger, Spartan, furnished with single bedstead, dresser, armoire, and old-fashioned dressing table made of rich yellow Quebec pine. Folded on top of the chenille bedspread lay a rather scandalous nightgown in bold reds and blues. Her spunky soul revealed again, I felt like an intruder and quickly left. The last door had been the smallest bedroom until renovated into a bathroom years ago: claw-foot tub, china sink, and toilet with a wooden handle. I took advantage of the opportunity. Back out in the hallway, it felt stuffy with the doors closed and the only light coming from the small window in the open bathroom. I would wait in the kitchen downstairs.

Jean-Paul's service was being held in the old seaside church in the town of St.-Jean on Île d'Orléans, with a reception nearby at his brother Antoine's farm. The coroner had not yet released the body but the family had wanted a memorial service to publicly honour him and express their grief. Practically speaking, the date also accommodated Jean-Paul's extended family.

Daniel drove just at the speed limit, not because we had plenty of time but because the main road connecting the villages on Île d'Orléans was only two lanes wide, a meandering route following centuries-old cart tracks. Why travel on land when the huge island was surrounded by the river? Not just a '*rivière*', but the wide St Lawrence, '*le Fleuve St. Laurent*'. Through the window I glimpsed a froth of whitecaps, and on the road, we had just passed a windswept pod of cyclists.

Daniel let Aunt Adèle carry the conversation, distracting us all from the point of this journey. Placing her hand on his knee as if telling a child to sit still, she recounted, with evident pride, each stage of Daniel's growing up, finishing with, "My nephew has always been a city boy, but you wouldn't think so, would you? He knows the value of hard work, he looks after family," and I could see her hand pat his knee with these words, "and he knows the value of money. You've kept this good suit for a long time, *n'est-ce pas*?"

"*Oui*, Aunt Adèle. But remember? I told you I don't need to wear a suit to work."

"You have a good, steady job. That's what counts, even if they let you dress like you don't care."

As she spoke, Aunt Adèle half-turned in the front seat from time to time to meet my eyes, and, as I saw from the flickering glances, to observe Meg. What concerned her? A safe bet that it had to do with the service. Meg sat beside me but with her back turned from the conversation, staring out the window.

"I was the eldest of five, and the only girl," Aunt Adèle was saying. "Our family suffered in the Depression but not so badly as those in town. We had a cow, chickens, a garden—we always ate. The maple sugar bush gave us sweets, the fields hay for the horses. I still remember those shiny black horses. I was so small and they were so big! Papa had them for ploughing and hauling. It looked like the maples were snorting steam when the horses stepped around them with the big sap barrel. We weren't dependent like today."

"On government programs?" I said.

"No, *ma belle*, dependent on cash. We could survive without much. We had to. We kept the horses even when we had a tractor. Papa and my brothers—did I mention I was the only girl? —they could fix anything. There were no fancy electronics in those days. And could my mother sew! Knit, crochet—everyone was the same as us. You wore the same clothes except to church, you wore them out, you made your food, you sold spruce trees at Christmas, made maple syrup in March, planted and hayed in the summer, put up your preserves and won prizes at the Fall Fair—you know, the rhythm of the seasons."

"Sounds good," I smiled, cozy in my penchant for history.

"I hated it," said Aunt Adèle. "I wanted only to get out. To be bold. To go to a city, to Montréal. To not have to look after menfolk, especially the little squirt who was this squirt's father." She smiled at Daniel. "You don't have a younger brother, Berry, do you? I wanted to tear up that apron."

"Did you get to Montréal?"

"No." Aunt Adèle's answer was forceful. "Too much to do around the farm."

"But at least you had your painting," interjected Daniel.

"I used to dream of going to art school. I'd do some work for other families to buy paints and canvas. I had a small talent." Aunt Adèle turned as much as her body and the seatbelt would allow. "But the real talent for drawing in this family lay overseas, didn't it, in Ireland." She smiled at Meg who continued to stare out the window. "You know I'm right. I've lived long enough to know what's art and what's technique."

Aunt Adèle turned back, grimacing. "Am I talking about myself too much? Now, Berry, you must have an art talent also to be repairing works of art."

"Not as much as I'd like," I replied. "Plus, I conserve objects, not paintings or drawings."

"What subjects does a student take in conservation school?" asked Aunt Adèle. "You must have done some art to understand your objects. How the artisans made them?"

"Absolutely," I agreed. "Conservators have to understand materials and how they were put together to figure out deterioration and preservation." In the front seat Daniel glanced at Aunt Adèle, not hiding an exaggerated roll of his eyes. I recognized the signal for my habitual enthusiastic pontification about science, art and conservation. Too bad, Daniel, your aunt asked a question. "And to even get into conservation school you need to have some art or photography projects for your portfolio as well as some science. My talent is miniscule, and only in certain areas anyway."

"Your false modesty is what's *not* miniscule," grunted Daniel.

Aunt Adèle interjected, "And your talent is in what areas, then?"

"There's always drinking tea," I joked. I'd satisfied my mission to explain conservation, and I shut up for the driver's sake.

"And wisecracks," said Daniel, "Then there's your talent for preaching the Good Word of Art Conservation.

A little self-flagellation each time you talk shop might be beneficial, at least for us."

"Too medieval," I replied tartly. "I don't wear a hair shirt."

"Do you want your listeners to wear one?"

"Don't worry. Your destiny with hair is that it's receding. You'll have a male pattern baldness shirt."

Aunt Adèle snorted and raised a black-gloved hand delicately to her face. Turning towards me with an impish grin, she said, "My destiny is to look like Réjean's renovated sugar bush. My own trunk will have lines attached, too, but I'll be lying in a hospital."

Daniel and I laughed. Meg turned from the window, then hunched back.

"Your destiny," said Daniel, "is in my hands, so watch it."

Aunt Adèle broke in. "Your strengths, then, if you won't accept the word talent." She took off a glove and adjusted her black hat.

"Well, all the time I was tutoring French in Toronto, I also did pottery."

Right then our car swerved into the oncoming lane.

The wheels on one side lifted off the road. The other side bounced on the uneven pavement and we lifted off again, flying, tilting, in the back seat two of us screaming at the dark flashes of trees and ditches.

—◦◦◦◦—

CHAPTER ELEVEN

For far too long the car rocked. I couldn't breathe. A high
mew escaped Daniel's lips as he wrenched the vehicle back.
He slowed, gravel on the shoulder spewing like gunshots
on the metal underside of the car, and managed to stop,
car upright. Moments later oncoming traffic shadowed
the other lane, the exact pavement four terrified people on
their way to a funeral had careened over.

"*Dieu merci*," murmured Aunt Adèle.

Daniel was bent over the steering wheel. "I almost
killed you," he stammered. "I can't forgive myself."

Meg spoke her first words. "You wouldn't have to if
we'd all been dead."

"Was something on the road?" My lungs lacked air
after this speech. What was wrong with me doing pottery? Was I conserving pottery the day I found Jean-Paul?
I searched my shell-shocked memory. No. But that
awful morning Meg had been sitting outside measuring pottery, waiting forever for her rendezvous. On his
very first visit to the dig the eminent historian had been
exclaiming over the Willow Ware. Was there some clue I
was missing, some link Daniel the journalist had never
mentioned?

Aunt Adèle turned to look at Meg. "My love," she commanded, "Would you and Berry mind walking up to that
farm and getting me a dozen eggs?"

There was no sign about eggs or any farm laneway in
view. Why had Aunt Adèle needed to contrive a private

conversation with Daniel? His driving certainly deserved a firm word but how could I subtly find out if it linked to my mention of pottery? I pushed over to Meg's side, flipped the handle and we hustled out and began tramping down the shoulder as if we knew why.

Farmers had inhabited Île d'Orléans since the 1600s and by now most of the woodlands had been cut. The open fields with their stone or wood farmhouses, the essence of the island's scenic history, created little impediment to the weather. The wind was cold, and I used this as an excuse to put my arm around Meg and hold her close. It helped steady us both. I hugged her hard, wondering if she knew how much I loved her rampant, spirited self despite my inability to cut her young moods enough slack.

"What was that about?" I said.

"Don't ask me. They're only family."

After fifty yards Meg nestled deeper into my black jacket. "What now?"

"No idea. Keep walking."

"I'm cold."

"You're dressed for the sun this morning. Thank God I brought a jacket for church. You want it? Do you still have to cover your head in a Catholic church?"

Meg said, "Got anything to confess?"

I grinned, "Plenty. You?"

"I'd rather hear about other people's sins and confess them."

"No fair."

"But more fun." Meg met my eyes. "Do you know what Danny's big sin is?"

"Daniel? What?"

"I don't know. I'm asking."

"How do you know he has one?"

"We were talking about not going to mass since we were kids and Danny said, "I'd go if I thought it would do any good, but my sin can't be erased so easily."

I halted. Did this have anything at all to do with the swerving, or the life we were commemorating today—to do with death? I vowed to watch Daniel during the service. Then another thought hit me.

"Meg," I mumbled, thinking of Daniel's shying away from commitment in our relationship. "Even today the Catholic church isn't fond of gay men. Do you think he's actually in the closet?"

"Gay? Danny?"

I nodded.

"Berry! He's in love with you." Meg was laughing. "You silly old moo," she said with affection. "Danny adores you."

Then why not he ever said it like that? I started walking.

Meg grinned and began to sing that Irish American favourite, "Danny Boy". I joined in, in my scratchy voice. When we got to the line about summer gone and all the flowers dying, Meg's voice dropped and she looked hard at the gravel shoulder. We walked on in silence until she said, "Do you know, Berry, if it's usual in this country not to name the illustrator of a book?"

"Say that again?"

Meg repeated her question.

"You mean, put the name in the book itself? Are you talking about Antoine's publishing your drawings of the flowers?"

"I had to ask him who did the drawings in his last book because it wasn't mentioned."

"Each artist probably has a particular arrangement."

"I don't know what to do. I want to ask him to put my name in, but if he does, I could get in trouble with Immigration."

"You should definitely be acknowledged," I said. "Surely he'll do that. Besides, Immigration can't monitor everything. How do they know you were even paid?"

"And in cash," Meg grinned. "A book credit like that in my résumé would be brilliant, wouldn't it?"

When Daniel's car pulled in front of us a few minutes later, I silently thanked Aunt Adèle for this sweet spell with Meg.

In the car there was no mention of farm eggs. Silently Aunt Adèle reached for the heater, then kept eyes front like a Xian tomb warrior. From the back seat I gazed at Daniel's salt and pepper hair and wished I were up front holding his hand. And that he would talk honestly about pottery.

"Your beau is a very good man, Berry," Aunt Adèle broke the silence. "Let me tell you a funny story." I was grateful her generation had been brought up well, because somebody needed to take over, like the host at a dinner party who needed to manage a guest's disagreeable mood.

"Do you remember, Daniel," she continued, "that long evening when Miam-Miam ate the mushrooms we'd fried up with the omelette?" Aunt Adèle broke into a smile. Miam-Miam had been her cat, the mother of Daniel's Faux Paws.

"A friend and I had spent a beautiful day gathering mushrooms, and I made the most delicious omelette for dinner. Fresh eggs, too. There were six of us, weren't there, Daniel?" She turned towards me. "Then I caught Miam-Miam in the kitchen licking the dirty pan right on top of the stove. I named her "Yum-Yum" because her abiding passion had always been her food. She'd cleaned out the pan, including some omelette we not had room for. I scolded her, of course," and when Daniel grunted, she said, "Like this," and cooed, *Mon beau petit minou.* I laughed. Meg had one ear cocked. "And then we came in to sit by the fire. A few hours later Miam-Miam stumbles in, and she starts to writhe on the floor. It was so horrible, and I knew what was wrong. She'd eaten the wild mushrooms in the omelette."

"And so had we, of course," Daniel chimed in. "Aunt Adèle's face blanched the purest white, and she said, I'll never forget this, 'I've poisoned you all! You go to the hospital, I'll get the priest.'" He started to chuckle. "She was serious. I don't know if you wanted to confess your poisoning us before dying or if you wanted us to confess our own sins, but we only persuaded you to go to the hospital by saying there was a chapel there."

"We spent until five in the morning having our stomachs pumped, and recovering," said Aunt Adèle. "With me on my knees in between."

"So when we got back, exhausted," Daniel said, "I offered to find the cat and remove the body."

"I began to cry," added Aunt Adèle, "My poor *minou.* We all waited outside."

"When I came out," said Daniel, "shielding something from view, it was obvious I was choking up."

"Daniel collapsed on the grass. But in gales of laughter, kicking his feet in the air, pulling only his big arm out of his jacket. I was deeply offended." Aunt Adèle continued, "So I threw the door open, and there was Miam-Miam nursing four newborn kittens."

"But I never ate Aunt Adèle's wild mushrooms after that," Daniel half turned towards the back seat, smiling. Then he abruptly swung his head back to the road.

At the church, the car crept into the parking lot and was forced to wait as men in dark suits and women in somber hats converged slowly towards the doors. Some greeted each other with muted words and others looked out towards the water. The stone church with its silvery-green steeple appeared to embody Unmovable Truth, one side making the road twist to get around the building and the other diverting the St. Lawrence River. People shuffled towards the open doors like schoolchildren after the bell has rung, obliged to enter but storing up each moment of blue sky to buffer against the acid reality ahead. Climbing out of a van, the archeology crew, scrubbed, nobody in jeans, still looked scruffy and stained, impossible to hide that they had been digging in the dirt all summer, a visible reminder of their link with the dead man.

Aunt Adèle put her arm through Meg's so that support and supporter were indistinguishable. Daniel and I did the same. Before entering the shadow of the church, though, Daniel turned his face towards me and took two deep breaths.

"Berry, I need to clear it up."

"I was hoping you'd tell me about swerving into the other lane. Death's on my mind, too."

"It is . . . about death. And love. That's what I need to know. From you directly, about the intimacy between you and Jean-Paul. Why haven't you told me yourself? What 're you hiding?"

I didn't need a script. I'd been avoiding this conversation for days. Pottery didn't matter right now.

"Daniel, there was nothing intimate, I swear, between me and Jean-Paul Nadon. I respected him, he was intelligent, he was interested in the dig and in my work . . ."

"Things I'm not?"

"Let me finish!" I shut my eyes. "Sorry. I hate funerals and I hate this because," I looked up, "what if you don't believe me? Jean-Paul and I met a few times and I didn't tell you in case you'd take it wrong."

"And because it was a little wrong?"

"Maybe," I admitted. He meant Jean-Paul and me flirting. An accompanying small flutter of the heart.

"Daniel . . ." We were almost at the church's high red doors. There was much more I needed to say, but how? 'We need to talk'? The words men hate the most. 'I didn't tell you because I don't know where you and I are in our relationship'? How clinical. Or the unspoken third: 'How much do you really love me?' One answer would be unbearable right now. I played the 'L' note in a minor key. "Daniel, I like you. Very, very much." And waited for what he would say.

Daniel looked up at the sky. "I almost killed you."

Mon beau Daniel would never knowingly harm Aunt Adèle or Meg. I gave up for now musing on this driver losing control of his car, on our near, sudden crash, and how Daniel would feel for the rest of his life if he had caused that accident.

"Staffage these days," I grinned. "Impossible to get a good chauffeur."

Daniel mouthed a weak "*Merci*."

"But you have to go to confession," I joked.

Instead of rolling his eyes as I'd expected, Daniel merely nodded. I bustled us into the church to find Meg and Aunt Adèle.

Despite the heat inside the crowded church, halfway down the aisle Aunt Adèle sat pressed against Meg, still arm in arm. Meg's eyes were fixed on the flowers near the altar. There was no coffin. Florence had told me that in his will Jean-Paul had stated his wish for cremation, and so the memorial service was much less tied to burial. She had added that the police had not released the body, that apparently the autopsy was not yet complete.

Unlikely, I'd said, that the coroner had not examined the body by now. Florence agreed and so had her brother in the Sûreté, saying only that it must be tied up with the investigation but he didn't know how.

What information could make a difference to the coroner in order to complete an autopsy? The police able to conclude whether Jean-Paul had fallen or been pushed? Surely a coroner could determine this himself, and if so, would already have reported it as evidence. But would it have been possible to ascertain a stumbling fall from a fall caused by a push? Or was this coroner simply incompetent? Searching for clues in any direction, I'd asked Meg if Antoine had mentioned why the ceremony was taking place today. She confirmed that the date had been chosen to accommodate the many relatives living far from Quebec City. I was no further ahead.

As I settled, Aunt Adèle bent her head and said, "May I ask what you and Daniel were talking about?"

She had no right to know, and did I really want to hear the matriarch's opinions on my relationship with her nephew? My hesitation finally produced, "Maybe later."

"It is none of my business," agreed Aunt Adèle as if she had read my mind. "But Daniel," she murmured, "needs to say something to you, and if he hasn't said it, I will press him. It's important for you both."

Her fixed stare made me sit up even straighter on the hard pew. I said, "Then please just tell me."

"It can only come from Daniel."

"How can I tell you if he said it if I don't know what it is?"

"Let me rephrase my rude question. Does the name Sylvie mean anything to you?"

"No." I took a deep breath. "Who's Sylvie?"

"Nothing to worry about."

"Can't you tell me?"

"Daniel will tell you," said Aunt Adèle. "As soon as he can. He's having a hard day today. Let this rest."

Daniel was sitting with his head down, absorbed in a religious book from the pew in front. He was slowly leafing through the pages. The book was upside down.

"Aunt Adèle," I said, "can't you just tell me a bit?"

She sighed. "This will be like candy, you'll only want more. Hard candy. The last funeral Daniel attended in this church was Sylvie's."

Her clipped words said that this memory was the extent of the conversation. Aunt Adèle was right. Sylvie, whoever she was, was dead and that was the first thing I needed to know. Not a threat, not directly, but also too awkward a situation for me to comfort or confront Daniel. Sylvie might be a former girlfriend, his first love, a beautiful bow forever on his heartstrings. Nothing to do with the man we were burying.

Silence fell in the church as Jean-Paul's extended family entered from a private sideroom. The group spanned four generations. They would all be cousins and second cousins according to the family tree in the memorial notice, some of them living in France now, all the others spread across

Canada except for the one person I recognized, Antoine. As the rest arranged themselves he remained standing at the front, staring at the assembly. His face was strained but there was no stiffness, only sorrow. He started to pace down the aisle, looking around, not entirely aware of the hands pressing his or the sympathetic glances.

I looked around, too. Where was Odette? What would prevent her from being here, for both the man who was dead and his brother who, distressed, searched the gathering? Police custody was all I could think of.

At our pew, Antoine thrust his arm out.

"Meg, please. Sit with me." He grabbed her hand and turned back down the aisle. Meg rose and floated a pace behind him.

The pew of archaeologists quietly devoured the scene. Gaetan's face exposed a sullen pout. Sitting stiffly upright Florence alone remained unaware, eyes closed under a black straw hat. Next to her Luc was licking his lips.

"Meg and Antoine Nadon—do you know anything?" I whispered to Aunt Adèle, who immediately laid her hand on my knee.

"Do me a favour and keep an eye on Meg at the reception."

"Why . . .?"

"I don't want her mixed up with Antoine any more than she has to for work. I don't want her thinking that *la province de Québec* isn't modern, that this back-to-the-land nonsense is the same as farming. Everybody talks about his wonderful cheeses. They cost twice the price of cheese at the co-op."

The choir stood as the organ played the first chords. The thin gloved hand that had been on my knee folded back into Aunt Adèle's lap. The priest began reciting. I turned towards Daniel. He slouched immobile against the wood of the pew.

An intimate loneliness rose and submerged me—memories of being a child waking in my parents' bed to find them already gone for the day, hearing the live-in student gabbing on the phone while she shoved cold cereal into a bowl; later, high school without one truly memorable prom date or pajama party. Forty years later I sat surrounded by a memorial service, an unwanted ritual in an unfamiliar place, among people I longed to be with but who had withdrawn each into their own cosmos.

As I had into mine. One thought had surfaced and reeled me in, one question I'd hardly dared ask before. Was the missing notebook in any sinister, hideous way related to Jean-Paul's death? Other than the fact that its disappearance had led me to examine the dirt pile? At this stage, the police wouldn't be particularly interested in searching for a mislaid piece of dig property. My questions would only be answered if I pursued them.

My fingers gripped Daniel's. The church mass was solemn, the voices beautiful. I took no comfort. But eventually my dark mood ebbed, chased away by the warmth of Daniel's hand. He was beside me, and we were alive. The horribly lonely person here would have been Jean-Paul Nadon, cold and forever isolated even as hundreds of friends and family surrounded him, and a few burly men at the back of the church surveilled who in this crowd might have murdered him.

CHAPTER TWELVE

—◦◦◦—

Near Antoine's house, goats of various denominations sized up the guests arriving for the reception. The house and barns were set back more than a field's length from the road where the cars had been signalled to park. A warm sun had come out and the winding laneway we walked down held a humid summer scent. I wished Aunt Adèle had come to the reception rather than taking advantage of a lift to town; this must be the same fieldflower smell of her childhood.

Near the house an old Quebec porch swing with its two facing banquettes was being rocked by several young women from the dig. With my good shoes grinding my toes, I hobbled towards it. Sympathetic smiles greeted my arrival and I kicked off the pumps. Nobody on the swing was speaking, just swaying in the sun and nature's afternoon silence of breeze and cicadas. Daniel waved and headed into the house. The slam of the screen door and the voices from the farmhouse receded with each measured creak of the *balançoire*. From my seat, Antoine's barn, outbuildings, a small orchard and an orderly vegetable garden were visible beyond the house.

A tray of white and red wine advanced towards us. Luc, pipe in mouth, dishcloth over one arm, played sommelier. The mood on the *balançoire* shifted as he approached, and one woman put a foot down to halt its swing. Luc bowed formally in his role and recited the two types of white and red on the tray. Circling to serve each woman from the left like a practised waiter, he spun the tray so that her choice was nearest. When he reached me he bent down. "I need to see you immediately."

Reluctantly I squeezed into my shoes and followed my boss. He stopped well before the first trees in the orchard—a collegial chat, all above-board, it would seem, yet nobody could hear us. At least from here I could keep the gang in sight.

"I need your help," Luc began. "And I'd appreciate it if you didn't tell anyone."

"Depends," I answered. He had broken the reveries of the swing, a pleasure I almost craved right now. "What's up?" I took a swig of my Riesling.

"Wine's just as good sipped," Luc admonished as if I was one of his young charges.

At this condescension I almost spit my mouthful on his polished shoes.

"Sorry," I said. "The wine's too sweet for me. I'll try the other," and lifted a glass of Sauvignon Blanc from the tray he held.

I was scoring points in the jostling that often underlay our conversations, but Luc was far from blameless himself.

He closed his eyes for a few seconds and then said in a slow, low voice. "Berry, I know you don't like me. And to be honest I find you one diffi . . ." He paused. "Different woman," he finished.

"Same to you. As a man. So we're even."

There was no need for me to stay snippy. We both looked drawn and forlorn after the long day. "Sorry. You asked for my help and instead the memorial service today is all that's on my mind. So I want to start with . . . even 'diffy' me can see how good an archaeologist you are."

His eyes opened wide at this compliment.

"I should have said that before."

"Thanks"

"Can I ask a related question? About the archeology? Before we get to the help?"

"Shoot."

"Archeologically speaking, what did you really think of the dirt pile Jean-Paul was buried in? Could the debris have been washed down in the storm, or was it deliberately placed?"

Luc dragged his boot heel hard on the ground. "Whoever that bastard is he won't get away." He lifted his grim face to watch my reaction. "Everyone's asked the same question. The answer is 'either'. That's what I told the police. There could already have been a pile at the bottom that my students just added to when they were cleaning up, or the whole thing could have been constructed. With the rain, there were no shovel or wheelbarrow marks. Nobody remembers where they were piling the dirt or rocks, they were working so fast to clean up before the next downpour." He looked me in the eye. "What do you think, with your conservator's eye for detail?"

"Frankly," I said, my tight grip on the glass easing, "the stones on top made the dirtpile look too tidy for my liking."

Luc pursed his lips, nodded as if considering my reply, and turned to stare at the ground. We both drank.

Eyeing me again, Luc said, "My turn now to ask a question, and I need a straight answer." He placed his pipe in his mouth but forgot to fill it. He began with, "We're not the same, you and me. Can we put it aside, you know, right now, and also that I'm your boss, and all that? I need to know about Meg."

My eyebrows shot up but I said nothing.

"She's way too upset about Jean-Paul. I'm worried. Is there anything you can tell me?"

"Why shouldn't she be upset?" My mood was sliding into wary. Despite what he'd asked, a small voice inside raised old warnings about my boss. "*Are you intending to make me upset to get your answers?*' I leaned on my less cramped foot. "Why does it worry you so much?"

Luc lifted his pipe from his mouth and concentrated on tamping in tobacco. "I'm wondering if she's concealing something. Something I should know." Luc added, "That might affect the dig." He lit the pipe and eyed me. His face betrayed genuine worry.

"You're right," I finally admitted. "Meg's doing drawings for Jean-Paul's brother. Secretly, so Immigration doesn't know she's working privately as well as on the dig." I exhaled audibly. "I've got worries about Meg, too. Why, really, is an eighteen-year-old meeting up with a guy who must be in his sixties? I think she was upset about the drafting table that day because she wanted to do some drawings on the sly. And also," I wanted to clamp my mouth shut but I wanted any gossip, too, "I caught her and Antoine in a café together."

But as I spoke my mind turned on different track about Meg and her young life. Here's Luc suspicious of information being cached and he asked, "Is it about the dig?" Did he mean, "is it about the missing notebook?" Does he think Meg's found it and isn't telling him? Maybe because the page with the drawing of the bathing slipper is wrecked and she's scared to tell him?

I said, "Do you have any clues to anything else she's been hiding?"

When he patted his heart, I jumped. "What, you think she was in love with Jean-Paul?" I swallowed. Had Antoine been only a means to get close to Jean-Paul? "Why?

"Was she?" he countered.

"Ask her! And for God's sakes, why would that affect the dig?"

"What was her relationship with Jean-Paul?" Luc demanded.

"Let's start with what's *your* relationship with Meg."

We'd slipped back into our usual sparring.

Luc paid too much attention to setting his tray down on the ground. The glasses rattled.

"I am," he growled, "the father of a nineteen-year old. You didn't know that, did you? Suzanne, my kid with an ex-girlfriend before we knew we were too young to act like grown-ups. My daughter barely speaks to me. She's very angry. Meg is very angry, or at least emotional. I want to know if Jean-Paul Nadon did something to make her so upset."

"Jean-Paul? Why would that courteous, sympa . . ."

He interrupted. "Ask her." He exhaled. "Please."

"Luc," I said, folding my arms, "what would this have to do with your daughter? Meg is from a different country. She's probably completely different from your daughter." His pronunciation of 'diff-erent' had surfaced in my tone.

"My Suzanne was a student of Jean-Paul Nadon's." Luc's voice betrayed genuine anger now. "Three years ago. At a Saturday group he started for high school students, each week taking them around Upper and Lower Town, explaining the history to them, forging more links for Quebec pride."

"So?"

"Jean-Paul came on to her. Big time."

"I don't believe it. At his age? And risk his reputation?"

Luc took his pipe out of his mouth and stubbed the ashes on the ground.

"Don't mix up your own relationship with Jean-Paul in this. I'm talking about my daughter. And Meg."

I wanted to ask what in hell he believed went on in my "relationship" with Jean-Paul.

"He had his hands all over Suzanne," Luc continued. "She said as much to me later. Or sort of said it, when her pregnancy showed." With each of those last words Luc banged his empty pipe against his palm. "I'm worried Jean-Paul had his dirty hands on Meg too."

I opened my mouth to tell him yes, I was putting aside his being my boss because he was completely crazy. Instead, two thoughts froze my tongue. First, if I was correctly following the trajectory of Luc's imagination, I might actually be facing the person responsible for Jean-Paul's death. Luc certainly had a motive if all this were true: avenging his daughter. Second, whether this was the case or not, Luc had leapt to appalling conclusions that involved Meg. Was he implying she might have murdered Jean-Paul if he had molested her? Or . . . if Luc himself had killed Jean-Paul over what he allegedly did to Suzanne, was I listening to the bastard shift the blame to Meg?

My body had solidified into ice, the kind so cold it burns instead. My face flushed with anger even as I welcomed what had suddenly surfaced in my mind. Why would a man guilty of murder or even of framing an innocent girl come and ask for my help? One thought was clear, though. I absolutely had to find out how and why Jean-Paul had died. Do my damnedest to make sure a killer did not escape justice. Because for decades Jean-Paul had lingered in my mind as an inspiration, and much later had been genial and generous to me in person. And because, like it or not, this *tête-à-tête* had brought me into Luc's mess. The archaeologist's muck had smeared Jean-Paul's name. First Odette with her Golden Dog refrain, now Luc. Whatever that muck was, getting to the bottom of it might give me the name of the murderer, and, so very important, unequivocally confirm Meg's innocence.

"I'll talk to Meg." I shivered.

Right now I needed time alone to think. More, I needed to see Meg's face, just to hold in my sight the familiar mischievous mouth, the tangle of dark hair over ruddy cheeks, the deep young eyes that devoured all visual detail.

The farmhouse was crowded, people still milling around family members weighed down by the day and the inescapable conversation. As at Aunt Adèle's, the living room was beside the front door hallway, and there my gut did a double-take. Jean-Paul was everywhere; a multitude of photos, framed honours, letters and clippings gathered over the years were hanging on walls or spreading out across tables. His publications covered the whole top of an old upright piano. I was surrounded by memories marking his vitality and tears welled up even knowing my own grief was small compared to others. But mine was real grief, too, and hadn't been consoled. Nor would I be, unless I opened up to someone. Daniel was out, the memory of Jean-Paul exaggerated as a rival for my affections. Florence was out; she'd known Jean-Paul better than I, her grief undoubtedly deeper, if better managed. Why hadn't she stayed for the reception? Comfort for me in this house would not come easily. I'd feel better when Jean-Paul's death was fully investigated and his killer found. I swore to myself, "I'll do everything in my power to hasten that discovery."

Through the crush of people I glimpsed Meg sitting beside Antoine on the couch, her face calm and relaxed. Meg was fine. There was even a gentlemanly space between Antoine and her; he was paying more attention to the group in front of him. I could forget Aunt Adèle's plea to look after her Irish Meg. It was as if the young woman had weathered the day's storms and was now in a safe harbour. I would talk to her about Luc's crazy suspicions when more time had slipped between all of us and the memorial service.

Antoine sat forward, wineglass in hand, talking as he faced several standing men. Daniel was one of them. My eyes took in Daniel's dark linen jacket, elegant on his slim body, and saw the way his slacks leaned in a slight curve as he stood, the way his hair curled over his blue shirt. "*Mon beau Daniel*," I murmured.

Shifting my gaze to Antoine, what I saw startled me. I understood the gaunt face from grief and from his strong features, but he sat so alert, almost like a cat ready to spring. There was no threat in this posture, though, no ferocity; it was the lithe grace that struck me, an animal-like quality of his whole body. Beside Antoine, Daniel appeared soft, accommodating in the way he held himself, compared to the sense of power and quickness in the brother. And Antoine's dark suit did not hide his rough, farm-work strength. A disturbing thought infiltrated my mind, one that had a mild effect on my body. The Nadon family, Jean-Paul and now Antoine, were unmistakeably, irrepressibly attractive.

My rational self tried to quash this response. It didn't work. Maybe being rational had switched off after seeing Meg was okay, or maybe my own emotions were so taut any touch spun them like a stretched string. Abruptly I headed for the kitchen, trying to distract my thoughts. My body was starting to bounce on some kind of sick trampoline activated by my mind, sending it flying where I didn't want my flesh and feelings to go. In no way could the next few minutes have me facing Antoine, giving him my sympathies while Daniel watched. Shit *la merde*, what was wrong with me? Boyfriend in the room and here I am, hot for the other man. In his house, on the afternoon of his brother's wake.

"How's Meg, Ms. Cates?" asked a thin voice next to me as I leaned against a door. I jumped.

Gaetan had insinuated himself into a space between my doorframe and a tiled kitchen counter.

"We're all upset." Including me. He could probably see that. "But she's doing okay."

"I feel really bad. I wanted to tell you this the other morning. I never should have asked for the drafting table. Luc was getting mad, though. Do you think Meg understands? I couldn't finish the stratigraphy drawings without its big slanted surface."

"It's not so much the table right now."

Gaetan hung his head. "I know. It's Monsieur Nadon dying."

I seized my chance. "The day he died, did you notice Luc, how he reacted when he first saw Monsieur Nadon's body?" For good measure I added, "He must have been very upset, and usually he's got everything under control."

"He puked! Didn't you know? He ran over when you started screaming and was kneeling by that dirt pile brushing away more of the soil. Then he crossed himself and got up real quick and just puked."

I'd been so immersed in my own reaction I hadn't asked about others. Was Luc's vomiting, though, from initial shock only? From seeing a famous colleague lying dead on his dig? Or from something more personal, his suspicions about his daughter and the dead man, that he might never know, now, to exact revenge? Or worse for Luc, had his revenge just been discovered?

Gaetan straightened. "Why did you want to know?"

"I'm just trying to put things together. There's a lot an outsider like myself doesn't get." My toes wriggled in my uncomfortable, half-chic shoes. "For instance, back again about the drafting table. Why didn't you just come to work? Use it in the trailer?"

Gaetan searched my face as if he wanted to see what hidden weirdness was producing these questions. "Ms. Cates," he said, "You didn't know? I've got to stay away for a while. Doctor's orders."

"I'm sorry, Gaetan, no. Hope you feel better soon." I gave him my best solicitous look while trying to wipe the curiosity off my face.

"Hah. I thought everybody knew. I'm the joke of the dig."

"Honestly, I haven't heard a thing," I said, "and neither has Florence." I figured she would have told me. "So it's not as bad as you think." I added, "Whatever it is."

"I'm doing it 'cause I love Meg."

I sighed. Undoubtedly another thing in the name of love that was dumb. It made me want to shake him by the shoulders and yell, "What? Do what?" Instead, I inquired, "And how *are* you doing, Gaetan?"

"Do you think she even likes me?" he answered.

"Meg isn't in a state right now to know," I sidestepped in a soft voice. I remembered her appalled reaction when I'd asked on the day the drafting table had gone missing. Meg needed to tell him herself what she thought, and I'd no cause to admit to my own feelings. I continued my evasion with, "She admired Jean-Paul, she does some drawing for his brother so she's close to the bereaved family. It'll take a while before she sorts things out." I saw Gaetan relax even with this non-answer. He was a redhead, with the kind of light skin and freckled complexion that can be their unique bane. Now his hand stopped worrying at the strands of flaming hair over his forehead. Had he been singled out and teased over his young lifetime for looking so different from the stereotype of a Québécois? I remembered Florence commenting on Irish ancestry in Quebec.

"And you," I dogged on, "How are *you* right now?"

"Remember I told you I was going to try something uncool? It's the shits, but they say the first part is the worst. I haven't had a drink in a week and I'm holding out here okay."

I couldn't help myself from glancing down. In his hands Gaetan held a can of soda.

So that was it. "That's fantastic," I exclaimed. "Bravo!" and added, "Is this what the priest advised you that morning I saw you coming out of church?"

"He'd invited me to a group for alcoholics who want to quit. Don't tell Meg. Maybe she doesn't know. But I'm going to get clean."

"That's courageous, Gaetan. Really." I wondered if alcohol was his only vice, but this was not the time to peg him as a type, nor to discourage his *amour* for Meg. "You, know, Gaetan, I don't have any kids, but if I did, I'd be so damn proud if they were doing what you're doing."

"Thanks," he mumbled as he took a slug from the soda.

"If people are making jokes about this, they're just jealous."

"That's what the doc said would happen. My buddies would try to get me down to La Taverne. So he said to stay away 'til I feel good and strong."

I leaned forward. "Luc's okay with that?"

"Luc's been fantastic. He really looks out for me."

I couldn't hold back. "So Luc's been good?"

"He gets it! He's the biggest friend I ever had."

I would square this version of Luc with my own later. "I knew you could drink quite a bit," I pursued. "What made you decide to quit? Apart from Meg, and Luc, I mean?" Maybe that was enough.

"You couldn't see I was a mess? Meg did, and she told me, straight. She was right. Luc said he'd help. Another boss would've tossed me out. I need to stop acting stupid. Gotta sort things out."

"Me too," I murmured, and gave his hand a squeeze. "Keep me posted."

My eyes caught Luc heading straight for us. No longer the sommelier, or maybe just careful as he came towards Gaetan, Luc had no glass and was grinning, making amiable small talk as he pushed through the crowd. He smiled at Gaetan and nodded at me.

"*Ça va*, Gaetan? Everything good? Maybe we should head back."

Gaetan grinned. "I'm ready if you are."

"Then let's go." Luc glanced at the can in Gaetan's hand, an involuntary check. "Glad you're my designated driver. Berry, come see me tomorrow morning."

Luc put a light hand on Gaetan's shoulder and steered him out.

Tomorrow morning, what? Shit *la merde*.

❧•❧

CHAPTER THIRTEEN

~⊶⊷⊸⊶~

The farmhouse kitchen buzzed louder, and Odette was in the middle of it. So she was not in police custody. Had Odette been the veiled woman slumped under a heavy coat in a front pew, creating privacy from prying eyes, like mine, at a service dark with emotion? Seeing her left me elated, and on edge. Now I could carry out, albeit rudely considering why we were all here, my half-baked idea to 'bump into' her and broach the one subject our conversation in the store and bistro afterwards had failed to answer. 'So you think you're the Golden Dog? Know anything about how Jean-Paul died? Something about he's bitten and now your time has come?' An animated crowd surrounded Odette. I backed out of the kitchen and wait for a more private opportunity to chat.

Daniel beckoned from the living room. He was still talking to Antoine and drew his arm around me as soon as he could. I stiffened and this time said my condolences. My too-straight back betrayed my secret, that the man on the couch held my eyes, right here beside my boyfriend.

"*Merci.*" Antoine's voice was warm. "I saw you the other day but I was in a foul mood. Please excuse me. Jean-Paul talked about you. My brother was interested in what you were doing. He told me all about how you could preserve the original surface on a metal artifact even when it was covered by corrosion. For him it was like seeing real history revealed."

Daniel half-smiled.

"Thanks for telling me," I replied. "He mentioned you to me, too. In fact, everyone I meet keeps talking about the excellent cheeses you make."

Antoine ducked his head. "They're all out for the reception. *Merci*." An impeccable host despite the occasion, he continued, "Daniel, you must be hungry and thirsty by now." Daniel tightened his arm around my waist and motioned me with his eyes towards the kitchen. I stood grinning at Antoine.

"Wait." Antoine paused. "I want to ask Berry one conservation question."

You can ask my id anything with those sculpted lips.

"I have some drawings upstairs and they're stained. Can they be fixed? Could you do any work on them that would make them look better?"

"Etchings?" I asked.

"No, just pencil or ink with some colour washes."

My cheeks flushed after my "come up and see my etchings" reflex. "Hot," I apologized, and took off my jacket. Stop undressing in front of him! And get your blushes under control. Find a support group, a Blushers Anonymous. But the participants would have to live without anonymity; the red cheeks would be a guaranteed give-away. I said, "I'm sure the stain on the paper can be reduced," and immediately regretted "sure". If the stain went through the painted area, it could be far harder to remove than if the work had been a print like an etching.

"But I'll have to see it." Any conservator would, before diagnosis. But at what point would I reveal that I did not treat works of art?

"Meg," Antoine turned to the figure nestled in her own thoughts against the sofa cushions. "Would you take Berry upstairs and show her the drawings, the ones with the brown streaky stains? Show her the ones you've done, too, that I framed."

"Daniel," Antoine continued, "Your Irish cousin's really good. Go take a look. I don't know if you've seen these drawings." As we left, Antoine stretched his long legs, stood, and walked outside.

Upstairs, the great rafters of the farmhouse had been uncovered and the tall space finished for a master bedroom under the steep slant. It occupied half the attic, the same layout as at Aunt Adèle's except that the two biggest bedrooms in this farmhouse had been opened to form one large room. The bedroom's dormers overlooked the garden, apple trees and pastures, all the way to the distant high haze of Mont Ste. Anne on the mainland. Between the dormers stood an antique dining table with neat piles of books and papers, one lamp and one wooden pressback chair. Other antiques had settled in their own wall or floor space: a pine dresser, a Victorian armoire. A night-table that had once been a cake stand now displayed a small beaded pouch of the kind nineteenth-century fancy ladies bought from Indigenous makers. In the far corner a brass bedframe supported high mattresses under a quilt. I slipped out of my tight pumps and began to examine the two dozen or so pieces of folk art scattered on the floor.

"Those belong downstairs," said Meg, "but there were too many people."

Daniel grinned. "He's got some nice art on his floor." He played his fingers through a whimsical weathervane to set a wooden figure cycling, and patted a placid, stolid cow. I pointed out a hand-painted two-engine airplane, or rather aeroplane from its time period. Then Daniel and Meg began scrutinizing the pictures on the walls.

"That's bad," he said, "The stain, I mean. It ruins the white on these plants."

Meg said it looked worse than before.

Daniel leaned over the big table to see the drawings. "Why does he hang pictures of these ugly things? Roadside weeds and a half-eaten toadstool."

Meg hardly let him finish. "He did them! They're incredible drawings, really—all those gills on the mushrooms, all perfect. Everything has to be illustrated. Plants don't think if they're good or bad. Only gardeners call them weeds. Antoine draws them all equally, and every stage of their life cycle."

Daniel nodded. "I guess. This one's from the top, the bottom, all the parts. I can even see the different seasons. A ton of work. For a weed."

"It's so you can identify them! Don't call them weeds, Danny, they're wildflowers. They all grow around a farm. That's his new book, 'Biology of the Wild in Farmlands'. Everybody's interested in the plants that are native." Her voice rose. "Especially if they're changing with the climate."

"Are the native leprechauns under these toadstools extinct?" Daniel stepped back to see all the drawings together.

"Danny, don't make fun. Antoine's a great artist because knows everything growing on the whole island. I couldn't ever do perfect drawings like these."

"I bet you could, *ma belle*. You just have to learn to love a toadstool."

"Well, somebody here sure loved lilacs." I avoided thinking about why I'd wandered over to the bed while I peered at the two pictures hanging over it.

"Meg!" I exclaimed. "You did these? They're magnificent."

"Oh fuck." Meg shook her head. "I was hoping no one could read the signature. I did them to help my portfolio, and then Antoine kind of went overboard." Red rose in her cheeks. I was glad I was not the only one with this syndrome.

Daniel's face lit up as he approached the drawings. "Now, these are my kind of paintings. I can see why Antoine had them framed." He looked Meg in the eye. "Bravo, *ma petite.*" Daniel kissed her on both cheeks. "*Et encore bravo.*"

"I like the way they turned out," Meg admitted.

I smiled. "I'm trying to be able to say in words why they're so good. So much better than the mushrooms and weeds, for instance."

"Native fungi and flowers," corrected Meg.

I was not to be diverted, even if such praise embarrassed her. "For me, yours have the hope of spring in them, warm weather at last after a long winter, green in the garden and summer ahead. The others over there are botanical illustrations."

"But that's what they are." Meg sounded peeved. "The point is so you can identify them. He's a real botanist."

"And you," I said, "are a real artist."

Daniel beamed. Meg rushed towards the stairs and yelled back, trying to hide the evident pleasure in her voice. "Bullshite. You told Aunt Adèle you didn't know much about art. So don't blather on about me being an artist."

"I'll remember next time," I called out. She had better get used to compliments. Turning to Daniel I said, "They're extraordinary."

"They are. I feel like a proud parent."

"That's exactly the problem. Meg hates that parental solicitude. The omniscient adult."

"You mean, know-it-all?"

"Speak for yourself."

Daniel grinned, "That's why I'm in radio. You only have your artifacts to talk to."

"Well, at least they can't email back. Let's go."

"*Ma belle*," Daniel put his hands on my shoulders and spun me around to face the frames above the table. "We're up here so you can look at stains on plant pictures."

"So we are," I said, concentrating on Daniel's lips nuzzling the back of my neck. This wasn't so bad. Then he gently pushed me forward towards Antoine's stained pictures, and received a backwards light grab in return.

I lifted one of the drawings off the wall. "Goodie! I know what's going on."

"You know it all?" Daniel said.

"You weren't supposed to hear that."

"What'll the press release say, then? Okay, now you're allowed to pontificate."

I did. "The pictures are mounted *à l'ancienne*, with thin wood boards backing the drawing. He probably used old frames. There's a space where the two boards meet. Air and humidity circulate there and the acids from the wood have migrated into the paper, right up to the front of the drawings. That's the streaky brown stains. They should wash out fine, even where they've run into the pigment."

Carefully rehanging the picture, relieved at the positive outcome, I contemplated the drawing. Antoine was good: the shading of colour, the precise detail. His skill and keen interest in his subject overcame a lifeless, static quality I found in botanical illustrations, at least when compared to art, like Meg's lilacs or even the few paintings Aunt Adèle had in her house.

Daniel grabbed one of my discarded shoes, kissed me, and took off. I chased barefoot after him and kissed him "*passionément*" at the top of the stairs.

CHAPTER FOURTEEN

Talk on the ground floor had dropped to a murmur. Everyone strained to hear the information from the man with his back turned sideways to his guests, head bent, grunting into the phone. As he took in each piece of news, Antoine turned to the family member closest and hissed a phrase or word that reverberated louder until they all knew. When Daniel and I descended, shoes on, grinning and decorous, we heard, ". . . apologies, calling . . . solid news." Antoine glanced at the whole crowd. "Before . . . leave tomorrow." Antoine asked the caller to hold a minute and covered the mouthpiece as his whole body went rigid, steeling itself against what he might hear.

"Let us know . . . autopsy confirmed . . . did not die before . . . caught in the storm . . . Injuries consistent . . . storm strength . . . tumbled? . . . falling debris? . . . still investigating . . . burial, dirt . . . apology . . . exact cause of death . . . not yet."

Daniel, gesturing towards the phone, whispered, "Police?" to the nearest person. She nodded. "A little more news." With pursed lips Daniel plowed through the crowd to find Meg. I hesitated for an instant, lingering at the bottom of the stairs. Most listeners were Nadon family and I hurried out, having heard enough and tasting my intrusion.

No news had reached the noisy kitchen. Meg stood at the front of an intent group, with Daniel now at the back of the ten or so listeners, his hands on his hips, lips tightly pursed. At the front, gesticulating, stood Odette. The thin blonde woman spoke with her hands as much as her voice. I elbowed closer.

"So you see, Meg," Odette was saying in a voice whose strength I hadn't anticipated, "when you ask about the legend of the Golden Dog, I could talk for an hour. But you don't want a history lesson."

Her smile dismissed her class and Odette turned her attention to the glass of wine in her hand. When she looked up her face was drained. Most of the people had disappeared except for me and Daniel, standing now quiet as rocks on either side of Meg. Odette nodded towards me.

Meg was looking at Odette with a plea in her eyes; probably well practised, I thought, when I heard her voice.

"I'm really sorry if I'm bothering you," she said slowly in English, ramping up her Irish accent as part of her act as a visitor, "but I'm, you know, so interested in the history here after meeting Jean-Paul."

Odette's cheek twitched.

"So, and this is my last question," Meg pressed on, smiling, "What does being the Golden Dog mean? When would anyone become a golden dog?"

She's playing it perfectly. What an assistant. What a sleuth! I shifted my weight to the other foot without moving.

Odette bit her lip, paused as she focused on Meg, and spoke in a voice low enough that, only a short distance away, I missed a few words.

"I know who you are," said Odette, "Antoine . . . your drawings. You were staring at me the day we found out Jean-Paul had died. At the dig, staring."

Meg swallowed.

"I was very upset. You heard me talk about a Golden Dog. I will answer you but then this will be the end of it," she said. "Agreed?"

Meg nodded quickly.

"Jean-Paul was a golden boy. Professorship at Laval, fellowships, books, interviews." Odette lifted her eyes for a second to Daniel. "And after he retired he ran programs in public history. Continued to publish. More interviews. TV. Québec celebrates its own, you know, very well."

Grimacing, she continued. "I never made it like he did, and we're in the same field. I had kids instead, and besides, Jean-Paul was always ahead of me, just that much older, more distinguished, the favoured son. Son, you understand. Favoured daughter is not an expression in French or English, I think. I've taught, I've published, sure, but 'Odette Fortin'? Always the bridesmaid, never the bride, isn't that what you say? Jean-Paul is gone and it breaks my heart. Truly. For *le Québec*, for his family I know so well, and for *moi-même*. I once loved him, I admit it. Now I'm older. Not much time left for my work. But maybe I can at least stretch one leg in the sun now, like an old dog, what do you think?"

My answer would be for Daniel's ears only. "I think you had more motive than most to bury Jean-Paul. Before the sand in your own hourglass buries you."

Meg extended her hand towards Odette and thanked her, and I marvelled at her transformation into the mature young woman. "I admire your honesty, I really do," she said, and Odette smiled, saying something in return but the noise level in the kitchen had boomed to deafening and I heard nothing. The ruckus subsided as suddenly as it had risen, and then rose again wave-like to smash against all surfaces. The police news about Jean-Paul's death had reached the kitchen. The waves rose higher with each retelling. Killed by a fall? What happened? Still investigating? Was someone with him? Scared, so they buried him? The next thought remained invoiced but inescapable. Cold-blooded killing, undeniable murder.

Meg turned and ran, but Daniel had his arms open and wouldn't let her past. It took a few minutes for Odette to process the babble, and as she did Odette lost her balance as if she were fainting. I caught her waist and yelled for help. Someone shouted out about being a nurse, and in a few seconds Odette was sitting, face pushed forward between her knees, moaning. A young woman was retching at the sink.

The wake for Jean-Paul slid into chaos. Instead of celebrating a life amidst friends and family, closing with precise stitches a section of the collective heart, a knife had opened the wound wider. Guests lined up to shake Antoine's hand, murmuring rapid good-byes before they could flee for their cars. Odette managed to stand up, waving her hands. Others shouted for quiet. Odette raised her voice.

"Wait! Everyone, please. We must honour Jean-Paul!" Odette gulped, "He deserves as many remembrances as we can give him." She stopped. "I can't think right now. Antoine and I will talk, but maybe I could do a city tour 'à la mode de Jean-Paul'. The history, his favourite places, the ones he's famous for writing about. If he had enemies, show them how much he meant to us. Soon! This coming weekend? Start at the Porte St-Jean, yes?"

Applause swept away the darkened mood. I vowed to go on this tour. Not just for Jean-Paul. Any chance to question Odette, or even observe her, would let me know more about this dog's bark and bite.

The house emptied more quietly while the dazed family pulled chairs together in the living room. When Daniel, Meg and I approached Antoine to say goodbye, he pressed Meg's hand. Meg, her maturity again taking me by surprise, asked if she could stay and help clean up for him.

"*Mille mercis*," he replied. He smiled up at Daniel and me and thanked us. Whether it was for coming or in appreciation of Meg wasn't clear, but a jolt of electricity ran up my spine when he looked at me and said, "Come back, will you? I'd like to ask more about the picture staining. You two come for dinner sometime." He added, "I'll get Meg safely into town tomorrow afternoon at the latest. Odette's staying too in case this might seem inappropriate."

Daniel and I left the farmhouse leaning close together but soon separated into our own thoughts and pace. Walking down the long lane, Antoine's invitation slipped to the back of my mind as Jean-Paul's death took over. The pasture was empty, the goats no longer near the fence line. The late sun highlighted the fields and trees in a warm glow. It seemed to promise happy endings. That just wasn't true.

"The sun's a liar," I said. "A false prophet. The end to Jean-Paul's days was horrible."

Daniel had moved over to walk in the other rut of the lane. "What's got into you? This last sunlight's beautiful. Just enjoy it, why don't you?" He shook his head. "Sorry I'm so irritable. Long day. This light..." He tried to chatter. "There's a word, *la brunante*. I think from the *habitants*, their origins. Today you hear *crépuscule*, too. Twilight, dusk. They're the same time of day, aren't they? And that's not right now. The sun's still going down. What's the word for right now, in English?"

"I don't know if there is a word. 'Gloaming' is Scots, but I think it means the same as '*crépuscule*'."

We came up with no more conversation. Arriving at the end of the lane, Daniel began fumbling for the car keys but his hand was just ferreting about while he stared at some spot in the distance. When he pulled out the keys and jammed them towards the car door, still not blinking, I wrapped my arms around him. Was 'The Hidden' about to be revealed? Was Aunt Adèle's prediction coming to the boil—was he going to talk about Sylvie? Would it be the same as 'Danny's big sin' that Meg had mentioned? My hug was all he needed to tumble out the secret.

"Married, I was married long ago, did I tell you? Four years. We had a farmhouse. Like here. Lived off the land, goats and a garden. Aunt Adèle almost disowned me. Then my wife died. The funeral was in the church we were in today."

"Aunt Adèle mentioned the name Sylvie." But this had nothing to do with Jean-Paul's murder.

He trembled, and his eyes swivelled to the trees by the laneway. "We both did pottery. Did I ever tell you I was a potter? No, I bet I didn't, but I didn't know, you know, you'd been one too. Big wood-fired kiln, but *merde*, the work! You can imagine, chopping all that wood, and then tons more in winter for heat. Sylvie loved the look it gave, the glaze like raku, but it was too much for me. All I did each day was chop. No time for making the pots!" Daniel's laugh was as shrill as a hawk's cry. "Chainsaw the logs to fit the stove. Trim with the axe. Split the pieces—hammer and wedge. Stack it all inside." He swore.

"Did you have an accident chopping?" My voice remained under control, merely curious.

"It was too much work, you know? So we switched to propane. Big new kiln. Easy to use." Daniel was talking to himself.

"Thanks for letting me know you were married." I should have chosen better words. "I mean," I said softly, "it's really good you're telling me this."

"With Sylvie. Four years."

"Then she . . . passed away?"

At last Daniel looked directly at me.

"I killed her."

———

CHAPTER FIFTEEN

—◦❦◦◦❦◦—

I stood staring at a murderer or my insane beau. But this was a man who takes spiders outside rather than kill them. I needed my smarts if we were going to talk through this disaster. And I did not need an audience. Stragglers from the reception were coming down the lane. Pressing a rigid Daniel in a half-hug with my left hand, my right extracted the car keys from his fingers. I grabbed his elbow, marched him around to the passenger side, and then shoved. He sat, head down, retracting his legs automatically. His exposed neck waited for the guillotine.

My shortness of breath told me I wasn't in great condition to drive and it had nothing to do with the wine. Shit *la merde*, where can we go nearby and be alone? Maybe the 'English' end of the island where nineteenth-century artists had summered. Nobody from the reception likely drove there. A radio host isn't necessarily recognized anyway. I wanted to shake the truth out of the robotic Daniel. Beads of sweat decorated my upper lip.

As we followed the old highway I did a sort of meditation to get calm, emptying my mind of worry and concentrating only on the road and the changing landscape. Instead of long thin fields, a New France land usage fronting each farm on the St. Lawrence, Ste-Petronille hid cottage country. Victorian verandahs looked west across the river towards Quebec City. Luxurious stands of mixed hardwoods had been preserved for shade rather than cleared for fields and firewood. I hustled Daniel past the painter Horatio Walker's brick house. The waves of the

St. Lawrence were receding and we stopped on the wet gravel beach, sitting close on a retaining wall.

"How did you kill your wife, Daniel?" The calm voice had to be mine despite the way my insides felt.

"With the kiln."

A film cel cartoon of a body flattened under a toppled, firebrick-lined kiln formed in my mind. First the distorted shape, then blood up here and around there, and how would it look if the kiln had been on? 1200 degrees centigrade? I reeled back and watched the river. Had Daniel said something?

"The vents," came the whisper.

The vents. I'd fired pots once in a propane kiln, and every year accidents with stoves and fridges at remote hunt camps made the news. With any propane equipment, if this odourless gas was not properly vented it would flood the room. After a while, whoever inhaled it would never wake up.

"You set the vents wrong?"

"She did. I thought she knew how to use them."

"But you didn't deliberately go and shut the vents?"

Daniel's head reared back as if he were a monster snake about to defend itself, eyes glinting with venom.

"You think I would—"

"No, for God's sakes! I mean, it means, you didn't kill her!" My hand on his jacket had formed a fist twisting his lapel.

"I left her alone!" Daniel screamed.

"So you weren't even there."

"I thought she knew how." His eyes flared wide with the effort of getting me to understand. "I should have gone over the venting more."

"It was an accident."

"I could have prevented it. And it was me who bought that kiln. No more wood chopping." His hands made a weak chop in the air and slid over to his face as if to cover it.

"And you would have, if you'd had any idea what was going to happen. Daniel, you know it, I know it."

He bowed his head, breathing heavily. "That's what my shrink said. He convinced me the way I feel's not rational. But her dying haunts me every day."

"I'm with the shrink, and we're both know-it-alls, remember?" I tried out a smile and added in a tender voice, "I love you," and let the words hang between us. In their silence, the St. Lawrence River played the beach stones like an orchestra.

"You forgive me?" Daniel's voice shook.

"You didn't do anything."

"That's what I've been saying!"

"No, eejit! *Idiot*!" I raked back my hair. "There was nothing you could have done. You feel terrible. You're a guy with a conscience. With emotions. Bravo. You sought help for your guilt. Bravo. Guys don't like to feel vulnerable. You have people who love you—look at Meg." I paused. "Or me," and quickly continued, "Bravo. You're still able to love despite this awful tragedy."

Then I started to laugh. His peevish look made me laugh even harder.

"I'm so happy!" I embraced him.

"Breaking news," Daniel headlined with wry determination. "Man may not have killed wife. Girlfriend so relieved she forgets he never told her he was married."

"I am relieved," I choked. "You've explained everything."

"Yes, well, the incident has had a little influence on my life."

"And mine." My mouth kept breaking into a grin. "Like how we don't talk about love when we get together. It all makes sense now."

"Us together didn't make sense before?"

"Ay! Like your swerving on the road today. Now I get it. I'd just told you I was a potter."

"We almost got it, too. Pure luck there wasn't any traffic."

"That's because," I rose so we would start towards the car, "we're lucky together." Then I insisted on driving back.

On the trip home I had time to figure out that in my circle, luck in fact held no meaning. An enticingly congenial acquaintance and cultural figure had died horribly and I'd been the one to come face-to-face with his body under an archeological dirt pile; my boss had huge secrets and a daughter who wouldn't see him because she'd said this same man was her son's father, so to Luc, Jean-Paul was a predator; the boss had implied that my impish assistant, a relative of my boyfriend, might have been involved in the murder; this boyfriend lived with the irrational belief he'd killed his wife; and I'd made the acquaintance of a thin golden dog of a woman who, after the murder, no longer had to chew the career bone thrown to her and was salivating to taste the meat.

What would luck mean for me? Something as mundane as having my work contract extended? No. Luck would mean I would discover a killer's name. That no one I knew was the murderer. And that no one else would die, including me, for a long, long time.

I faced off against Luc Monday morning, the trailer already stuffy with pipe haze and humidity. On my arrival he sent everyone out, workers back to the dig and his assistant scurrying, first making a show of giving me more budget money for supplies. Bogus needs, I figured; the season would end soon and there were still unused cartons piled above the cupboards. He had to be setting the stage for something big. Now, puffing tobacco clouds, Luc slowly waltzed his chair side-to-side in the quiet trailer, waiting for my response to his first and only question.

He repeated, "You promised you'd talk to Meg and tell me what her relationship was with Jean-Paul Nadon."

"No can do," I murmured. I worked on my slouch near the door. "She deserves my trust. Not tattling to her boss."

Luc appraised my answer with a few more puffs. He swivelled the old wooden desk chair around to look out the window at the workers in the trenches. A minute later he was back scanning me, eyes gleaming.

"I'd really like you to stay on," he said, warming his voice to heat up the temptation.

"I certainly can stay." My eyes fixed on his face. So much was hidden by his beard. Straightening up tall, I said, "My work's gone well, and I could tell you right now what's left to be done. I want to do it."

Luc spent a moment shuffling papers on his worktable as if to emphasize that this conversation was all business. Was there smugness as his mouth set into a smile?

"As long as you talk to Meg at least seven days before the dig ends, the job is yours." He added, "Find out exactly about her and Jean-Paul. She'll talk to a woman. I have to get back to work." He continued to smile.

"First one question." I was not ready to leave. "For a man to answer. If there *was* anything going on, would his male friends just have sniggered and protected Jean-Paul? Or would they have tried to stop him playing around with such a young woman?"

"Depends. That's all I can really say."

I needed to find out if Luc was in any way connected to Jean-Paul's death, but I also, for so many reasons, needed my job to continue.

"Just spit it out," Florence grumbled, hands raised over her keyboard. "I mean you," she turned towards me, "Not this infernal computer—that's what IT means—Infernal Torture. Look how it's just brought up an old file I didn't want. Berry, you were talking to yourself." She added, "I couldn't hear it all."

Rolling my eyes didn't hide the red on my cheeks. "So I'm getting old."

"Here, then." Florence aimed and launched a blue plastic-covered pad at me.

"Watch it!" The sailing adult diaper was one of several products made originally for quite a different purpose that we found useful in archeological conservation. I warded off our flying disposable table padding. "You might hit the coins."

"The ones you haven't been working on for the last half hour?"

"The ones . . ." and I noticed that the coins had been reinserted into their specialized holders. "I meant the nails."

"Good riddance," replied Florence. "There are more than enough boring nails in history."

I agreed, reading off the closest boxes to buy time. "Nails hand wrought; nails drawn; large heads, hammered; nails industrial." But the cleaning of rust from nails, square or round, big or small, had given me time to think, time I needed.

"Well?" Florence smoothed her lab coat over a clean beige pantsuit. "So what were you saying to yourself? You already told me about the supplies."

I contemplated the nails while I bought time and carefully peeled off my surgical gloves. They had captured miniscule splinters of fibreglass shed by my jeweller's cleaning brush. "Why weren't you at Jean-Paul's reception?"

"That's not what you were muttering about."

"Tit for tat. You first."

"Berry, I arranged to babysit a friend's grandson so I'd have an excuse not to go. Death for me is best handled by seeing new life. Your turn."

"Luc had a daughter," I said.

"What brought this on? I only mentioned kids now."

"He told me at the reception he has a daughter, Suzanne."

"So?"

"So, well, I didn't know before that he was a father. I mean, what kind of father is he?"

"Why?" Florence's fingers played at her perm.

"He said his daughter wasn't speaking to him." Let's make it sound like cozy gossip.

"That's old news," Florence replied. "There was some scandal three, four years ago, and his daughter ended up . . ."

"What scandal?"

"Let me finish. Suzanne ended up in Chicoutimi. It's a long drive in winter."

"What's that got to do with it? Shit *la merde*, just tell me."

Florence turned her chair to face mine. "You know it already, *ma chérie*. You know it has to do with Jean-Paul or you wouldn't be asking."

"Break-time! Let me make you some really good coffee."

⌘ ⌘

CHAPTER SIXTEEN

Over hot drinks, cushioned in the ratty chairs, Florence related what she knew and what she figured had happened. Luc's daughter had been in high school, not doing too well and not caring much about it. Luc bribed her to go to the Saturday history group run by Jean-Paul Nadon; she'd make new friends and fit in easily because she already knew a lot of the subject via her father's work. Suzanne went, and got pregnant when she was fifteen. She wouldn't tell her friends exactly who was the father, but rumours circulated that she said Jean-Paul had 'touched' her. Florence knew because her youngest daughter had been a senior at the Saturday club that year.

"What did Jean-Paul say?"

"He dismissed the whole thing as absurd lies. The rumours dropped out of sight."

I leaned in towards Florence. "What's the truth do you think?"

"I don't care who the father is. In the circumstances, I think Luc has done everything for his daughter and her little boy that a parent could."

It was a good clear answer, but not enough.

"So why isn't she talking to Luc?"

"Ask Meg."

"What! You're telling me Meg from Ireland follows old Quebec scandals?"

"Berry, Meg and Suzanne are friends. Suzanne's going to art school now, or maybe it's design. Anyway, I heard them in Luc's trailer talking about illustrating, right after Meg first arrived. I went into the trailer and Luc just had this happy grin on his face, pretending not to watch them. He told me later he hadn't seen his daughter and grandson in ages and maybe with this visit things would change. I guess they haven't, but hasn't Meg been up to Chicoutimi on a few weekends?"

I slapped my forehead. "God, I'm so out of the loop I don't even think to get back in. I figured she was just seeing the province, you know? I'll ask Daniel what's up."

"Whatever. Why does it matter?"

I sat upright. It did matter. To Meg's future, and mine. "Did your daughter like the Saturday group? Did she ever say anything about Jean-Paul acting inappropriately to *her*?"

"I asked her, of course, once the rumours started. She was as shocked as I was that people could even think that of Jean-Paul. My daughter idolized him. She's in History now at the Université de Québec. Her fiancé does house renos. His skills better support her through a lot of schooling is all I can say."

"And the Saturday club continued. The parents must have had confidence in Jean-Paul."

"Exactly."

"So the parents didn't think Jean-Paul had done anything wrong?" My eyes met hers. "Has anyone commented on Luc's accusation?"

"Berry, they'd have told the police long ago if they thought there was a problem."

"Florence . . ." I leaned back. "You know a lot. Ever think of going one step further? You know, asking questions now that Jean-Paul has died, being the detective who figures out who killed him?"

Florence slammed her cup down. "Berry, never. It would only make enemies and I've lived in this town all my life. You, now, you're an innocent newcomer. You keep asking your questions." She saw me grin. "Just remember, though, if a trout keeps its mouth shut, it won't get caught."

Pretending my teacup was a mic, I leaned towards Florence. "Some fish can be slippery. And I've got plenty of questions. Like, why were all these young people so enchanted with Jean-Paul? Answer me that."

Florence sighed. "He was a star, Berry. He was a real *personnage* here, like Daniel—who knows how many people love Daniel from his radio shows? You might have competition, you know, *ma chérie*." She laughed. "Québec's its own world, and Jean-Paul was loved for unveiling so much of 'Québécois' right in front of our eyes. At the Saturday club, each week they'd go around town, Jean-Paul with all his energy explaining the buildings they were looking at or the *quartier,* and he'd read from eighteenth-century records, nineteenth century romance novels. Then they'd all go lunch somewhere and joke and ask questions and afterwards go to the old Seminary building. Laval's auditorium, one floor up from my lab. The students would have fun with what they'd seen." She closed her eyes with a smile at the memory. "They'd dramatize how the romance had ended or pretend to be the merchant writing the record. But keeping as true as they could to the times. Then they'd go off to the computer room and add it all to their website. Scripts, videos, cartoons. Gaetan's drawings are still up. They had fun. Jean-Paul was charismatic, that's the word. And handsome. Even my daughter thought he was good-looking."

"Wasn't he a bit old and hairless for her?"

"Nonsense. Kids get crushes on their teachers."

"In high school? In this cynical age? Earlier, maybe."

"Hey, thirteen, fifteen . . . romantic notions happen at any age." During this last sentence Florence fixed me with a sardonic smile, and my face began another slow red flush.

I started cleaning the hand-wrought nails. Something still lay hidden that had caused Luc to want to know about Meg's relationship with Jean-Paul, something Meg had not told him, or why would he have asked me? And Meg liked Luc, if not idolized him, and apparently had gotten to know his daughter. The day Jean-Paul was missing and Meg had been so upset, I'd found her in Luc's trailer drinking in his paternal warmth. What was so secret? Why was I discovering that the more I learned, the less I felt I knew Meg?

After the university's formal but heartfelt tribute to Professor Jean-Paul Nadon, Daniel and I found a bench outside and sat in the fresh air.

"Motive, Daniel." I was thinking out loud. "Tell me, what possible reason could there be for Meg to be involved in Jean-Paul's death?" Daniel fidgeted beside me on the *Terrasse Dufferin*, the huge boardwalk that faces the castle-like Chateau Frontenac hotel, his frustration at not having a good answer evident as his legs crossed and uncrossed. The Friday afternoon tourists milled about in front of us marvelling at the panoramic view the Terrasse gave them of the St. Lawrence and the smaller city of Lévis on the far shore. Seated, my visual field was less enticing: the backs of several woman sloped by their carryall purses, shorts rucked up on two hefty men, and various commercial logos on T-shirts. I looked around and saw groups fixing their smiles as they leaned back against the boardwalk's railing while one of their number jiggled a camera or phone. Through this throng a more visibly chic crowd headed home after work or to a bistro for a '*cinq à sept*', an enjoyable 'five to seven' drink with friends, but also carrying the older, more illicit connotation of a hidden amorous rendezvous. A memory buoyed my mood: Meg's question early after her arrival, whether instant coffee had been a popular Quebec tradition, because she'd heard about a special event beginning at five o'clock called "a Sanka set". Perhaps Odette's walking tour tomorrow would last into a Sanka set of the drinks kind. If not, I had to find the right time in the history tour to 'bump into' her and ask casually, to see her reaction for myself, about being bitten, about a Golden Dog, about a death.

"Of course," Daniel replied when asked if he was coming on the tour. "We're going together, no?"

"Of course." Imagining Antoine there too. And me the amateur sleuth questioning Odette.

"Berry," said Daniel. "Let's go somewhere where there's less people."

We retreated to the park beside the Chateau Frontenac and sat on the grass near the monument with General Wolfe's and the Marquis de Montcalm's names back to back, like a perpetual duel.

"Motive," Daniel continued. "Meg wasn't angry at Jean-Paul. From what you say she was beside herself he didn't show up. There's absolutely no indication she was involved in his death. No motive. Luc's crazy, or hiding something."

"All right. Next question: what?"

"Sounds more like his daughter's doing the hiding. Hiding something from him, maybe the name of the kid's father, maybe something else. And hiding out from him."

"Luc's dying to find out. So he's jumping to conclusions, for instance about Meg. He's driven to know. Why?"

"It's his daughter!" Daniel said. "Anyway, 'dying to find out' doesn't make sense when it was Jean-Paul who died. Why would Luc murder his prime source, his best source, since his daughter won't talk to him?"

"If Luc finds out what he's after, maybe he can make his daughter come back to the fold. That's why he's so determined." My voice quickened, "He's trying to win his daughter back."

"It seems to me finding out could make it worse. His daughter has a secret, and he discovers it, how does that help? Especially if it's about murder."

We went over this for another half hour. It was as if we were wading in a tar pit, sinking slowly, nothing firm to grasp onto.

"We're getting nowhere," I admitted. "Plan A—you talk to Meg and see if she knows anything secret about Jean-Paul. Like if he ever fondled her. You're her guardian and close relative here—it's appropriate. Then you or I can ask Meg if it's okay for me to tell Luc, and why."

"And how do I wriggle this intimate news out of her?"

"Daniel, you're the professional journalist."

"And you're off the hook." He continued the plotting. "So let's go to Plan B, too, something for you. All we're trying to find out is if Meg is in any way implicated in Jean-Paul's death. Right? Wipe out Luc's suspicions that Jean-Paul touched her like he did Luc's daughter, and Meg in some way took revenge."

"I want more. To know my boss's secret."

Daniel gave me a look.

"It would tell me the man I'm working for wasn't involved in any death. I want more than clearing Meg. I want to know who murdered Jean-Paul."

Daniel frowned and gazed out over the park. "That's for the police."

"It is," I conceded, "but nobody's heard much. And the least I can do for Jean-Paul is to keep my ears open and my brain working. Like the Golden Dog, look like I'm just chewing away, but one time maybe I'll bite on something that'll avenge Jean-Paul."

"*Formidable*," muttered Daniel. "Do you have any suspects?'

"Well, frankly, yes. We still have Luc." I emphasized the 'we'. "Meg's off my list. I won't believe she's involved, but we have to make sure. And what about Odette, whose life perked up as soon as Jean-Paul died?" I left out that this would be a good time for Daniel to get over thinking he had killed his wife. Or for me to quit ignoring if instead there was a thread of truth in what Daniel had recounted, rather than my own self-interest helping me believe that Daniel could never murder.

"All my suspects," I continued, "are pretty unlikely. But it's a place to start. I'll try to suss out more about Luc."

"He's your boss. Don't ruin your chances. Wait till he gives you the contract for the rest of the year. So then Plan C's Odette. A Golden Dog finally stretching her leg now that one sun has conveniently set so hers could rise? I'm definitely going on that history walk tomorrow. We'll compare notes."

The rest of the year! No Louisiana? A warm glow overwhelmed any thoughts of Antoine. Until Detective Laflamme strode across the park towards us like an adversarial Wolfe or Montcalm, her cold presence dousing my own inner fire.

—◦◦◦◦◦—

CHAPTER SEVENTEEN

—◦⊙◦⊰◦⊱◦⊙◦—

Laflamme lit up and held out a cigarette to me as she sat down. We had not invited her to join us and she did not care, either. I shook my head at the gift she had guessed I wouldn't take. Daniel remained silent. Bad Cop Laflamme had already neatly established her advantage.

"Since we're all here, I can do this now or take you down to the station. Your choice." Laflamme pulled out her phone, said, "Agreed?" and immediately began recording. I bristled but figured she would find other ways to persist, like exactly what she'd promised: the station. Laflamme stated the date, time, location and our names. "Bérénice Cates," she said, formally, "I'd like to make sure we have the correct information about you and Jean-Paul Nadon. That you'd met together several times before the evening of his death. Tell it to me again. If there's anything more you haven't said, I warn you, now is the time to say it. Did you and Professor Nadon have an intimate relationship, for example?"

I jumped up, hands on my hips. So this was why Laflamme had engineered meeting up with me when I was with Daniel. I faced her and my beau, whose set face was intent on my answer.

"Absolutely not!" I said.

At least Laflamme's "correct information" wouldn't shock him. On the day of the memorial service Daniel had confirmed he knew Jean-Paul and I'd met for a few drinks. But now would be the worst time for more details.

"As I've told you, I first saw Jean-Paul Nadon maybe twenty years ago, at a graduation ceremony." Daniel knew this old story, too. Then I said Jean-Paul had been a welcome visitor to our dig and I'd seen him several times "in that context". If Laflamme wasn't satisfied with this general statement, I would drag out again a few more reminiscences of the first week of the dig when Nadon had come to the conservation lab and seen the Willow Ware and the gold cross. This was all she would get.

"I think you'll need to come to the station to explain what you call the context," Laflamme said, making it sound serious and watching Daniel's reaction, but when there was no shock, she did not look happy. She hadn't finished her cigarette and didn't move. The police station was an empty threat. My hands shifted to behind my back where my impatience could hold them steady.

"Detective Laflamme," Daniel's terse voice intervened, "Can you let us know how the investigation is proceeding?" He was telling me he was on my side and part of this conversation.

"Monsieur Tremblay, the media are informed when we hold a press conference."

"I'm more than media. I understand that after my interview you investigated me personally. About whether I actually went to Radio-Canada the night Jean-Paul died. I gave you the name of a colleague who would corroborate my presence. Am I a suspect?"

I lowered myself onto the grass in case I didn't like the answer.

"Monsieur Tremblay, your friend of course would say you were there. Security verified your presence. You are not a prime suspect."

"About time I found out," Daniel muttered.

But my relief was cut short by realizing Daniel was now free and clear to go to Louisiana. Earlier, hearing his words, "the rest of the year", I'd jumped to thinking he'd stay here if my contract was extended. I'd better keep a careful watch on how Berry the Sleuth drew conclusions.

In a cool voice Daniel said to Laflamme, "So, your investigations *are* proceeding." He rose. "I'll leave. Berry has a right to know the details, especially if you're suspecting her on some level. More than the trauma of finding his body, I mean."

"She doesn't have any right to know where we are in our work. She's not immediate family." A thin, tight smile formed on Laflamme's lips, or maybe it was just the way she dragged on her cigarette now.

My eyes moved to her casual slacks and summer-weight sweater. I'll distract her further from her questions, I thought, and her threat about going down to the station. I'll draw the right conclusions. My hand opened slightly to signal Daniel not to leave.

"Are you in plainclothes today, Detective?" I tried to sound innocently curious, but my mind was going over what, exactly, Laflamme must have plotted in advance about this encounter. Did she think I'd spill if she made me squirm in front of Daniel? She must have been following us. How much had she'd heard of all of my and Daniel's discussions?

"The plainer the better." Laflamme was now the one with the pale, set face. "Interview ended." She closed her phone.

She had not heard anything, I figured. Her tactic in speaking to us had failed, giving us information, not the other way around. She had probably not planned this meeting but had seen Daniel and I, and decided on the spot to confront us.

I now had the advantage but couldn't think of a smart or even smart-alecky way to use it. All I came up with was, "Plainer is better? Sorry, I don't understand." And I didn't, it wasn't part of my act or what I knew of French Québec's flair for chic.

"Ms. Cates, plain is not a concept I hear jokes about in the police force. Did you grow up looking like I do?" As she spoke, even the ordinary act of sitting up straight brought attention to her high-cheekboned face with its blue eyes, and emphasized her tall body, good bosom and small waist. "Crimes solved will speak for me." She stood, grimaced her goodbye and left without further mention of the police station.

I finalized my birthday gift to Daniel. It was getting closer to a big number birthday for him and he didn't like the thought. I figured this out when he said he wanted to celebrate at Aunt Adèle's—where else was he as close to his experience of unconditional childhood-ness?

Aunt Adèle intuited this. "For someone who's almost six today, you're looking good," she greeted Daniel.

"Five plus," he corrected.

"Five point seven," I clarified. Pedantic, possibly mean, but I excused it as honesty. I did want to make sure he stayed older than me.

"On the logarithmic scale." Meg at least could be gleeful about aging.

"Exactly!" I said. "Like the logarithmic scale we use to measure acidity in old books. Going from pH five to pH seven arrives at the neutral center." I was attempting to divert the conversation since Daniel was sensitive about today, but did anybody really want to know this scientific detail? I should have absorbed the body language, the sets of arms folded and waiting, before I rattled on with, "Seven is ten times less acid than six, a hundred times less acid than five. I'm glad he's five point seven and not five point four."

Aunt Adèle brought herself up to her full height. "I'm five two. Feet, but once it was in years, too. I used to stand five four. So on your pH scale, I'm getting more acidic. What a metaphor for aging." I gave in and laughed.

After dinner Daniel declared, "A perfect birthday!" as he unwrapped Meg's gift of a pastel interior view of his apartment. He had almost cried when he opened Aunt Adèle's box of molasses cookies, a favourite from his childhood. My present was a big risk, even bigger since it would be opened in front of an audience. I hadn't realized that Aunt Adèle's son, Réjean, and his family, would drop by too. Fidgeting behind a rigid smile as Daniel untied my box, I practiced my lines about how if he didn't want it, it could be exchanged. The store manager had said no problem, they had lots of other things there, some smart watches for instance. I had to avoid the insinuation that I was giving him a keepsake for his ring finger. Too easily a ring's implication could frighten, end up as dead air on my radio. But I needed him to know, visibly, that he was my love, and that anyone else in Quebec, like Jean-Paul, had been an acquaintance. And Antoine too, despite whatever crazy tack my menopausal body sailed on.

Out of the box came a man's silver ring with one edge extended so its shape rose to complete the head of a loon. The feathers had been patinated black in highlights and the circle around the loon's neck was shimmering gold. I might as well spend my salary well. Daniel stared at the ring, at me, exhaled, held it up to the light, got up without a word and gave me a long, long kiss. Everyone applauded, as at a wedding.

"*Merci, ma belle,*" Daniel said with delight, slipping the small ring easily onto his left pinky finger where I'd hoped it would fit, too small for the significant ring finger.

"You know the loon is my favourite." He broke the sentiment building in the room with a loud imitation loon call. The sound woke up his old cat, Faux Paws, sleeping by the fireplace. Her summer holiday in the country, by unspoken consent, had been extended. Faux Paws accepted a pat and ambled away to find new sleeping quarters.

A few minutes later I heard a noise. "That reminds me . . .", and I dashed into the kitchen. "*Maudit*! Faux Paws, get down!" A fat thump. The tricolour cat came charging out, stopping to lick her paws when she reached the safety of Aunt Adèle's chair.

"I forgot it on the counter." I entered with the butter dish. "This cat, Aunt Adèle, has licked the whole surface. She'll be sick."

"You're such a little monster," cooed Aunt Adèle.

The end-of-evening rituals began. Meg announced, so we could all hear, her intention to do the dishes, and Daniel offered to assist.

"No, it's your birthday. I'll help," I said.

"*Mais non.* I'll do them *because* it's my birthday. It's my tradition, to do the dishes on my birthday. Because it comes only once a year."

I groaned and let fossil man escape. I'd have to use that line on my own birthday. The stocky Réjean and his petite wife said their goodbyes, their girls dutifully kissing each adult. Aunt Adèle carried a few dishes into the kitchen, and for a moment I caught a glimpse of her holding Daniel's hand, his new ring held close to her eyes. Wondering what it cost? A loud voice carried over the running dishwater and I heard Aunt Adèle describe what a blessing a consecrated marriage held.

Aunt Adèle came out to knit in her comfortable chair, giving me a rare chance to talk to her alone. Only slightly regretful that decorum and the rules which used to smooth social behavior had not been part of my upbringing, I plunged right in with personal questions.

"There's something I'd like to ask you about, about your own feelings when friends or your husband died, because I'm not dealing very well with my feelings about Jean-Paul Nadon's death. Do you mind, though? And is this a good time?"

"We're alone."

"But I don't want to make it painful. It's been such a great evening."

"I live with that pain each day, *ma petite*."

"Well, it sounded like you've dealt with it, had closure. These days everyone wrings their hands over closure."

"Closure is for zippers."

I knew I could proceed. "So how do you deal with death? Without being bitter?"

"'Dealing with it' came after my time also. I've made my peace with the accident that killed Claude. By accepting that there're several ways to see what happened, and that how I tell the story becomes the kind of person I am." Aunt Adèle reached for her reading glasses, picked up her knitting, and found her stitch. "If I let myself grow bitter it'll seep into whatever I do. Eventually it becomes my life. Then I'll enjoy that bitterness. I'll take pleasure in meanness, sourness, disappointment. Who wants to spend time with a woman like that? Not even me." She raised her head in a brief smile.

"But that doesn't mean," Aunt Adèle continued, needles clicking, head bent, "that I've forgotten. You must know Québec's motto, '*Je me souviens*', '*I remember*'? It has another meaning for me, deeply personal." She glanced up, wool immobile. "Is it too poetic if I say I have a hollow where something that sustains life itself, in my heart, has been taken away? But I've bandaged it up fairly well. I've accepted what happened to Claude. And to me, not to someone else, and that it's something I have to live with."

"Bitterness is so powerful. You got over it by sheer willpower?"

"Of course not." The needles were clicking again, with Aunt Adèle peering at me every few stitches over her half-glasses. "First, is it just my pride thinking I've gotten over it so I can square my shoulders and show how strong I am? Number two, I'm talking about it. But intellectualizing means I'm using my brain. Is that a mask, a good excuse not to feel? I don't know right now if tonight, when I'm in bed, even after such a wonderful evening, my guard will plummet and I'll start to cry."

My bottom lip began to twist and my own eyes welled up. I rose and awkwardly hugged Daniel's aunt. How to move between talk and this intimacy otherwise, to resolve those divisions between head and heart, younger and older?

Aunt Adèle accepted a short hug. She cocked her head so she could look me directly in the eyes. "Did Daniel tell you about Sylvie?"

I nodded. "His wife."

"Good. The important first marriage."

I caught my breath. "He hasn't had a second wife, has he?"

She laughed. "You are incorrigible. Why don't you ask him?"

—◦◦◦◦◦—

CHAPTER EIGHTEEN

As we walked to meet the group for the history tour, I put my arm around Daniel and squeezed tight. "Do you know the expression in English, 'my main squeeze?'" He didn't, so I explained, using it as an intro to my next move. "You've only been married once, right?"

"I told you."

"Just confirming," I said, "that you didn't have six or eight additional wives."

"Ah. The conservator who can't believe her good fortune, to find a live artifact that hardly shows wear."

"An artifact almost sixty years old, to boot," I said, but my mind was elsewhere. On the not-alive. Today Jean-Paul's death would niggle away at me all day as Odette led us around in his footsteps. Had he survived a fall? Maybe if someone at the dig had worked late that night, he would not have died. I'd declared a mission to discover who had killed him and to clear Meg's name, but how much chance would an amateur like myself have? Daniel was sputtering something about not being even close to sixty, and I yes yessed him and returned to my obsession. How would Clueless Cates recognize a clue?

I said this to Daniel, adding, "Odette's one Golden Dog and I'm another. I'd better not be the Golden Dog who just watched and filed it all away for future reference and never got any further."

"You?" Daniel imitated my hard squeeze. "This is a day for watching, sure, but it's to see what unfolds on the history tour. And if it's me kissing a woman on both cheeks, just remember, she's never been my wife, I'm only saying hello."

"I expect to see you *not* kissing women today unless it's good-bye."

Savouring bowls of *café-au-lait* to prime us for the rest of the history walk, Florence commented that Jean-Paul would have loved Odette's first choice of what to show us. After gathering at '*La Porte St-Jean*', the 'gate' on St.-Jean St. that was one of the main entrances to the walled Old City, our real stop had been just paces away, the open court-yard of the ChantezPortes bistro, one of Jean-Paul's favourites since the 1970s. Even I, the tea-drinking *Anglaise*, sat happily sipping a *café au lait* while Odette explained the city's stone walls opposite. Though medieval-looking they were picturesque reconstructions of what had been austere, functional military fortifications hundreds of years before. Like Jean-Paul, Odette had a gift for public oration.

"Remember," she concluded, "what you'll see today is a living being, a city always changing, where history is made by new additions or re-construction as much as by what was originally here. Jean-Paul still lives: through his work and his students. He used to say to them, 'history is uncovering the cover-up'. The nineteenth century covers up the eighteenth, the eighteenth the seventeenth, and on and on. But remember, even old buildings that are now visible were never static. They've been inhabited by generations who alter them or simply hang out new signs. As we walk, try to imagine what went on before that you can't see now. Think of stone and brick as the solid remnants of peoples' lives and the events they lived to witness."

Daniel and I exchanged looks. "Cover-up" had struck us both as a slip-of-the-tongue tribute to Jean-Paul's death.

Clouds and cold had cut our anticipated numbers, but the thirty of us were in a bright mood when we set out through residential streets for our next destination, the Ste.-Ursule convent. Odette made sure we confessed out loud how our legs felt on the steeply sloped street. As we climbed, Odette pointed out that the backyards of the houses ran alongside the west wall of the Convent, and that these buildings, jostling each other shoulder-to-shoulder, showed styles spanning hundreds of years. Whatever their age, each entrance had a small stoop fronting directly on the sidewalk and an iron railing attached to the bricks at waist height that ran along the width of the housefront. In 1682, she said, other exterior additions like staircases had been forbidden by law because they collected garbage and blocked traffic. Later, the handrails we could see were permitted to be attached, for winter pedestrians on the steep icy slopes. These were well maintained.

Would I be here this winter to use them?

At the Ursuline convent we filed into its museum and saw the still-shiny coins people had put on collection plates four hundred years before, and designs on cloth and birchbark that showed the influence of both the nuns and their Indigenous converts. Jean-Paul's name had given us access to the extensive inner courtyard to marvel at the oldest buildings and the grounds. Two nuns appeared from a dark doorway, bent towards each other, talking. They were dressed in old-fashioned, faded garb that covered them head to foot, and although they were walking towards us, we were completely ignored.

Florence turned pale. She didn't appear frightened, just stunned. I looked at Daniel. His mouth hung open. I couldn't understand what the nuns were saying, and suddenly I knew why; they were speaking an accented older French I'd only seen written, like the inscription for the Golden Dog and in a few old books as well: for milk, "*du laict*" instead of "*du lait*", and other archaic forms such as "*nous trouvasme*". Just as the nuns reached us, a young man dressed in torn trousers and a blousey collarless shirt ran up with a wicker basket and bent down in supplication. He was speaking old French too, but his hand gestures uncovering the basket where a baby lay, were clear enough. A nun picked up the swaddled baby and cradled it, and half our group gasped. The young man bent down again, obviously thanking the Ursulines.

Odette raised her voice. "For hundreds of years this scene was acted out many times on the very ground we're standing on. A child of any age being delivered to the good Sisters for care and instruction, perhaps an orphan or the youngest that made too many mouths to feed. Some of you recognized, in the dramatic tableau here, an old illustration in our schoolbooks. I imagine you haven't thought about that drawing in thirty, or fifty, years. Thanks to Jean-Paul Nadon and our actors from the Saturday history club he organized, you remembered it today. We all help create history, and history lives inside us."

The two nuns and the young man held their final pose and then faced us, and all three bowed deeply, one holding the doll from the basket. Odette began to applaud. "Let us thank these fine players, past and present members of Jean-Paul's club." Our group clapped loudly, shouting bravos. The actors pulled back their head coverings and bowed again. It was my turn to be amazed. The young man, with unmistakable red hair, was Gaetan.

Lunch was held not in one of Jean-Paul's favourite small restaurants but at the Chateau Frontenac. The nineteenth-century grand hotel had come up with a succulent buffet that celebrated the best of Quebec *gastronomie*. Not *haute cuisine* but simple, superb produce and products. All labelled for this occasion in the best scholarly research style as to maker and origin: salads and herbs fresh from gardens; moist slices of pâté: goose, venison, and hare, and the version eaten by those who were poorer or might at least work off the calories, the delicious fatty pork *cretons*. All of Antoine's cheeses were here, and others made from sheep or cow's milk that had been ranked with imported delicacies when I'd lived in Vancouver. Quebec law still allowed unpasteurized cheese to be sold commercially, and I'd learned why: its taste was unmatchable. Waiters circulated with glasses of sparkling wine and Quebec cider.

The room fell silent as we heard Odette's voice. "*A la mémoire de Jean-Paul Nadon!*" She raised her glass.

"*Vive Jean-Paul!*" we shouted back several times, and drank.

"*Et un grand merci à Antoine, et à toute la famille Nadon.*" Odette finished. She turned to a corner of the room, and there stood the Nadon my eyes had been searching for all morning.

Daniel talked to Antoine during lunch, and briefly to Odette too, but I lacked a journalist's facility to be persistent in asking near-strangers amiable but inquisitive questions. I vowed to learn fast. At least I could question Daniel. In the afternoon, despite my misgivings regarding Odette's excuses in front of Meg about "the Golden Dog", I was wrapped up in her poetic sense of history and found myself, more than once, at the front of our group, listening intently. The treed park beside the Chateau Frontenac, she told us—where Daniel and I had sat on the grass just yesterday—existed as a formal French garden over three hundred years ago. On busy rue

St. Louis the whole crowd of us bent down to run our hands over a huge iron cannonball buried in tree roots now adjacent to the sidewalk. History through the kinds of artifacts we had been finding all summer became one continuous story when a Parks Canada archaeologist showed us the excavations below the boardwalk of the *Terrasse Dufferin*.

Just as we were about to leave the Terrasse, Luc, the second 'missing person' from my private list of history tour attendees. showed up to speak about the last ten thousand or so years of human habitation here, the original First Nations of the area. It hit me then that Quebec City's history stretched in every direction and dimension, forward and deep into the ground below us. Its memory rose on high hills. It was tangible in the width, depth and height of each building and wall, and present everywhere in the dimension of time.

"I owe a lot to Jean-Paul," I told Florence. "I can't believe how much this afternoon made me appreciate his passion for the history of this place."

"Don't forget Odette, she did Jean-Paul proud. Or Antoine, not that you'd overlook him." I stuck my tongue out at her grin. "This whole tour had to be orchestrated, you know," Florence continued. "Thanks to their hard work, even you drank coffee, we ate superbly, had a wonderful time and we can't help but love and admire Jean-Paul. What better tribute."

We continued over to Montmorency Park to gaze in a different direction, out at the St. Lawrence and the port. The first '*habitants*', we were told, had farmed the soil under our feet four hundred years ago. Between that era and when Daniel and I had walked here the night after Jean-Paul's death, when the yellow dog with its master had passed us, buildings had occupied Montmorency Park's site, including a parliament: important history now gone, reminding me of Odette's admonition to remember the unseen. The not-to-be-forgotten.

Many in the group stood staring out over St. Lawrence while others took photos as tangible records of this moment's existence. In the distance the magnificently visible St. Lawrence River flowed past as backdrop, and I, finally, found myself standing beside Antoine. I had only a ridiculous opening line ready.

"Thanks for all those excellent cheeses at lunch. I probably enjoyed too many," and I happily patted my belly. Not exactly the witty or sexy come-on my id might have liked, but how could he be other than glad to see me?

"What if I told you I provided the whole lunch? Would you still tell such pretty lies?"

"Did you?" was the only way I could think of responding to his rude reply.

"Odette told me what she'd planned for the day, and I thought, I can make this contribution to honor Jean-Paul." It sounded like a prepared speech.

"Well, you certainly did that."

"Thank you very much," the speech continued. "I looked up to my big brother, I always wanted to be equal to him, and today I wanted to give as good a lunch as he would have. The ChantezPortes went well too, *n'est-ce pas*?"

"Your idea?" How to make honest small talk with someone demanding praise?

"Odette's. But I booked the terrace and the coffee." He paused. "I'm sounding pompous, aren't I?" His strong features broke down into a wry grimace. "Sorry. It's just I've been so up and down and I want it all to be over."

"You sound like you thought of all the right details." I smiled and picked up on the end of his sentence. "Is there any more news from the police?"

Antoine shook his head and stared out over the river. "They keep in touch and they say, "The investigation's proceeding. Regretfully we have to keep Monsieur Nadon here for now." He turned with a defeated, hollow look. "What else could they possibly find?"

I had no idea. All I could answer with was the comforting, "The stains on your watercolours are definitely cleanable."

His eyes lit up. He asked if I would do the work.

"The pieces are worth being cleaned by a specialist in paper. I'll arrange it." I turned the conversation to my other priority. "Are you going to use those illustrations in your new book?"

"I'll decide later. If Meg's final drawings are good, I'll use those. Can you ask to get that conservation work done soon, just in case?"

"I'll phone Monday. Now, I can't remember . . ." since I knew this only on Meg's say-so, "but in your last book, was the illustrator mentioned? Will I be able to boast about her drawings in this one?"

"You mean, will her name be in my book?"

"Yes."

"Does she want it in?"

"Yes."

"In spite of Immigration?"

"Yes."

"We talked about it, and I thought she was worried about Immigration."

"Did your last illustrator have a problem with Immigration?" I kept my voice sweet.

"A different arrangement." His speech slid into lecture mode. Learned from his brother? "Often we had numerous small illustrations on the same page and to make it clear, I would have had to credit each individual one," he said.

"You understand? Which ones were mine and which his. And he wasn't all that pleased with his work, to be frank. There were so many details and he felt he'd worked too quickly. Also, he wasn't going to declare his income. So he was just fine with not being named." Antoine glanced at his watch. "I have to go." He started to walk away. After two steps he halted, half-turning back.

"I'm horribly abrupt. Forgive me. And please, also for the day I walked out of the bistro when you came to see Meg. I've been very rude. I'm still so upset and it overtakes me. My only brother . . ."

Odette had begun to talk about the statues in *le parc Montmorency*. Antoine didn't move, probably seeing disappointment lingering on my face.

"You do excuse me?" he said softly. "I thought I could master my grief, but I've discovered it's not an adversary. It's a companion who travels with you. Whether you like it or not. I really have to go. Please come and see me about the pictures." He ducked through the crowd.

I nodded yes. If I stretched my mind in a blacker direction, though, I stumbled against a shadowed wall. This city tour proved Odette and Antoine worked as well behind-the-scenes as in front. At least one had the skills of a master planner. As did chief archaeologist Luc.

I found Florence, told her only that Antoine could be rude and her early advice was right: stick with Daniel. I said that, right now, I didn't care if Daniel had had a second or a seventh wife. I pushed the "what if" out of my mind; what if I discovered Antoine's behind-the-scenes planning skills meant no more than innocent cheeses and theatre?

⌘ ⌘ ⌘

CHAPTER NINETEEN

Passers-by had joined our group in Montmorency Park, drawn by Odette's ringing voice and moving hands. We turned to look at cannons, monuments, across the road to the Seminary, and then back to the battlements and the view of the St. Lawrence beyond. This time, when two people in centuries-old dress appeared, we were prepared. A young man and woman were walking arm in arm, and I whooped with delight. Meg had been her usual stubborn self this morning, refusing to join Daniel and I, expounding pointless arguments. Now I saw why; she had joined up with her peer group, the Saturday history club. In a loud voice and unmistakable Irish-English she declared she was an immigrant from Ireland and asked her 'brother' to make sure she found a good husband. The brother was Gaetan, his red hair put to excellent dramatic use. Gaetan responded in English and French so those listening would understand the scenario; yes, I will find you a husband, but he has to be a farmer, not a *coureur de bois* who will leave you for months and years chasing furs in the west. Gaetan had injected an Irish accent into his lines and sounded like a music hall Paddy. He got a spontaneous hand and much laughter. Just then a bearded man flew out from the crowd and on bended knee asked Meg in French for her hand in marriage.

"What's he saying, now?" asked Meg.

"Will you be his wife, to be sure," replied Gaetan.

"Does he farm?"

"He says he farms goats."

"Does he now. Is he Catholic or Protestant?"

"You don't have to ask that question here," replied Gaetan, to more laughter.

The bearded man began to speak, "I am not so old, I don't get too drunk, I have a hundred hectares, I need a wife. Can you bake bread?"

Gaetan translated. Meg put her hands on her hips, threw back her thick dark hair and said, "Can I bake? Can he love?"

The man rose and stood towering over the petite young woman. "What do you think?" He posed theatrically, half muscular wrestler, half modern celebrity, and winked at the audience.

"So?" translated Gaetan.

"I think you'll do," appraised Meg.

We all clapped, Daniel shouting, "Bravo!" When the actors took their bows, I was genuinely surprised. The suitor removed his false beard. He was Antoine.

Odette signalled for all of us to follow her to our last stop. Antoine, sweating and smiling, pushed his way towards me as we crossed the road. He clasped my hand. I almost pulled it back in shock.

"You must forgive my appalling behavior earlier," he said. "I was so nervous about this acting, I never do this kind of thing. In our family Jean-Paul was the man in the limelight. I was the one who had to practice answers in case I was asked a question. I made Meg and Gaetan go over our scene a dozen times. And I couldn't tell you that, of course. Our little drama had to be a surprise."

"You were terrific."

Florence, off to one side, shouted her agreement.

"You act really well." I wanted him to know I'd been impressed, but now I was the one getting nervous, with

Antoine still holding my hand. We were crossing the road towards the old post office opposite. Was Daniel with Florence? Could he see us?

"Do I?" Antoine's voice sparkled. "Thank you. I'm so relieved. It almost ruined my day. Wasn't Meg excellent?"

"Yes she was," Daniel piped up from behind. "But why did you agree to be an actor, then?" Antoine's grip released.

"I wanted to, I guess." Antoine waited for him to catch up. "A good question, why. Maybe, to be honest, because I'm the youngest, the 'benjamin' as you know we say here, who still wants to be the man his older brother was. Now that he's not here," Antoine coughed to hide the catch in his voice, "I thought I should try." He shrugged.

Odette clapped to silence the chitchat. "The verse about the Golden Dog," she announced, "carved in stone above our heads, has many interpretations." Odette fixed her eyes on Meg. "Let me tell you a few historical facts. In 1688, a surgeon, Timothée Roussel, built a house on this site and apparently placed this carving with its inscription on it. In 1734 the house was sold to a merchant, Philibert, who kept the stone carving. In 1748, a French marine officer killed Philibert during a terrible quarrel. There are many versions of this story of intrigue, murder and revenge." Our group buzzed. Odette held up her hand.

"In the next century," she continued, "a post office was established on this site, and although our Buade St. post office continued to operate here, the original building was demolished and replaced in 1871. But the stone carving with its inscription was kept and re-erected. Now, remember Timothée Roussel who first put up the stone in 1688? He was born in the south of France. In a town not too far from his birthplace, there exists a sculpture of a dog with an inscription that is almost identical to ours here. The date for that sculpture is 1561. It is not too far-fetched that Roussel erected the stone carving on his house in Quebec in memory of where he grew up. And that region in France may have been carrying on an ancient Greek tradition of placing carved dogs at entranceways as a symbol of protection."

"The Golden Dog didn't protect our late historian," I said to Florence.

She nodded. "I wonder if it was a *crime passionnel*, or if somebody bided their time, like the Golden Dog, and got revenge on Jean-Paul. But for what?"

Late in the evening, Daniel, Meg and I sat down to a conspiratorial pasta dinner at his place and compared notes. Daniel related how at lunchtime, with separate questions, Antoine and later Odette had divulged virtually the same story of their friendship. It expanded what I'd heard from Florence. Jean-Paul had not consciously come between Antoine and Odette in their relationship. His part was unwitting. He had simply fallen in love with someone else.

Years ago Antoine had been passionate for Odette, but it seemed they could never get together without her asking about Jean-Paul, and Antoine concluded he had no chance. Odette confirmed she was so smitten with Jean-Paul that she and Antoine were like friendly ships hailing each other with a sea between. Jean-Paul, however, married a woman from Trois-Rivières who'd died since, a decade ago. Meanwhile, Antoine, not wanting to be second choice for Odette's love, had kept in the background. He retreated even more when Odette married a cold academic, including when they divorced. But throughout all this the two had kept in touch.

"Odette described their relationship as having developed into one of mutual support," Daniel said, "and the honesty that settles between old friends when games no longer need to be played. They understood each other. Odette said she and Antoine would talk wistfully about his young dream of being a famous artist or a biologist at a university, and his disappointment at earning his living, in his fifties, as a goat farmer. She spoke of the disillusionment of ending up as a mere sessional lecturer instead of a full faculty member."

Meg poured us all more wine.

"They would commiserate over family as well as unrequited love. Their parents had lived conservative, rural lives where schooling brought mixed blessings, starting early when classes were on during haying season. Odette and Antoine both were desperate for a university education so neither stayed to work the family farm, and both disappointed their parents that way. Jean-Paul's success showed them they had been right to dream, but to the Nadon parents, it only confirmed how intelligent their eldest was."

"So did you ask Antoine about my illustrations?" Meg demanded.

Daniel's warm radio voice answered, "I wanted first to get him to trust me. I had to bring them both to a comfort level where they'd open up."

"I asked," I interrupted. "I made sure he knew you wanted the credit."

"Will he do it then?"

"Remains to be seen. We'll keep bugging him."

"So, Meg," Daniel shifted gears, "Now I need to ask you a question." I sat back to see how he would handle this.

"You're angry at Antoine," Daniel said, "Because he might not credit your drawings. Are you angry at Jean-Paul for anything?"

Meg frowned in serious thought.

Daniel said softly, "Anything upset you?"

"His dying like that."

"Of course, *ma petite*. But anything, for instance, he wanted from you?" Meg sat, thinking in silence. Daniel's usual patience had thinned from fatigue, if not the wine. "Try another question," he said. "Has anyone here in Quebec made sexual advances to you when you didn't want them?"

"You mean Gaetan?"

"Has he physically touched you when you said no?"

"I touched him, physically as you put it. A slap on his bloody face. Am I in trouble?"

"He hasn't pressed charges. Next question then: has anyone here who's older, at least ten, twelve years older than you, touched you inappropriately?"

"What's inappropriate over here?"

I swallowed. Meg was serious innocence. Daniel said, "I mean, sexually, instead of friendly. When he's a lot older than you." The insinuation was hard to miss.

"What if I wanted it?"

A vise squeezed my ribcage. Was she romantically attached to a seventy-year-old? "Describe it," my throat croaked.

"Well," said Meg, getting up to nestle herself in the couch pillows, "It hasn't exactly happened, so. But I've thought about it. Sinned, have I, Danny?"

The chokehold eased up, but Daniel muttered, "Good." Then, "Thinking's good. But that's between you and a priest. Let me ask it another way. Has any man—or woman—on the following list propositioned you or touched you sexually? Here goes."

"Ready." Meg looked intently at the ceiling.

"Odette?"

She burst out laughing. "During the little drama rehearsals, you dope? Or in public, people thinking I was having it away with my mother?"

"Antoine?"

"He's too scared, but I think he'd like to."

"Jean-Paul?" Daniel's voice remained calm.

"Now there's my sin. Mistress to a handsome, famous man."

"I need to know." Daniel growled. "Did he?"

"Oh, no, alas. Just a dream. Now we'll never, poor fella." Meg's voice held such deep, young regret.

"Luc?" I broke in.

"Go on with you!" Meg almost shouted. "Luc a dirty old man? He's more a knight riding to the rescue."

What did she know about the so-called scandal that had tarnished Jean-Paul, and Luc's involvement in it? Daniel had finished. It was up to me to describe the gossip, and my voice was matter-of-fact until Meg interrupted.

"That's old news. It was utter rubbish anyway."

"Luc doesn't think so." My loud statement grabbed her attention. "He believes Jean-Paul fathered his daughter's son. She won't say. You know her, don't you?"

"What if I do?"

"Here's the problem." I lowered my voice, and my eyes scrutinized Meg intently. "Luc is so angry his daughter won't tell him who the father is, and the scandal said it was Jean-Paul, that people are saying Luc killed Jean-Paul to get even. If Jean-Paul was such a great guy, he should've had the guts to acknowledge his son."

Meg's indrawn breath was audible.

"It gets worse." Daniel took up the story. "There's talk that if Jean-Paul was a sexual predator, anyone he came on to might have gotten so angry they could have killed him." He paused. "Including you."

"Fucking lies!" Meg screamed. "Surely to God you don't . . ."

Daniel got up and knelt on the rug beside the couch, putting his hand lightly on Meg's, and said, "I swear I don't, Berry doesn't, absolutely we don't. But we need to prove it. About you, and about Luc."

"What does Luc say?"

"It's more what his daughter will say." I went over and sat on the rug by Daniel. "She's the only one who knows."

"No she's not."

My heart almost beating louder than my voice, I knelt and reached for her hand. "Meg, please tell us."

"Can't," she said. "It's nothing to do with me, it's between Luc and his daughter. She's a lovely woman and a brilliant mum and he should just leave her alone." Meg folded her arms. "And I've been sworn to secrecy. Anyway, Danny," she turned to him, "I'm helping and the situation's getting better. Just give it time."

"Okay." Daniel smiled patiently. "It's your business, not ours. So let me explain something else. Luc is blackmailing Berry."

Meg gasped. "Luc isn't like that!"

"When he really wants something . . ." I began.

Daniel broke in, saving a blow-up between me and Meg. "Extortion's more accurate. Berry has to find out your relationship to Jean-Paul and tell Luc something or she gets no contract for the winter. So he wants to know if Jean-Paul in any way approached you in the way the rumours say he approached his daughter. And I have to know the same thing, because I'm your chaperone over here and I love you."

"We don't need to know anything else," I said. "Except what you'd like me to tell Luc."

"You don't need to know if the rumour is right, if Jean-Paul is the father of Suzanne's boy?"

"I don't even want to know if you're certain," I said.

Daniel remained focused. "Tell me, *mon ange*, my little angel, what Berry is going to tell Luc. Did Jean-Paul make advances to you?"

"Never," Meg said, "And that's the truth. Well, he might have flirted, but he never ever touched me like you're asking."

"Honest?"

"I'll go to confession and you can listen."

CHAPTER TWENTY

❧⋯⟨0⟩⋯☙

"Jean-Paul never touched Meg."

Luc didn't reply. His pipe needed new tobacco. Apparently.

"Ask her yourself," I said.

"What did she say about my daughter?"

"That's not what you asked me to find out." I gazed through the window of his trailer and saw diggers refilling one of the excavation's trenches. The end of the archeology season. In another hole, the tops of the workers' yellow hard hats were barely visible; the bottom of the trench was being sampled and photographed, readied to be backfilled and smoothed over, returned to being city parking.

I'd delivered my side of the deal. It was Luc's turn. I said, "Would you like me to wrap up the artifacts and the reports of what I've done, to make it easier for someone else to continue in September? Or will my contract be extended?"

He took a long time lighting his pipe. "Give me a few days."

He got a work week. Florence, cataloguing the last trays of potsherds, advised I should wait longer; Luc was extra busy with the dig finishing. And 'asking' came across to him as 'nagging'.

"Luc's playing me like a fish," I responded. "He's got all the power and I've got a life to organize." I was in no mood to soft-pedal. Everything was stalled. There was not even more news from the police about Jean-Paul's death. Why? Top secret, or increasingly cold case? Florence, Meg, all my contacts knew nothing.

"Patience, Berry," Florence said, bringing me back to the present. "Let Luc come to you."

"You're talking to the wrong species. I've already made an appointment with him at eleven."

Florence concentrated on the earliest pottery on the site, playing her fingers lightly across fragments of lead-glazed earthenware. "See what you can do with these. Are any of them from the same pot? Their locations were side by side." All business.

I began searching for similar edge shapes and matching irregularities in the shiny, mottled green glaze. I fit several sherds together rapidly and glanced at Florence. She wasn't looking, so I exclaimed "goodie", as if to myself.

Florence laughed. "Why don't you just say, "Watch me, Mom! Is Daniel as much of a child as you still are?"

"'Youthful' is the word, Florence."

"'Spry' might be more accurate."

"'Fun', 'free', and 'alive' will do just fine." I added, "Daniel's worse. Come to his comedy routine tonight if you want it spotlit."

A worker poked her head into our room. "A *dame* here to see you, Berry." She winked. "She's talking to Gaetan right now at the drawing table."

I didn't know any ladies here, or women who wouldn't have just come up to the lab. "Odette?" I said to Florence. We peered out the window but the awning hid whoever was under it. I scrambled over to our mirror, rapidly combed my hair, powdered my Rudolph-like nose to matte, and charged out. I almost flattened Aunt Adèle coming up the stairs with Gaetan.

"*Bonjour, ma belle* Berry," she said. "I'll greet you at the top. I move slowly but I have to keep the momentum up. I'm part of the slow staircase movement." Grinning,

Gaetan headed back downstairs and I backed up to the landing, waiting to introduce Florence at the top. She suggested tea or coffee, knowing it would give Aunt Adèle a chance to sit, me my liquid amber addiction, and her a chance to be nosy with her captives.

"Am I interrupting?" Aunt Adèle asked.

"A welcome interruption," I smiled, and before I could say more, Aunt Adèle explained she had seen a notice in the paper that Daniel's comedy act was at Le Club this evening. She wanted to witness for herself his passionate hobby and wondered if she might hide between me and Meg, if that wasn't an imposition. She thought it would be interesting to see the dig and my work first. And Meg. Where was Meg?

"She's out buying art supplies. Back I'm not sure when. She traded today off for working a Saturday."

"Her boss is very flexible."

Not with all of us. I changed the subject to what a visitor could see of the work we did here in the artifacts room. The gold cross went under the microscope, and after that it was ten minutes before we were allowed to have tea. When Florence excused herself to check that the morning's finds had been logged in, I said,

"I mentioned to you already that Daniel told me who Sylvie was." Aunt Adèle gave me her full attention. "But he says he killed her. What," I said, "do *you* think?"

Aunt Adèle smiled. "And you? You know him as your beau and I still see him as the little boy horrified at seeing my mousetraps. "But mousies are my friends!" How could this man kill a woman he loved? Now, give me your opinion."

"Deliberately kill? Impossible. He doesn't have it in him." I shied away from thinking what else he had in him, like love for Sylvie.

162 Chapter Twenty

Her smile broadened. "Your Daniel," she said, "is a treasure. Warm, kind, responsible, at least to old aunts. He can put aside his own needs, and his 'to do' list. He can enter, I think fully," Aunt Adèle squinted, as if unsure how to phrase her thought, "that dimension old-fashioned me thinks of as love."

I stood staring. "And he loved Sylvie deeply."

She nodded. "The worst thing that could happen to him did. A man like that makes one mistake, and it ended in tragedy."

"But Daniel didn't make the mistake! How could he have known?"

"'If only I hadn't done that', or, 'why was I so stupid'. How many times have you looked back on something and said that?"

"In French or English?" I avoided answering. "So you do hold him responsible?"

"Not one bit. But he holds himself responsible in the most human of ways, because he is one of the most human men I know. He's tried to overcome his guilt, to come to terms with just how irrational it is, and he's better. But he's not over it."

"What can I do? I'm no good at doing helpless."

"What can any of us do that we haven't already tried? Love him, believe in him, and cut him some slack."

"Words to live by." I started to embrace Aunt Adèle just as the door banged open and Luc charged into the room shouting obscenities.

My face turned scarlet, but Aunt Adèle's expression was bemused and curious. I caught her mood and announced, "My boss. And Meg's." Her eyebrows rose.

"Berry! *Maudit*! Christ! Get over here," Luc yelled. "You were supposed to see me at eleven. Where were you? They've just found human remains in Sector 5."

My blood disintegrated into glacial shards.

"Dammit, don't look so worried. The bones 're old and deteriorated. Just get to work. Make sure they're safe while I call the *maudite* police. This is going to hold up everything."

Luc finally registered that an old lady was in the room, albeit one dressed in svelte pants, trim blouse and silk scarf, all somewhat faded but neatly pressed. "*Pardon, Madame. Je vous en prie. Une urgence.* Weren't you with Berry at Jean-Paul Nadon's memorial service? Are you Berry's mother?" Luc's face started to sink.

Aunt Adèle introduced herself and shook his hand, saying she completely understood, she wouldn't hold me up a second longer. As soon as he was out of the room she said, "Can I watch you work?" and then, "That was abominable. How can you trust a man who flies off the handle like that? You really want to keep working for him?"

"Of course you can watch me work on site." I left the rest to simmer.

Aunt Adèle stayed, engrossed, until I'd finished and the police had arrived. Then she insisted on taking me and Florence to lunch. The Beau-Port restaurant knew the dig and did not even glance at my filthy clothes, although they sat us in a corner far from the window. It wasn't until I'd finished dessert and a cup of tea that Aunt Adèle said, "Would you have time to show me more of the dig or would it be better if I said goodbye now?"

I hesitated. The report on the skeleton had to be done for Luc.

Florence said, "I'd be delighted to take you around."

Afterwards, when Florence reeled off the long list of what she and Aunt Adèle had seen, I wished I'd been able to go along. Almost casually Aunt Adèle had asked where the dirt pile was that Jean-Paul had been buried in. She had looked up from there, commented on how she had stood many times directly above, in Upper Town on Rue des Remparts, enjoying the panoramic view over Lower Town and the port. Wasn't that the bastion with the two cannons directly overhead? Such a low stone wall they had built there. She had hated taking Daniel when he was young, but those were the cannons he wanted to play around, the wall short enough for a child to see over. "Of course, for historical accuracy, cannon have to reach over a bastion's wall, even in a reconstruction, but I would never let Daniel climb on them. It ended in tears each time."

Around three-thirty I managed to send Aunt Adèle off with the key to Daniel's for a restorative nap. I finished the condition report on the bones and left an hour later by a different route, hoofing it up Côte de la Canoterie and along Rue des Remparts. Aunt Adèle knew her city; the stone wall forming the bastion with the two cannons was not at the same height as the rest of the ramparts. Here the wall measured only two feet high. And the top of the wall sloped, the far edge pointing down, down the *Falaise* at one of our dig's sectors with its dirt piles a hundred feet below.

Later, over wine at Daniel's, I explained that the skeleton found today on the dig was several centuries old but that police forensics were examining it because of "the first incident with a deceased." Aunt Adèle was narrating her encounter with Luc when the apartment door burst open with the shout, "Fuck, I'm glad it's you. So I am, so."

Daniel rolled his eyes. "If Meg's been speaking French too long she reverts to her native tongue at home. My home."

"Just got to phone," Meg declared, kicking off her shoes and dropping rolls of paper and canvas bags onto the floor, followed by her sweater and more packages. She noticed

Aunt Adèle and to her credit blushed and held a shushing hand over her mouth. Continuing obliquely into Daniel's bedroom, Meg hauled the door shut as she said, "There's cheese in the carry bag for the cooler." Daniel shook his head, then rose to stow the perishables in the fridge, returning to the livingroom with a bottle of Beaujolais.

Meg emerged in a matter of minutes, apologizing for the mess. She'd run into Antoine in the art store and he had given her some advice on supplies, three cheeses from his car's cooler, and then he'd taken her out for coffee. "Just like Jean-Paul used to, like Antoine said he would. Oooh. It gives me the shivers." Meg hugged herself. "I thought I left some pastels and two of Gaetan's paints at the café, but they don't have them, and Antoine's not back yet, so if he calls let me know right away, now, would you?"

She bounced over to Aunt Adèle and gave her a huge hug. "Are you coming to Danny's show, then? Do we have time to eat?" Meg reached around and sipped from Aunt Adèle's wineglass.

"Barely," Daniel answered. He had to be at Le Club by seven-thirty and we would follow. "I'll grab some cheese. Are you finished with the drawings for Antoine?"

"One more day's work and I'm done!" Meg exulted. "Antoine wants me to go out to the farm Sunday. He said he'll show me a proposal about crediting the drawings then. And pay me the balance. Can you give me a lift, Danny, best cousin in the world?"

"How is Antoine?" Aunt Adèle asked. "Have the police been able to give him any news at all?"

"Not as he's said." Meg visibly slowed at the thought. "More wine, anyone?" She poured herself a glass.

⸺◦❦◦⸺

CHAPTER TWENTY-ONE

An hour later, at Le Club, Meg was ordering more beer, returning flirtations with the table next to her and yelling bravos at the stand-up comics on stage, even though she missed much of what they said in their rapid-fire French. Aunt Adèle attempted to translate but soon realized Meg's fun was not dependent on the words. When Daniel came on, Meg screamed her enthusiasm and jumped up, clapping and banging the table. The mostly male crowd applauded her performance as well as Daniel's entry.

"*Allô, allô!*" Daniel shouted, dressed up in his trademark fake lumberjack outfit: plaid shirt, jeans, and big boots.

"*Allô, allô!*" the audience and Meg yelled back in unison. "*Comment ça va ce soir?*"

The audience told Daniel they were ready for anything.

Daniel hung his head and began wailing about summer ending and needing to go camping one last time. Two friends joined him on stage and they became the Three Musketeers, their names coming from the famous tale but the twist being that instead of swords, they held high three plastic fly swatters. '*Mousquetaires*' were musketeers. '*Moustiquaires*' were for killing mosquitoes.

Daniel continued the modern version. "Today a brave band of Moustiquaires cannot just be men. Women hold up half the tent," and invited an audience member to join them. An uncertain woman was pushed towards the stage. I gasped. Odette. She played her part, though, even joining in at the end with the famous line, "All for one and one for all!" Daniel motioned his Musketeers to sit on the stools behind him, and the spotlight surrounded him for his closing monologue, a riff about moose hunting in the fall. There are a lot of hunt camps in Quebec. Daniel bowed to loud applause.

After the performance, at the table, Meg and I and Aunt Adèle recalled the jokes, even the bad ones, revelling in Daniel's success. Gradually Aunt Adèle's laugh slowed and her face betrayed a tired body. Reluctantly she rose to leave for the friends she was staying with, blowing Meg a kiss across the table, touching my extended hand, and making us promise to tell her nephew how wonderful he was. It was close to midnight before Daniel, sweaty and smiling, reached our table, people clapping him on the shoulders and grinning their bravos. Meg jumped up and hugged him hard across the empty glasses.

"You're a terrible man, Danny," she laughed.

"Am I now?" he replied, imitating her Irish accent even in his imperfect English. "*Et toi*, Berry?" he leaned over and kissed my cheek, "What did you think?"

What kept me from saying, "I loved you"—too bald a statement that could be misconstrued? Was it the lingering sense of difference, that the jokes hadn't seemed as funny to my outsider, non-hunter, urban female outlook as they had to the audience? "I love the way your face moves with your character, and your pacing."

"It went well," conceded Daniel.

"You in particular. Aunt Adèle agrees." I gave him her apologies for not being able to stay.

Daniel brushed back his damp hair and sighed. Streaks of stage make-up remaining on his face shimmered in the light.

"You really are good," I said.

"You're brilliant." Meg kissed him.

"*Merci infiniment, mes chéries.*" Daniel gazed at me. "Now if I could only get you to listen to my radio program, maybe you'd marry me."

Topsy-turvied without warning, I tried to smile. "Say that again?" After my last experience with a husband I'd sworn off marriage contracts. But not co-habitation. "*Danger,*" I said in French, "This is a no-joke zone." I wanted to wag my finger to exaggerate my "no-joke", to lighten my mood and draw a laugh, but knew from experience, from Florence to be exact, that this also might be taken the wrong way.

"You two love-birds sort it out while I visit the loo." Meg extricated herself from the crowded tables and chairs.

Daniel clasped my hand, "I know you're waiting for the commitment a real contract means."

I gasped. What the hell? Was he going to propose? Here? Now?

"So when Luc finally hires you, I'd like to celebrate. Just the two of us." Daniel's eyes shone, and I smiled weakly while my heart thudded onto the ground with the seesaw of our relationship. He kept grinning but didn't say more. His eyes had strayed off to the distance.

Odette was making her way to our table.

Kisses on cheeks and compliments about her performance followed, especially from Daniel who called her a natural actor. She joined us for a drink. Meg returned and complimented Odette again on the history tour. Now all I wanted was to be alone with Daniel to delve into our last conversation and talk about the low rampart wall.

Odette and Daniel gabbed away, expostulating on similarities between comedy acts and teaching. Meg and I listened. I was deep in a fog, a funk, maybe it was the wine, but my eyes remained on Daniel across the worn table, my brain inadequate to figure out this guy I called my beau. Tonight, with Odette sitting a few feet away, I was sinking fast. One heartache had gotten mixed up with another and I could not join the ebullient mood at the table because Jean-Paul was stone cold dead, his murderer free, and someone who perhaps knew something sitting in the next chair.

Earlier I'd been buoyant and relaxed and had gotten into a very personal conversation with Aunt Adèle before Daniel came on stage. What was your life like on the farm, never able to follow your dreams of going to the big city? Was it 'dull', or just 'hard work'? Do you mind me asking? Looking back, do you ever feel disappointed with your life? "I mean, what's your advice if you feel you want more out of life?"

Aunt Adèle had slowly shaken her head and replied, "I think you and Meg are both too young to understand. Everyone makes up a story about how their life's gone. 'I'm a big success' or 'I'm a big failure'. If I'm a failure, it's usually because so and so did it to me. Or she had chances I never had. Or, 'if only'. Well, if only my wonderful husband not died in the accident, if only I'd gone to art school—these could have been my themes. Excuse me if I preach. 'A good aunt never offers advice to her relatives'. You know that's not me."

Meg had giggled and leaned forward to hear better, both elbows planted on the table.

"Do I want to live in my younger past, in whatever my best years were? Sure, the way I think of the past, running my own household as a married woman before Claude was hit by the truck in the mine at Thetford. He should have stuck with farming, shouldn't he? Instead of renting the fields to neighbours. Do I still want to kill that truck driver? No. I used to. It was very comfortable, satisfying, to dwell on revenge. Then one morning I woke up and said, 'I'm addicted to this story, the endless versions I tell myself of how awful it is for me now, for my dead beloved Claude, for my young son, how I'll make justice triumph in the end.' And you know what? There's another story. It was an accident, and, I'm very old now, and, I enjoy my beautiful family and being *gran' maman*. And I enjoy my garden, seeing the pink eyes of the new potatoes and their translucent baby skins and sniffing the bold smell of tomato leaves. I'm conscious my time is limited. And today is as much my life as yesterday. Do I want to use it up dwelling, or living?"

I remembered this as I sat fixated on Odette. Jean-Paul took over, though, and in that moment I knew I wanted more than justice. I was no equal to Aunt Adèle. I wanted to avenge Jean-Paul's death. To me, bitterness over injustice was fair and square. I'd stepped into new territory, though. I'd become an addict with a compelling need: for vengeance.

"A penny for your thoughts, Berry." Daniel looked quizzical.

"Am I really an addict?" I asked him. "Or is it perhaps only a dedication disorder?" I tried to smile.

"I think we'd better go home now." Daniel rose. "I have no idea what you're talking about. Can you stand and walk, Berry?" In confusion, he glanced at my empty wineglass as if it held evidence of a dozen drinks I might have guzzled while he was onstage.

"No, I'll leave," said Odette. "I'm sure my presence has made you think about Jean-Paul, Berry. The only other times I've seen you have had something to do with him and his death."

I nodded my thanks.

"You're not like the poem on the inscription at all, Odette. You're no waiting Golden Dog," announced Meg. "You're like Daniel's moose in his skit, you know what's really going on."

"You can't forget that old symbol of Quebec City, can you?" Odette said, still serious, turning to the young woman. "Will you finally forget my shock that day, what I said? Will you accept I'm not a Golden Dog who lay in wait for Jean-Paul? What do I gain by his death? Not a position at the university, not an inheritance, nothing material, nothing even intangible." Meg, now staring at the table, frowned.

"Intangible, like love." Odette's voice was crisp and dry. "I don't know if it's you, but you're the one who asked questions about the Golden Dog after Jean-Paul's service. Someone's spreading rumours that maybe I'd something to do with his death, biding my time like the inscription says until I could get my revenge. Malicious gossip! I want you to know the truth, and whoever it is to stop lying in wait for me."

During this speech, Daniel was shaking his head and muttering about misunderstanding. I was musing on Hamlet. "The lady doth protest too much, methinks." Daniel started to speak just as Meg opened her mouth, sullen, glaring at Odette. "Fuck, if somebody's got it in for you, it's not me. You said 'Golden Dog' first anyway, I didn't. I only asked because you were going on about it on the dig." Meg kicked her chair away and hurried through the tables towards the door, Daniel chasing after.

CHAPTER TWENTY-TWO

—◦◦◦◦◦—

Sunday I took the place of the 'best cousin in the world' and drove Meg out to Île d'Orléans. Daniel was with two of his "Musketeers," so I'd had in mind a pleasant afternoon exploring the island. I also pictured myself chatting with Antoine about reframing his plant illustrations after their cleaning. While Meg would be packing up the last of her artist's tools, I could be convincing Antoine to replace the wood backing on the drawings with non-acid material to prevent more staining. I dug out samples of thick, neutral-pH matboard and neutral white corrugated plastic sheets for the backing. Show-and-tell would take up time, and give me more opportunity to bring the conversation around to finding out whether Odette benefited by Jean-Paul's death. I wanted corroboration before writing her off as a suspect. Would Antoine give away any clues? Not if they were in cahoots.

Île d'Orléans looked like paradise in the sun and light breeze and I wished I'd brought a bicycle with Daniel's car. When we arrived, Antoine already had Meg's last drawings that needed finishing touches spread out on the kitchen table. I left them to it, saying I would be back in a couple of hours, and shortly after cursed myself for forgetting to ask Antoine where to stroll without being on either private land or the highway. Maybe I should actually join the modern world and get a cell phone. I did have a guidebook, though, which listed historic sites, but when I arrived at the first, a seventeenth-century farmhouse, a tour bus had just emptied its crowd into the courtyard. The next, the magnificent Porteous house with its murals, was now owned by a Catholic order and closed for a retreat. So I parked back near Antoine's farm, as far down his laneway from the house as I could, and took my time ambling in the field-sweet air towards the buildings. I could blissfully swing on the *balançoire* for the rest of the afternoon.

I stopped before the goat fields, breathing in the scent of a roadside plantation of Christmas trees, its blown needles piney hot on the gravel lane. With luck, or Luc, this Christmas I would be here in Quebec enjoying a family Noël with Daniel, Meg, Aunt Adèle, her son and family: *toute la famille*. Did people still celebrate Christmas traditionally, going to midnight mass, with a big meal afterwards, maybe *tourtière* or goose? For a present I could get Aunt Adèle some canvases, and now there were water-soluble oil paints that didn't require turps or other toxic solvents.

Cicadas hummed and a goat bleated as I neared the house but I didn't see anyone. I stopped again, wondering if I should make my presence known since I was early, or return to the laneway and stroll down it one more time, the walk such a treat for the senses. Suddenly Meg came rushing out of the barn. Antoine was chasing her. He seized her hand. I stood paralyzed. Meg shook her head like a half-tamed horse trying to avoid the bit.

Loudly Antoine pleaded with Meg to stop, to just give him a chance to speak. Meg did, but whether it was because she couldn't free her hand or she wanted to hear what he had to say, I could only guess. Antoine was now down on one knee, going on in a low voice about something I couldn't hear, but for all the world it looked like the scene out of the pantomime of the Irish immigrants arriving and looking for a husband. Meg tossed her head 'no' back and forth even while Antoine continued to speak. Then she broke free and ran for the house, slamming the door and for all I knew locking it.

Antoine rose slowly, brushing off his pantleg. He didn't follow her but began wandering around the front yard, distracting a black goat nibbling grass. The goat approached and Antoine bent down, collapsing on both knees. He leaned his head on the animal's warm back. His arms hugged its neck. I heard the pain in his sobs.

Stepping as silently as I could back up the lane, jogging when the car was close, I gunned the engine to use dust and noise as my arrival signal. Nothing more was going to happen. When I got near the buildings, Antoine stood up, wiping his face. The goat wandered off. Meg came flying out of the house with her bags and yelled a fast goodbye to Antoine. "We must be off," she said to me, sliding into the passenger seat. "There's something I forgot in the city," she added by way of excuse. I waved to an immobile Antoine, backed the car around and floored it.

We drove in silence, Meg staring out the side window. When we got stuck in the Sunday traffic returning to Quebec City, I opened with, "How was Antoine's?" The answer was noncommittal, not much more than a groan. I can spend endless hours using small dental tools to clean artifacts, but for the big questions, my unruly impatience wants them out and over with. I'm no philosophical Golden Dog. Confessing to Meg what I'd witnessed, I reached out my hand and said, "It looked to me like you handled a difficult situation really well."

"You helped. The car arriving."

"Lucky timing. But you, that was good thinking."

"I wasn't thinking. I was in shock."

"Let me be part of it."

I'd not been far from the truth in believing Antoine was acting out the *habitant* farmer wanting a bride. He had indeed proposed to Meg. Declared his love passionately, leaving Meg astounded. She'd said it was all too much and she had to think. Like me, Antoine was not the patient type either, apparently, because he kept insisting on an answer, or at least an indication. Meg said she was too young, he was a wonderful man and she liked him very much but not in that way. He said he could wait if she'd say yes. He wanted the book to be their book. That's when she broke free and fled. Now words tumbled as she tried all sides; how solicitous Antoine had been, emphasizing how much he liked her artwork and would say so in his book, but all the time his hand had been squeezing hers; how he's basically a good man, brilliant with his goats and cheese and generous, but he shouldn't have forced her to answer. "Sometimes I wish Antoine would just," she began, and ended with a forlorn "piss off". Maybe, she continued, thinking out loud, his brother's death pushed him to make good his own dreams, but he's terribly awkward around people, isn't he? And she'd been so very close to finishing the drawings, too, most people would think they were done, but they weren't, she wasn't quite satisfied, and in the rush she'd left some there. What would happen now? His book would be first class, but would he still talk to her after today? "I do think the world of him, but . . ." she shook her head in disbelief.

"But it was extortion, linking marrying him with getting credit for your drawings." I, too, had seen the good in Antoine and had feelings for him in ways I was loathe to admit. I turned towards Meg as the traffic inched forward.

"He was counting on your admiration. Oh, Meg," I bit my lip, "you don't deserve to have a mentor turn out like this. He's good in so many ways, and Jean-Paul's death seems to have really hit him hard. But today was inexcusable. You, though," I added, "were fantastic. You did everything right."

In Upper Town I parked in the first free spot I saw, and Meg and I limped towards Daniel's.

On Monday, Luc began delivering his final lectures to the dig crew. He summarized the history of rue Sous-le-Cap but now integrated it into a show-and-tell of our archeological finds. I didn't know that our street, begun as a narrow path at the foot of *La Falaise*, had been originally named '*Ruelle des Chiens*', Dog Lane.

"Any link to the Golden Dog inscription in Upper Town?" I asked. Luc said no, although the carving had been there at the time our site had been part of Dog Lane. What a coincidence. What colour had dogs been in New France?

"Picture Dog Lane," Luc boomed expansively. "In the 1600 and 1700s, Lower Town was overrun with the livestock people kept, and their dogs, too. You can imagine how the streets looked, filthy and crowded in spite of the laws, and occasionally soldiers had to be sent out to regulate the waste. Disasters—fire, cholera, typhoid—swept the town well into later centuries." He held up artifacts: the charred end of a wooden beam, a collection of animal bones, a medicine bottle, a surgeon's steel saw, and worn examples of daily living: broken stoneware beer jugs, white clay pipes and barrel hoops; buttons and needles that had slipped through floorboards; gun flints, and the one small gold cross. "By the nineteenth century," Luc was ending his saga, "Sous-le-Cap came to be considered picturesque with its old houses, laundry lines and wooden stairs crisscrossing above *les misérables*, the lives of poverty, all on view in the street's narrow diorama." Florence stood up and passed around copies of archival photos, the street exactly as Luc had described, scraggly urchins, diapers and shirts on laundry lines, and at least one dog in each picture staring out at strangers.

I spent the rest of the afternoon cleaning a small hoard of children's marbles made of stone, and a policeman's badge. Many more artifacts needed to be restored for display and study. Luc had finally signed my contract to work in Florence's lab in Laval's Seminary rooms in Upper Town until the end of December. But I had not been careful in what I wished for in fighting for that contract. Starting work in the lab, each day I would walk in and out of the Seminary building, one minute away from Rue des Remparts and the bastion with the two cannons. From its low-walled height had Jean-Paul met his death, and how?

CHAPTER TWENTY-THREE

That evening Daniel and I reviewed the evidence. Our dinner together celebrating my contract had descended into death talk. Yes the dig's walkways were temporary but they'd been well built, collapsing only with the violence of the storm. A fall from their platforms would not have killed a man. Unless he'd had a heart attack as well, or perhaps, in the fall, a broken neck. Surely bruising on the body would distinguish a fall from a walkway with one from the high cliff. A hundred or more feet above the excavation, on Rue des Remparts, the bastion wall with the cannons was low enough to be dangerous in the dark. But it was two feet high, not six inches. No one would inadvertently tumble over it even in a bad storm. Was he drunk? And whatever conclusions the coroner reached, Jean-Paul's body had been covered by a mound of dirt that night, a mound that might have been shaped by human hands. Undeniably, we concluded, someone else must have been there. By now that person had had enough time to come clean to the police, confess utter panic when Jean-Paul had slipped, the guilt of not saving him, and the terror that blame was certain, causing him—or her—to hide the body until a calmer plan could be devised. But I'd found the corpse before that plan. The key to this scenario would be more information that confirmed death came from a long high fall and only a long high fall. No one had come forward, and the police were saying nothing. Not to us. I did not want to "bother" Detective Laflamme, but Daniel and I conjectured that Jean-Paul had been pushed.

Our next thought was equally disturbing. Was the murderer a stranger to us, someone from another part of Jean-Paul's life? Or was the killer someone we knew? From the dig? What kind of danger would I be in if I kept trying to find out?

Our last week on the dig was spent cleaning the site. "We aren't leaving the street like the pigs and dogs did in the eighteenth century," Luc admonished. The students washed each trowel and bucket, a small backhoe refilled the trenches, and Florence and I systematically secured and marked all the boxes containing the finds. We had three days to empty our room for Friday's move up to the Seminary, an impossible time limit in my opinion. Dozens of packing cartons lay open and half-filled as we removed the special artifact trays and bags from the dig lab's shelving and sorted them by material into their correct location and time-frame box.

"We're so damn organized we've created the picky-ist, prissy-ist job I've ever worked on," I said to Florence.

"Would you prefer Earl Grey, green, or regular?" Florence reacted automatically.

"We're boxed in."

"Very clever. By the boxes for packing or the boxes of tea? But we have to work fast if we're going to finish. Plug the kettle in and make yourself a strong cup. And keep it on the desk, not near the artifacts." Then she smiled. "I mean it, you are clever. You can joke in both official languages. But sometimes it's like listening to someone making puns—the more there are, the worse they sound."

"Are you telling me to shut up?"

"Just fill your mouth with tea instead."

"I'm going to be drinking a lot of tea this winter."

"Yes, *ma chérie*, you are. That story you told me, about your grandmother making you put pennies in a jar when you swore? You have your choice here—drink tea or donate money."

"What would you put *your* money on?" I countered. "That Jean-Paul's death was accidental, or that someone else might have been involved? A person we know? Who?"

Florence stopped packing. "An accident is unlikely. I've seen Jean-Paul walking the city alone as well as with his students. For him Quebec City must have been like a movie you're seeing for the hundredth time." Her eyes were wet. "Someone else either killed him accidentally or deliberately."

Florence quickly wiped a sleeve over her face, stood up straight and said, "What have the police found out?" The question was rhetorical because we both knew the police hadn't divulged more information, at least not publicly. The investigation appeared about as active as a turtle on a sunny log. "Our own suspects are limited," she stated. "It's probably someone we don't know."

I needed to lighten the mood as well as pursue my line of thought. "That's no fun," I said. "We can't talk about them. Let's start with Odette."

Florence joined my game. As she picked up a bag of potsherds, carefully placing it in order in the carton, she said, "Did Odette profit? She told you no." Florence of course had winkled out what I knew. "But we aren't certain. Keep her on the list."

I'd already made a mental note to do just that if I ever saw Antoine again to ask. "Luc?" I said, and glanced around the room to make sure he wasn't within earshot.

"Speaking of Luc," Florence looked at me cupping my mug of tea. "We've got to keep working while we're talking, *ma chérie.*"

"You didn't answer my question. What do you think of Luc? And his daughter Suzanne?"

"You told him what Meg said, swearing that Jean-Paul never touched her, and what was his reply again while you were signing the contract? 'It doesn't mean Jean-Paul didn't molest *my* daughter.'"

"But Meg's certainly not a suspect, right?"

"Nothing would make me think she was. Nor anyone else we know. But," and she stopped momentarily, "we have to admit bias."

I thought of my need to have Aunt Adèle repeat in no uncertain terms that Daniel had not killed Sylvie. Just a detective being thorough, I said to myself. He was no murderer, *mon beau Daniel*, although love, as Florence had pointed out, might be making me blind. Aunt Adèle, too, had warned me that evening in the comedy club about skewed perceptions and their influence. I changed the subject.

"Do you think anyone in Jean-Paul's family might have killed him?" I asked.

"What, to inherit? I heard his money is going to be divided equally among the branches of the Nadon family, as well as a lot going to his history group, and to charity. Besides," Florence said, "if you're worried about Antoine, he must have known he was named as executor. Jean-Paul's death gave him a huge amount of ugly work. An estate for the benefit of a whole extended family, a club and a charity? He doesn't get much money however you measure it."

"You certainly have your sources, Florence."

She smiled. "My family and I work as a team. Speaking of teams, why has your assistant abandoned this big pile of paper and drawing stuff?"

"She'll clean it up this afternoon. She promised. Meg said she had to work with Gaetan this morning."

"Gaetan? I saw him drive away hours ago. And yes, Meg was in the passenger seat."

"He doesn't have a car, Florence."

"They were in Luc's truck, *ma chérie*."

"Then there must have been errands to run that he needed Meg for. I'm glad they're at least on real speaking terms."

"Did Meg ever find that notebook she thought Gaetan stole along with the drawing table?"

"It's never turned up," I said. "Maybe we'll find it in this cleanup."

"A good time to sneak it back, that's for sure. Do you want to bet it shows up this week?" Florence turned from the window where she was packing files. "Ten dollars?"

"Ten to you if the notebook shows up but the money goes to me if I find it."

"Anything to get you to work faster," was the response as we each deposited our money in an old teacup. Before I could think of a smart aleck comment to throw back in return, Florence yelled, "Hey, there's Luc's truck now. It's back. And here's Luc running out of his trailer. Boy, does he look steamed. He's shouting something about he needed his truck at eleven and what the hell's going on."

By now I was over at the window, too. Luc was tearing a strip off Gaetan while Meg was quietly sneaking out of the truck and disappearing. Coward. We heard Luc bark, "Gaetan, get the fuck into my office!" and the next second a few workers who'd been inside the trailer came scurrying out, tails between legs, glancing back as Gaetan was force-marched through the door. We all waited, pretending we weren't. Five minutes later Gaetan burst out of the trailer, shoulders hunched, face red, stumbling towards Luc's truck. Luc was yelling from the door stoop, "Just ask, you dumb shit. Go through the bag yourself. And be back here on time for once."

"Something's really wrong," I said. "Luc likes Gaetan."

"It's sure set him off. Have you noticed how Luc's been on edge? Maybe bringing this season's dig to a close is tough on a prof whose real field is prehistory. Or maybe it's the death of Jean-Paul. Maybe Luc thinks he's the next victim. Maybe there's some ancient curse on this site."

I snorted. "Maybe your gossip antenna could nose around this afternoon and find out what's up? This week's going to be hell if Luc's rabid."

"I'll ask the students, you ask Meg. She's the one in the know. And get her to clean up her stuff."

I did search for Meg, twice, because she never showed up in the collections room as she had promised. Each time I found her she was engaged in earnest drawing or a "terribly important" conversation. "Later," was her curt response when I interrupted. For a supervisor, what was the line between wuss and control freak? When did you trust your staff and when did you order them around? Which made for a more productive work atmosphere? Good for a discussion over tea with Florence, I figured, as I returned from the second trip.

Pushing open the door to our lab I noticed a smell of old dirt. "It's stuffy in here," I said, and looked at the wall clock to see if it was break time.

"I closed the windows," squeaked Florence.

Her strange voice caught me. She was holding a tissue close to her eyes, the other hand pressed on the phone.

"Berry," Florence said, "Come and sit down."

Lyrics floated at the back of my mind. "There's no panic like real panic," it sang. Lighten the rising fear, the visceral dread. Over which you have no control because something has happened and some kind person is here to tell you.

"Daniel?" I whispered.

Florence shook her head. "Safe. He wants you to call. Come and sit down," and she turned her chair to face me.

"What's happened?" I shuffled forward.

Florence said, "Oh *ma chérie*," and bent me slowly down into the chair. She hugged me. "Daniel called. I have sad, sad news for you. Aunt Adèle has passed away."

"What happened?" The voice might have been mine but I couldn't tell because I couldn't breathe.

"She died . . ." Tears streamed down Florence's face. "Someone shot her."

I screamed. Florence held me for a long time. Eventually she said, "I'm going to find Meg," and I could hear her hurrying along the hall just before I broke down bawling.

CHAPTER TWENTY-FOUR

The week reeled on with one shock after the next. Whoever had killed Aunt Adèle was a murderous criminal, whether he had brought his own weapon or not; he—or maybe she—had shot Aunt Adèle at close range with her late husband's old hunting rifle. The police surmised that Aunt Adèle had heard a noise in the house, grabbed the rifle, gone to investigate, and the gun had been wrestled out of her hands by the intruder. Further detective work would answer if she had been robbed. It didn't seem so at first glance. The police reported that the house looked immaculate except for the area of the crime. Right now they didn't want the family to see the living room, but they had questions about trampled papers they would ask when we were ready.

After two days I made myself go to work so distraction would blot out our immense loss. Daniel did the same, although in the first raw week his radio program had a guest host in to provide the chatter while Daniel hid in a back room, ostensibly working on scripts. I made artifact boxes. The careful measurements and precise cutting of foam liners to fit each piece required concentration, and any mistakes resulted merely in a loss of supplies, not historic evidence. At night both Daniel and I slept badly, me especially when I was at my place alone.

Aunt Adèle's son, Réjean, after conferring with Daniel, authorized an autopsy, and by the end of the week her death by gunshot wounds was confirmed. My faint hope had been a massive heart attack before the intruder fired: surprised, instant, gone. That this thought could be called a hope appalled me; life was so relative as well as temporary. Daniel kissed me when I made that comment.

"Relative is right, Berry," he tried to joke in English, using his *comédien* persona. "She was my aunt, and that's why it hurts so much."

Daniel's attempts at humour to keep us from going under were worth another kiss. We were lying on a foam mattress in my cheap apartment in St.-Jean-Baptiste. Meg had taken over Daniel's bedroom at his place, collapsing on hearing about Aunt Adèle's death, and Daniel and I grabbed small bits of privacy here. Just days ago, before the murder, my daydreams had had as theme a new apartment for the fall—with Daniel?—since I'd be staying in Quebec. Now, at this moment, comfort came when I pressed myself against his warm body and we hugged so tight I was inhaling not air but him, our being alive and with each other.

"Sex isn't the only thing," I said into his shoulder. "The media, advertising, have missed this."

Daniel pushed away so he could look me in the eye. "What are you talking about?"

"Hugging is underrated."

"Hugging you is . . ." Daniel said, "as much as I have strength for right now. Not forever, don't underestimate me. At this point I'd even light your post-hug cigarette if either of us smoked."

The word "cigarette" made my gut clench. Laflamme. The death of Jean-Paul Nadon. Now Aunt Adèle. What was going on? We cuddled, each touch a reminder that for us it was life happening right this moment, that holding onto it in each other stretched it out like an open road.

"I want to shut off my thinking brain," I said, when our lips were speaking instead of seeking.

"You're thinking about Aunt Adèle?"

"My hope now," I admitted, "is that the murderer is found quickly, and with irrevocable proof. I want revenge."

"Careful, Berry. It's a dish best eaten cold, *n'est-ce pas?*"

Cold, heartless, in cold blood, cold-blooded murder. A tap dance of words. That someone should be able to kill and just walk away was hideous, except that I knew it happened often enough. Worse, in its own way: had the killer enjoyed it, the power, and the ultimate omnipotence? "I want revenge for Aunt Adèle, and for all the other victims."

"You're incorrigible, Berry, an incorrigible innocent in this case. An idealist."

"I love humanity just as much as the next idealist."

Daniel laughed, and it started us kissing again, touching, fishing for pleasure in life. He held me close and said, "You have to deal with the world as it is, not just as you want it to be." He crushed me against his warm body. "An idealist might like it better in a cloistered nunnery. On second thought, forget I said that. Don't take holy orders. That wouldn't exactly be good for us in the future." Daniel's plain words shocked me into happiness, but the break in the clouds was brief.

"Okay, I want revenge only for two victims. Aunt Adèle and Jean-Paul."

Daniel and Aunt Adèle's son arranged the funeral. Réjean insisted on the near-by church in St.-Édouard so all the neighbors could come. He asked Daniel to deliver the eulogy. Daniel said he was honored, and would also organize others who wanted to speak.

We arrived at a church protected by the tinned diamond-shaped shingles common in old Quebec roofing. Here the diamonds did not gleam in any lamplight. Grey and stained under a heavy sky, they mirrored my mood. Even the metal trim was dulled, and the church's century-old elegance spoke not of comfort, but of times lost. Its pealing bells were a summons, not solemn beauty. A damp cold pervaded the vast building. Had the summer sun ever penetrated its musty walls?

Aunt Adèle would have been pleased with the eclectic assemblage—people with nothing in common but her life, decade by decade. At the reception later I would be introduced to her many neighbors, to an old school friend now in a wheelchair, to friends of her son and his wife's relatives, and to two of Daniel's workmates from the radio station. Florence was the one friend of mine who I counted on being there. At this funeral, I was part of the family that entered the church at the last moment from a private room off to the side.

We shared the front row with an exhausted-looking Réjean, his wife in black hat, black mini-veil, grasping white tissues, and their two solemn, confused girls in Sunday best. In my pew Daniel and Meg were on one side of me and a too-empty space on the other. A plain pine coffin, closed, rested at the front, surrounded by clouds of flowers. To me its blatantly dead, cut wood brought home the finality of Aunt Adèle lying inside, almost within reach but forever gone. I could hardly move to wipe away the tears.

Daniel squeezed my hand and murmured, "The flowers, so beautiful." Someone had known Aunt Adèle intimately; the blooms were fresh from fields and gardens. Store-bought displays of magnificent exotics had no place. A few late tomato plants had been dug up and potted, too, and some last stalks of corn. On the coffin itself a deep cobalt blue vase held a squash plant that draped its magnificent yolk-yellow flowers in numerous trails. Blue was Daniel's favourite colour in ceramic glazes. The vase must have been his pottery from years ago, undoubtedly a gift to Aunt Adèle from him and Sylvie.

The religious part of the service was simple. The priest knew Aunt Adèle and built on what had been important to her. After the mass he invited Daniel to the pulpit. Daniel's heartfelt voice deepened the somber mood as he began to recount Aunt Adèle's life. Then a chuckle surfaced when he told a story about her impressionist paintings, close-ups of the voluptuous insides of green peppers, oils that had been refused, when she was twenty, for the Thetford Fall Fair's arts and crafts section. The judges had told her that this was an agricultural fair and if she thought painting provocative subjects in green was going to hide their immoral nature, it was not proper in this township. Aunt Adèle's presence filled the church, all of us either in tears or bursting out laughing as Daniel recounted the tragic, the wonderful, and the spunk in Aunt Adèle's life. He performed a superb tribute. It had become a marvellous funeral. I sat in love.

Neither Réjean nor his wife were in any shape to speak but when Daniel asked if family wanted to say a few words, Meg stood, pulling down her short skirt and tight blouse as she approached the lectern. At least her clothes were black. She faced the crowd with confidence and I exhaled with relief even before her first words, watching as her eyes made contact with the audience. She had been a mess when we were preparing to leave for the church, fussing, crying and needing Daniel's calm presence, but here I saw how close she was to him in other ways. She had a stage presence older than her years, a control today over her public persona that made me appreciate just how much she had shown her unselfconscious soul to me at other times. I felt intimately trusted, was glad she had decided to take a year of French at Laval and would be staying, and equally relieved that I was no longer saddled with a supervisory role.

"*Je ne parle pas très bien le français,*" Meg began, and then read from notes. She spoke on behalf of Aunt Adèle's relatives in Ireland and said how glad she was to have had this summer to get to know her great-aunt, as she called her. "It's hard enough to figure out my actual family relationship to her," she explained, "let alone say it in French." The congregation murmured its appreciation when she stepped down from the platform.

Then a few people stood up in their places and told anecdotes. We were all rather enjoying ourselves by now, as if so engrossed in a feature film we had forgotten time. The school chum wheeled herself to the front and recounted an episode when she and Aunt Adèle were both newly married and she and her husband had been invited for dinner. It was the only time in her long friendship with Aunt Adèle that she could recall her swearing. Aunt Adèle had been trying out a new pressure cooker recipe for pot roast, and her "*Tabarnac!*" scream from the kitchen had paralyzed all of them, although not the piece of meat that had come sailing out, propelled by the released steam pressure.

Daniel invited anyone in the audience to share reminiscences of Aunt Adèle. Many did. At the end, I stood up. I did want to pay tribute to Aunt Adèle, and besides, I figured it satisfied the silent curiosity of the many who knew Daniel and were seeing me for the first time.

CHAPTER TWENTY-FIVE

❦

"I'm a friend of Daniel's," I began, "And like Meg, I'm also one of those who met Aunt Adèle only this summer. I loved her boldness, her generosity of spirit and her *joie de vivre*. Although I have to admit I was really scared of her at first."

Daniel, a few steps away, laughed with the congregation. I described having to pass muster, and then beginning to understand how wise Aunt Adèle was. I mentioned a few of the things Aunt Adèle had said that impressed me, about dealing with the past and wanting to live, not just dwell, and then I turned to Daniel and said I was so glad this philosophical bent had been passed on in his family. I recounted what Daniel had said to me in my apartment: "You have to deal with the world as it is, not just as you want it to be."

"None of us wanted this amazing woman to die so horribly, but it's happened, and we have to deal with a world without Aunt Adèle, and on behalf of my own love for her, and others who feel the same, I'd like to ask you all to please help the police in any way you can to bring her murderer to justice."

Even if it meant assisting Detective Sergeant Laflamme, but I didn't say that. There were several burly men at the back of the church watching this funeral, too. And one tall, beautiful woman with cold blue eyes.

Daniel stepped to the lectern and put his arm around my shoulders. His eyes were moist. I half-turned to sniffle into a tissue as he leaned into the lectern's microphone, using a Québécois expression everyone understood, "*Ma blonde! Merci.*" My hair was never blonde and now it's faded mainly to grey, but the word had little to do with real hairdos, and announced that we were a couple. The congregation applauded as Daniel kissed me on both cheeks. Aunt Adèle's funeral had become my debutante's ball. At the reception afterwards many people congratulated me, telling stories about Daniel as well as more about Aunt Adèle.

The interment came first, though, and it was hard to make it through. So much for being strong for Meg and Daniel. Or in front of Laflamme. The graveyard seemed an ominous extension of the moldy church under the dark sky, so many dead surrounding us, the shovelfuls of damp earth burying the remains of a vibrant woman. Trudging back to the church hall for the reception, grateful that the funeral clothes Florence had forced me to buy included a jacket, I held tightly onto Daniel's warm hand, the free one that wasn't wrapped around Meg. Once inside, the three of us huddled together without words for a few minutes. Then we joined the rest of the family. The guests' kind words in the warm and well-lit room began to blunt our distress. There was no longer any sign of the police, or perhaps I just wasn't looking.

"Would she have minded that Daniel made such a big public deal of saying I was his girlfriend?" I asked Réjean, not wanting to take anything away from Aunt Adèle's final celebration, the real reason we were here.

"Not at all. *Maman* would have said something like, 'I love Daniel and he loves me, but it's about time my nephew had a younger woman in his life again.'"

I smiled my appreciation. Maybe later I would change the subject, ask Réjean if Aunt Adèle had ever been threatened by anyone, young or old, but my voice dried when I looked down the line of people offering condolences. I was filled with gratitude that Florence had stayed. Behind her, though, stood Odette, Antoine, Luc and Gaetan, and I shocked Réjean when I muttered, "What the hell is that line-up doing here?"

Antoine's grim face said by itself how difficult the unjust death of a loved one was. His hands clasped the mourning family one person after another, each time bowing his head to murmur private condolences. When he reached me he said, "Berry, I am so sorry for your loss. Let me say, though, that you spoke beautifully. Thank you."

"We have to stop meeting like this," I said in English. I hadn't planned on him knowing the phrase but a slow smile spread over Antoine's face. It made his features handsome again, as I'd thought when I first met him, like noticing the shine of an artifact through its worn surface.

"Yes, let's have no more funerals for a while," he agreed. "I'll go light a candle to that." He was about move on when I said in my sweetest voice, "I didn't expect to see you here," and placed my foot casually in his way. His brother had been killed and now Aunt Adèle. Did this add meaning to the police presence? To witness possible connections between the deaths?

Antoine didn't seem offended. Maybe he had already been asked why he had come. He gestured towards the buffet; he had, I was not surprised, brought an array of cheeses. "When I heard, I offered," he said simply. "It was the least I could do for Meg. For all of you. I feel so badly we've had a few disagreements, after Meg did such good work for me. And now I know you and Daniel better too." His face fell. "I have some experience . . . with what you're going through."

I stepped back. He smiled grimly and was about to move on when I stopped him with, "It's too close, our experiences. Do you think there're any possible links?"

The pause lengthened while Antoine tried to find words, his head bent down, and when he lifted it his whole face had collapsed, on the verge of tears. He shook his head quickly, muttered "killed" and walked away unable to say more.

Odette, standing beside him, did not wait for my query about her presence. A woman giving her name as Adèle, she immediately began, had called her before the history walk for details. They'd had a marvellous conversation, at the end of which, "I advised, 'Don't wear jeans or you're going to be wet all day if it rains.'" Aunt Adèle had laughed and told Odette how old she was. "I haven't been embarrassed like that in ages," Odette blushed. "I thought she was an older student keen with questions. I wished she'd come on the tour, although I worried after that call that the walking would be too much for her. When Antoine told me he was going to the funeral, I had to come too." She sounded genuine.

Down the line, Luc was speaking to Réjean's family. Behind him, Gaetan stared at his shoes. Luc finished, glanced at Gaetan, and tapped him lightly on the arm. Then it was as if the young man sprang into a pre-arranged pose. He repeated it with each person: hand extended, one short sentence, then head hanging down again even before they'd politely replied. What was going on here? A fiery heat flashed through my body, driven by adrenalin, asking, "Have the murderers returned to the scene of their crime?"

Florence, shuffling forward in the line, might have gossip. Luc had only met Aunt Adèle that one day on the dig. It didn't follow that his outburst of obscenities had embarrassed him enough to come to her funeral, nor that it prompted him to drag along Gaetan, who obviously didn't want to be here. When the duo reached me, I waited to witness their act.

Instead, Luc said, "Take whatever time off you need, Berry. I can put you on sick leave. Family's more important than work." Then he glanced at Gaetan.

The young man looked up, relieved eyes searching mine, a familiar person at this funeral, and whispered, "I didn't do it! You believe me, don't you?"

Jaw open, I stared at Gaetan cringing in his ill-fitting funeral suit. Immediately Daniel stepped in, rescuing me with, "Thank you for coming, Luc, Gaetan. Is it all cleared up? Have the police finished interviewing you?"

Gaetan nodded, his thin frame folding over again, hiding a blotchy face.

"They'll be back," said Luc, grimacing. "That Laflamme doesn't care who she collars as long as she gets somebody. Now she's directing the two cases. Thanks for letting us come here. I told Gaetan that since he didn't do anything, there was no reason not to pay our respects. Damn the police for showing up. I think they've fingered Gaetan; they insisted he must know something. Being here shows he's not afraid, just was in the wrong place at the wrong time." Luc smiled over at Gaetan, "It's tough, but he's a tough guy, despite people pointing him out."

"Did they?" said Daniel calmly. "Then they're going to get a big surprise." Daniel signalled to Meg. She smiled and threw her arms around Gaetan.

In French phrases Meg must have prepared, she said, "Don't let them get to you. I know you're innocent." She twisted, looked up at his collapsed face, and said in a voice so low I barely heard, "I'm really to blame. I asked you to go." I could have fainted except I was too enraged. Daniel had told me nothing about any of this.

"See me in the corner, sweetheart," I hissed.

Daniel turned me around with a loving gesture and walked me a few paces away. "You snored right through this two a.m. drama, *ma belle*. Scotch can do that."

"You're hardly a teetotaller," I said in dignified English, not remembering the word in French.

"You, *ma blonde*, are tea and a totaller. You totalled that bottle of scotch last night. Stick with the tea."

I wasn't going to appreciate his facility in both languages. "Mickey," I replied. "And it was almost empty when I started. Daniel, shit *la merde*, what did Meg say last night? Made Gaetan go where?"

"Later. Right now we just have to get through this afternoon."

I was furious but backed off. Daniel was Aunt Adèle's closest relative and this was his day more than mine. If I could pull myself together to act maturely, I would tell him that. But if my inner pout wanted one more kick at the can, I would snicker a clever reply. I forced myself into maturity. Florence was approaching, reminding me that one person had at times called me juvenile. Besides, my age was, after all, a perfect cover for acting maturely.

Florence and I hugged, comforting each other with a warm silence deeper than words. I whispered, "Have you said hello to Antoine and Odette?" and raised my eyebrows what I hoped was a significant amount.

Florence looked around to see who might be listening, and replied, "What are they doing here?"

So she didn't know anything. I had to explain. "Gaetan and Luc are here too." I pointed to where they and Meg were now conferring and waited for her response.

"Gaetan showed up for work two days ago with this massive hangover," Florence said. "Then yesterday Luc phoned me to say he was at the police station with Gaetan and would I put an "away" message on his door and his university landline. Luc turned up at the end of the day and all he would say was that Gaetan was apparently the last person to see Aunt Adèle alive."

My sleuthy self kicked in. "That was the day with Luc's truck!" Florence nodded gravely. I focused on the details. What had Meg just whispered to Gaetan? "I'm really to blame. I asked you to go." All I said to Florence was, "I'll find out more and tell you."

That evening I drove an exhausted Daniel and Meg the sixty kilometers back to Quebec City. Meg, wrapped in the car blanket, was asleep against the side window in the back. Daniel sat beside me trance-like. I just drove.

"I feel good," he eventually said into the darkness of the country road. "We did as much as we could for Aunt Adèle. For a funeral, it was okay."

"I don't know how you could have been better. And considering what you must have been feeling."

"I'm fine in the public eye, like a shy kid who can do theatre. Give me a role and I'm not inhibited. But in private, sometimes I just don't know how to express myself."

When we chatted like this, relaxed, honest, we were each other's best friend. I put my hand on his leg and caressed it. There were more ways than words if he wanted to communicate.

"You were great, too," he continued. "I got a lot of compliments, you know, at the reception. What a nice person, what a good choice."

"I behaved, didn't I?"

"For almost ten hours."

"A personal best," I agreed.

"I want you to come to Aunt Adèle's house and pick out something to remember her by. Réjean suggested it."

"That's so kind."

"*Quelle politesse.* You're still behaving. Why?"

"Wait till morning. I'm giving you mourner's privilege till then."

"Thank you so much. You are so kind." Through the dark of the car I could half see him grinning. "We do have lots to talk about," Daniel said. "I'm completely done in, though, tonight."

"I know you are." I tried to sound compassionate rather than smugly mature. "Talking like this is enough right now. For me it's intimate. Like hugging the other night. I felt very close to you."

"Me too."

I waited for his next words. This was the exact point in our conversations where he would remind me again of a cat who, when the bird has flown, pretends its real interest all the time has been in cleaning its fur. In the same way, Daniel would switch to another subject to make an honorable retreat from embarrassment or discomfort. Had today's events and emotions, his words at the lectern, meant he was no longer reticent to express his emotional commitment to me? Could I imagine a day when we might move in together? Or had this funereal day resurrected Sylvie's shadow? He started to joke, predictably sidestepping anything more about commitment. "Of course you felt close. You were smothered by my shoulder. Berry, don't worry. I'll get back to real sex soon."

"Lately I've been feeling my age," I said. "Don't wait too long."

⋄⊚⋄⊚⋄

CHAPTER TWENTY-SIX

I stumbled to the bathroom at five a.m. but someone was already using it. Not Daniel, a lump beside me on the camping mattress squeezed out on his living room floor. It must be Meg. Propping myself against a wall, I waited, until something moved around my legs. My sleepy brain and eyes without their glasses felt rats, or was this the farmhouse and it was a snake, or was that in the story in my bedtime novel? A plaintive mew stropped my ankle. Faux Paws. After the tragedy Daniel had brought his cat home from St.-Édouard. Faux Paws' summer vacation catching mice had abruptly ended, but her reward was Daniel. He whispered sweet words to her and enfolded her in his arms at every opportunity. I was not a big fan of cranky precious cats, but she was softening me up. At least, better than a rodent would have.

Meg emerged, startling me by being fully dressed. At five a.m. I'm likely to strap my bra around my knees, the first bumps I hit. With a nonchalant, "Couldn't sleep either? I'm making coffee," she headed for the kitchen.

I followed, stating the obvious. "You're dressed." I was pleased enough I'd kept my voice low because of Daniel. "Are you going out?" I said, standing feet apart, arms crossed like a sentry at the gate.

"You're such a little monster," said Meg to Faux Paws in exactly Aunt Adèle's tone.

"Outside at this hour?" I repeated. Anything was unreasonable this early.

Meg picked up a purring Paws and said, "I'm 'on my moon', isn't that the Indian expression, and it wrecked my nightgown."

"Aboriginal. Indigenous. First Nations, First Peoples. Shit *la merde*. What a pedant I am, even at five in the morning. I give up." Sleep wouldn't return, and this was a good opportunity to have a chat with Meg without Daniel. I said, "Let's blow this joint," immediately feeling foolish, as if I'd shown off a new belly tattoo on my fifty-four-year-old body. "Let me take you out for coffee," I clarified. I could at least be a nice crone to the young, extra points for it at five a.m.

"At this hour?" Meg imitated me.

"Something'll be open by the time I'm dressed. Maybe a hotel. Let's try the Chateau Frontenac." If breakfast wasn't being served, it would at least be a nice walk.

"Jaysus, fancy schmancy." Meg showed off another expression she had picked up, and did a light dance step. I was glad to see her North American phrase collection expanding from her first tryouts of useful indicators like "son of a bitch" and "schmuck".

"Yer darn tootin'," I replied, giving her more vocabulary.

We avoided rue des Remparts with its bastion and cannon even though the view of the dawn would have been spectacular. My excuse was that it was too early, and we would see the light anyway from the windows of the Chateau Frontenac. The cool air held the freshness of morning, a new day indeed unfolding. Yesterday was yesterday and behind us. It occupied our thoughts, though, because after innocuous small talk, before I could frame a question about Gaetan's "I didn't do it", Meg came out with, "One murder feels different from the other, doesn't it?"

I stumbled. "Say that again?"

"Well, you were, we all were, a mess after Jean-Paul, and now you're, like, brilliantly together. But you were closer to Aunt Adèle." She could not mask her curiosity. "Weren't you?"

"I don't have words for how much I loved her. And inside I am a mess, and I've been trying hard to act mature. But I'm no Florence."

That last truth was my undoing. Sobs like huge gulps rose. I turned to hide my face against the wall. Trying to lean against it, with each welling of tears and grief I slid further down the cold brick. Slumped kneeling on the sidewalk, I felt Meg's small arms tightly embrace me. She was saying something in Irish I didn't know, lilting and soft, a song whose lines broke too often as her own voice choked.

Shakily we untangled and stood, searched for tissues, said nothing while we retrieved our daily faces and began walking. Lucky I was an amateur in this detection business. It was not just the learning curve but my whole being, my emotions right now, were so far from being a hard-boiled kick-ass on this case.

I said, "I was hoping to be strong. So Daniel didn't have to be. Now you know the real me."

"Likewise. You've heard my awful singing."

I shook my head and took in Meg's face, pallid and still slightly wary. "You really helped. I needed to open up. Needed you. And your song. Thanks, Meg."

"You can scare me anytime. I hate it when people 're polite." She hesitated. "Can I ask a rude question, so? What's it like later on? When a person gets old, do you naturally want to just sit around? Where's your fun gone?"

"Your *joie de vivre*? Meg, you have nothing to worry about. Maybe when you're seventy you'll begin to have your answer."

Joie de vivre at seventy. Pale fingers reached out to me from the blackness of a burial. I swallowed hard. Jean-Paul, a man I so admired. A death I was going to avenge by discovering the killer. Ideas smothered in the cellar of my mind by fresh grief.

Meg had stopped, observing more pain skim my face. Leaning against a wall again, I said, "Meg, you out of all of us understand how images can override the thinking part of the brain, how powerful they are, and you already have a lot of good pictures to fuel the *joie* in your life." I straightened up. "Back to what started this. If I'd actually witnessed Aunt Adèle the way I found Jean-Paul Nadon, you'd never have needed to ask your first question. No way could I have even pretended to be strong and together. Now, how are you feeling?"

"Like I've aged a decade," Meg replied. "And I didn't want to."

"It's not exactly the summer you came over for."

"Ah, that's for darn tootin'." Her pace slowed, and her hand darted to her face to wipe away tears.

"Let's get some take-out coffee and sit on the Terrasse," I suggested, heading for the familiarity of the bench Daniel and I had occupied not so long ago. "Then I'll treat you to breakfast in someplace warm and elegant."

Meg snuffled, "with a bathroom?" and tried to joke about the great compromise take-out would be for me since tea that way was generally awful. Her voice was breaking, though, her eyes flooding. Could I handle this situation and say the right thing now without being too motherly, condescending, or mouthing empty platitudes, any of which would cause Meg to close down and flee? Emotionally open was exactly where I needed Meg to stay so I could discover what had gone on between her and Gaetan the day Aunt Adèle died.

The pale yellow light over the St. Lawrence was tinged with pink in the east. The west still dissolved into night, although with the streetlamps, stone buildings, and trees, the colours were simply versions of dark. I wiped the dew off the bench with my jacket and we sat sipping our hot drinks as the sun rose and the mist lifted off the river below.

"I hated the graveside part," I said.

"The worst."

Silence followed. The sun gained enough height to surveille the city and favour us with its immediate warmth.

Skirting around what I needed to know wasn't going to work. Once again I thought how useful Daniel's questioning skills were: his investigative tools, and his professional armour to protect against any resultant explosion. My own mouth instead did its usual march forward in a straight line, directly over the top.

"Gaetan," I began, "said to me, in the reception line, 'I didn't do it.' Why would I ever have thought he had?"

Meg sat. She hadn't sworn, she hadn't gotten up and run away. I hardly wanted to glance at her, afraid to intrude as she assembled what she would say, her own tools and armour.

"Remember the day Aunt Adèle died?" Meg started cautiously. "I wasn't on the dig site part of the morning? You came looking for me?"

"Sure."

"I went with Gaetan."

"I saw you coming back to the dig in Luc's truck. I figured you were running errands with him."

"He had some stuff to do for Luc. I persuaded him to help me."

My face asked the question.

"Go to Antoine's," she blurted. "Give me a lift so I could get my drawings."

"You went out to Île d'Orléans?"

"That's why Luc was so pissed. It took fucking hours. Much longer than Gaetan was supposed to be away."

"Did you get the drawings? Was Antoine there?"

"He must have been off in the woods or something. He didn't show. I just dashed into the house and left. Berry, I stole a bunch of your corrugated plastic from the lab, the white stuff that looks like cardboard? To hold the drawings flat. I took some rubbish bags too."

I could have said, 'Stealing dig supplies?' but I was still priding myself on acting mature. The sheets were not expensive. "I didn't miss them," I said, and then, "No wonder you didn't want to talk to me afterwards."

But the supplies were not the point. "Why did Gaetan drive off again?"

Meg wailed, "Jaysus, it's all my fault."

"It's not your fault, Meg," I didn't know what 'it' was, but my tight breathing guessed.

"We didn't go directly back to the dig with my drawings. I hid them at Aunt Adèle's."

I froze. "Did you see her?"

"Yes! She was fine! She took them and the sack with my drawing stuff and said she'd hide it all behind the couch in the living room. Nobody would think to look there. 'I won't have to clean,' she was laughing, and I could come and get them any time. I can hear her saying it." Meg's voice cracked. "Then Luc made Gaetan confess why we were late, and he made him go back to Aunt Adèle's. To see if . . . you remember my notebook we never found? Luc really needs it or else we're missing information. He made Gaetan look through my sack for the notebook." Her voice faded. "Luc didn't trust me."

"What happened when Gaetan went back?"

"Nothing! Jaysus! Gaetan said Aunt Adèle let him look through the bag, they both saw there were only pencils and that kind of thing. And the drawings." Meg gulped back a sob, but another escaped.

"So Gaetan was the last person to see Aunt Adèle alive." Florence vindicated.

"Everyone thinks he killed her!"

"Luc doesn't. The police?"

"They interviewed him the whole day."

"They let him go," I said. "They must believe him."

"Do you?"

"Yes." The firmness in my voice felt good. "Daniel does too. Let's go find breakfast and a bathroom." I wanted to walk and think. If Luc was after the notebook, and didn't trust Meg, would he have trusted Gaetan, her co-conspirator? Might not Luc have gone out to Aunt Adèle's later to see for himself what Gaetan had told him? Was his solicitousness around Gaetan at the funeral a cover for what he had really found. Or worse, done?

—◦◦◦◦◦—

CHAPTER TWENTY-SEVEN

An uneasy routine permeated our new workspace in the Seminary. Florence and I unpacked and organized the artifacts and whenever Luc dropped in, I busied myself while Florence headed him off. She agreed that the only immediate real course had to be letting the police discover whether Gaetan or Luc, or neither, held the truth about Aunt Adèle's death, but in the meantime I'd remain watchful, alert for any clues, connections, or missing pieces that would lead to conclusions about Jean-Paul's murderer. Or Aunt Adèle's. Build my case behind the scenes. A real detective was paid to act; I was paid to work for Luc. Could I be sneaky, subtle? At my age, the way my hearing kept worsening, I couldn't even eavesdrop properly. But trying to figure out Jean-Paul's murder meant that for hours at a time I avoided thinking about the death of Aunt Adèle.

Florence and I discussed Jean-Paul time and again but made no headway. Were the cops as stalled as us? As far as we knew. Even when asked by Aunt Adèle's family, Laflamme stated they had no new information but of course were pursuing leads.

My trying to act sharp and coolheaded dissolved around Luc. He behaved as if nothing was wrong, that my short answers and nose-to-the-rusty-nails attitude were normal. I wished Florence would fill him in about my low marks in patience when the subject matter was important, and he would just confess. Or prove his innocence. Then I wouldn't see the hands of a murderer each time my boss entered the room.

Daniel had called me an idealist, and my hoping for an outright confession certainly belonged in that category. An old Hollywood happy ending. The alternative made me sick. It was one thing to watch revenge in a movie, but to have actual murder touch my real life and loved ones shattered any romance about retribution. Especially if it involved more violence, more killing. But my heart demanded revenge. Would a jail sentence satisfy my anger, my anguish, my *je me souviens*—my own "I remember"? Would a distanced court-determined outcome appease? A settlement I would have to live with for the rest of my life? For me it had to, or there would be no difference between me and anyone else who rampaged believing their viewpoint had to be right and that making others suffer didn't matter. Let the police bring the killer to justice. But I would keep secretly tracking down clues. Anything to unmask a murderer. No more Clueless Cates.

In the hours spent setting up our new workspace I'd had too much time to think. "Grief is unpredictable," Florence comforted me, "You never know how it's going to affect you, or how long it's going to last." We followed the police investigation into Aunt Adèle's death as closely as we could, keeping lists of who had mentioned being interviewed and discussing all the "who had said what to whom" we knew. And everyone we knew had been interviewed, some several times.

Laflamme had made Florence one of her targets. Not, we figured, because Laflamme actually suspected her. But Florence was closer than anyone else to many people on the dig, the sympathetic woman who knew them from work this summer and perhaps from before. Florence would return exhausted from the police interview and practically weep on my shoulder. Laflamme's monotone relentlessly prodded my stellar workmate for dig information. One day she held up the butt of a chewed-up placebo cigarette and said to Florence, "Would you like this? This is all you'll get in the holding tank, and a lot worse if you keep repeating stale news. You've got eyes and ears. Who's talking about the murders?"

Florence was not about to repeat rumours and innuendo. But in the evening she would phone her brother's son in the *Sûreté* who would assure her Laflamme had no evidence with which she could possibly make good on her threat to jail Florence.

The police kept hauling in Gaetan, too, and Luc hired a lawyer. I wondered if I should share my suspicions of Luc with the police. Tell them about the notebook, how much Luc wanted it in order to complete the field season, how he might have gone out to Aunt Adèle's himself to check. But I had no definitive proof, and Aunt Adèle had warned me about skewed perceptions. Instead, I speculated with Florence.

There was one fact I didn't share with her. I was not just grieving, but quietly raging. Avenging Aunt Adèle had grown into an obsession. Despite my rationalizing about not taking revenge, an anger management program would have been way too tame for the way I felt. Detective Cates was not planning violence, though: simply cunning. Occasionally this daydream broke up into little voices: "So, Berry, what next?" "Can't think? Menopausal memory you say?" "Isn't Ms. Hot Flashes getting enough sleep?"

With each passing day a perpetrator was less likely to be found. Rumours circulated that there were jurisdictional disputes between offices, municipalities, counties. And undoubtedly galaxies. I was determined to go my own sweet way. I would be mature about it, sugary to those

I needed to talk to, but shit *la merde*, any progress would be better than sitting all day pretending the priority in my life was rust on wrought iron nails.

My brain plotted as much as it was able. My gut was now in a familiar clench. If only this counted as exercise for the abs. I'd tell that brilliant joke to Florence, but there was a serious bit I was not ready to share—my conviction now that Aunt Adèle's murder had to be linked to Jean-Paul's. The facts didn't fit together yet, but that must be because I didn't have enough pieces of the puzzle. So, facts were what I decided to find first. My mission: fill in the gaps. I did that well enough with broken pottery. What did Aunt Adèle and Jean-Paul have in common? The answer: Gaetan, Luc, and the whole notebook non-incident. Meg. And me.

Somehow Laflamme found out my plotting. I was called in the middle of the night and commanded to be at her office at eight the next morning. Not showing up for work at the Seminary would be *my* problem to explain.

Laflamme kept me waiting an hour. Alone in a dank, windowless room. When she showed up I was desperate for the toilet and almost shaking with anger. Laflamme asked a good quarter-hour of unnecessary questions before a female constable led me away for relief. Returning, facing Laflamme, the interview tightened like a tourniquet. Probably every dig person who had been questioned had been made to confess site gossip, and my name had not escaped. The Detective Sergeant had noted the incidents. She had found out exactly how often and where I'd met Jean-Paul for drinks. She'd found a couple of eavesdroppers, too.

But Laflamme wanted something more. Her cold blue eyes were as effective as her voice. "Stop snooping immediately." She sat back, arms folded, and waited for my denial. Or my telling her I just wanted to be helpful.

"What do you expect?" I replied, my voice steady but hoarse. "You aren't sharing anything with the family. Families. We're left making our own way trying to figure things out. We haven't even been told why a detective sergeant whose turf is the city is in charge of a second murder in a village on the South Shore."

Her sardonic smile surprised me. "You really haven't been told anything, have you? Those St.-Édouard cops. That jurisdiction was supposed to keep Daniel as well as Réjean informed. The guys there aren't working with me. Surprising, isn't it?" She bent forward. "Tell a family member, Daniel or Réjean, to contact me if they want the details." She placed two business cards on the table.

"What I can say to you is this," she continued. "In the city we have a gang problem, a drug problem, and the older problem of the death of Monsieur Nadon. My boss, in charge overall of the Nadon case, has been promoted to gangs and drugs. I'm now him. In St.-Édouard they have few police, and a gang problem, a drug problem, and the case of a woman who was murdered. The gangs are related and the drugs are related, like everywhere. Stopping these is priority. I still have a few officers on my murder investigation team, if this is the word I can use, so it works if I take the St.-Édouard case. There are links here too. As you know, since you're one of them." She leaned towards me. "We know that Aunt Adèle attended Monsieur Nadon's funeral. Why?"

I explained, repeating as well as I could remember that Aunt Adèle said she had heard him lecture, admired him, and wanted to attend. My immediate follow-up was to ask what the police had concluded so far about her death.

Laflamme said she had to deliver information directly to the immediate family, and skidded the business cards so they fell in my lap. "Will you quit asking questions now?"

I fingered one card, my thumb running over the crest of the police unit, all official, all the power in their hands, the family reduced to supplicants at their phone-loop altar. I bowed my head. But it was to avoid answering.

"You're grieving, but if you in any way interfere in police investigations, I will have to have you charged. Don't think I can't. This is not some game for amateurs."

"Then show us some professional results," I wanted to say. A year and a half ago, when I'd worked in conservation at the Museum of Anthropology in Vancouver, an Indigenous spokesperson had pointed out that regalia repatriated from museums was often in poor condition. That museums, calling themselves professionals in heritage care and conservation, had done a lousy job. Here in this investigation it was the police pretending they were the best, contrary to the evidence showing itself to us. I was determined to keep my head down but continue sleuthing.

On the next bright September Saturday, Daniel, Meg and I drove out to Aunt Adèle's farmhouse to choose keepsakes.

"Réjean isn't allowed to sever the land to sell it," Daniel said. "And it's too soon for him anyway. In fact, he'd prefer to keep the farm intact. So, I'm renting it."

"You're moving to St.-Édouard?" That would put a few cracks in our glaze, living sixty kilometers apart. And if I stayed the night at the farmhouse, Quebec's notorious winter was coming, and I had to be at work early. The roads on the South Shore were famous for blizzard conditions. But why worry? I didn't own a car.

Daniel let me wait. He knew this was not simply a polite enquiry, and I knew, only too well, that he was a comedian who enjoyed teasing. Or, I fidgeted, was there actually some momentous proposition he was going to come out with? It was a big farmhouse, after all. But with Meg in the back seat listening, surely this was not the time to propose, even in a whisper, that I come live with him.

Right now, would I want to move anyway? Unrequited love and unfulfilled daydreams had common ground. They were romantic, and happy endings could be dreamed. But the reality was that my contract would end in December and I would need employment after. And Daniel was probably off to Louisiana.

Besides, I did love having my own space. Even if it meant living out of boxes and suitcases as I'd been doing for the past two years, first in Vancouver and now here. A friend's basement in Toronto stored a few memories from my parents' home and even fewer from my marriage, that existence before my husband left, formerly known as life. Those two geological records had totaled close to fifty years. So before I went back to school and trained as a conservator I'd pared down my possessions to only those memories I wanted to keep, and because of buddy the ex, there were damn few. Yet despite ending up post-fifty without a house, comfortable furniture or other common Canadian middle-class comforts like a fridge that did not need defrosting, my cheap apartment in St. Jean Baptiste was still my home. I left it messy, I left it neat, I didn't need to care or compromise. It remained my refuge.

Daniel glanced over to see if I looked nervous. I might at times be able to put on a mature act but I have to really work at a poker face. He smiled. "I'm renting Aunt Adèle's as a country place. A ski cabin or a place for nice summer evenings."

"Is a chalet what you want?" He'd never mentioned a rural retreat.

"No. But the heat has to be kept on in winter or the structure will suffer. Somebody has to pay. I thought you'd enjoy a place to go to. You like the country."

"I love it. Like now." In the early afternoon sun as we drove south, the hills slanted the autumn trees into a bazaar of crimson shot with gold, tents against a turquoise sky.

"But I am moving," Daniel added.

My loud swallow made him grin.

"Just to a bigger apartment."

I waited, but again, he paused.

"Where?" My voice quavered. "You have a beautiful place, a great location in Upper Town." He knew I meant, 'why?' The whole 'it's a big house' scenario that had just flitted through my brain rewound itself.

"I want two bedrooms." Daniel gestured towards the back seat. Meg had started French classes at Laval and still had her own cheap room but came over to Daniel's a night or two a week. Then Daniel would sleep on the couch or camp out on the floor. He liked looking after Meg. This routine had become an antidote to the evil that had touched them both. Like Persephone, they lived now tainted by an underworld. Daniel whispered, "And I want my privacy with you, too, if Meg's staying."

Réjean met us at the farmhouse. He and Daniel became engrossed, or Daniel acted a bravura performance of it, in the electrical and the plumbing, the storm windows and basement drainage. Meg and I wandered from room to eerily empty room, finally sitting in the big farm kitchen to wait. Joining us, Réjean politely asked what we had chosen as a memory of his mother. With equal gentleness I asked what he and Daniel wanted to keep. Réjean replied that his family had already taken a porcelain figurine, a lamp and some photos, but they preferred the modern. Daniel said he was content to keep whatever was left after we had selected. Did I want any furniture for my apartment? I shook my head. The old dressers and chairs belonged here, not in my makeshift camp in the city, however homey.

"Are there paintings?" I asked. Aunt Adèle had hung only five in the house. I guessed Réjean had some and that she had given many away over the years. I was curious to see the attic.

Réjean gestured instead to a door off the kitchen. Meg opened what had once been the pantry. Shelves displayed dozens of clean mason jars waiting for their annual preserves. Lower shelves held a pickling kettle and its paraphernalia, carefully saved jars from grocery store condiments, and a strainer for jellies. On the highest shelf sat a wooden paint box and two stained pots filled with brushes. Meg carefully lifted the artist's materials down, and we all knew what she wanted. Réjean said, "I think there's an easel out back."

Between the shelves, the space was completely taken up with a wooden rack. It had twenty or so slots, and each one was crammed with canvasses. One by one we leaned them against the kitchen cupboards. Daniel bobbed behind Meg and I as Réjean watched. Meg exclaimed over a sunny painting of fields, the view from the back porch. Daniel picked a dozen oils to hang in the house. I chose a large painting of the inside of a green pepper.

Bouncing out to the car and back, Daniel loaded up Meg's paints, several platters too beautiful for a recreational house, and a stack of family photos and documents. With a great show to Réjean he declared that the conservator was in charge of wrapping the paintings securely. Réjean took me to the linen closet, and with sheets and towels I cushioned what I could. The art was in excellent condition, no flaking or fragility, and I silently congratulated Aunt Adèle on her art techniques and knowledge of painting materials. When I looked up, I saw Meg's face looking even sadder than mine.

"The house feels empty," I commented.

She nodded. "It *is* empty." Her dull voice brought a concerned look from Réjean.

"Come back often, Meg," he said. "It's yours now. Aunt Adèle would want you here."

Meg replied, "I can't find it."

She didn't hear my 'what?' because Réjean, who had trouble with her accent, asked if Meg needed a map to find it. Her mind was somewhere else. She didn't answer or move.

To break the awkwardness I said, "Let's go get something to eat. Poutine?" Meg was a big fan of the province's best known and least snobby delicacy.

Meg muttered, "It's not here." She squirmed, and I could see her effort to reconnect with the room and us. "Réjean," she said slowly in French phrasing she had worked out so he wouldn't misunderstand. "Have you seen my sack?"

I held up her new backpack, slung on the back of a kitchen chair. Meg shook her head. "A green rubbish bag with some drawings, and my big zipped-up rucksack with my pencils and everything?" Hoarsely she added, "It was behind the couch in the living room."

Réjean's grey eyes held mine for an instant. "I think Aunt Adèle was looking at some drawings in the living room when she died. She had them spread out on the carpet. All of that is at the police station now."

It was not just because of the unspeakable absence of its occupant that the house felt empty. We had come in through the door beside the living room. My mind had registered its order and cleanliness. Now I realized the old oriental carpet was missing as well as several chairs and undoubtedly more. Any signs of blood and struggle were gone. It was not a surprise when Réjean said, "Meg, I don't think those drawings are good anymore. They got, well, messed up when *Maman* died. You need to ask the police."

"All of them?"

"The police told me two were okay, and a signed book on plants in a plastic bag. I didn't know they were yours. They found out the author lives on Île d'Orléans, so they were going to see if he knew anything about them."

When Daniel came in from the car, Meg wailed, "A bunch of my drawings are ruined and Antoine knows it and he can't put them in the new book. My work's gone! My whole summer's fucked, so."

We drove back in silence. The forest colours, still beautiful, signalled the death of everything green, the inexorable coming of winter.

—◦❦•❦◦—

CHAPTER TWENTY-EIGHT

I woke up cold Monday morning after the visit to Aunt Adèle's, tense with determination to go ahead with my plan of filling the gaps and discovering the murderer. Dogged Detective Cates had solid leads this morning, or at least a seemingly intelligent way to proceed. After a family member asked the police for explicit details about the drawings that were at Aunt Adèle's, I'd have good information to judge whatever Antoine said about his book and its future. What was he going to do to replace the wrecked illustrations? At the same time, we'd hear the latest on any progress in the investigation of Jean-Paul's death, if that wasn't too much to ask Laflamme.

As uncle and Canadian chaperone of the person who had done the drawings, Daniel was my co-conspirator here, even if he was afraid nosing around might get me in trouble. Nobody must suspect I was teasing out information, he warned me several times. He didn't just mean the police. He didn't need to add, "Least of all the murderer. Or murderers." Jean-Paul's death still lurked on the edges of my daily work.

But my determination to avenge Jean-Paul Nadon was falling victim to a big reality check. The police already viewed me as amateur interference. Luc would protect Gaetan, whom I saw five days a week in the dig's computer room in the Seminary. Meg? She would remain in control of her secrets, selecting the bits of her life she would share. I would not let the depression of impending failure, even if usual under the circumstances, roll over me like a cloudbank.

One step at a time. Break the problem into small steps and you've felt you've made progress. Let humour mask pain. Berry, lighten up. "Cwaaazzy," I sang as I dressed, belting out, "Cwazy to find yooouu."

Even so, the most immediate problem for me would be keeping up "normal work" appearances in front of Florence. Not perhaps my forte at the best of times. What, anyway, was "normal"? Save the philosophy; I needed to see Luc to discuss the next phase of my tasks. My contract was for the restoration of an impossible two hundred artifacts by December thirty-first. "Whatever," I'd murmured signing the coveted document, thinking I'd start with his priorities, get him pleased, and the rest of the artifacts would be a finish-up. As in, a contract extension at least until fiscal year-end in March. Who else was he going to get in frozen January, anyway?

School had begun and students were lined up outside Luc's office door in the former Seminary building, so I emailed for an appointment. He responded almost eagerly. Tuesday at nine I was in his office asking what information he needed most—for instance the shape of the eighteenth-century shaving bowl now in small pieces? Which objects ASAP for his exhibit labels? To show the lab was bustling I described the electrolytic cleaning of the iron cannonballs, but while these bubbled in their tank, "I will certainly make room for whatever you choose first to be conserved."

Luc took this all as standard and asked me to lay out the pieces he had originally wanted for review that afternoon. He didn't know when he'd have time to write up his field notes, but at that point he'd need more artifacts cleaned and restored. I acquiesced with a smile, adding that it might be difficult to fit them all into the agreed timeframe. The lovely old, 'yes, but' good employee routine. "*Yes*, boss, of course, will do for sure, *but* I want to let you know about some things that might come up."

Luc cleared our business fast. It was soon apparent why he'd welcomed my email. "Have the police given you any more news about their investigation in Aunt Adèle's farmhouse?"

"Nothing. It's proceeding. Apparently, they've canvassed all the neighbors but nobody heard anything or even saw a vehicle." I lightened my voice and shrugged in sympathy, "Other than your truck."

Luc reached for his pipe. He still wore his dig clothes, carefully laundered since school began. The uniform asserted to students and faculty the importance of archeology even after the field season had closed. "They impounded my truck and did every test in the books. They've re-interviewed Gaetan how many times now? I think they're satisfied we had nothing to do with it." He began tamping tobacco into the pipe bowl. "I mean, Gaetan told them exactly where the green garbage bag was hidden and exactly what he saw. As he was leaving her house Aunt Adèle was taking out some of the drawings and laying them flat on the carpet. Gaetan said the last words he heard were exclamations about how good they were." Luc sighed. "How are you and Daniel doing? And Meg?"

I was about to take this opportunity to delve into, "How's Gaetan doing?" but Luc seemed genuinely interested. "We're doing okay," I said, and filled him in briefly on Meg's new life at l'Université Laval. "And you?" I began, "Is there still any flack from the police because the body was found on your dig?" and waited for his reaction.

"Just endless routine questions." Mine had not seemed to upset him.

"Glad to hear it."

Luc nodded. We sat in what, to my astonishment, was an almost companionable silence while he finished filling his pipe. "Want to go outside while I . . ." and he gestured with his pipe towards a 'no smoking' sign hung by Admin in his office.

"Wait," and he rose to plug in a kettle on the floor in a corner. "I've got a bag of tea here somewhere." It might end up a lousy cup but I was touched by the sentiment and thanked him. We chitchatted about how he was going to survive the winter smoking outside, and continued our pleasantries once the kettle had boiled and we were out the door. My hands cradling the mug, we leaned against the old stone building, warming ourselves in a crisp sun. Finally I moved our talk to Gaetan. Luc breathed in deeply, saying how relieved he was it was all over. Gaetan had gone on a binge right before the police came to interview him one time and everyone, Luc included, had taken this as a sign of his guilt.

"But they found nothing in what Gaetan said to give any evidence he knew Adèle would be dead an hour after he closed the door."

"Why did he go out there?"

"Meg didn't tell you?" Luc was surprised. I wanted him to confirm what she'd said. The scientific method: repeatable results equal the truth. This time I was not as adept at lying as I could have wished. I should have learned my limits long ago, along with my lack of a poker face.

"She did," I confessed, hoping I might win employee points for honesty. "But I was wondering, actually, if you had any reason to think Meg would have the missing notebook back in her possession and not told you? And hidden it with her things at Aunt Adéle's?"

"Well, Meg never said diddly," Luc replied, "but I was concerned about Gaetan." Seeing my confusion, he continued. "Remember that whole scene with the drawing table, when Meg thought Gaetan took the notebook, too? He swore he didn't, but he was in bad shape, and hopelessly in love with Meg. A few weeks ago they were talking to each other again. I asked Gaetan what changed. I remember his words exactly because he was so pleased. 'She likes my decision not to drink. She says I'm a different person than she thought, strong enough not to let it ruin my life.'"

"But I thought," Luc continued, "there's got to be more than that in this blossoming friendship. Maybe Gaetan *had* taken the notebook, and finally given it back to her. And now here they were at the end of the dig in possession of a notebook they knew I was looking for, but now they were buddy buddy and didn't want Gaetan to get in trouble. So they hid the book temporarily with the rest of Meg's stuff while they figured out how to get it back without being fingered as culprits."

"That's pretty devious. They could've shoved it in any packing box."

"Maybe they just found themselves in a tight spot. If the notebook suddenly appeared I'd start asking tough questions. Anyway, I was wrong. The police found nothing, and I've given Gaetan every bit of support I could think of to get him through this crap with them. You'd think he'd trust me enough to tell me about a lousy notebook."

"I think he trusted you a lot before."

"Can't tell. Me, as a kid I never had an adult I could trust. I have no real idea what someone his age—I call them the 'semi-mature, fully-self-absorbed'—are thinking."

I laughed, and then remembered Luc's willful daughter not speaking to him. He was talking about her as much as anyone, humour masking the pain. Thin ice covered a deep pond. I said, "What was going on when Gaetan first came back and told you he'd been out to Ile d'Orléans?"

"I was so pissed at him." Luc shook his head. "I had a doctor's appointment in Ste.-Foy and missed it because I kept expecting the truck to show up. I was trying to clear up loose ends on the dig and sent him out to check various storage areas to see if the notebook or anything else on the list had turned up. Then I see Meg hop in with him and I thought, perfect! If Meg knows anything about the notebook, Gaetan can find it out. Then he comes back way late and says Meg had drawing stuff out on Île d'Orléans, and admits they took a bag of it to St.-Édouard. All the time the dummy hadn't even looked in the bag. I really lost it, and you're right, I didn't believe him. I sent him off again."

"You really want that notebook."

Luc's eyes flashed before I realized how he'd interpreted what I'd just said. My phrasing left open the unvoiced accusation that Luc himself might have gone to St.-Édouard, desperate for the notebook. It was obvious my few words had slammed the door on our budding friendliness.

Luc sneered. "If you're going to ask what I did after work, if I went out myself to look through that bag, let me just say Detective Laflamme has it on record that my doctor saw me at 5:30 since I'd missed the morning and they had a late cancellation."

Heat flashed through me but my voice kept steady. This was real information, easy to corroborate, and I smiled back. "Thanks for telling me straight." I'd enjoyed our camaraderie, while it had lasted. Since the police had corroborated his alibi, why not trust Luc? Putting that question aside, he still deserved an explanation. "It's just that, since Meg and Gaetan were friends again, if you doubted that Meg was telling you everything, then you might have doubted Gaetan too. Including that the notebook wasn't in the bag. So you might've gone to Aunt Adèle's to ask her yourself."

"I didn't," he said. "Make sure Daniel knows that, and Meg." He turned on his heels. I retreated to my lab.

With a bottle of white from Languedoc, a chicken and some other ingredients and spices for a Provençal dish, I created a sumptuous weekday supper so both Daniel and I could plot my next move. I needed to do better than my bust-up with Luc, losing the goodwill of my informant to gain one bit of information.

"Why do you think Luc's so protective of Gaetan?"

"I'm the same way with Meg."

"But she's a relation. You're sort of her guardian right now. Do you think Luc has, well, an unnatural interest in young adults?"

"Like he accused Jean-Paul of? No. He's led enough digs with students that there'd be rumours if he'd acted like that. Meg's told us he's a great guy, a mentor. You said Luc mentioned he had no adults he trusted as a kid. Maybe he's making up for that."

Why did everyone trust Luc's goodness except me?

Playing the next-of-kin card, Daniel phoned the police about Meg's drawings found at Aunt Adèle's but he learned little. A couple of drawings in the bag were unharmed, the rest badly damaged, stained and torn. I pictured the struggle, two people scrabbling, tumbling, grabbing for purchase, the drawings underfoot, ripping, sliding. Daniel was assured it would be best for us not to see the pieces of paper. There was not in any case much left to see. Besides, the police were testing the papers for evidence and preferred no possibility of contamination. They had some partial stains of bloody shoe soles, and possible prints.

"What about the two pictures left in the bag?"

"This is what's most interesting. The police interviewed Antoine for anything he knew about the book he signed, and the drawings. Antoine identified the pictures as his."

CHAPTER TWENTY-NINE

My next move was easy, or more accurately, obvious. Discover Antoine's motives for claiming Meg's drawings as his. "*Quel* schmuck," I said to Daniel, offering no translation. "Does he think we wouldn't notice if he printed her pictures in the book?" Antoine had already made me uneasy at times: his rude arrogance in the park before the play, for instance, and especially his propositioning Meg. But for both he had apologized sincerely.

"I'll have to ask Meg if she usually signs her work." Daniel was clearing the dinner table as his brain meandered along each alleyway of the situation between Meg and Antoine. I stood at the sink rinsing the dishes, taking comfort in ordinary daily life.

"I don't think she signed the illustrations for Antoine. That's one reason her lilac pictures over his bed were unusual. Meg said he'd cajoled her into signing them before framing when I asked, because I didn't remember her signature on any others she ever showed me. Or Antoine's on his own work, thinking about it." I stopped and wiped my hands on an embroidered apron Florence had made and given me. Daniel was snuffing out the tapers that served to make my old kitchen table elegant. "Did she ever sign that contract for publication credit?"

"Not as far as I know. Did Meg mention to you she'd signed anything that day out at the farm, before Antoine tried proposing? Then Aunt Adèle died, and she hasn't even seen him since the funeral, has she?"

I gave Daniel my crafty look and theatrically rubbed my hands together. "I'm calling Antoine first thing tomorrow, to offer an estimate for the work on those drawings he wanted cleaned."

"You're not a paper conservator. How can you give an estimate?"

"I won't. I'll go out there, take notes while I'm snooping, and tell him I have to figure out a price. And call someone who knows. Like a paper conservator. Who 'll do the work later."

"And how exactly are you going to extract a confession that he's claiming Meg's drawings as his?"

"I'll think of something."

"After you call someone who knows?" said Daniel, reaching over to poke me playfully in the ribs. "Why don't we both just plan it out now?"

Daniel could be such a plan-every-last-move worrier. Worse than a picky conservator cleaning treasured artifacts. So I said, "Because you have to ask Meg first if she signed anything, which it looks like she didn't but it still needs checking. There's the question, too, whether Antoine's ever raised the subject again of signing the contract." I sipped the dregs of my wine and rinsed the glass. "Maybe he's hoping Meg 'll forget about it. But I don't know what my next move is until I know what's what. What's up. Where we're at."

"Latitude and longitude?" said Daniel. "I see your point about more thinking. Try it using nouns and verbs. It's what's what in radio."

I stuck my tongue out at him but it wasn't enough. My finger darted towards his ribs, and he blocked my arm. I grabbed a dishcloth to whip around as air defense, but he deftly feinted, circled his arms and spun me around.

"Let me give you a few pointers on street fighting," he said as he tightened his grip.

"What do you know about street fighting," I coughed as I struggled. "You soft-bellied, over-educated, Westmount boy?"

"Who you callin' Westmount?" For one year when his father was posted overseas, Daniel and his mother lived with rich friends in that largely English-speaking enclave in Montreal. He'd improved his English in school there but remembered most his loneliness.

Turning me around again so I was backed into him, Daniel said, "If someone's got you like this, give him a kick with your heel to his instep. Or his groin, if you can reach it. Easier if you're facing him. Just don't try it on me."

"Truce, then," I panted. "If I can't try out my moves."

"Truce," he agreed. He opened his arms, freeing me just enough to swirl me around once more, his lips now brushing mine.

"Bedtime!" I announced. The bed wasn't far away in my tiny apartment, and we ignored the phone that had begun to ring. The two of us entwined tonight was perfect.

The next morning, half-asleep even after breakfast because now I did not want to give up the night, I listened to the phone messages.

"He beat us to it," I said. "Antoine's invited us for dinner this weekend." Daniel stopped putting on his coat. "All of us. I'll have to tell him Meg's going to Chicoutimi. See if he still wants us to come."

"I hope so," Daniel grinned. "It would be extremely convenient. Tell him how much we look forward to seeing him again."

"He said he had a surprise for Meg."

We stared at each other.

"The contract?" Daniel said.

"The pictures? Would the police have handed them over if he said they were his?"

"Surely not until the case was closed."

"Well, confirmation that he saw the two surviving pictures and they're in great condition would be a welcome surprise for Meg."

Daniel said, "We're going out there with or without an invitation, even if I have to buy a kilo of his cheese. Tell him I have a good Bordeaux in my cellar."

"Ace reporter ups ante." Daniel did not have a wine cellar, nor did he really like goat cheese.

Antoine, disappointed but charming, kept the invitation. He had, after all, had good conversations with both Daniel and I at the Nadon funeral reception and even at its horribly chaotic end was able to say, "You two come for dinner sometime". But Antoine on the phone did want to make sure Meg knew she would be missed.

Saturday we packed the car with a red Bordeaux, and a Côtes du Rhône white in a cooler bag, and headed out of town. At the farmer's market we bought a pot of fall asters as a present, and a double chocolate treat for ourselves in the hope we could ramble along the north shore of the St. Lawrence for the afternoon before heading over the bridge to Île d'Orléans. If private property stopped our exploration, the chocolate would soothe our spirits.

"Too bad the medieval alchemists didn't know that the universal solvent is chocolate," I said in the car.

"They were trying to find gold. Good chocolate today costs gold."

"I rest my case. They would have had gold *and* an elixir if they'd had chocolate."

"Or illuminated parchments about pimples," said Daniel, braking hard and yelling "*Idiote!*" at a black car dashing in front from the left. The car immediately signalled and headed for the right-hand lane but was stopped within seconds by unyielding traffic. It revved up again and managed to insert itself then jerked back its speed. I glimpsed blonde hair and a taut face. In an instant the road signs ahead determined our route. Not the north shore. Daniel signalled and swerved into the right lane too, hearing brakes and horns. We followed Odette out the exit towards Île d'Orléans. When she barrelled down the dirt turn-off to Antoine's farm, clouds of dust hid our lone car as we drove on out of sight.

"Did Antoine tell you he was inviting Odette?"

I shook my head. Did we have to revise plans? I'd held to my opinion that we shouldn't make too many, whereas the experienced radio host preferred a storyline. We agreed to play much of the evening by ear since an added person changed the balance. Another unknown was how Antoine would respond to Daniel's journalistic curiosity combined with my "good cop" conservation flattery about cleaning his wonderful illustrations.

"Two against two," I concluded.

"A fair contest."

Antoine asked if we had ever seen how Quebec cheeses were produced, hinting to Daniel that it would make fascinating radio.

"I've learned how to tour from Odette," he said, bowing in front of her. He reeled off "did you know?" facts as he guided us to a small white building set off from the house. Odette called out after us, "Just a glimpse: the hors d'oeuvres are ready and the wine's open!"

A glimpse was all we wanted as Antoine explained how, for the full tour of his cheese-making "factory", we would have to don hairnets, coveralls, gloves and shoe covers. Like police officers at the scene of a crime. Inside the doorway I had to keep my hands from touching the room's gleaming walls, as clean and sterile as an operating room's. The interior smelled both clean and stinky. The stainless-steel vats and countertops were immaculate and there were rows of neatly shelved equipment Antoine named that I'd never heard of. He was trying an experimental batch next, adding fresh-picked herbs, red peppers and chanterelle mushrooms to make a savoury cheese that might replace quiche in a summer lunch. He was explaining how he made only one type of cheese at a time and was glad his factory was small, as each time he had to clean it completely for the next batch, when Odette appeared with a bottle of wine in each hand, tempting us back to the house where the glasses awaited.

The scent of the cooking made me never want to leave the big farm kitchen, and tasting the food confirmed it. Flaky pastry morsels wrapped around a melted Brie-like filling were mouth-watering. Squash, red cabbage and apples from the fall garden and a *tourtière* with a tomato relish were followed by a magnificent crème caramel and an assortment of new cheeses. Each course was accompanied by a different wine, and the dessert with port. Since Daniel had previously made rude references to my behavior after a few glasses I'd offered to be the designated driver, and I ate well to compensate.

Daniel used his journalistic skill to get Odette to explain again how she had become such good friends with Antoine and his family, and the intimate sentiments that surfaced, as much as the facts, grabbed my attention.

"I was in love with Jean-Paul," Odette freely admitted, "but he hardly noticed me. Didn't blink an eye when all the best contracts for work on the history of Quebec City—I do that too, as you know—flowed to him and not to others."

"He just assumed it would," said Antoine. "An older brother naturally assumes the more grown-up privileges belong to him and not to the youngsters."

Odette said, "We all know men go after younger women. Jean-Paul married someone else, and then she died early. He would have been better off with me, *n'est-ce pas*?" A faint smile crossed her lips. "In the meantime, I married someone else too, had two kids, had to quit full-time work because my husband did nothing but his research, so we broke up and now here I am. Last week the City gave me the contract for a historical brochure Jean-Paul had been interested in. A horrible fluke has given me back my career."

Antoine grabbed Odette's hand, "And you'd have been better off with me. Admit it. Was Jean-Paul better looking? More charming? Was it because he was a full professor at Laval and I'm a goatherd?"

"Let it go, Antoine," Odette said amiably. "We've been through this so many times."

He sighed. "You forgive Jean-Paul everything because you loved him."

"Antoine," Odette's voice became low and stern. "He's not here. You've had a dark day. There's no sense obsessing about the past. Let it go. We have guests." She turned to me. "Antoine has some ups and downs."

"Don't we all," I murmured, watching as Antoine brushed a shaking hand over his pained face. The hand was the only part of him that moved now, as if a welling up of grief was paralyzing his body.

"My brother," he whispered. "My beautiful brother. When will they find his murderer?"

Odette took over, rising to stand behind Antoine, resting one hand lightly on his rigid shoulders. I thought about Aunt Adèle's perspective on how a person chooses to view their life. We hadn't talked nearly enough about the web that depression, whether from disappointment or much worse, traps you in. About if, when, and why you're finally able to free one limb and then another and eventually rethink and rebuild. Antoine was still in the grip of grief. Odette, time and circumstance giving her more distance, was much less caught, and this was evident as her light voice put our dinner party back on balance.

"Once, we were sitting around when Jean-Paul had just finished reading this English novel. He was talking about the expression 'as different as chalk and cheese'. None of us knew it. Antoine got it into his head that Jean-Paul was making fun of his cheeses and calling them chalk." Odette shook her head. "We had a good laugh about it when it all got sorted out. I've made awful mistakes with my English too."

"Amen," said Daniel.

"Then it was because he was a great lover?" Antoine's voice was low and desperate as he looked up.

"Antoine," Odette said calmly, her face set as she pressed her hand firmly down on his shoulder, "We don't need to talk about this." Looking at us she said, "But I guess now you're curious. Daniel, would a journalist agree the era of free love lasted a long time in Québec?"

Daniel nodded.

"Jean-Paul and I did in fact spend one crazy night together. During a history conference. He walked out on me before I woke up. He left me a clever note to make sure I knew it was all history, and in his view history didn't repeat itself." A rueful smile appeared on Odette's face as she looked at how Daniel and I were taking this intimate news. "My conference paper bombed the next day, but it was equally my fault, wasn't it, for taking the risk the night before? Passion over reason, in the wrong context. So I apologize for saying Jean-Paul took no notice of me. He did. But only once. And long ago I put that in the past."

Had she? And how had "the one crazy night" affected Antoine and Odette's friendship? She had obviously told him, but how much did I really understand? The handsome couple opposite me could not have known how, early on, Florence had described them to me as 'both wanting things out of life they never got'. They might not even have remembered talking to Daniel during lunch on the history tour. Now I was seeing Odette and Antoine interact, as well as hearing the details of their friendship from the actors themselves. It confirmed my trust in Daniel's interviewing skills and Florence's gossip, but I knew there was a lot still hidden.

Had Antoine arranged this evening to play through his and Odette's set piece, giving them the certainty that Daniel, myself, and the invited Meg, had heard their story as they wanted it told? Explaining the triangle between the two brothers and Odette added to the innocence of her 'Golden Dog' remark this summer, especially as Odette had not been at all embarrassed when "the one crazy night" was revealed. She did indeed appear to have put it safely in the past. When Antoine was not submerged in grief, had that crazy night been much of a factor in his and Jean-Paul's brotherly competition? Or, between themselves, had they also relegated it to the past? Like Daniel, I was an only child and had witnessed enough sibling rivalry in friends' families to know it could exist no matter what, and to make me grateful for my own situation.

"Do you have an older brother, Daniel?" asked Antoine, shaking his head as if he were sloughing off a bad dream. "It's tough when you're young," he continued, before Daniel could answer. "You can't help but see it as privileges for the older boy you can never be—later bedtimes, favouritism in sports. And then growing up, of course, favouritism in a woman's love." Antoine sighed theatrically in Odette's direction, tried to smile, and then his face tightened. "Now I lose him, and it's awful still. And there's no closure."

Daniel tried to speak but Antoine plowed on. "It's like he's still alive. Maybe it'll change when I can wind up the rest of the estate. The family isn't even allowed to rent out his house in case the police actually think of something. Decide they need to go over his life one more time. Of course, renovations for renting would cost."

"So, the police aren't getting anywhere?" I asked.

Antoine didn't hear. "I'm paying bills, for God's sakes, because the bank's keeping too much of his money tied up. And you, *mon amie*," he turned towards Odette, "are now the best freelance historian here but you're still in Jean-Paul's shadow. It's not like you've been given a permanent job."

Antoine looked over at us. "Sorry. It's so unspeakably awful. Losing him so suddenly. Odette's right. Excuse my mood."

Odette nodded and brushed blonde strands from her face. "Colleges hire the young who'll have decades to publish, not me who'll be pensioned off in a few years."

Daniel tossed a smooth non-sequitur into the awkward silence that followed. "Antoine, what about that surprise you said you had for Meg?"

—◦◦◦◦—

CHAPTER THIRTY

❧⟶❧

"What can I tell Meg?" Daniel smiled perhaps too amiably at Antoine. "You mentioned a surprise when you called." I silently admired his phrasing: not 'can I tell her?' but 'what'. I would rub in later how effective was his use of the 'what' word.

Antoine shrugged. "Well, it's not much of a surprise, really. Just a *tisane*, plants from the Island. I've dried them into a herbal tea and I wanted Meg to name it. But don't let her know. *La tisane de l'Irlandaise*, maybe. But she can come up with something better. Maybe even in Irish."

My impolite guffaw earned a round of curious stares, but Meg's "piss off" promised too much fun to be ruined by an explanation.

Antoine said, "I'd like to market it along with the cheeses."

I murmured something innocuous. Daniel said, "Ah. I'm glad I didn't mention to her what I thought. I figured it was the contract and her name on her drawings."

"Daniel," Antoine opened his hands palm up on the table, "That's been ready for weeks. I hope there's no misunderstanding. If your aunt not died before . . . please just tell Meg to come and look it over and sign."

Daniel and I stole a glance at each other. "Thanks," Daniel said. "But do you have enough illustrations? We heard Aunt Adèle had some of Meg's drawings, and they were ruined when she died. Then there was some question of whether they *were* Meg's drawings."

Antoine shifted in his seat. "You heard this from the police, I suppose? They asked if I knew anything about the drawings and a book I'd signed for Meg. They found them beside your aunt. I said yes, I could identify them. But I didn't want to mention Meg's name as the artist in case they asked further questions and found out about her working illegally. The whole immigration thing. So, my white lie was, the drawings were mine. Two of them are still fine. Is that what they told you?"

Daniel replied in his pleasant radio interview voice. "I guess that apart from those two drawings, there's still enough to sign the contract for? How many were destroyed?"

I expected a scowl but Antoine leaned back with a sigh, his face relaxed but sad. "Meg did a bunch but they're not all equivalent. Some were just small botanical outlines of the leaf shape or arrangement. I could redo those myself if I have the time. I'm going through the reference photos now to see what's missing. The two the police found intact are 'art' drawings, different plants together, like they'd be in a natural scene. I had Meg do them to make the book more than an ordinary field guide. I know my limitations." Intently, he explained. "I'm in discussion now with the publisher about whether we should just use photos for the drawings that are gone. But it might not work. For instance, there are the ones Meg did that showed the tubers below ground as well as the full plant. Do you think she'd do those over? I have photos, and some of the plants are still alive, she'd just have to put them together, and she'd remember what she did before."

"It's up to her," Daniel answered, and changed the conversation to, "Could I try the *tisane?*"

"*Moi aussi,*" I chorused with Odette.

Antoine shook his head. "Meg should be first. It's hers, after all. I'll contact her about more drawings, but," Antoine glanced at Daniel, "I don't want to get in the way of her schoolwork." Lifting his wine glass, he changed the subject to what was ever-present on his mind. "Here's to Jean-Paul, how I wish he were here tonight. May he rest in peace."

Odette continued the toast. "So many reasons in our hearts and souls why we miss him." We clinked glasses, each in our own thoughts.

Antoine murmured, "Please, God, let me do my best to take his place in my family." We raised our glasses to Jean-Paul again, looking for all the world as if we were posed for a photo, such good friends at a supper table.

It was going on towards midnight when we left. Tonight there was no moon but the stars were brilliant over the fields. The four of us stood outside attempting to name constellations. Daniel claimed he saw a shooting star; I kidded him about red Bordeaux astronomy. In the car, he nodded off as I drove, concentrating on the road and the evening's conversation. There was still so much we didn't know. And we had forgotten something. What had been Antoine's reaction when he learned the drawings were missing and had been found at Aunt Adèle's?

At work on Monday Florence interrogated me. I extolled the food at Antoine's, admitting I hadn't thought to ask who cooked which dish. I described Odette's forest-green shirt which brought out the tints in her eyes, how elegant she looked even in jeans, and Antoine's loose Scandinavian-style striped shirt.

Florence snapped, "Stuff *la mode*. And I don't want to hear what the goats were wearing, either."

I rambled on, saying how much Odette had liked my indigo blue outfit and how Daniel looked great as always. Florence unplugged the teakettle and marched it over to the window, opening it wide despite the cool air outside, about to drop her hostage overboard.

"Tell me why he invited you!"

I gave in and she sat down, but when I launched into details of whom I would call to get a paper conservation estimate, Florence bluntly yelled, "*Arrête!*" She scuttled her office chair over to my table. "Can't you tell me what's up, *ma chérie?*"

That perceptive, say-it-all 'what' word again. "What's up?" I repeated. Florence refused to help. She sat back, arms folded. My inane substitute for real conversation had fooled no one. I'd been a dope to think I could keep secrets from my smart workmate. And I should have known by now that Florence was also one of my most trustworthy allies.

I swore her to secrecy and then related my plans to help discover who had murdered Aunt Adèle. Details we had learned at Antoine's would be just the beginning, although I glossed over questions we should have asked at the dinner. From my purse, I extracted my new notepad and read out the text as if the items were brilliant ideas we would now act on.

"1: Antoine's reaction? To pictures found at AA's.
2: Will Meg want to redraw ruined pics?
3: Meg—Antoine? Anything there?"

If my menopausal memory and Daniel's penchant for wine were a bad combination in detective work, lists would help. Persistence led to solutions. During my year at the museum in Vancouver, a curator had told me I was like a terrier with a bone. Here it worked for a carved Golden Dog.

Florence said, "I knew there was a reason you were looking better these last few days. Determination is your strong suit. But please be careful! I'm glad you're so stubborn, though. Better putting that talent to discovering a murderer than in brushing rust off nails."

"I scoff at nails."

I still had to work, however. Luc had narrowed the artifacts down from two hundred to a hundred and twenty, but the pair of dainty, owl-eye spectacles alone would take me weeks. Their gold-plated frames were bent and the tiny edges of the broken glass gave little room for the adhesive, even if the hard-to-get special glue for glass came in the form of a thin liquid. A liquid epoxy with a very short shelf-life that would be compromised by the slowness of this job. Already I was way behind schedule, and my mind was fixed on something else entirely.

To make matters worse, in the lab I had a bigger concern than the glasses. The waterlogged shoe Meg had gotten so upset about on the dig was a unique find, a rare rubber bathing shoe from the beginning of the rubber industry in the 1800s. When her notebook went missing Meg had cried over the loss of the drawing that showed the shoe lining's shadowy imprint in the freshly revealed mud. The cloth covering on the inside of the shoe had dissolved in the potent environment of the latrine in which it had been discarded over a hundred years ago. The fill in the latrine had composted over time into innocuous organics and had later been destroyed by the storm. Before beginning to preserve the shoe, I had to be sure there was absolutely no remnant of lining or weave imprint on any dirt still inside; the treatment designed to clean and conserve waterlogged materials would ruin the traces. And the dig photos of the inside of the shoe were too dark to yield information. If any imprint of the lining remained, I had to record its survival.

New photos, taken in the studio conditions that were so much better than on the excavation, had been equally disappointing. We had tried re-shooting using various filters and even infra-red, but they made no difference. We examined the photos under ultra-violet with no better results. My last chance lay in different technology. Enhancement via computer, what used to be called 'fiddling' when processing older paper-print photos, might bring out features in the images. This kind of technology was not my forte; I'd also resisted spending money on cell phones that weren't yet perfected. I went to see the geek.

Gaetan was staring at his screen in a dark room, neck arched at a stiff angle, hand palsied over a mouse. I winced but made no comment; he would hear a mother admonishing the child to sit up straight. Luc I would tell, though, and since he was so protective of Gaetan, maybe he would find the budget for an ergonomic desk and chair, and a room with some daylight for its user. For me it would take more guts to hunch day in day out in this dark space than to quit drinking.

"Let's see what we can do." Gaetan eagerly inserted the flash drive.

I pulled over a chair. "It must get boring just working on the database for the artifacts catalogue." In one of the pauses between our banal chitchat and my genuine concern for the weave of the textile lining, I would question him about his trip to Aunt Adèle's.

Gaetan's fingers moved on the keyboard more quickly than my aging eyes, so I sat back and let 'im give 'er. Now, that's an expression Meg would enjoy. I closed my eyes and allowed questions for Gaetan to rise in my brain. A slow intake of breath, a timid "Ms. Cates?" and Gaetan's embarrassed face as I opened my eyes told me I'd been snoring.

I grinned an apology. On his screen was a faint criss-cross pattern showing in a muddy blur. Without my asking, Gaetan increased the contrast, then changed the image to complementary colours to create a more distinctive pattern.

"Can you save that?" I leaned forward. "Plain weave, the lines of yarn in the textile running over and under—do you see it? Can you print that?" Gaetan was way ahead of me.

I studied the picture Gaetan produced while he sat justly basking in my praise. He'd added an accurate measurement calibration in the image. "Lunch is on me tomorrow if you're free," I said.

"Can I ask for something?" He bit his lip.

"Just about anything." I fluttered the paper.

"Will you tell Meg what I did? Maybe it'll help make up for her notebook still being lost."

"Definitely. You've worked wonders. But Gaetan," I leaned towards him, "the clearest record of the weave is in that notebook. Meg drew the fibre traces when the evidence was fresh. If you know anything about where the book is, please . . ."

"You're blaming me, too!"

I touched his arm and shook my head. "I don't care who's got the notebook or how it comes back, just that it returns. And I'm even willing to become an accomplice to bring it back. How about if I take the blame?"

Gaetan's voice broke. "I don't know anything. You've got to believe me."

"I do. But will you let me know if you hear anything? I squeezed his hand and stood. "If you print out a couple more copies of the weave, I'll give one to Meg. She'll be so delighted."

I waltzed back to Florence to show her our find. Even if nothing of the actual lining remained visible in the shoe, the imprint in the mud had shown a pattern called plain weave. A little more research into bathing shoes of that period would tell us exactly what the textile had been. I placed my bet on canvas. Florence upped the ante, demanding that I stipulate the grade of the material from the line width, and whether linen or cotton.

Gloating, I propped up the image where I could easily see it and took samples of the remaining dirt inside the shoe. If Florence wanted cotton or linen, I would find it. She could do the book or web research and I'd look for remnants of cell structure under the microscope. Or ask a biologist at l'Université Laval to examine the sample. I had excellent experience phoning colleagues for help. And tomorrow at lunch I'd question Gaetan about his visit to Aunt Adèle's.

I caressed the image, allowing my fingers to trace the pattern of the weave's warp and weft. "Speak to me," I murmured, having bet more money with Florence that it was cotton.

The paper fell onto my worktable and I sat bolt upright. The picture had responded! The kernel of an idea seeded itself in my brain. If I could retrieve this small grain lost somewhere in my fifty-four-year-old compost bin, it might grow. I sat still, eyes closed. Like the first fish to crawl out onto dry land, the idea surfaced. In my mind's eye I clearly saw a moving weave pattern, a crisscross, lines intersecting and side-by-side. Like people.

Who crossed Aunt Adèle? Who crossed Jean-Paul? Who crossed them both?

—◦◦◦◦—

CHAPTER THIRTY-ONE

꠷꠶꠷

On Tuesday, Daniel and I met Meg at the Beau-Port for supper. It was strange to be back in the vicinity of the dig, my former workroom so near to where I now sat. Coming here we had strolled down Sous-le-Cap, past the now-invisible excavation areas reverted to unpaved parking spaces.

Meg chattered about Laval and how good her French was compared to others in the class. It was the perfect distraction for me from brooding on the unwelcome thoughts that had surfaced when we were walking, my eyes straying to search for traces of dirt piles. Now the three of us sipped Côtes du Rhône and kidded around at the table. We played with Meg's descriptions of courses and teachers, building up an entirely new arts and science program Laval could offer in French for Irish residents only. To the amused glances of the other restaurant patrons, Daniel hummed and did a short spectacular imitation of how students could learn new French vocabulary by describing Irish dancing, and learn it even in their seats since only the feet moved. "Brewing 101" would compare *les bières irlandaises et québécoises* and there would be homework.

Later, with dessert, came the questions. Meg's weekend in Chicoutimi? Yes, great fun with her friend Suzanne and her boy. It had been the son's fourth birthday. Meg enthused about the party and the enchantment on the faces of the other small boys during a DVD of enormous trucks. Then they had gone to an actual work site where one boy's uncle drove during the week, and each child got to sit in the cab of a huge vehicle, smothered by a hard hat, touching the controls.

"And the best," said Meg, "is going to be the surprise for Luc."

"Can you tell us?" I spoke too rapidly.

"Suzanne's going to tell her da who fathered her boy!" Meg's smile took up her whole face. "And I'm the very one who made it happen."

"Bravo," said Daniel. "How did you do that?"

"Well, it wasn't exactly just me. But it wouldn't have happened without me."

"So who is it?" My excited feet were doing their own little Irish dance, betraying my usual lack of patience.

"Oh, well now, it hasn't happened yet. So I can't say."

"A hint?" said Daniel.

"Well, Danny, it'll be obvious who the da is," Meg teased. "Do you want to meet Suzanne? She's coming down here in two weeks if Luc's okay with that."

"He'll be ecstatic," I said, "And all of us at work will be, too, if he's in a good mood. Thank you, Meg." I saluted her with my after-dinner *tisane*, a French brew of mint and linden. "Meg, why is Suzanne doing this now? Because you persuaded her, or did something else change in her life too?" I was curious if Jean-Paul's death had helped her and her father reconcile.

"Something else changed in someone else's life," Meg giggled, still in teasing mode.

Daniel changed the subject. "Speaking of surprises, I tried to find out what Antoine said was the surprise he had for you." A shadow flitted across Meg's face. "But he wouldn't tell. Said you had to be the first to know." My cup of herbal tea rattled as I set it down, almost drawing enough attention to give the secret away.

"He also said," Daniel continued, "that he only claimed the drawings were his to keep your name out of the police records. In case probing further brought in Immigration."

Meg nodded. "Did he say which drawings weren't ruined?"

"The two art drawings with the plants like they are in nature."

Meg squealed, looked around in embarrassment at the other tables, and leaned towards us, eyes shining, "They're the best, Danny. I didn't lose the best."

Then the shadow crossed her face again. "What's he going to do about the others?" she asked. "The wrecked ones?"

Daniel related what Antoine had said, finishing gently with the question uppermost in my mind, "Do you want to work for him again?"

"Why not? If he gives me a real contract."

"Meg," I intervened, not caring if I sounded like a concerned mother, "he propositioned you, remember? What if it's not just work he's after?"

"Oh that." Her scorn rose. "He's seen the consequences. He didn't take no for an answer, and suddenly his drawings go missing. He can piss off on that account."

"I'm not sure Antoine sees it that way."

Daniel turned to me, "Can you find out exactly what he does see? When you give him the estimate for cleaning the stains off his pictures?"

"Detecting 101," I replied. "What's the homework?"

Meg reported the next day that Antoine had emailed her about doing five more drawings. I asked her to hold off answering him. When Florence caught me staring into space, I admitted to being stymied. How could I ask

Antoine to leave Meg alone, to have only a normal work relationship and trust him on that, if he was still in love? What would be the words that would make him agree?

Florence answered, "No comment. I don't set up blind dates for friends, either. The messenger gets blamed if something goes wrong." Anticipating my response, she stuck her tongue out at me first, followed by a pleasant, "How's the restoration of those spectacles going?"

"Just fine," I coughed.

"Mind you," she said a half hour later as we hunched over our workstations, she frowning at a computer screen and me with eyes equally glazed from moving tiny shards of glass into positions where they might fit each other correctly, "you've gotten results before using your normal approach."

"And what's that?" I demanded, irritable from finding too many fragments of thin glass missing.

"Well, maybe it's your fallback, not your usual thoughtful way." Was Florence trying to assuage my mood, or was she being sarcastic?

"*Alors?*" I wouldn't let her get away with it.

"Be direct. To the point. Stubborn but civil. Just tell Antoine in a tactful way to lay off. He'd know Meg would have told you and Daniel about his proposal."

Sometimes it takes a best friend to tell you what you were blind to. Like your long hair being thirty years too young for you, or the too-tight pants emphasizing your belly. Berry, are you calling obsessive thinking 'planning'? Just get on with it. I hadn't even gotten all the information yet on pricing stain removal for Antoine's drawings.

Immediately I called two conservators specializing in works on paper, one at the *Centre de Conservation de Québec* and one in private practice. Their answers made it obvious; I had to go back to Antoine's for a closer look at the pictures. What kind of paper had Antoine used for his illustrations? Well, that question I could ask him over the phone, and it gave me a perfect intro for my call. But the conservator in private practice who might do the work needed more. What colours did the stains go into? Some pigments were more fugitive than others. Could I see his paintbox or pencils to get the brand and exact colour names? Was any initial sketch visible, and what was its medium? The list of questions took up a full page in my notebook.

Scribbling the information, I hadn't noticed that Luc had come into the room. "Conserving some paintings?" he asked from the chair he had plonked himself into during my long calls.

"An emergency." I was satisfied my brain had responded to my boss listening in to an obviously personal phone call on work time, a potential emergency for many employees, although Luc might think I meant emergency for the paintings.

Luc drew his pipe out, fingers patting it like a favourite pet, and a smile spread slowly over his face. "My daughter called. She said Meg had visited on the weekend, been a real help at my grandson's birthday party." His eyes sparkled. "She said he really liked the DVD I sent, 'Big Trucks at Work'. Suzanne's coming down not this week but the next with my grandson. He got on the phone himself. She must've coached him. '*Merci beaucoup, grand-papa,*' he said. He wants to see me! Suzanne said Meg convinced her it was time. I want to thank Meg."

"I'm really pleased for you."

He bowed his head. His voice dropped. "Maybe everything I said to you before wasn't necessary. Maybe I don't need to know who the father is. Having my little grandson back close to me is enough."

"It's the best beginning, anyway."

"I came to ask, should I send Meg flowers?"

"That's lovely," I replied, "but she's at school all day. Why don't you phone or drop her a note and just invite her for a meal or something. You could give her flowers then, too, if you want. And Suzanne also. She made the decision."

"Another thing," Luc said. "You must still be thinking about your family's recent bereavement." I liked the way he called us 'family'. "I know it's easy to get distracted from your work here. Suzanne's been on my mind all morning. Are you going to be able to finish those artifacts on time?"

"Actually, I don't think so." I was thrilled he had asked, and that Florence had reminded me about direct, honest speech. I hoped I was being tactful enough. "Even without Aunt Adèle's death, there are just too many of them."

"I'll see if I can find money to hire you an assistant. Would that help? As long as you do the fine work."

"I could do all the work," I said, "if there's a way to extend my contract till the end of the fiscal year in March. Because I don't know if we could find a trained conservator to help for a few months in the middle of winter."

"I'll see what I can do." He heaved himself up off the chair while he reached for his tobacco pouch, and headed outside.

Florence watched him go and said, "*Incroyable!* You've tamed the wolf, *ma chérie.*"

"Bear," I said. "And I wish I could take credit. You'd owe me big. But it's Meg who's worked her Irish magic."

"Let's hope Suzanne's visit goes okay. Just in case, if I want anything from Luc I'll ask him during the next ten days." Florence was so savvy.

Antoine returned my call after researching the product number as well as the grade of the smooth paper he preferred for his illustrations, betraying his scientist's love of factual detail. I could examine the stains again anytime. What about Sunday, with Meg if she agreed to come out to the Island and work on the pictures? I hesitated. I did not particularly want to spend all of my day off making conversation with Antoine while she painted, but maybe I could drive Meg out, disappear for a researched-beforehand walk, and pick her up later. Chat with Antoine only over an afternoon tisane. But this scenario included confronting Antoine right now to ensure everything would be above-board.

"Antoine, one thing. If Meg goes out to your place, it's just for work. You know what I mean? She's only interested in drawing."

I'd prepared myself for silence at the other end of the line, or snarling curses. Not laughter.

"Ah, Berry," chuckled Antoine, "Am I an old goat or an old fool? You tell me. I apologize from the bottom of my heart. I was so stupid. What was I thinking? Dreaming, I guess, as if I were young again, ramping it up. A selfish obsession. Unrequited love. If you'd prefer, I'll bring everything into town and see Meg with a chaperone."

"I'll talk to Meg."

"I'm so ashamed. Has she told more people? I've as good as shown the rumour about my brother was true, that there's something in our family where we go after young girls. I've messed up again."

I said simply I would call back. Did he go after old girls when he had been warned off the young? My inner devil started to poke through my closet asking what I would wear.

Antoine phoned back fifteen minutes later, insisting that if Meg agreed to do the drawings, he'd come into town and meet her and me on our territory so there'd be no further questions. He'd bring the worst of his stained plant pictures, too. Meg chose to meet at Daniel's, with its old comfort and beauty, its view and natural light, and most of all, its big table where she could work. Daniel had looked at a few new apartments but his commitment to moving wavered according to whether his mind or heart was ruling the day.

The next Saturday while Antoine set up photos of the plants in bloom beside now gone-to-seed specimens, unearthing their roots from the pots and discussing with Meg how the drawings should look, I propped up the two stained paintings he had brought and went through my check-list of questions for their conservation. Daniel made coffee and discreetly hovered. Eventually, when Meg put on her music and began sketching, Antoine left her to concentrate. Daniel and I couldn't stand the mechanical thump thump of the sound Meg liked, and we shortly followed.

"How are you ever going to live with that," I asked, "if you get a bigger place and Meg moves in with you?"

"This Christmas she gets the latest device and those big earphones. We'll both be ecstatic."

We walked past the ChantezPortes and saw Antoine inside with coffee and a newspaper. Two policemen went by on the opposite sidewalk and my body flinched as if I'd been burned à *Laflamme*. We headed out of the Old City gate and resumed strolling along St. Jean beyond the stone walls, into my St.-Jean-Baptiste neighbourhood. Here, outside the walls, stood the poorer buildings, joined houses often with two or three apartments, their old red bricks fronting directly on sloping one-person-wide sidewalks. The stores on St.-Jean, though, catered to all tastes, from those who had lived there all their lives and never made it beyond, to students, to their professors. Daniel and I stopped to peruse the fresh produce, the bulk foods, the European delicacies, and buy cheese sticks at a *pâtisserie*. All these stores were old, treasures that had adapted what they sold to changing tastes, and had survived well for as many years as I'd been alive. Aunt Adèle, too, had adapted as times changed—— radically quickly in the case of Quebec, from the religious and rural to the urban, moneyed, and globalized. Many like Aunt Adèle had been gladdened by this progression, ready to leave behind a close-knit conservative society that some called xenophobic. But to arrive, after this 'progress', at a situation where, in a small village like St.-Édouard, a stranger could murder an old woman and not be caught? I told Daniel I needed a cup of tea and, jackets half open, we sat outside in the sunshine of another crisp, unusually warm sunny day, savouring *croissants au chocolat*. Fresh and delicious, they should have been perfect, both of us sipping and smiling at each other between bites. The other tables were full: people enjoying the day, the café, and their companions, including the two dogs casually eyeing each other from the feet of their owners. But then I heard another dog chanting,

I am a dog who gnaws a bone,
As I chew, I take my rest,
A time will come that is not yet here,
When I will bite him who has bitten me.

I couldn't rest in the sunshine anymore, doing nothing. "Let's go back and see how Meg is."

⤙⟐⬦⟐⤚

CHAPTER THIRTY-TWO

─◦⟨◦⟩◦─

"Antoine's come and gone." Meg's head was bent over her paper, clearly hoping we would imitate the botanist. We did, unpacking the food bought on rue St.-Jean but scuttling out for our own lunch. If Meg didn't eat all the groceries we would have a fine summer-memories supper: cheese sticks and the fresh baguette, cold cuts and pâté, and more artisanal cheeses from Île aux Grues and elsewhere in Quebec. After a long lunch we ventured back into the Old City, ignoring the tourists, seeing no police. Daniel spent time in a bookstore while I shopped for a flirty blouse in SiBelle-SiBon.

When the sense of waiting it out became too obvious—"I don't have the patience of the Golden Dog," I joked—we headed back to the apartment, whether Meg had finished for the day or not. At first I thought she was out, but then my own gorge rose as I heard the putrid sound of retching. Daniel ran to the bathroom door. "Meg! Ça va, ma petite?"

"I ate too much," she wailed, and vomited again.

"I'm coming in," and before she could say no, Daniel was cuddling a racked body off the floor, her knees sprawled, no strength left, mess on the tiles, panting between heaves. I arrived with a blanket from the bedroom and a large bowl, and together we trailed her out to the couch where she crouched in pain in a fetal position, holding her stomach, gasping.

A young woman pregnant? Antoine? Luc? Her uncle? I swallowed back my own rising puke.

Meg was in real pain. Not simple morning sickness. Something she ate?

I racked my brain to remember the bacteria that caused food poisoning by contaminating meats and cheeses. I could only think of two, *E. coli* and listeria. Both could be lethal. Newspapers this summer had been quick to report stories about *E. coli* in undercooked hamburger, and listeria contaminating dairy products. Had we brought home any artisanal cheeses that were unpasteurized?

My hand flew to my mouth to cover a cry. Whose cheeses had been contaminated? Antoine's? His place was so scrupulously clean. And Antoine was devoted to Meg. He would have come with his best.

"I ate the stuff you bought," Meg mumbled. "Didn't look at the dates."

"Did Antoine eat anything?" I could phone and see if he was sick too.

"Nah," she managed, and between gasps, "I ate your food, and then we had the herbal tea he's going to market, and Antoine had half a cup of that. It's heaven. Did you know he wants me to name the new *tisane*? He left before I could think of a good one but it's not for right away."

Daniel was already on the phone to an *Info-Santé* nurse, who advised bringing the patient to a hospital immediately. "She says it's unusual for either bacteria to act so quickly. She wonders about some sort of poison. Did anything taste funny?"

Meg said no, not really.

"Did you have any alcohol?" I asked.

Meg admitted she and Antoine had opened a bottle of Daniel's white wine they'd found in the fridge. "But we finished the bowl of almonds, so we had food with it. I forgot, Berry— Antoine did eat some almonds."

"The white Bordeaux? The whole bottle?" Daniel's eyebrows rose as a sheepish blush suffused Meg's face. "In the morning? With a few stale nuts?"

Meg tried to grin. "It wasn't morning. It was already past noon. Look, I'll pay you for it. I'm not drunk. I ate a bunch of the real food you brought after."

Daniel frowned and listened to the nurse again. "We have to put anything left of the food and drink in the fridge. In case the doctors need to test it." He made a hurrying motion with his hand. "*Vite!*" His voice softened as he watched Meg hug her belly. "It's your turn to get tested."

"Noooo. I don't want to go."

Daniel hung up. "You have no choice, *ma petite*. Your health is precious to me." We tossed together the remains of our purchases and stowed them in the fridge along with the empty wine bottle. The slice of pâté was already gone, but I found its wrapper.

"Any *tisane* left?" I asked.

"I finished it this afternoon."

I sighed, drained the cleaned teapot into a plastic container, and hoped there would be enough traces to be worth testing.

Five minutes later we were trundling Meg out to the car. I tried to distract her during the drive, chattering about how the Meg-named brew must be zesty, bold, with an underlay of sweetness and Irish-green. I thanked her regretfully for her efforts to clean up the kitchen before she got sick. Exemplary behavior on her part had meant we had less to get tested.

Clinical procedures over, Daniel insisted Meg move into his apartment for the week. Each evening on his way home he bought fresh food and inveigled her to eat his delicious dry toast, working up to eggs and mild pasta with a little butter and salt, and a smooth cooked carrot concoction flavoured lightly with cardamom and cinnamon, one of my favourites. I was put out with myself for feeling a tad jealous of all the care Daniel was lavishing on Meg. She needs it, I reminded myself, and it speaks well of Daniel. Then one morning in my little apartment I woke up sweating, dreaming of being eighty and bedridden in a care home and hearing Daniel whispering sweet nothings to my roommate. I would get a photo of Aunt Adèle for my wall to remind me that aging was not necessarily a nightmare, or at least not all the time.

Meg recovered well and the clinic stated further testing of the food and drink was unnecessary. Throw it all out, including any bags. It was likely a mild case of food poisoning, some bug picked up through one of myriad possible pathways. They had not had many similar cases this past week; there was no locus of contamination. I was pleased, too, not least to be staying over at Daniel's again several nights. Florence was content to hear as many details of 'Foodgate: St.-Jean' as I would tell, enduring time and again my pun on "*La Porte St.-Jean*", the gate to the old city.

My *beau journaliste* had surreptitiously found tidbits of information the police were not releasing. The investigation into Jean-Paul's death was moving slowly but had by no means stalled. Through contacts Daniel learned that the autopsy showed his fall had definitely been from a great height, and that two dark-raincoated males had been seen looking out over the bastion around 10 p.m. on the evening of the storm. Jean-Paul had been deliberately buried shortly after death. The police knew he had been murdered, and they were keeping everything under wraps, outwardly in stasis, unsuspicious, as they continued.

"We'd already figured Jean-Paul had been murdered," Daniel said, hands on hips, and swore me to keep the police information secret. It pained me to tell Florence only that the police were apparently trying to prove that Jean-Paul's death was murder and were continuing their investigations. This she knew anyway from her nephew in the *Sûreté*. To feed her, I talked about Daniel and his yes/no about a new apartment, and Meg's contract. I repeated what Meg had said; Antoine had needed to work out the details with her first, and then he would put the offer on paper.

Florence said, "And when will that be?"

"It's happening as we speak," I replied. "Antoine was supposed to bring her more plants to draw this afternoon." I didn't mention my continuing Antoine-Meg worry, but my face probably showed it in high definition.

Meg had no classes on Thursday afternoons. That was inconsequential in the sense she had already missed half her classes this week, but why had Daniel buckled in to her demands that Antoine be allowed to bring work over to her at his apartment? My own gut flip-flopped, thinking of the two of them together for several hours while both of us were at work. Had Antoine truly gotten over his passion for her? Daniel's office was close to his apartment and I, at quitting time at the Seminary, already had my running shoes tightly laced. When I arrived at Daniel's at 5:07, my beau was just taking his jacket off.

Meg was in a marvellous mood. Two drawings were complete and she proudly set up the plant scenarios again and held her pictures next to them. Bubbling with delight she explained the trick she had pulled: on one, a small grasshopper was destroying the succulent new growth on a leaf, and on the other, a tiny leprechaun was sheltering under a toadstool. That's where she had placed her initials.

"Meg," said Daniel severely, "did you and Antoine have any wine?"

"Oh yes, but this time he brought it," she giggled.

"Meg, that's all you did, right, drink and discuss?"

"Aye, aye, Danny." Her glass-hand saluted.

"Is Antoine coming back today?"

"He left like you wanted. He headed back before the rush hour. He brought lunch and wine and cleaned up and was a perfect gentleman. Ever thought of running a strict boarding house, Danny?"

"I do already, sweetpea."

"Jaysus, I'll be getting a curfew next."

"Did he bring any more of your *tisane*?" I asked.

"Not this time, but he brought more stained pictures for you," and Meg pointed to some frames in a corner. "I am to tell you he would like a written estimate. For his records." Meg giggled. "Mrs. Boarding-House."

I would enjoy engaging Daniel on the subject of his wish to move to a bigger apartment and live with Meg. I started fingering through the three paintings, indulging, sotto voce, in responding, "We are not amused. We are not drunk, either." Then a better response surfaced. "Speaking of invoices, can I see your contract? Are you allowed to make alterations, like leprechauns?"

Confusion crossed Meg's face as her hand scrambled through the papers and pencils on the table. "I did sign it."

"You don't have a copy?" asked Daniel with a resigned look that meant he already knew the answer.

"Yes, well, no." Meg slowed to explain. "Antoine said, now I've read and agreed to the contract, and we penciled in a few changes, he'll photocopy it for next time, and also, this is the thing too, he'll bring me a fair copy with the changes in and we'll both sign that one also. So," Meg held up first one finger and then the next, "I'll have a photo-copy of the original, and a hand-signed real contract."

"That's not exactly standard business practice, Meg." I wished one of us had been here to question Antoine.

"Well, Jaysus, he's not your standard bureaucrat now, is he?" Meg's heel hit the floor. "Do you think he makes his cheese in a fucking cubicle with a computer screen?" She stomped into the bedroom, flinging the door wide open so she could slam it shut.

"Sorry," I whispered.

"She's on the mend!" Daniel laughed. He waved his hands as if over an invisible crystal ball. "An image is appearing. I see a trip in our future. To Île d'Orléans and a goat farm."

The doorbell ruined the rest. Daniel frowned and went to answer. "Berry," I heard from the bottom of the stair-case, "would you put on some coffee?"

He never asks me to make coffee, not trusting my tea-drinking self to that art and science. Daniel ushered a dishevelled Odette into his apartment.

CHAPTER THIRTY-THREE

Odette pleaded "*mille pardons*" for interrupting Daniel at home as I clanked cups in the kitchen to remind her they were not alone. Daniel answered her murmured question that yes, Meg was here as well. The journalist in him waited for her to thread the silence that followed. All I heard was Daniel telling Odette where to find the bathroom. While the coffee machine gurgled I leaned against the kitchen table with its unobstructed view of the livingroom. When Odette re-entered, hair combed, lipstick fresh, it was the Odette I recognized, poised and elegant.

We exchanged small talk and I sat beside Daniel, dispensing coffee. A private conversation between these two was not in my books. Had Florence's early joking about rivals for a radio host's affections made me insecure? Daniel and Odette's *tête-à-tête* after his comedy act? I chose instead my belief that an investigator shouldn't miss a thing.

At first all Odette talked about was the historical brochure the City had asked her to write; she'd like to make the project available as an audio-visual tour as well as a printed text. "Would you do the narration, Daniel?" His eyes lit up, and they discussed possibilities. Daniel would be good here; he had the voice and enthusiasm for the subject. I kept a smile glued on, though, with a special liquid epoxy I too often found hard to get, for my mind told me this was not the reason an acquaintance stops by a home she has never before been invited to enter. Eventually, more silence. More coffee.

Odette leaned forward. "Meg can't hear us, can she?"

Daniel pointed his shoulder towards the bedroom. "Probably not, but no guarantees." Odette lowered her voice and I bent to hear.

"I'm worried about Antoine," she said. "He's never sunk as low as this before. And I think he's flipping his depression into a fixation on Meg to help him feel better. He was supposed to meet me twice now when he said he was coming into the city to bring work to Meg, to meet me afterwards, but both times he hasn't shown up. I didn't know if I should talk to you." Her fingers mussed through her hair.

"You want to know what's going on?" Daniel explained enough to give Odette the impression it was all work and too much wine. Hearing about the wobbly contract would only be gossip against her friend.

"It's worse," she kept her voice low, "and it's not just because I feel slighted. Antoine's been talking Meg this, Meg that, non-stop. It's not all positive. He's just like my son was when he was a teen. One minute Charles was extolling his new crush who was beauty and talent personified, then whining she was much smarter than him and smirking about her complexion. Bouncing from one extreme to the other, obsessed like a kid whose toy has been grabbed by another kid and no other toy will do."

Daniel reached for his coffee, his hand straying along my leg. "I don't know what to say, except I'm planning to go out to Antoine's and have a talk with him."

"You've noticed it too?"

"Well, there's more complications," Daniel admitted. "There's a whole history around whether Meg 'll get credit for her drawings. You know some of this from the evening we were there, but it's a long story."

"Ah." Odette sat back, thinking. Her voice lowered even more. "Is that why Antoine's pictures were at your aunt's place, then? Meg drew them and Antoine wasn't going to credit her? His last illustrator had some disagreement with him too, but they settled in the end. So, she made off with them?"

Smart woman. I said, "They're both kids in a tug-of-war over whose toy it is."

"Antoine's suffering tremendously from his brother's death." Odette sighed. "We've known each other for so many years, but I can't excuse this kind of behavior. He's old, going on oldster like the rest of us, and this book is important to him. I think he's afraid it's his last. He's desperate for it to be good. But he'd better do what's right after he's had his little tussle to show just how big a boy he is. Jean-Paul would have been ashamed at any whiff of plagiarism."

Odette shook her head, and when I saw her fumbling in her purse for a tissue, I realized how deep her worry was. And her feelings still for Jean-Paul. And Antoine.

"Odette," I said, "We've never talked to Antoine about the paintings being at Aunt Adèle's. Would it help to clear the air if we did? Let him vent?"

"He must know why they were there. He just can't get over it very well. Or his brother's death. God, I wish the police would find Jean-Paul's murderer." She dabbed her eyes. "Please forgive me," she murmured. "It's been so hard on all of us. Maybe an arrest and conviction would be satisfying enough for Antoine to see how out of balance his life is getting. He's drinking far more than he used to, did you know that?"

I didn't say that we'd seen some of the evidence right here.

"This might be too personal, but is he seeing a therapist?" Daniel had been going once a week since Aunt Adèle's death.

"I've given him names, retreats that might help. But I'm only a friend, not his doctor. Antoine does what Antoine does. If only the police would catch the killer. That's what would help."

An image of the *balançoire* at Antoine's farmhouse floated into my mind, and I was on its slow rhythmic swing. Gently, melodically rocking, the porch *balançoire* so different from the wild plunges of a pumped-up playground swing. *Pauvre* Antoine, medicating his moods with alcohol. Frustrations piling up, pushed into the center like dead autumn leaves raked together, a perfect fire-starter, and blown wildly out of proportion each time a bitter wind rose.

"Thank you for coming," said Daniel. "I mean it."

I smiled and stood and kept my mouth shut. Distressing Odette further right now with my own thoughts about 'le schmuck' would lead nowhere good.

"*Merci, Daniel et Berry*," Odette said. "Here's my card. It's got my contact numbers. We'll talk more about the audio-visual tour." She glanced at the closed bedroom door. "Don't tell Antoine I was here, please. If he doesn't want to keep his rendezvous with me, I'm not going to persist. But I've alerted friends, and if he gets really depressed, I'll contact his doctor. There're the goats to look after, too, if he's in a bad way. If you see him I'd appreciate hearing your impression."

Meg, Daniel, and I drove to Île d'Orléans on Sunday. I had wanted to park at the far end and walk the dirt laneway but a light rain was falling and the wind made the autumn air even cooler. We drove right up to the house and I was glad of my winter jacket. Meg almost stumbled protecting her finished paintings as she ran inside.

Antoine was still unshaven. He offered us coffee but seemed almost too weary to make it. I'd heard the expression, "The black dog of depression," and I saw the animal in front of me. Meg displayed the two completed drawings and that cheered him, but when she asked for tisane instead of caffeine, he lapsed into silence, rousing himself after a long pause to say simply, "Can't." After another pause and a shrug, "Haven't made up the recipe again." Noticing the apples and green tomatoes on the counter behind him, I asked if he'd been working in the garden. "No". Finally, "Friends," he said. "Friends are helping."

"Are they putting up some of the produce?" I could give him Aunt Adéle's canning jars.

He barely managed "no". Antoine's handsome face had the gaunt lines and distracted look I'd seen at Jean-Paul's funeral, only today he looked worse: listless and grey.

Daniel tried to engage him over coffee, enthusing about the new car Antoine had outside. "Oh that," he responded. "Jean-Paul's. Gives me a lift. Get it? Good on gas. Not like the truck."

"You seem tired," Daniel said outright. "We won't stay, but I'd like to get Meg's contract. The new fair copy needs signing."

Antoine raised one eyebrow, murmured, "Of course," and shuffled away. We sat in silence, and when he returned, in silence, none of us really wanted to look at the documents. Daniel did duty, however, nodding as he read, reaching for a pen and then proffering the sheets first to Meg and then Antoine. The photocopy of the original was there, as Antoine had promised. Our business was done.

"The paper specialist who's cleaning your illustrations, the art conservator I told you about, hasn't finished them but I'll call you when I hear from her," I said.

"Next week would be Jean-Paul's sixty-ninth birthday, did you know?" Antoine roused himself. "I've got to go, too," and he stumbled out of his chair. "Check on the goats."

At the car, I watched his retreating back as he plodded towards a far field. Daniel called Odette as soon as we returned. She said she'd phone his doctor, get him to call Antoine on the pretext of an annual exam. This time it would not be just a physical.

CHAPTER THIRTY-FOUR

Meg plunged into her school program and Daniel and I concentrated on our own work. On October tenth, a police officer actually called Daniel with a report. They had received more tips about vehicles seen near Aunt Adèle's and were in the process of checking them out. Using my own experience in a detail-driven profession, I figured that meant meticulously, but only when time permitted. Or when Detective Laflamme permitted. Recently there had been shootings of innocent bystanders in a rash of drug-related crimes in the suburbs, and I said to Florence that Aunt Adèle should have joined a street gang if she wanted any attention.

Days passed and autumn crisped colder towards winter. One particularly woolly day I finished gluing the spectacles, and they looked, I used the English word to Florence, spectacular, despite some missing pieces. I arranged all my work in a neat sequence, having started a half dozen gluing jobs so I could move from one to the next while the first adhesive dried, and went to find Luc to show off.

He'd been rising and falling with the tides of his daughter's news. First she was coming down from Chicoutimi. Then her boy was in bed with a cold. If Luc had had a good phone call, he would be attentive and supportive at work; if not, he barked like a drill sergeant. The most recent time he appeared in our lab, though, he was glowing. Florence got all her catalogue changes approved, I got the artifact list reduced even further. His grandson,

Luc boasted, would have the coolest Hallowe'en costume. Luc had managed to find out how tall the boy was and what he wanted to dress as. Advised by several parents, he had found the perfect 'king of the jungle' costume, all furry yellow fleece and tail with an eared hood trimmed in lion's mane.

I was thinking about all this and wondering if Florence would get the pun if I asked, "Is this a good Luc day?" when I saw his office door open down the hall. Goodie. He was in. Then a man backed out of the office, literally crawling on all fours. Luc! Even at this distance I could see his face was a mask of terror.

I flung myself towards the closest office and squeezed tight against its locked door, my hiding place four inches of worn wooden doorframe. These were university corridors even if they were in a building still called the "*Séminaire*", and horrific shootings had happened on campuses across the continent. I heard low noises and peeked, hoping the gunman would be headed towards the sunlit exit at the opposite end of the hallway. Luc was backing in that direction down the corridor, his assailant crawling after. Growling and roaring, a yellow furred figure advanced on his retreating grandpa.

I heard laughter and pulled my drained body out for a better view. Three adults were now silhouetted in the light from Luc's door. Backlit in the corridor, I couldn't distinguish the taller two but the short one I recognized as Meg. Skipping school. Shit *la merde*. I strode towards Luc's office.

Meg saw me immediately. A huge grin animated her face, and she gave me a two-thumbs-up. Lifting her hands around her mouth so I could see her lips, she formed the word 'Suzanne', and jabbed towards the young woman beside her. I smiled back, gave her two thumbs up in return, and moved closer. The last figure near Luc's door could be identified now. It was no surprise to see who had traipsed after Meg. Gaetan. He gave me a big smile and held his finger to his lips, motioning me to keep still, pointing at Luc and the boy. Their game was ending, though, with Luc saying, "truce" and brushing off his knees, and the boy proudly running back to his mother. As she hugged and lifted him, his lion's hood fell back, revealing a face shining with pure delight as only a child's face can. His hair glowed a gorgeous red. Just like Gaetan's.

"Aah." I grinned like a goof. Meg had her arms folded triumphantly, whispering to Suzanne who had leaned towards her to get the goods on the jaw-dropped, middle-aged innocent coming up beside them. Gaetan was making faces at his little lion. I barely pulled myself together as Luc introduced his daughter Suzanne, and I invited them all to come see the completed work in my lab. I hustled back to Florence with the best gossip of the year.

All of them turned up in our lab around three. I put on an extra show, highlighting Gaetan's work on the photos of the textile lining, and gently held one of the four-year-old's hands under the big standing microscope so he could see fingernails magnified twenty times, a sure-fire gross-out. "Lion's claws!" I said. Gaetan and Meg were talking a few feet away, one eye on the child. Luc examined the artifacts, in archaeologist mode again. I tried to get Florence's attention. She, however, was wrapped up in conversation with Suzanne over in the corner and wouldn't respond. It peeved me Florence was keeping Suzanne away and all to herself, as if I were here to strum background music while she occupied the main stage.

Luc clapped his hands, congratulated me, and the visitors all trouped out. I turned to Florence, blocking any exit she might attempt.

"Spit it out!"

Florence plugged in the kettle and settled herself into one of the ratty chairs.

"What did you find out?" I stood over her. In a minute I would grab the emergency flashlight we kept nearby and shine it directly in her eyes.

Florence knew what I meant. At lunch we had huddled over a hundred questions after I clued her in that Gaetan, never Jean-Paul, was the father of Luc's grandson.

"Suzanne remembered my daughter from the history club. She let me in on her life. Suzanne's excited to try and get together, all three of them, my daughter, her, and Meg." Florence paused and concentrated on her instant coffee, teasing me.

I waited, eventually losing my patience and breaking the silence with, "Suzanne must have red hair in her family, too." I was pleased at least to remember my high school biology's discussions of recessive and dominant genes.

"Know-it-all," commented Florence. I did not mention I'd heard that before.

"You were the one who told me about the Irish backgrounds here," I retorted.

"Call me a know-it-mostly."

"Then cough it up, you with your daughter knowledge," I said. "Why did Suzanne never tell Luc who'd fathered her boy?" When Florence still sipped her coffee, I gave in. "You have a storyteller's knack for keeping the hook trolling, then flashing the fish out of the water only at the end." I refilled my tea and sat.

"Once upon a time," Florence mocked me gently, "Suzanne the wild teen had her first morning-after revulsion about the guy asleep next to her. Those are her words. She said she was worried from day one because they'd used no protection, and she saw her life unfolding tied to an immature drinker. She's smart. After swearing never again to let herself or her guy be careless in the throes of passion, she had her worst fears realized by a pregnancy test. She needed a plan. She was living with Luc, her mother having moved to Sept-Îles with a new man, and she knew her dad would go through the roof."

"She could have had an abortion."

"She was only fifteen. With a lover! At least Suzanne knew she was too young to make such a big decision alone. She was too innocent to know where to turn for advice and too afraid of making Luc angry at her."

"His daughter having a baby at fifteen would please him more than her not having one? I never pegged him as a conservative 'family-values' man."

"I asked the same thing. Suzanne said it has nothing to do with beliefs. He was apparently abandoned as a child. His parents simply dropped him at his grandparents one day and drove away. All he remembers is a big black car leaving. When *grand-mère* got ill, he was shunted from one relative's home to another. Nobody would answer his questions. They didn't realize it hurt him more believing he was the worst kid ever, who didn't deserve a mom or dad."

"So he's spent his working life digging up other people's past lives." It was as if some knot in my ribs had let go and I was breathing more easily here at work. "With great success."

"And is fiercely protective of young people who come his way, passionate about being an understanding adult."

I nodded. "It took him a while with his own daughter." I now comprehended Luc in a way I never had, and knew I liked him more. It was all coming together, a mended artifact made whole after a disrupted life. But there were pieces still missing in the puzzle. "Why didn't Suzanne tell him it was Gaetan? He likes Gaetan. Why spread a rumour about Jean-Paul?"

"Gaetan was in trouble then, already a heavy drinker. Even when you met him at the beginning of the dig he was a mess. Suzanne wanted nothing to do with him. Jean-Paul was rich and famous, an ideal father everyone, including Luc, might be able to live with. Or so a teen thought. That's why she never made a direct accusation, only hints, then clammed up. She was so young. She never realized what the ramifications would be."

"So now Jean-Paul's dead it's okay? She tells her father?"

"No, *ma chérie*. Meg convinced her to give Gaetan another chance now that he's got his life more together. With Luc's help. Meg pointed that out, too. At least let both Luc and Gaetan be part of her boy's life. They have that right, and Suzanne knows her son wants it too."

I grinned. "Meg really was the key, wasn't she? She likes Luc. Been mentored by him herself. And she knew how much it meant to Luc to resolve this paternity question. More important, have his family talking to him again." I wanted badly to hug Meg. "To know also Suzanne's not been violated. She took Gaetan's crush on her and . . ." I couldn't finish. I was going to say, "And used it to lift Luc's immense burden." But Jean-Paul had been killed, and Luc's innocence in the affair would still need to be clearly established, at least to me. Aunt Adèle had been murdered, and Gaetan was an initial suspect. Luc's burden in no way absolved any role he might have played in these deaths.

Back at my worktable I chided myself for thinking all that of Luc. Ever since Aunt Adèle's death, his and Gaetan's names had been in and out of my mind as suspects. Maybe those names should be replaced for good. Both had been cleared by the police. Neither had crossed Aunt Adèle in any way that would lead to murder, according to their stories, which obviously rang true for the cops.

No, not yet. I'd keep an eye on Luc for a while longer, be the Golden Dog chewing and waiting. After Luc's euphoria from the reunion with his daughter and grandson lessened, would his moods still swing, would he still suddenly rage? And why? Anger from his childhood I now understood, but if he had anything to do with Jean-Paul's death, would it come out now, from guilt over an innocent man's death?

CHAPTER THIRTY-FIVE

—◦❂◦◂◦▸◦❂◦◦—

Basking by the window in my small kitchen, soaking up every minute of weak November light to make a full hour of sun, I had the whole day before me. Sunday morning church bells pealed through the *quartier*. My second pot of tea sat cozied on the table. I dawdled over yesterday's papers. Today I was having my favourite 'Berry good day' as an irresponsible, unrepentant slug, an indulgence permitted only to me and a few others who weren't at work, had their health, and lived alone. If I didn't feel like getting dressed, I wouldn't. Snacks of whatever could replace meal prep. Daniel and his gang were at Aunt Adèle's house developing a new skit. They went out in somebody's van so his own car remained in town in case I wanted to join them. Rehearsing meant, I figured, that my invitation was for cooking and cleaning. I opened the Arts section.

Aunt Adèle's house had stood empty all fall. Réjean made sure the heat was on, no raccoon had nested in the house, and Daniel, up to his vocal cords in radio work, repeated, "Wait for the snow, then we'll go skiing."

My bowl of cereal with pears in maple syrup empty, I ambled over to the fridge, found last night's leftover soup, and put it in the microwave for brunch. A loud noise started up but it was a different machine, the damn telephone. I should just get a cell with a cute ring tone, but on days like today, I didn't want to be found. Unfortunately for me, a ringing phone emits a force field strong enough to move me towards it, the proverbial horse following the carrot. As soon as I picked up, a bouncy voice announced she had finished Antoine's drawings.

"Bravo!" I mustered some energy.

Meg had already spoken to Antoine, he was at home and expecting us so could we go out now and she could take the drawings and get paid?

"Say that again?"

"Danny left his keys, but he warned me they're only for you since I don't drive on the wrong side of the road. If you're here soon, we could be at Antoine's for lunch."

"There's nothing left in Daniel's fridge?"

"Well, there's that, but I'm done! It's such a relief, so, and he said he would pay me, and tomorrow I could get that brilliant outfit I showed you at SiBelle-SiBon." Meg was out of breath.

What could I say? The voice on the other end of the line wheedled, "Please?" and then, knowing how to make it stick, "Please, Antoine said he'd love to see you again and hopes you'll discuss more conservation. He's got questions about his folk art."

"Shit *la merde*, Meg. I'd other plans for today, but okay. I'll be there when I get there."

I stowed the leftovers in the fridge, a different voice rising in my ear. "The slimming black jeans with the sparkly top?" Why not? I wanted to feel good no matter what mood Antoine was in. I took out my clothes, kidded myself about not having done laundry in a week so my only clean underwear was lavender and lacy, harnessed up my two tired girls in the bra, put on the rest, and didn't look too bad except for the dirty running shoes. Since we had to spend the day in the country I was determined to take a long walk in the fields or by the river.

The weather was cloudy on Île d'Orléans but Antoine, this time, was not. I was relieved to be greeted by his old self, solicitous about our drive and excited and generous with praise when he saw Meg's work. Maybe his doctor had him on meds. It was two p.m. by the time we sat down to a simple, delicious lunch. By three I was ready to go, keen for the walk and increasingly uncomfortable with my appreciation of his handsome face and solid shoulders. Meg wanted her *tisane* but Antoine still had not mixed a new batch of the plants. I was rising from my chair when he said, "Wait!" and fetched a bottle in which berries and fresh leaves had turned the liquid a rose-amber. He chose a crystal wineglass. "Call it a cordial," he said. "It's almost the same as the *tisane*. Tell me if you think this is marketable. The vineyard down the road makes ice wine and could do the distribution."

Meg let me taste first. "It's too sweet for me," I shook my head after one small sip, "but anybody half my age would love it."

Indeed Meg did, downing the glass easily and proposing Jello shooters, horrifying Antoine, but he acquiesced to her command for another glass. It was time to take our leave. He told us how to go down a private road to a beach along the St. Lawrence; nobody would be at the chalets to stop us.

The wind had fallen although it was still cold and overcast, and with the retreating tide, the wide stone beach smelled of the sea. I loved being out on this untamed shoreline. We continued on for almost an hour, Meg griping as she slithered over patches of seaweed on the exposed smooth rocks and stumbled on the pebbles deposited in between. I figured being here was the reward for giving up my Sunday. I ignored most of her whimpering and simply enjoyed the challenge to my sidewalk-stunned legs, the sights and the sounds: the wide vista of water and the rhythmic slap of waves on the shore, then the million tinkling bells as the water trailed back out through the pebbles.

"I'm really cold," Meg announced, "And I'm going back to the car."

I didn't want her to return by herself. I wasn't convinced either of us alone could find the car anyway, since we had cut through someone's property, and how many brown chalets had we passed? The light was fading, although we would always have some until evening since we could see far to the west as well as to the east down the St. Lawrence. But it was November, I reminded myself, and darkness and cold spread early. The deciding factor came seconds later. Large, soft snowflakes began to fall. I'd begun to freeze, too.

"Wait up!" I yelled, and as we walked I proposed we should perform some ceremony to the first snow. Meg had never seen snow like this, and we stopped briefly to raise our faces to the sky, hold out our tongues and accept this communion with winter. Laughing when we finally found the car, we jumped in, turned the heater on full blast and started up the winding hill towards the highway.

The humid air near the river, the cold descending with the dusk and the snow now falling in curtains made the road slick and the visibility a felted white. The first little skid was fun, but then the wheels began to whine when the car slid, not finding any purchase on the steep hill. I geared down and gave the vehicle a little gas and it bolted forward, hitting more slope but climbing slowly. As the car rounded a sharp curve shadowed by trees the wet snow underneath compacted too quickly into ice. We shot in a straight line off the road.

The slope of the hillside stopped us, car nose pointing up towards the treetops. No flames, no screams, no caught in mangled metal, but I was gasping for breath. The hillside had once been bulldozed to widen the road and the exposed soil had slumped loose. Its tumble to the road seemed to embed us now in dark sand and small rocks. Trees leaned menacingly above us, half their roots exposed. I turned the hot engine off, all the time panting, "Oh shit la *merde*." The car did not slide back onto the road.

"Are you all right?" I turned to Meg, and she nodded. "I'm so sorry!"

"You're not half as good as Danny," she said. "He really cried when he practically killed us."

Jagged scenes flashed: the conversation with a very alive Aunt Adèle, the swerve into an oncoming lane, the careening forever, the gravel spurting, Daniel breaking down, Sylvie's ghost, Jean-Paul's funeral.

"I guess now's the point in the film where we get out to buy some eggs," I joked. Gingerly we pulled ourselves out into blinding snow. I retrieved the silvery foil-like blanket from cautious Daniel's emergency kit in the trunk for Meg, and found the summer's picnic blanket as well. She still shivered. So did I. I examined the car as best I could with the flashlight Daniel kept in the glove compartment. One wheel appeared bent. The front was buried. We had better get walking.

Meg looked a little green, and I huddled her protectively under my arm. "Nothing hurting?" I asked.

"My stomach," she moaned, and in one quick collapse she was down on her knees vomiting on the road. Quickly with the flashlight I checked for blood in the puke and found none. No internal injury: the shock of the skid and the cold had overwhelmed her. My own shocked and frozen mind was grasping at something else, though, even as I shielded her from the snow, pulled the blanket under her legs and held her until the retching subsided.

"Let's keep this film running," I said as soon as possible, lifting her, and she gamely walked twenty steps before vomiting again. We worked our way another few hundred feet up the hill like this, me supporting her so she wouldn't fall when she bent to puke. Dry heaves had started by the time I could see a few lights from the odd car passing on the highway. Meg stumbled weakly, me half-holding, half-dragging her, whispering that we were going to be fine in no time. But another film had been playing front and center in my mind: Meg vomiting after an earlier visit with Antoine. Just like today, towards the end of what to all appearances had been a pleasant afternoon, with a man who knew his plants.

This was crazy. Antoine had drunk some of the tisane that time, and I'd tasted the cordial. Besides, Meg and he had a good working friendship now.

Standing wobbly beside the main road, for the first time all day I was cheered by the unexpected. Barely a minute had passed when headlights appeared, braking hard at the sight of one woman enthusiastically waving while she tried to hold another doubled over. "*Mille mercis*," I said to the tattooed young driver and his one-ear-ringed companion who was shoving a beer can under his seat. "*L'hôpital?*"

"*Pas de problème*," the driver said, eyeing Meg. I opened the rusted door to take our chances.

The driver watched us from his rearview mirror, asking what happened. I barely understood his strong Quebec accent and pointed to Meg, saying, "*Irlandaise*," using her poorer French as my excuse, and added the useless half-truth, *"Accident d'auto"*, knowing as I said it that a caution about the weather would not be their interpretation. The two men in the front seat argued as the car sped. The gist, I divined, was whether to go directly to the hospital on the mainland, to stop at the police station for this emergency, or to go home and call 911. Earring nixed the police idea with a clink of his foot on what sounded like several beer cans and the exclamation, *"Ma bière!"* The driver didn't want somebody to die in his house while they waited for an ambulance, so we sped towards the hospital.

Unlike myself, though, Tattoo was in complete control of his car. The blue imprint of a dragon's tail that extended down the back of his hand barely moved on the steering wheel. He obviously knew the route well, and the heavy old beater hugged the road. Meg began to retch and Earring turned around, a look of genuine concern on his smeary face. Tattoo glanced briefly in the rearview, and I caressed Meg, knowing her belly was full only of pain. Someone in the front seat put on music, and Earring turned again, hopeful that it had made Meg feel better. She managed a weak smile.

A half hour later I was giving information to a nurse at a big hospital while Meg was whisked to an examination room. Seeing my own cold condition, the nurse hauled me into a chair and wrapped a blanket over my shoulders before asking her questions. I swore out loud when I realized I'd left all Meg's ID and insurance information in her backpack in Tattoo's car. I was too exhausted by now to make up a credible lie, so I admitted Meg was not a Canadian citizen, stumbled over details of her Laval student medical coverage and her backpack in some saviour's backseat, and shut up when the nurse gave a look of pure delight.

I should have known it wasn't for me. Two miracles, my work-shirted angels with blue reptile hands and gold ear insignias, had reappeared behind my seat. Earring extended a wet backpack, and Tattoo a cup of sweet milky machine tea for The Anglophone. I thanked them well past the point of embarrassment and thrust into their pockets some twenties which they had earlier refused, my hands shoving money into their clothes as if they'd been belly dancers. At least I could recompense gas and buy them a few beers. This scene was far worse than the ride in the car and they fled.

CHAPTER THIRTY-SIX

—◦⟨◦⟩◦⟨◦⟩◦—

Alone now in a brightly-lit waiting room, warm and tea-comforted, the whole day still didn't make sense to me, but what mattered was that Meg was recovering, gastric samples were being analyzed, and I'd left a voicemail for Daniel. I gave up trying to think and curled on my side over two chairs, collapsing into sleep.

Moments later, or so it seemed, a nurse whispered I could see Meg. "It's all good news."

In the room, the nurse shared more details with both of us. "The initial tests show only traces of a possible harmful substance. It's a compound found in rheumatism medicine. Does this make any sense?"

Meg lay there, me holding both her hands. Bleary but no longer in pain, she said, "Antoine complained about arthritis in his fingers, probably from all the milking. Maybe he used something and didn't wash his hands."

I was not going to discuss Antoine at this point, but my relief was palpable. This made sense. The nurse made a note to ask agricultural authorities for a farm inspection. In a few days the rest of the hospital tests, longer and more accurate, would yield their results.

Familiar male voices stopped just outside Meg's room. Another voice, a woman used to authority, said. "She claimed she was your wife so I let her in to see the patient. No wonder she said you were the guardian."

I heard Daniel answer, "Our divorce hasn't come through yet."

In stormed my beau, almost pushing me aside to reach Meg. It took Meg and the nurse considerable time to assure him everything was going to be fine, the force of their answers finally landing him smiling onto the edge of Meg's bed, smoothing out scraggles in her hair and caressing her pale face. Eventually he turned to me and rose. "Outside for a minute." He jerked his hand towards the efficient hospital corridor.

My heart sank. I toted up today's damage. I'd wrecked his car and almost killed his beloved cousin, not to mention myself, after taking her to a lunch that made her violently ill. I'd dragged her through freezing conditions and into a stranger's car race through a mini-blizzard. It wasn't all my fault, but this was not the time to explain. It would fall on deaf ears. Let Daniel vent first. I had certainly damaged his car and endangered Meg. Standing there while Daniel fussed at the bedside, it didn't matter I'd remembered one key detail. Antoine's first visit when Meg got sick had been in the city. Was it a stretch to think he had milked his goats then and not washed his hands? Arthritis medicine must be the wrong track.

As we exited, there sat Luc in a chair outside Meg's room. Chewing on his empty pipe, he half-rose to question Daniel. Daniel shouted as he rushed me past my boss, "Meg 'll be fine! Go on in!" I attempted a friendly voice and an innocuous question as I was hurried further down the corridor. "What's Luc doing here?"

"He gave me a lift."

"Not one of your actor friends?"

"Long gone." Daniel trekked me into a small, cold hallway leading towards doors to a rear parking lot. No one else was there. At least it was a space with no bleak relatives of other patients absorbing themselves in our *tête-a-tête*.

I flattened myself against the wall as Daniel faced me. I'd never seen him so explosive, and I braced my arms in case this different Daniel should lose it completely.

"What the hell were you thinking?" he yelled. "No note when I got home saying where you'd gone or when you'd be back? Then I go outside—in a snowstorm—looking for my car, and when I come back in there's a voicemail saying you've been in an accident. And that Meg's probably having her stomach pumped. At an unnamed hospital. Nothing about how bad anyone's hurt!"

I hung my head. It was a trick I'd learned in Vancouver from a museum colleague, and it usually worked to show enough contriteness and guilt to calm the offended party. Not Daniel.

"I sat by the phone I don't know how long with your first message," he shouted, "calling everyone on my cell to see if they'd heard from you. When I phoned Luc to see if you'd left a message with him, he came right over. He didn't know a thing about you and Meg but he had his truck and his shovel and he arrived to help. I found Meg when I phoned the hospitals. Luc didn't hesitate to give me a lift out here. Now," Daniel reached a hand towards me, and stopped, "tell me exactly what happened."

"I'm really, truly sorry," I said between clenched teeth. He'd had his say and now it was my turn. I flung his hand down. In as neutral a tone as my exhaustion could muster, I explained Meg's wanting to go to Antoine's, the lunch, the walk, and the weather change. The car had skidded, and there wasn't too much damage but I'd pay for it all. I told him about Meg suddenly starting to vomit. I described our angels, my exhaustion, and apologized again for my lapse in not trying to reach him more often, but I'd fallen asleep. Then I swung the door open that led to the main hospital corridor. Daniel grabbed my arm. I shuddered. Both his arms enclosed me, and with all the strength I could muster I raised my elbows to break his hold. Glaring, I had no further resources to make nice. "Don't you dare," I said.

Daniel trailed me into the fluorescent glow of the building and again I felt his hand on my arm, a light touch only this time.

"Berry," said his practiced radio voice, "I just wanted to hug you."

I fell into a plastic chair outside some clinic. "In the mood you're in? And what was that about divorce?"

"I didn't understand what happened."

"So you went ballistic. Thanks for the trust."

"I was so worried! Berry, it seemed like hours when I didn't know if I'd lost you and Meg." His pained eyes tried to hold mine. "Maybe that's why you never called back." Daniel crouched by my chair. "And I couldn't find you. I couldn't do anything!"

All at once I saw not a new adversary but my familiar, wonderful boyfriend kneeling beside me holding his heart out. I could almost see the mess in his hand. Not a real heart, not an "I ❤ you", just the few red, raw bits that would have remained if something had happened to Meg and to me after losing, suddenly and tragically each time, all the other women in his life.

"You aren't still angry?" I needed to make sure while I tamed my own temper.

"Just promise me you'll never do this again, leave unexpectedly, with no note and no way to find you."

"Promise!"

"And you'll carry the cell phone I'm buying for you."

"And turn it on?"

Daniel grinned. "I know how hard this is for you, the modern era, for a preserver of the past. Do I have a deal?"

"As long as I don't have to buy you a new car."

"We'll see about that," said Daniel. "We'll start first with a coffee. Okay, tea. We can go to the cafeteria after we check on Meg."

As we walked the long hall, I said, "Luc came through for you, didn't he, and you hardly know him."

"He became my best friend tonight."

Outside Meg's room a large note was scrawled and left on the chair seat where Luc had been sitting. 'Meg sleeping. Gone outside front smoke.'

"Look," Daniel said. "Luc knows how to make sure there's a clear message, *n'est-ce pas*?" He gave me a warm, impish smile.

Meg was asleep so we headed to the cafeteria. Tomorrow, when we both had energy to face the dark and certainly when the tests came back, we would talk about how she got sick. Right now, cups in hand, we basked in the ceiling's fluorescent sun, on a far shore we had all reached safely. We had survived and Meg would get better. I held my tea as if it were a lit votive candle, staring at this man opposite whom I hardly knew and knew so well.

Daniel said, "A penny for your thoughts."

I hung my head, then glanced up at him through the tops of my glasses. Now was the time to whisper, "I love you." But the long swim to this sunlit shore had been frightening, and I was still too unsettled, too vulnerable to chance his answer.

"I was thinking that things aren't always what they seem," I said. "They don't fit the ideas you have, the stereotypes or even the conclusions you've come to." I moved on to safer ground so it wasn't obvious this was about the Daniel I'd witnessed tonight. "That cup of tea the driver got me, you know, awful tea from the machine in the lobby? That was the best cup of tea I ever tasted."

Daniel smiled, and reached across the plastic table to touch my hand. When I pressed his, he said, "I'm sorry I got so angry."

"Thanks. Really, thanks." I could see he wanted more, but I was too exhausted. My apologies were done.

"What do you think of me now?"

All I could say was, "You really want to know?"

I could see Daniel straighten in his chair. "I'm ready."

The over-bright, disinfectant-smelling cafeteria was not the place I would have chosen for this lemon-squeeze, as we called it in high school. Telling the other teen what you really thought of her. And this was not the time for the kind of honesty the listener heard as critique.

Daniel said, "You can blame me."

I sighed. The proverbial hair shirt again. He was indeed bracing himself for a lemon-squeeze. He knew his rage had shocked me. But I shook my head. "If I can appreciate tea from a machine, then I'm going to dwell on the fact that Meg's okay and we're sitting here together. The teacup half full, that's what I want to think about. I'd never seen you angry like that, but we'll . . . ," I slowed for comfortable words, "sort it out another time."

Daniel's eyes searched mine. "I'm ready," he repeated.

"Not now."

"Yes, now." He took a long look at my weary face. "I'm ready to tell you what I've been thinking for so long." Daniel was pulling one of the paper napkins out of its metal dispenser and twisting it. He placed the circle on my finger. "How much I love you." His hand caressed my cheek.

A gasp rose from somewhere deep inside. The near-empty cafeteria gleamed its delight in chrome and primary colours, but this gesture, now, the white ring on my hand, could not have better reflected love, or better embodied all I needed for a wedding. And Daniel was wearing the loon ring I'd given him.

"I'm ready, too," I said. "I'll keep this forever."

"With the help of a paper conservator," Daniel joked, his face still tight and nervous from waiting to see how I'd respond. But as he watched me fondle the ring, tightening and smoothing it, he whispered twice, "I love you." My stunned happy smile told him everything. He grinned and squeezed my hand. I didn't mind that he did a little sidestep with more joking. "I had to say it now before it's too late. Jaysus," he said, imitating Meg, "I don't want my future to haunt me as well as my past."

I reached over the table until our lips met and spelled out, "I love you too."

CHAPTER THIRTY-SEVEN

❧⟡❧

The numbers one through seven in the a.m. are not my best hours. Daniel stayed at Meg's bedside and Luc drove me home. During the trip even basic conversation escaped me, although surfaced enough on arrival to thank Luc and tell him I didn't think I'd make it to work the next day. He took it like a friend, not a boss. Beyond weary, I staggered up the stairs, dozed off in a hot bath, and, half-drowned, blissful, crawled into bed. But sleep eluded me, adrenalin-filled film cuts scissoring through my head, or maybe those were my dreams, because it was the bright noon of a different day when I awoke in a panic. Why did I hurt so much? The soaked jacket and heap of clothes on the floor reminded me.

I left a message for Daniel meticulous in its precision as to the time I called, needing to go for groceries, back by three, wanting to know how Meg was, and, since now he demanded exactitude, wanting to see him. Once moving, my bones performed some semblance of walking, propelling me up the steep street to St.-Jean, where I treated myself first to an excellent quiche and pot of Earl Grey and then did as much grocery shopping as I could carry. A tasty larder would be a comfort as was the spree at the bakery. Back, a message from Daniel said Meg was discharged and he was bringing her home. I wondered how much the taxi would cost. At four o'clock I remembered to phone Florence and let her know I might not come into work tomorrow either. She chuckled a thank you and threatened excommunication if I didn't show up soon and tell all.

At Daniel's that evening Meg was princessing it amid cushions on the sofa, asking for a morsel of this and a sip of that, but so obviously on the mend I bowed with grace to her wishes. In the bedroom Daniel was napping, or, since he now demanded explicit detail, snoring. A garage on Île d'Orléans had towed the car and called with the kind of detail I did not want. The blue book price of the old vehicle was probably less than the repair bill, but I was committed. Everything was falling into place except the answers I needed. Would Antoine deliberately harm Meg?

Florence the next day figured out one reason he might have done this. First she made me consider that maybe it wasn't Antoine at all, or if it was, he didn't wish to harm her. "Don't condemn him until the rest of the hospital tests are in." With that out of the way, we dove into the alternative, that deliberate ill was intended. Antoine liked if not still loved Meg, but she had rejected his early proposal, and had gone on to win their battle for a contract and credited drawings. Perhaps this was petty revenge. He knew his plants, and gave her just enough purgative to make himself feel masterful again.

"Eeww."

"And if you want to go worse than that, he sweetened his act until Meg redid the drawings, and then showed who was boss."

To think of Antoine that way pained me. Here was a lonely man grieving for the loss of a brother, overcome with depression but making efforts to surface, often generous with his compliments as well as the produce that was his livelihood. I started cleaning the hammered nails. It gave the appearance of work while I replayed the Antoine sequence: asking Meg to sit with him at his brother's funeral; her complete comfort beside him at the reception; their fun immigration scene with Gaetan on the history walk; Antoine's later real proposal and her refusal; Meg's still obvious admiration for him, and his for her talent; his reasons and reluctance to give Meg credit for her illustrations; her making off with the drawings and hiding them; her special tisane, and his excuses, if that's what they were, so nobody else tried it, and Meg getting sick; his mood swings, the improvement this past Sunday, but then, after our lunch, there was the cordial with berries and leaves, and Meg getting sick again, and not me. But I'd only had a small sip, and a big meal.

Where was the key to the castle? Its drawbridge was descending, clanking and grinding, as its chains and gears, like those in my brain, turned over and over.

The noise of rusty metal. The nail in my hand. It fit like a key. As I'd once explained to Aunt Adèle, to figure out deterioration and preservation, conservators were trained to understand materials and how they were put together.

Plants were often boiled or soaked to extract botanical essences. The liquid varied. Whether making perfume from rose petals or dyes from other fragile plant parts, alcohol was one excellent extractant. Another was water. Plants and boiling water could make healthy tisanes, or poisonous infusions, as with hemlock, for instance. Substituting alcohol for the water could be equally effective. A cordial.

"Florence," I said, "I don't feel so good. I'm going home."

"Just keep an open mind until you hear back about the hospital tests, *ma chérie*. Phone tomorrow if you aren't coming in. Before noon, if you can manage it. Do you want a lift?"

I shook my head. I would go to Daniel's, so close by inside the walls of the Old City. Although it always took me a few minutes extra to avoid Rue des Remparts and the bastion, where Jean-Paul had fallen down the cliff face.

Meg had gone to classes today and I grabbed the sofa and stretched out. I needed a brief reset, as Daniel called afternoon naps in an effort to not feel old. A short down time would refresh and focus my fired-up energy. I willed myself to concentrate on the pleasures of the sunlight, how my body aches were now cushioned and comfortable and I was one with Inertia, my personal goddess of the late afternoon. But my mind refused to meditate. I took a break instead by losing myself in mundane details. I made tea, found a dry croissant, softened my snack in the microwave, and checked my home voicemail. Only one message, but my heart plummeted. The paper conservator had finished removing the stains from Antoine's drawings. Could I pick them up right away? She had too many works in her studio and more were coming in.

Let Antoine pick up his own damn drawings. But he was on a farm where running errands fit between chores. The conservator was my friend, had jumped Antoine's work into her queue in a crowded schedule, and I'd facilitated the whole escapade. It was up to me. That evening Daniel reluctantly handed over his courtesy car keys so I could fetch the cleaned and framed pictures the next day. He had arrived home with my new cell phone, conducted a long technical lesson, and entered his home and work phone numbers on speed dial.

Nervousness still pecked away. "I have to take the cleaned pictures back to Antoine. What if something he gave her is what made Meg sick? The tisane or the cordial. He knows his plants. Why would he do that?"

"All we can do is find out," Daniel said, and ever the optimist, added, "He might have done real damage, but he only made her a little sick."

"A little frighteningly sick."

"But she's okay." Daniel was working hard to maintain his principles; in this case, that Antoine should be innocent until proven guilty. "We need to know how he explains it. Otherwise we're making up stories. Thinking the worst. To be extra safe, can the paper conservator go with you? There's no way I can miss any days from work and we're covering the outdoor concerts in the evening."

In the end, I phoned the safest person I knew for this situation, Odette. And for something else.

"I'm going out to Antoine's tomorrow to take him his cleaned paintings. Any chance you're free to come? See them with Antoine?"

"Berry, I just can't. I'm working full out. There's a deadline on that history brochure."

"Can I bribe you to take a half day off? Name your wine. Wines."

"If this wasn't such an important contract, Berry, you'd be getting the list. But I have to show the City I'm the person they want, not somebody younger now Jean-Paul's not here."

"Any chance at all, Odette? I'm a little worried going there if Antoine isn't feeling good."

"If it's any help, when I talked to him yesterday, he sounded fine. Impatient to see the pictures. Ah, *merde*. I've wanted this history work for so long, Berry. Here it is, and the downside of working is here too. No time off for another ten days. Which means now I should hang up."

I couldn't let her go. "There's something I was going to ask you about. You don't have to answer, though." How curious will she be?

"Can you make it quick?"

"Sure." Would she tell me if she had seen, or intuited from Antoine's voice, what exactly had been his reaction when his paintings went missing and were found at Aunt Adèle's? But there was something more urgent I needed to know first. I left out the nice explanations and said, "Did you ever know Daniel's first wife, Sylvie?"

There was an abrupt intake of breath, and a long pause.

"What was she like?"

"Québec's a small place. I met her several times. She was an artist."

"I know the story's surface, but not its depths. Or shoals. Do you think Daniel ever got over her death?"

"I don't know him intimately, Berry. I know he had a hard, hard time. I was suffering inside my marriage then, and to be honest, my first thought was, 'lucky guy, his spouse is gone'. Don't ever tell him, please. I was so appalled at myself, that the idea had even entered my head, that the death of someone you had loved, trusted, and who had never deliberately harmed you, that this might be a good thing. I tell you, I didn't even make it to the toilet in time."

My belly cramped, not in sympathy, but in horror. Not too long ago it had crossed my mind that Daniel had had a motive for wanting Jean-Paul gone if my flirtations had taunted him. After all, this was the Daniel who had convinced himself he was a killer.

"Did you know Jean-Paul befriended Daniel at that time?" Odette continued. "It was one of the first interviews Daniel did when he started working again. Daniel kept skirting around issues related to a loved-one's death, asking questions phrased like, 'As a historian, do you get angry at people who destroy heritage?' and 'How can the past be kept alive when everything 's changed?' It was so poignant. I remember how slowly and deliberately Jean-Paul answered. He said more or less, 'The present is going to be different from even the day before. Inevitably and uncontrollably. Living in the past doesn't help the past or the present. I like to think that remembering, especially celebrating the richness of the life of what's no longer with us, is the best way to honor what's gone. But at the same time we have to live in the present, and with an eye to the future.'"

Even if I would have to go out alone to Antoine's, I knew now Daniel could not possibly have been involved in the death of Jean-Paul Nadon.

"Thank you, Odette, for sharing that."

Quickly she said good-bye. I had to leave my question about Antoine's missing his paintings until another time.

I determined to make it a very brief visit delivering the conserved drawings to Antoine's. That way I could handle it. I would eat and drink nothing and ask him no questions except to confirm that Odette had not benefitted from Jean-Paul's estate. I hated myself for this, but at least it was a line of inquiry that in no way involved Meg.

The next day I smugly called Florence by ten, trying to sound unwell. I was determined to pick up the drawings and get the whole business over with. Do the deed expeditiously, and, I reminded myself, wash my hands thoroughly at Antoine's farm and not eat or drink anything. I told him to expect me around two. Well between meals. Then I packed a herbal teabag in case a polite fallback was needed for a situation that should look like a normal social afternoon. I would excuse myself by saying that the tea was special, formulated for an irritated throat. My explicit note to Daniel included several ways I loved him, how I didn't like it that his style was influencing me to be prudent and over-prepared, Antoine's phone number, when I'd be there, and that we should go to the Beau-Port for supper. Hunger would be dogging me because I wasn't going to eat or drink until I'd driven back to the city. I signed my note with a picture of a dog chewing a bone and XOXO. Packing the new cell phone in my purse, I went back to my apartment to find fresh clothes, trying to remember again the last time I did laundry.

I planned on 'power clothes', not in the business sense, although I wanted to look professional, but an outfit for personal power. My newest shoes suited my plans perfectly, a recent find, red with cute straps and a solid low heel for country ground. I matched a loose but jazzy skirt with a fitted cotton sweater and grinned into the mirror. Why was I even thinking about how I looked? For the paper conservator who had seen me often enough in summer dig clothes? I knew better. I dreamt those test results would erase my suspicions about Antoine. He would be the man Odette knew so well, at times captured by depression, at times immature emotionally, but not malicious. So what if I hid a bit of dress-up under an outfit chosen for my paranoid "just in case I have to run"? The only items left in my underwear drawer had been midnight blue with magenta lace. I wanted this day uneventful and over, but I was glad to feel good.

Outside the conservator's studio I stopped dead. Not from braking too late at a stoplight and almost hitting another car. What was I doing? Antoine simply depressed, not malicious—why was I convincing myself of this?

Planning not to eat or drink anything at his house showed I suspected him. He was an expert botanist. Plants can nourish, depress, inebriate, or drug a person. Antoine was blaming his current depression on his brother's death, but what if this was a mask? If he had been jealous enough of his older sibling—and he had referred to his brother being famous when he was a goat farmer, and how an older brother gets privileged over the younger—maybe it was not just Meg who got sick after drinking his plant infusions. Had he brewed up a concoction to make his older brother sleepy and doped enough to fall off a cliff? I wanted to stay away from the other supposition until there was more evidence—that Antoine had deliberately pushed Jean-Paul.

But there were key questions to find answers for at the farmhouse. And details to keep in mind. Farmhouse: the farmer was an aging back-to-the-lander. Who hugged his goats and made excellent cheese. With not one war-like jacket in camouflage colours visible on his coat rack. No stuffed, glass-eyed hunting trophies on his walls, either. A man who might possibly wield a herbal tea as his weapon of choice. Yes, there was the apparent stupidity of my going to Antoine's alone, but even if he tempted me with a good Earl Grey I would decline. No potion of any kind would affect me. His brother's death might well have been accidental, even if Antoine had played a role—hadn't this been Daniel's situation with Sylvie?

Besides, Odette had said that Antoine was in a good mood these days, not depressed. The opportunity for a perfectly ordinary visit, like we'd had before, had presented itself with the need to return his artworks; this was not some risky scheme Clueless Cates had concocted. I would leave quickly after dropping off paintings he was clearly excited to see. He had no reason to harm me, and I had no reason to peg him with the worst stereotype of a power-hungry lone rural male. My plan was solid.

At the studio the pictures were ready for transport. It was impossible to glimpse anything through the bubble-wrap, especially with its inner layer of tissue preventing the frames' newly cleaned glass from being marred by the plastic bubbles. It would have been reassuring to gauge in advance how Antoine might react to his precious drawings but I was loath to disturb the careful covering. I took my time going over the documentation, including the "before" and "after" treatment photos. The conservator had done a marvellous job, and I sang out my thanks.

The sky was a brilliant blue and the wind on Île d'Orléans like a souvenir of fall's crisp, sunny days. I drove slowly, not wanting to arrive too early and not feeling comfortable with leaving Antoine's pictures in the car if I went for a walk. I hungered to park in the old spot and walk the serene laneway, but I had my cargo. The leaves were off the trees now, and pale fields unfolded gently in all directions towards the river. Nearing the house I opened the window to hail Antoine.

He apologized for having me park behind the barn. It was muddy there, with no gravel, but some farm vehicles that would need the driveway were coming. All day, he said peevishly, he had been expecting a load of feed as well as another farmer who needed hay. He wasn't sure, he griped on, of the size of the vehicles or if the farmer would bring a truck or a tractor and wagon, but he had to leave room to turn as well as park. Directing me as if his arms were signalling an airplane, Antoine guided my car over what looked more like an enlarged goat track on the far side of the barn where his own car and truck were parked. I got out into wet dirt bordered by tall grass and wished I'd not worn my new shoes. He apologized again for the parking spot, swore at the farm vehicles being late, and vowed he'd valet-move the car himself onto the good part of the lane when it came time for me to go. Antoine carried all the paintings over the mushy ground around to the house and into the living room, expertly kicking off his shoes as he stepped onto the old waxed floors.

It caught my eye how neat and clean the house was, like the well-maintained barn I'd just walked past, with its stacked, sorted lumber outside, tools and farm appa- ratus nailed purposefully under an overhang, and beyond, the whitewashed cheese "factory" and the precise rows in the garden with labels as big as the plants. No wonder this orderly man was frustrated by the no-show farmers. Everything said, "Here lives a careful man of science". Antoine gestured to the rag rug beside the door where shoes and boots were arranged in pairs, and my paranoia caught me. If my shoes were off there would be no quick escape if this sensitive man did not like the look of his cleaned drawings. Besides, we'd all worn our shoes during Jean-Paul's reception, even if it wasn't house rules.

"Antoine, show me where I can wash the mud off my shoes. I'd rather keep them on. The doc told me to wear orthotics 24/7." It was true. I'd just not done anything yet to get them.

Antoine pouted but he was more interested in the packages.

❦

CHAPTER THIRTY-EIGHT

Antoine hurried outside to bring the second load of paintings in from the car. Quickly I slipped off my shoes and ran upstairs. After scrubbing their soles in the bathroom sink and ruining a beige towel in the cleanup, the conservator bounced downstairs with apologies. Antoine paid no attention. Slowly unfastening the paintings' wrappings, his long fingers gliding as if they formed a sharp letter opener, he was exclaiming like a boy at Christmas.

Antoine had propped the pictures up in a line against the couch and was repeating *"très, très bien"* as each new drawing caught the light. He thanked me more than was necessary and asked if the paper conservator might like a gift of cheese when he went to pay the invoice.

The work she had done was indeed excellent. Almost all the stains had disappeared, and the remaining few lessened greatly. The pictures looked clean and lively; the whole paper had been treated, not just the stains. I handed him the client's copies of the documentation and immediately he wanted to know what this term meant, and that one, and why a particular procedure had been done, his scientific mind excited. I found myself answering questions about each piece while Antoine read out its documentation sentence by sentence, sometimes stumbling in the treatment summary but filling his curiosity. This was the Antoine Meg had first described. He stood absorbed in new discoveries, the lines of his face animated, his hands touching the details of each painted plant, making the connections between the report and the drawing. He was especially pleased with the watercolour of the mushrooms where the pure white ones were no longer yellowed and botanically misleading.

"That could be serious if someone misidentified them because of the colour. My field guide would be useless." Stacking the documentation, he said, "I need a coffee," and raced into the kitchen. "Tea?" he called. "You take tea, right?"

I followed him, remembered my somewhat paranoid plans, and declined his offer. He insisted, as any good host would, and I told the sore throat lie, said I couldn't stay long and went to retrieve my teabag, my purse having been left in the living room with my coat. Back in the kitchen he held the noteworthy teabag up to the light, then sniffed it.

"It smells like mint, with something lemony. I can give you instead fresh mint with a little lemon thyme. Thyme has anti-aging properties, did you know?" and then his handsome face reddened. "Nothing personal, please, that's just a plant lover's remark. Forgive me."

Already my plans had gone awry. I hadn't been in the room when he filled the kettle. My strong-tasting tea would cover any rogue scent. Was this really a problem? Shit *la merde*, Berry, if you're so concerned about your health, you might as well have worn an anti-viral mask and scrubbed up to the elbows with disinfectant. I felt my face getting hot. Asking for new water to be boiled would not exactly appear normal. I would just be flexible about my so-called safety planning.

My eyes caught the family photo on the wall.

"Antoine, you know, Florence and Luc were saying how they'd like some memento of Jean-Paul for our work space, a photo maybe? If there's something the family doesn't want."

It was the wrong thing to say. Jean-Paul's name or the word "memento" brought a visible grimace to Antoine's face. I pressed on with what I needed. "Is the estate settled yet? Does the family have what they want, and Odette?"

"Odette? What does she have to do with this? The estate goes to the family. I have to do all the work."

"Well, I thought, maybe a photo . . ."

"I'm sure she's kept lots from our younger days."

Odette inheriting nothing had been fairly well confirmed. I took one pleasurable gulp of tea before I remembered the promises I'd made to the cautious Daniel, and myself, but one taste had teased my addiction. With a streak of brilliance I upset my cup, apologized profusely, bustled around, cleaned up, acted scatterbrained which was not difficult, threw out the kettle water and refilled it myself. My used teabag was on a saucer and I rhapsodized about how weak tea was just what my throat needed. Antoine was over at the counter slicing peppers and mushrooms, drinking his coffee and shaking his head. By the time I was sipping my new cup, veggies and the herbs dried from his garden were sizzling together in a big cast-iron frying pan. The aroma was seductive.

"You'll stay for dinner, of course?" inquired Antoine.

I shook my head. I couldn't cave in now. We back and forthed a bit until he said, "But why not? You look hungry."

I was in fact drooling. My plan had been to arrive at two and be gone by three, and with all the discussion over the pictures it was now late afternoon. I was thankful there would be dinner at the Beau-Port. Glancing outside, the approaching early November dusk was my understandable excuse to leave. For myself, I didn't want to miss seeing the sunset as I drove, the spectacular end-of-day fade down the St Lawrence that illuminated the fortress of Quebec on its high promontory. *La ville sur La Falaise.* My eye caught another family photo on the wall and in it the figure of Jean-Paul. My throat did suddenly swell into soreness, the ache of grief.

Antoine kept glancing at me as he stirred the vegetables; the pan was full, the scent marvellous, and I hadn't accepted his invitation. I don't know what I looked like, except never having been good at hiding my emotions, he would see the sadness on my face coupled with my lousy, lying excuse for not staying.

Luckily for me, his phone rang. Flicking off the stove, Antoine went to answer. I remembered him standing in just that spot during Jean-Paul's funeral reception, at the foot of the stairs in the central hallway, speaking to the police, beginning to learn the hideous details of a murder. This time perhaps it was the over-cautious Daniel trying the number I'd left him. From what I could see, the house had only one phone on the main floor. I wouldn't interrupt. When he was finished I'd get my bag from the living room, ostentatiously show off my new cell phone by checking for messages, and say good-bye.

I heard an exuberant Antoine greet Odette and exclaim into the phone details of his restored pictures. I listened in, it was better than drooling, but I needed to leave. In his enthusiasm Antoine was telling Odette more aspects of the treatments than she could possibly have wanted or had time for. If he wasn't off soon I would just get my things quickly, wave and go.

There were several field guides at one end of the kitchen table, and to give him a few more minutes I leafed through them, trying to find the plants pictured in the cleaned drawings. *Forest and Wetland Plants of Quebec. Fungi of Eastern North America. Native Wildflowers and*

Roadside Weeds. The common names in French of plants and birds comprised a specialized vocabulary I'd never learned, and it came in handy that Antoine, the scientist, had used their scientific names on his drawings. I might recognize the English names, though, and the Quebec field guides contained both the French and English common names. The fungi book was an American publication.

Starting with the drawing I liked best, a particularly unusual plant with a dozen or so big white berries branching out on crimson stalks from the central stem, I found its unique form in the forest plants. In English it was called "Doll's Eyes", I guess because a dark round spot formed the center of each white "eye". Next I looked up something "Americana" in the wildflower and weed book and was pleased to find "Phytolacca americana", or Pokeweed. "Native", the book said, and "common to fields, fences and roadsides". Pokeweed, how appropriate: the leaves and berries looked vaguely like what I'd seen poking out of the bottle of Meg's cordial. Remembering the rest of that afternoon, I shuddered, and went down the entry to "Medicinal Uses". "Found in drugs and preparations used to treat skin diseases and rheumatism". Of course! Maybe Antoine made up his own arthritis preparations. Had he not washed his hands, or was it actually the same plant in the cordial?

The next words hinted at the answer.

"Warning: the roots and leaves are especially poisonous, but all parts should be considered toxic". The book's pages shook as I read the symptoms which included being able to make a small child deathly ill, but what stood out for me were "severe cramps, nausea and prolonged vomiting". "Symptoms start after two hours", I read, and suddenly the smell, sound and pain of Meg puking was right in the room. Somewhere in the background I thought I heard the notes of Daniel's intro to his radio show.

I grabbed the fungi book to look up the text on the white mushroom in one of the paintings. Even though mycology was one of the few "ology" fields in which I would readily admit limited knowledge, the mushroom's name had begun with "amanita", to me meaning, "never eat". It was worse than I thought. "Amanita virosa often inflicts on its victims no symptoms until it is too late, after the poison destroys liver, kidney or heart sufficiently to make recovery impossible."

It was soon evident that most of the cleaned drawings had depicted poisonous plants. "Amanita virosa . . . until it is too late . . . recovery impossible."

In the room, a cloying smell from a frying pan filled with plants.

Alarm stabbed me as if an earthquake had suddenly rolled the floor, flipping legs, eyes and heart as everything on my planet slid and crashed. But a calm voice from the next room was saying, "A history tour of St-Jean-Baptiste—isn't that a good idea, Odette?" Now my mind pictured the earthquake hitting the *quartier*: city streets slanting impossibly, buildings leaning and stones falling, snow sliding off tin shingles, giant icicles like frozen fear cracking above me. My fault for being in the wrong place. I'd ignored the signs, "*Danger chutes de glace*", just like Jean-Paul might have ignored signs that could have warned him, "Danger, falls from *La Falaise*".

I got up from my chair but had to sit right down again, realizing that the Amanita virosa, the less poisonous poke-weed, and the pretty doll's eyes were all toxic. Add a man who recognized each plant on the island. My key was the white mushroom. The drawing should have been left with those yellow stains. Antoine had mastered a Golden Dog, a perfect poison that lay in wait with no symptoms until it could have its revenge, giving a killing bite to the person who had first bitten into it.

By the time my panting breath and spinning head slowed, my mind understood that Daniel's musical intro I'd been vaguely aware of was the ring tone he'd installed on my new cell, stashed in my bag in the living room. If ever I wanted to call him, it was now. But in that instant of clarity I became aware of a shadow peering over my shoulder, seeing the mushroom book open at the stark white "Death Angel" photograph. I started to rise, and a thin voice, mine, skirled from far down its squeezed hollow chamber. "Another time I'll tell you about Daniel and Aunt Adèle and the cat who ate a mushroom omelette," I said, closing the book and looking towards the back door. The shadow mouthed some formula about "not going already?" and moved closer behind me. I kicked out backwards like Westmount Daniel had taught. Antoine sprang to one side, chiding, "Ber-ry." I turned to knee him in the crotch but he was two steps too far away, grinning. My careful planning had forgotten his physical farm strength and agility. When I faced him, I knew I was looking into the eyes of a killer and the trap had been sprung. This man was indeed a hunter. One who could hardly wait for his next trophy.

CHAPTER THIRTY-NINE

I stepped out from the table to have a direct route to the back door. Antoine sauntered over to the stove as if to turn the heat back on, then stopped. Closer to the door than I was, he reached out and put his hand on the knob, like a genial host poised to open it for his guest.

"Thanks, Antoine," I smiled, my voice strong now, "I really must be going."

"Got your purse?" he asked in a mild voice. "Your keys?"

I am not a good actor. He probably heard my inhaled, "shit *la merde*".

"I'll let myself out," I said, turning to make a beeline for the living room, my coat, purse, and the other door. There was a click. Instantly knowing it was true but wanting to deny it, my mind told me Antoine had locked the back door.

He lived here, and as I raced into the living room he followed closely but with an almost imperceptible detour towards the front door. The noise of the second click was so inevitable I was already planning my next move. Were his locks deadbolts with handles, or keys on the inside? If keys, they would be in his pocket. I would have to either overpower him or get help. Feinting so my back would block his view, I lunged to snatch my bag with my cell and Daniel's number on speed dial inside. But instead I froze.

Half-hidden in a corner with some papers lay a book, a book I hadn't noticed earlier in the chaos of bubblewrap and tissue and Antoine's exuberance. Meg's dirt-covered green notebook from the dig was sitting in Antoine's house.

I grabbed the unmistakable object and for an instant my venomous curiosity overrode my bag, my cellphone, and myself. "How the hell did this get here?"

Antoine didn't smirk. He smiled as if the whole world were normal. "I found it today cleaning up! It's the one Meg wanted, right? Please tell her it's here. She can come get it and we'll celebrate."

No way. "I'll take it," I said. Glancing over to where I'd left my purse, I shoved the book inside.

"No," said Antoine, advancing and ripping the bag from my hand. "I found it. It's mine. It's mine to give to Meg."

He was pouting like a child. And I didn't believe he had just found the notebook. Antoine must have snuck it from her art bag when she was here one time, a Meg keepsake from when he was desperately in love. A fail-safe if anything went wrong, bait for Meg to come out to Île d'Orléans one more time. Or had he stolen it himself, earlier, seen it among the dig's storm-strewn equipment the night of Jean-Paul's death? While he was looking for a shovel, for instance? I was making this up, but my survival right now depended on obliterating nightmares like this. I concentrated on the minutes left to me.

"I'll tell her you've got it," I said. Managing a 'boys will be boys' resignation in my voice, I continued with, "Did you take this book?" My answer was clear in Antoine's embarrassed shrug. I inched towards the central hallway where both exits would be in view. If they had been keyed shut, there were ground-floor windows. As if seen by a snake, though, my movement alerted Antoine to danger, and he darted into the hallway ahead of me. Then with one deft movement he pulled his phone from its jack.

"How 'm I supposed to tell Meg, Antoine?" I said in an even voice. Keep a calm exterior, don't set him off.

"I just want to explain. Please. Just hear me out. Come into the kitchen, I'm smelling food. The cast iron keeps cooking even when the heat's off."

I gave in, having no choice, following my purse, phone inside, and an unpredictable strong, agile man carrying it into the kitchen. The proverbial carrot again before the horse, but as well, the horse afraid of the master's violent hand. As long as Antoine kept up this polite charade of talk, though, I would, too. My strength might be in conversation. His lay in unpredictable power.

I stood at the table, arms folded. Sitting would give him an even more physical advantage. Antoine hurried to the stove and checked the pan, shoving my bag so it hung behind him and away from the cooking. Ever careful.

But he was silent. Breaking four eggs into a bowl, he whisked them together, poured them over the vegetables and turned the heat on low under the pan. I waited. Eventually he spoke. When he said, "You'll join me for dinner", it was no longer a question.

"No, Antoine, I have to go," I repeated. "Daniel's expecting me."

He kept cooking, stirring. "This'll just take a sec."

I whirled and ran. Again Antoine was quicker, blocking me at the door, now with a hot cast-iron pan in a gloved hand.

"I just want you to know, I would never hurt Meg. I love her, even if she doesn't love me."

"You did hurt her." I backed up slowly towards the hall. "What do you call making her sick?"

"It wasn't real harm. I didn't kill her or anything. She stole from me. She could've just asked for the drawings, but no, she didn't trust me. I let her know I didn't like that."

Florence had been right. Florence, I murmured. My heel, as I backed away, hit the first step that headed upstairs. When would I see her again to tell her?

Antoine's free hand reached for a door near his now-useless telephone and shoved it open, showing stained steps leading to a basement, airless damp releasing its musty smell. My legs stiffened as I placed one whole foot onto the other stairs up to the bedrooms. Maybe I'd have to jump from a second-floor window, crawl into the woods if I lived.

Antoine didn't try to threaten me down in the direction of the cellar. But with clear deliberation his long fingers reached out to a metal panel at the head of the steps, unclasped its small door, and threw the big black switches. Lights everywhere went out. I fled up towards the bedrooms.

I didn't remember this house much from Jean-Paul's funeral reception, I was focused on the pictures, and in my quick trip to the bathroom to clean my shoes I hadn't bothered with specifics. But I knew Aunt Adèle's farmhouse. I whipped into the first room and tried to open the dormer window but it was painted shut. I knew where the main bedroom was, and there Antoine would likely have a window that opened. Or would it be blocked with a big summertime air conditioner? And that was the room where the poisonous pictures normally hung. That was his most intimate space, with the innuendo of his now hateful bed.

I ran and locked myself safe in the bathroom. A stair or floorboard groaned under Antoine's feet. He had taken his time. He knew I was trapped. I tried the window. And it opened for me.

"*Dieu merci*," I breathed, until it dawned on me it wouldn't go any further. An exterior window had been fastened in place, a heavy storm window insulating against fast-approaching winter. Old wooden houses with old wooden windows. My hand found the narrow panel at the storm's bottom covering the four small breathing holes in its frame and I lifted this access to the outside air, my fingers the only part of my body able to escape. When I withdrew my hand the small covering panel fell part way down again, the hint of fresh air from its holes cut in half, as if to point out how trapped I was, and that my fate included being slowly suffocated.

Scrambling my arms through the sink cupboards for something heavy enough to break the storm window, I found only a can of shaving cream and the remnants of a bag of crystals. A bachelor farmer's bathroom: probably Epsom salts. Berry, concentrate! Stop analyzing the artifacts; that kind of escape doesn't help here.

On the counter my fingers touched a china soap dish, and I found a half bottle of shampoo in the shower. Heavier. Goodie. As well as the six small glass panes making up the storm window, I'd have to break the wooden frames around each.

I heard Antoine's labored breathing outside my door. A rumble that made the whole floor vibrate told me he was moving something heavy.

"Don't think about opening the door, Berry," he said in a workman-like voice, "It's blocked. I'll be back in a minute."

I knelt and felt the shadowed floor around the toilet but there was not even a long-handled cleaning brush, nor anything remotely heavy like a weigh scale. On the racks nearby, two thin, neutral-coloured masculine towels were identifiable in the fading November light. Through the window dusky grey-peach clouds silhouetted the trees beyond the front yard. I could wrap my hand in one towel while I broke the glass, use the other to cover any jagged bits while I climbed out.

A voice outside my door said. "Don't try anything. You know why?" And a bullet shattered the bathroom ceiling, raining shards of plaster and lath.

"I've aimed high," he said, "But I don't have to. Papa bagged moose every fall with this three-ought-three. A big moose weighs over a thousand pounds. Five hundred kilos." The well-informed naturalist. "Even bigger than you, Berry, so just keep quiet."

Goddammit. I slumped to the floor. Insulted and then shot? Hey, I would be hidden by whatever furniture he had moved to block the door. And the bathtub, could he kill me in there? I would wait him out. Daniel's comedy skit moose would rescue me, revenge all his brothers and sisters that the rifle had killed. Berry, concentrate! Daniel's moose was funny long ago, impotent here.

A loud crack shattered the silence. Puke turned me inside out and I crawled to the toilet, diarrhea starting, too. The ironic niceties of still being alive, properly using the toilet, not soiling myself. Slam hammer bang again, and a third time. It wasn't the rifle. Antoine was pounding nails into the doorframe.

"Don't try anything," he repeated. "You can't get out. You heard the barricade go up."

I flushed the toilet, and heard him pause at the noise. Whatever was going on, my only chance was talk. Maybe comedy had its uses. Get Antoine in a different mood instead of pumping out hammerblows and shots. Keep myself alive as long as possible, more chances, maybe later he'd sleep.

"Antoine, you know, Meg really admires you."

No response. "I have a story about plants she'd like you to know. It's about Daniel and Aunt Adèle and her cat. Can I tell you now? I'll make it short."

No response, so I stood vainly glancing out the window and began trying to make mushroom poisoning sound funny. No more nails were beaten into my coffin while I spoke.

At the end, Antoine said, "Idiots! What did the mushrooms look like anyway? Only a few fungi give no symptoms until it's too late for the antidote. If they'd been poisoned by mushrooms that looked edible, they might well have known. But they weren't feeling anything. Mushroom poisoning is painful."

The old smell of "dinner" downstairs smothered me. I fell heavily onto the rim of the bathtub.

Half-sitting, half-lying, I fished desperately for something he'd like to talk about. I needed a miracle, or to wake up from a nightmare. But this was no dream. Like Daniel's hunter in the comedy act, I had to get my assailant on my side. Bring Antoine around to believing I thought murder could be justifiable. His murder of Jean-Paul—my true guess but not absolute certainty, having witnessed in enough actions and in his eyes a confirmation he was capable—now fit in with an idea building in my mind. We had all been presented with an Antoine utterly depressed over the death of his brother. Did this make sense if he had murdered him? Yes, it did, if he had not achieved what he had wanted by that death.

On the other side of this door was a man susceptible to swings of extreme emotion. Including being hugely jealous of his brother. And of Meg. Here was a grown man who wouldn't give an eighteen-year-old credit because she happened to be a better artist than him. Trapped in his world myself, what more did I have to lose?

I'd start out on his side. Obliquely, softly. Who else had ever really sympathized with his deep grievances against his famous older brother?

All sound had stopped. I said, in the calmest voice I could muster, "Antoine, tell me why your brother was so mean to you."

"You liked him, didn't you?" He spat out the words.

The anger in his voice was good. Now, displace the anger back onto Jean-Paul.

"No," I said, "Well, at first, like everyone, but remember the dinner you and I and Odette and Daniel had? It sounded like Jean-Paul was really mean to you as a kid." Old memories that entrapped. Let him vent. Maybe it would be a purgative. A catharsis that would leave him calm. The risk was, it might pump him up even more.

CHAPTER FORTY

~⊸⟨◦⟩⊷~

Antoine fell for my ruse and stood, or sat, in any case stayed outside my door ranting about his brother. I made soothing noises agreeing with him as he climbed the ladder of his festering childhood hurts, age four being ignored by *maman* because Jean-Paul already won prizes at school, age six Jean-Paul taunting him because he still wet his bed, and on and on through ten and fourteen and it had never stopped. My voice sympathized in between. "How awful for you," and "That's terrible. Completely unfair." He had kept count of the injustices, piling his bitterness neatly, fact upon fact, like the stacks of lumber behind his barn, until one too many had caused the balance to tip. Like Jean-Paul, I was trapped under his pile of dirt.

I said something I couldn't forgive myself for. But it was my last chance. "Maybe you were right to kill Jean-Paul."

Antoine didn't answer. I didn't dare to move in case a creak of the floor or a knock on the tile distracted him. Then one word turned me upside down.

"No," Antoine said.

I had him completely wrong. Or had I misunderstood? No he didn't kill or no it was wrong to do it?

"No, what?"

"No, it didn't help. I don't feel better." The hard slap of a fist against wood shook the wall.

I had my definitive answer. And I couldn't do anything with it.

Far off a noise rolled on gravel. I heard it through the storm's half-open vent holes, an unmistakable sound in nature's November dusk. Antoine heard it too. He swore. Then I heard stomping and the metal bang of his hammer as he headed downstairs. My chance at calming him was finished, dead as a doornail. But maybe the feed truck was finally arriving or the farmer had come for his hay. Antoine would be distracted. Could I get the visitor's attention? Without getting Antoine's and the gun's? I glanced out the window and there *were* headlights. Coming slowly down Antoine's lane.

This is it, Berry. It's only in this direction the truck will be facing the housefront and you'll have your chance. But maybe with the house all dark they'll turn around instead. Now, foggy-brain, quick! No lights for signalling. Shaving cream on the window? I reached for the can, excited. There's still some light in the sky. A chance. But would they see it with the dark of the bathroom behind? What could catch the driver's attention?

I reached down and whipped off my undies. Holding my breath to stop shaking, I wrote the emergency number '911' in shaving cream on the midnight blue surface. Grabbing the lightest coloured towel, I pinched the fingers of both hands to hold my panties flat against it and began waving my flag up and down at the window. I could feel the lace waltz. Then the shaving cream started to slide. My flag had a short shelf-life. If it looked like they hadn't seen it and began to leave, I'd break the window and duck the shot.

Footsteps on the porch below. Antoine growled, "Fucking Luc."

Luc? My heart raced. A minute later I heard a door slam and Antoine from the porch greet the vehicle with business smoothness. I couldn't see over the porch roof running below my window, but I could see the outlines of a pick-up beyond and hear Luc saying, "Hey, Antoine, is everything OK? Watch that rifle."

A mute laugh like a hoarse cackle escaped me. "Luc!" I waved. "Look at my underwear!" Was death always this amusing?

"My power's out," said Antoine. "Just my house. I thought you were vandals."

"I'd like to get some cheese."

"I'll be lucky if I don't lose it all. The sooner the power's back on, the better. Sorry, the fridge doesn't get opened."

Another door slam, and a tight but still controlled radio voice said, "Have you seen Berry?"

Yes, I wanted to yell, yes. But a rifle shot would be louder.

"She left hours ago."

"Know where she was headed?"

"No. But I could tell you where the road is she and Meg took to the beach the other time, if that 'd help."

"No thanks. We don't want another big repair bill." Chuckles all round. Then nothing except a slight creaking of porch boards and a scuffling of gravel.

"Well," said Luc, "Her car's not here. Your car, I mean, Daniel. What next?"

I collapsed, dropping my flag and towel. If I hadn't been afraid Antoine would shoot us all, I would have shrieked. But maybe they weren't leaving. No one was moving, no sounds from below. What next, Antoine, careful scientist, planner of extravagant lunches to honor a brother you hated, plotter of drinks to make Meg sick even as she delivered your final drawings, liar fibbing me into parking where no one would see my car?

Antoine had planned perfectly except for this interruption. What did he have against me? What did I know that he wanted kept secret, the mushrooms already picked for dinner? He must have thought I guessed he poisoned Meg. He was right. But a botanist could have explained that away with some excuse. Even good scientists make mistakes. I didn't know he had the notebook, not until this visit. And I hadn't wanted to believe he'd killed his brother, tussling or tumbling him off *La Falaise* over some perceived wrong. Fabricated wrongs built upon wrongs, like sharp stones making a wall. Then Antoine having the nerve to retrieve the body and bury it under a dirt pile. But we found it sooner than you thought. Except nobody's got enough evidence for what happened, so you're safe.

"Can I use your bathroom?" Daniel's voice floated up. Oh yes!

"The plumbing's out." Silence. Then Antoine, cluing in on his cold behavior to friends who had shown up, said, "There's an outhouse back behind the barn." Immediately, though, it was, "Wait, no. I forgot. It's boarded up. It got full." Antoine on the porch and me upstairs were both swept up in the thought of the car there. He directed Daniel over to the trees.

A chance again! Daniel would move away from the house, maybe having a clearer view of my window if I could get him to look up. I snatched up towel and panties, foamed 911 on the side not already smeared with shaving cream, and began my odd dance behind my veil of towel. Because I couldn't see into the dark enough to know if it was working, my heart pounded out a desperate rhythm to the dance.

More gravel noise, and I saw the interior lights of the pick-up go on as a door opened. Daniel and Luc getting into the truck. The visit over. Antoine yelled good-bye, slamming the front door of the house. I burst out bawling into the towel. Then the front door slammed again.

"What's the matter?" Antoine shouted into the dark.

They hadn't left. I pulled off my sweater and started dancing for real in front of the window. Maybe flashes of bare flesh would be light enough to catch their attention. No jive this macabre dance of death.

"Got any hay?" inquired Luc. They were both back out on the gravel again. "I just thought of it. We ordered some but I'll pay you double if I could get it now. We need to cover over the dig area some more, as soon as possible. The City told us pipes we ran into could freeze if it snows any harder."

Liar. The only pipes we found were for smoking. Hundreds of years ago, and Luc's own. What the hell? Then my lungs opened in a long, silent, joyous, scream.

Luc was lying for me.

I jumped now, jittering, electricity pulsing through my whole body. Antoine wouldn't turn *this* power off. Dancing, sweating, shivering, flailing my arms, spinning, listening.

"How many bales?"

"As many as I can get in my truck. You make the old square ones, right?"

"You got two hundred dollars on you?"

"You're a hard bargainer. Jesus, Antoine. But I need the goddam hay. Glad I thought of it. Maybe between me and Daniel, we can do it." I heard boots on the porch.

"Let me see," and I could picture Luc talking out his wallet, "What have I got here, can you see in this dark?"

And when Antoine peered at the bills, Luc must have hit him hard. I heard a bellow of pain, the big man from the dig taking the strong farmer by surprise. Thumps, a sharp crack, gasps now between moans, screams rising to roars and howls like animals, fleshy bloody savaging of bodies on the gravel.

In hours or minutes one voice panted, "Daniel, my rope's in the back. Flashlight's in the glove."

I sent the soap dish sailing out my window, piercing the night air, glass tinkling as if I were toasting the trees. "Daniel! Luc!"

Fingertips caressed under my nailed door. I started jabbering everything I knew to Daniel until he interrupted with, "I'm getting a hammer to break the door down."

"Daniel, wait. I'm okay." Daniel couldn't see my rotten poker face. "Let the police have the real evidence."

Luc limped up the stairs and I cheered my voice to recount the story of the notebook. He left us to our privacy, heading down to turn on the fuse box, get the book, and guard the moaning Antoine.

I had to keep breaking up my narration to Daniel with assurances I really was okay. He told me his side.

"We saw a towel with this bikini pattern moving in the upstairs window. Some adolescent joke if it hadn't been for what looked like 911. Then Antoine came out with that rifle. Did he have some scared teenager upstairs? Luc works with students. He said, "Something's sure up.""

"We had to figure out what next." It had taken the interlude in the trees to realize a plan, and a quick huddle in the truck to call 911 like the towel said.

"Berry, we would never have left."

Each incident Daniel related comforted me. "Why did he want to kill me?" Daniel had no answer. That I'd figured out Meg's vomiting didn't seem reason enough to commit another murder. The evening replayed in my head. And one sequence was out of order.

"Antoine knew it was Luc even before Luc got out of the car!" I exclaimed. "I heard him swearing at Luc on the porch before a door even slammed."

"He'd recognize the truck. You know how small Québec is. Everyone knows who drives what."

"But it was dark. Sure, it was a pick-up. But he knew exactly whose." My thoughts kept surfacing. "Because the truck was important to him. Significant. Oh Daniel," I wailed, and before I could soften the words it was out of my mouth. "He murdered Aunt Adèle, too."

⚬❦⚬

CHAPTER FORTY-ONE

So many people shouting and snapping to commands, photos quickly being clicked away outside my door, medics asking me calmly about bleeding, feeling clammy. Then thunderous ripping sounds and the door sprung loose. Daniel's arms enfolded me, his hot face buried into me, kissing and kissing, the medics and a cop gently moving him aside but I wouldn't let go. More medical questions and prodding, and I was helped downstairs as if I were fragile gold, away from my ordeal, to talk to the police.

As we passed the kitchen one voice seared me like fire. I glanced through the door and there Antoine was, seated at the table, one arm extended solemnly like a priest or emperor offering dispensations. "Luc, you I forgive. You tricked this old farmer fair and square. Now, I don't forgive you loaning your truck for the commission of a crime, namely stealing my drawings, but I forgive you jumping me outside like that." He made the sign of the cross as if blessing the archaeologist.

The kitchen table was laid out with food, a ritual altar. Antoine's shirt was off and he was bandaged in rows as if beige, bloody medals hung from his chest. A temporary sling immobilized his left arm, his cut face starting to swell. Antoine dropped his good arm onto the table, picked up a fork, and scooped into the food piled on his plate. "Mm mmm. Good thing, Luc, you didn't break my jaw."

Antoine saw me staring. "You in the doorway," he said calmly, pointing his fork at me. "You can rot in hell."

I pulled away from my escort and stepped into the kitchen. "Same to you. Since you were the one who saw Meg take back her drawings. Then poisoned her with your drinks." The police officers lining the kitchen shifted silently, alert. Against a far wall, Detective Laflamme slouched, looking as usual as if she'd been hauled out of bed. But a spark of interest also played across her face. A weary smile surfaced when I walked unaided into the kitchen.

Antoine chuckled, "Rot in hell? That's just what I plan to do. And please, *my* drawings. She made them for me."

"You followed their truck, didn't you, after they left here with the pictures?"

The police in the room were quietly scrambling to make sense of this conversation, hustling down words as fast as they could write or record—voices, photos, videos. One cop with a cell phone whispered what was probably a play-by-play to someone at the other end. Detective Laflamme made slight movements with her hands as if conducting an orchestra, the rest of her intent only on us.

"She stole my drawings and then kissed that loser right in front of me!" Antoine continued scornfully, "He's supposed to be her brother and I'm supposed to be the lover. That's the play's story."

"You followed them to the dig."

"As soon as I could. And it wasn't their truck, it was Luc's. I knew it was headed back to the dig. Luc, thank you for calling that jerk a dumb shit. You yelled so loud I could hear the whole thing even from where I'd parked. TV parking, can you believe it, in Lower Town? You sure told him where to go."

"And you went too, didn't you?" I persisted. "Followed him to St.-Édouard, to get back your drawings."

"The dumb shit didn't take them or anything else. He talked to the old woman and left empty handed, to match his brain." Antoine laughed.

"So you went in. You killed Aunt Adèle."

"I did not!" Antoine banged his fork on the table. "She had the rifle. It went off in her hands."

"You wanted your drawings."

"That's right, Berry. *My* drawings. She wouldn't give them to me. She started mouthing off about good technique and good art. The old bitch." Antoine forked up another mouthful.

I stared, stunned. And the only thought that could override this gross insult to Aunt Adèle, did. Unbelievably, the police were letting my captor just sit and feast and drain a glass of wine.

"Ms. Cates," Detective Laflamme interrupted, noticing my appalled glance. "Monsieur Nadon is talking, and in return we're letting him eat before taking him to the station. We've agreed to let him have his supper, and he's agreed to give us his confession."

"But it's poison! Meg was poisoned!"

"Charges are pending," said Laflamme. "And Monsieur Nadon is giving us information."

"But—"

"We have a deal," said Antoine smugly through a full mouth.

Journalist Daniel interrupted. "What did Berry have to do with all this, Antoine? Why lock her up?" I noticed now that Laflamme was holding her hand flat, halfway raised, signalling to the rest to let this scene play itself out. Phone held at unobtrusive heights continued recording.

"I'd rather have locked up your little cousin, Daniel. Just joking," he smirked. "But this one," and he waved his fork at me, "Wouldn't let me get near. This beady old chaperone sticking her nose into my privacy with Meg. Right from the beginning, too, and making Meg like Jean-Paul better than me."

"What?" Daniel looked as confused as I felt.

"Sure, both of them always with Jean-Paul. Jean-Paul takes the drawings to Meg, not me. Jean-Paul meets Meg for coffee, not me. From time to time she comes out here but someone else is always around. I go to town and see Berry here talking to Jean-Paul, and he has some of Meg's finished drawings. Nobody invites *me* in. One day I walk past the ChantezPortes and there's Jean-Paul sitting with Meg by the window, where *tout le monde* can see, and he kisses her!"

"You've got it all wrong," I said. "Everything. Don't you kiss to say hello?"

"One thing I don't have wrong," Antoine replied, "You did your best to make sure Meg didn't marry me."

"She didn't want to!" I shouted.

"Because you let her spend time alone with Jean-Paul. So she'd like him better. With me, you stuck to her like glue. You know Jean-Paul got whatever he wanted. He wasn't going to get my Meg."

A calm voice by the wall said, "What did you and Jean-Paul do the night he died?" Laflamme's face betrayed only interest.

"I opened my heart to him!" Antoine swivelled towards the detective, his voice cracking. "I did everything a brother could to give him a really good evening. Thought about each detail—see a film, go for dinner later, walk, talk, and the right words to ask him to please stop seeing Meg, how it was tearing me apart. But he laughed at me. Dismissed the whole thing. 'You're acting like a baby.'

I showed him, though. I fought him like a man." Antoine drooped his head over his plate and murmured, "It's not fair. He keeps laughing at me."

Daniel and I clasped each other against this barrage of crazy talk and misunderstandings, Antoine still haunted by the man he'd killed, a brother he'd made into the captain who shipwrecked his life. My police escort tugged at my elbow but I was determined to have the last word. I opened my mouth, and then it struck me what Antoine had done while he talked.

I looked at the stove. The frying pan was empty. He had eaten far more than he had ever given Meg, and it was food, not a weak *tisane*. On his plate sat one last morsel of omelette. Omelette intended for me. Containers of vegetables from the fridge littered the counter, undoubtedly with more mushrooms spread out now for his own funeral feast.

"Don't anybody eat anything," I yelped. "Or drink. Before it's tested." Officers glanced at Laflamme and each other. "I'm no expert. I need to talk right now, in another room." But nobody budged, no signal from Laflamme.

How to make sure there's justice in the end? Should I make it clear, before it's too late, that it looks like he's just ingested deadly toxins? That these might show no overt symptoms until death is inevitable? If I said more they'd rush Antoine to the hospital to have his stomach pumped. Would justice, his family, his victims, be served any better? The scientist had made his decision. He could tell them about poisons right now if he chose—he was confessing everything, they'd said.

Was I going to respect Antoine's evident wish to kill himself rather than face scandal and the rest of his life in prison? Respect—or Revenge? Did it amount to the same thing—that I liked he faced harsh punishment?

Whose side was I on? If Antoine's, which side exactly was that, then, life or death? My own? Which side was that one? Speak out now or not—would it be a legal crime if I didn't immediately state my clear conclusion that he'd eaten highly poisonous mushrooms? If it wasn't a crime, would keeping silent, or raising the alarm, follow Aunt Adèle's wisdom and permit me to 'live, not just dwell'? Which decision, which outcome, would be inseparable from the rest of my life, would become my personal '*Je me souviens*'?

I was in no state right now to balance with wisdom this question and my intense wish for revenge: for Jean-Paul, Aunt Adèle, and my own near-death. In the next few moments I would give the cops my statement. I'd start with the mushroom dinner, work back from there. That would let the police take over. Let them make any decisions. I turned and half ran, half hobbled to the living room, shouting again that I needed to be interviewed right away. Laflamme was at my heels. Was I mistaken or was that a pat on the back? My police escort was already testing another recorder. The cops would have the last word, if it not already been determined by a biting dog, in this case called Amanita.

--❧◆❧--

CHAPTER FORTY-TWO

At home, everyone did their best to stop the nightmare. Daniel smothered me in his warm love; there were no more incidents of sidestepping. Meg sat by my bed opening up her heart as she relived her young knowledge of Antoine, at a loss to explain the man and his deeds. At night she drew furiously but showed the pictures only to Daniel. I praised Luc's strong command as boss of an archeological dig whenever I saw him, having lived to see its skills applied in a different situation. At work, cards, messages and flowers arrived from complete strangers.

Florence gave me news and gossip. And paid her bank debt willingly—I got the money for finding the notebook. Later I would win the bet for the shoe lining, too, doubled when Luc published Gaetan's photo with my description: "linen, a type similar in fibre width although not quality to that used in artists' canvases of the period."

But my real fate was irretrievably tied to Antoine's and I tried to keep this obsession hidden. Right after my ordeal, believing I would recover my happiness had been as far-fetched as thinking I would deposit the paintings in Antoine's grateful hands and drive home for a dinner with Daniel. The police had clamped down again, this time on information about Antoine, and this made the situation worse. Not knowing if he lived or died hung in the air. I knew it would stay with me for the rest of my life. What had my decision in those last few minutes in the farmhouse led to?

Daniel went to see Detective Sergeant Laflamme, ostensibly to thank her for "all she had done" in the investigation. He took Odette as a witness. Daniel figured, confirmed by Laflamme when she made them both sign confidentiality agreements, that Laflamme's words would not be for public consumption, but having the excuse of being a Radio-Canada journalist, he pretended surprise. He'd been especially curious to have one point answered. Daniel told me later he'd phrased it as, "Do other police investigations involve not releasing a body to the family for months?" And then, "Wasn't this highly unusual?"

"Yes to your second question," Laflamme had replied. To the waiting silence she said, "You were both part of the investigation. And as a journalist, M. Tremblay, I expect you to investigate details. Here is my answer and it will go no further." Laflamme had reached in her pocket for a "soother" cigarette. "Initially many people were suspects. Both of you included. You, Odette, and others, all of you mentioned in interviews Antoine's jealousy of his older brother. Nothing unusual in families, but enough to put him also on our list. To clear suspects we need good evidence, of course. I regret the time the investigation took. But we certainly did not want to release the body to Monsieur Jean-Paul Nadon's murderer. We came up with excuses, and we were lucky that family travels and the type of memorial service helped."

"When did you begin to suspect Antoine was the perpetrator?"

"Not soon enough. I regret this especially for your fiancée."

As my beau told me later, her tone had changed from its earlier neutral formality to a pained lower voice as she continued with, "In addition, as you know, Jean-Paul Nadon was a well-known, much loved, popular celebrity here. We did not want to disrespect him in any way. We needed to be certain of our conclusions." Laflamme had paused. "As you, Monsieur Tremblay, know from one of our conversations, I've experienced disrespect myself and worked to make this police force understand." Odette would ask Daniel about this later. "And then your aunt died. Antoine had no connections, as far as we knew, to Mme Adèle, as everyone called her. But Antoine's name pops up again. His book, and someone's plant drawings, found at her house. Antoine rose on our list of suspects, but we had no clear evidence of any convincing links to either death. Until you called."

Days later the police made a public announcement and made sure we and all of Quebec City knew one detail.

Antoine had survived.

But harmed by the poisons in the mushrooms? Suffering physical pain? Mental? Or pleased that he could now "rot in hell" as he said he would, whatever his fate.

For "medical reasons" Antoine was allowed no visitors, none that we knew of at least, not even from Odette who had asked. Whether any family members had tried to see him, she had no idea. Odette shared her own mental anguish only once with Daniel. She was convinced Antoine had become severely mentally ill. She wouldn't abandon him, he was a man she had known over too many years and through other clouds, thick and thin. She made an effort to remain a friend, his golden dog in the best sense. Her allegiance took on what had to be done. She arranged for his goats to be cared for, the cheese "factory" to be carefully cleaned and sterilized for someone's future use, and a neighbor and food bank in the coming year to make use of the maple trees and plant and harvest the farm's field and garden produce.

We learned one more piece of news about Antoine; a judge committed him to an unnamed locked psychiatric facility. His doctors confirmed it would take some time before an assessment could be carried out and have long-term accuracy. With no timeline announced, this ruling served to stave off clarity about Antoine's future as well to mask, to us, his exact whereabouts.

My fate was the opposite. Quebec City residents and not a few tourists recognized my face and knew, or thought they knew, my story. On the street those first few days my eyes welled up from the empathetic hugs, kisses and overwhelming friendship of a small, close city. Emotionally I felt fragile, though, and within a week I curled into a recluse, hardly venturing outside. My job provided distraction, but if I wanted to stretch and breathe fresh air by walking to or from work, I did it only with Daniel or Meg there to field others' well-meaning questions and give voice to my silent gratitude.

Then after a few weeks no one bothered me on the streets. It took Florence to prod me into admitting I was almost disappointed. Someone else in the city had been crowned with the double-edged celebrity title, "Victim". It meant, though, that Antoine slipped from my hourly thoughts.

It was time for me to do something with my current life other than withdraw. Somehow both Daniel and Meg had picked up on this moment, too, for me and also for them.

"If you don't get out and enjoy nature again, you'll be insufferable," from Daniel.

"If you don't get out and exercise, you'll get fat," from Meg.

Daniel and I went cross-country skiing in the winter's last snows at St-Édouard. On the best days, soft blue light lit the white fields, and Réjean's two girls joined us, unknowingly feeding us nourishing glimpses into childhood's delights and sweet hopes. The worst days belonged to Aunt Adèle's ghost.

Odette had hired a botanist and secretly, Meg. Together, they were determined to have Antoine's last botanical book published; enough had been completed. If they were able to prepare a good manuscript, a lawyer or doctor could show it to Antoine. People knew how important this book was to him, and it might help restore the Nadon name and perhaps Antoine's sanity. In doing this, Meg found a focus for bringing words and pictures together.

She started making art again with less dark emotion. She became passionate about design and text as well as continuing to paint and draw. She moved into my apartment, larger than the one she had been living in and better suited to spreading out her artwork. Inspired by the book project, she came to terms with the fact she could best study and write in English, and was accepted into one of the foremost Canadian art schools, in Nova Scotia.

I moved in with Daniel. I sort of never had moved out after he brought me home following my ordeal. Would Daniel perhaps look for a bigger apartment, one better suited to two people living permanently together? Just as I was rediscovering my old soul, enjoying rather than enduring each day, the future settled out like a cloudy solution layering into clear water at the top and dark particles at the bottom.

Daniel decided to leave for Louisiana. I came home one day and found him bounding around the apartment in his excitement at finalizing the one-year stint as a radio host there. Daniel asked if I would go with him, but almost in the same breath worried that I couldn't get a work visa for the States without a job offer first.

"What are you going to do?" he asked, as if the decision were all mine.

I walked slowly into the kitchen while Daniel watched.

"Finish my conservation contract," I said, pouring myself a long glass of water and drinking half. "Then I'll let you know."

I had to work, we both were well aware of that: to support myself, to bolster my CV for future employment, and to maintain my own sanity. The memory of my desperate year-plus wait before I got a make-or-break job at the museum in Vancouver was deeply embedded. Could I fault Daniel for taking up this once-in-a-lifetime Louisiana opportunity? Wasn't I passionate about my own work? After all, his stint down south was only for a year. But no one said I had to like it.

Luc's term as visiting archaeologist in Quebec City would end soon when the regular prof returned and he had invited me to join his next excavation, a site a thousand years old south of Montreal that an Indigenous community had discovered on its land. I was pleased, and the first decision I came to suited this well. I was determined not to stay in Daniel's apartment surrounded by all his things, as if there to guard the place for him. I would leave, too.

But instead of Luc's dig I decided to expand my future and applied for a position in a completely new area of conservation for me—natural history specimens. Not just collections of bugs and birds but a whole range of creatures. When I won this job competition I became the one bounding around in excitement, and in my running shoes, too.

Best of all, the contract was only for six months. Daniel could decide then how lonely he was, and I could decide the same. Whether a long or short visit to Louisiana, Mardi Gras was conveniently timed. If no visit, I would survive, unlike the precious specimens I'd been warned during my interview would need extra protection as certain species were now extinct. I assured my new boss I would give everything the best conservation I could.

But deep down, my own history would be encased there, too. Skeletons and stuffed natural history specimens would be excellent reminders of the care and protection all beings need at different times in their lives. And even then, sometimes catastrophes cannot be averted. At the new workplace the skeletons would be evidence enough of what happened to even large, sometimes well-armoured creatures. I would be starting by preserving dinosaurs.

Within days of signing the contract another type of predator became extinct. Another final, unique loss to the world.

Antoine died.

Death due to natural causes, the official certificate stated. None of us outside the case would ever hear more than the rumour that Antoine had lost his will to live, to come back and be part of the human world, even if it meant the exacting world of justice. Or perhaps he had ultimately died at the hands of the world he so loved and enjoyed, the natural world of both wondrous and deadly living things.

At the museum in Vancouver I'd first come to terms with the truth that once you know something, you cannot un-know it. Now my whole self would never escape the memory of an expert botanist and sympathetic goat farmer, and a monster run amok. But some species do survive, some survived even the disaster that wiped out the big dinosaurs, and for myself, I knew this too: at my age, I hadn't come through this much, as well as enjoyed so much out of life, to disappear without putting up a damn good fight.

Acknowledgements

Every book, even a work of fiction by a single author, is the product of more than one person. I could not have written this book without the generosity and help, whether they knew it or not, of the archaeologists, their crews, and the conservators and other professionals who worked for Parcs/Parks Canada preserving the history of Quebec City, and the Forges du Saint-Maurice at Trois-Rivières. There are too many names to mention but I am especially indebted to Céline Cloutier, Yvon Desloges, the late Pierre Nadon, Françoise Niellon, Marcel Moussette, and Gisèle Piédalue. My loving gratitude in particular to Alison McGain for her unfailing support, contributions and dedication to this book.

I am truly indebted as well to all those, too numerous to mention here, who read drafts and made suggestions, whether writers such as Cynthia Flood, Wayne Grady and the late Nancy Richler, professional editors or translators such as Jane Macaulay, and the many other friends whose valued contributions I relied on.

My heartfelt thanks to Kitty Lewis of Brick Books for sharing her knowledge. I could not have completed this book's journey without her. In addition, special thanks to Maggi Cheetham and Élise Dubuc for their insights on characters and setting.

I've saved until last my loving thanks to John Donlan, a poet with a special interest in nature and geology, and he has been my rock.